TIDEWATER

D1024272

LIBBIE HAWKER

TIDEWATER

*A Novel of Pocahontas and
the Jamestown Colony*

LAKE UNION
PUBLISHING

This is a work of fiction. Names, characters, organizations, places, events, and incidents are either products of the author's imagination or are used fictitiously.

Text copyright © 2014 Libbie Hawker
All rights reserved.

No part of this book may be reproduced, or stored in a retrieval system, or transmitted in any form or by any means, electronic, mechanical, photocopying, recording, or otherwise, without express written permission of the publisher.

Published by Lake Union Publishing, Seattle

www.apub.com

Amazon, the Amazon logo, and Lake Union Publishing are trademarks of Amazon.com, Inc., or its affiliates.

ISBN-13: 9781477829929
ISBN-10: 147782992X

Cover design by Salamander Hill Design Inc.
Illustration copyright Lane Brown

Library of Congress Control Number: 2014921617

Printed in the United States of America

In memory of Judie Guich. When my time comes to face the inevitable, may I do it with as much courage, humor, and love as you.

And for Paul, always.

SMITH

April 1607

Prologue

He was far away, reclining on a bed of cool silk, the sweat drying on his skin. The window was unshuttered. A breeze moved the long wisp of curtain, carrying a scent of rosemary into Antonia's chamber, bringing with it the rich perfume of Constantinople in elegant decay: the dust of hot brick; ancient incense from the church on the hill; fish offal sharp and salty at the wharf; the inoffensive, homey tang of horse dung drying on the bare streets.

Antonia moved from behind her screen and dipped a rag into a basin. The water fell like stars over her smooth skin. *I should like to see it*, she said, her voice distant and wavering in his memory, an echo from a lost shore. He could no longer recall her face—not with any accuracy, though he knew that she was beautiful. He did remember her voice. The subtle rich smoke of it, the water running down her shoulder, tracing over the curve of her hip, puddling under her small foot. *See what?* he asked. His Greek was nearly as bad as his French, but she understood him well enough. *The world*, she said. *All of it. I want to see it all.*

He could smell her still—her and Constantinople, and the rosemary. The memory shut out the stink of the brig, the reek of peat tar and his own piss. Antonia's bed was much softer than the narrow plank where he huddled. He no longer felt the damp roughness of the wood, nor the splinters pressing through his clothing.

The *Susan Constant* heeled. He cursed and braced himself; the chains of his fetters clanked. A cry came through the thick boards of the deck, muffled, but even in the brig he could hear the joy and relief in the man's voice.

"*Land!*"

He pressed himself against the *Susan Constant*'s curved rib, ducking his head to peer through a chink in the wood. But he could see nothing, and the sunlight hurt his eyes. Tears streamed down his face and into his long, matted beard.

He heard footfalls on the deck above. A grunt, an oath, and with a squeal of hinges, the trap opened. Light as bright and shocking as the cut end of a lemon fell into the small chamber. With it came a great gust of fresh air, carrying the scent of a new world: rich and green, damp, spicy, fertile. It startled him, how much it smelled like the coast of England.

"John Smith."

"Aye." His voice grated like the hinge.

He waited for an explanation, perhaps even a word of acknowledgment that they had made it, after everything, to the New World. A ladder dropped into his rathole; it was a sad thing made of worn rope and faded dowels. He climbed it gingerly.

Wingfield was waiting on deck. He stood straddle-legged, the sun gleaming on the neat jut of his red beard, his body moving with unconscious ease as the *Susan Constant* dipped into a gentle trough of a wave and rolled up to its white crest. Edward-Maria Wingfield rode a ship as easily as some men ride horses. The damnable creature was pointed ever upward as surely as a compass needle points north, as if God Himself had tied a line to Wingfield's helmet to keep him permanently in divine plumb. He was the only shareholder of the Virginia Company to set sail for the New World, and he thought his wealth had given him the right of leadership. There were five score and four men divided among the three ships. Too many of them agreed with Wingfield. It seemed that even on the open sea, blood counted for more than brains.

Wingfield did cut a dashing figure in his perfectly polished steel armor, Smith grudgingly conceded. A foolish figure, too. One storm, one slip on a wet deck, and Edward-Maria Wingfield would find himself and his fine armor beautifying the seafloor. Smith had advised him not to wear the stuff aboard the *Susan Constant*. The warning had been scorned and dismissed, as ever.

All the men were on their feet. Even after so many months at sea, they swayed with less grace than Wingfield. The deck was crowded—the whole ship was crowded. It was a freighter, a trade ship, and not a large one at that. Its hold was outfitted to transport goods, not men. The Virginia Company had purchased it for a song, and songs were a good bit less dear than gold. Beyond the crowd, Smith could make out the two sails of the *Godspeed* ahead, already entering the deep-green arc of a bay. A thrill of dense woodland spread north and south, fading far off into a blue haze. Southeastward, lagging behind, the *Discovery* was a white smudge on the horizon.

"Clackety-clack," one of the men jeered, pantomiming his own hands in chains.

"In fetters again, Smith," another called—a smoother voice, one of the many useless gentlemen who plagued the voyage. Smoother, but no less mocking. "Just like in the Turk's fields, eh, lads?"

The men laughed. No one believed him about what had happened after Antonia. He was already a slave when he'd been gifted to the woman, taken as booty after a misstep with the Tartars. Smith's too-trusting master had sent him to Constantinople to act as door guard for the Turk's beloved Greek mistress. It wasn't Smith's fault that she'd fallen in love with him; though what Antonia had seen in

Smith, short, broad, and hairy as a half-grown bear, he still could not say. Once their master realized the truth, it had been the cane for Antonia—that soft, white flesh marred by red stripes—and sale into hard labor in the Crimea for Smith.

Let the men laugh. Their scorn changed nothing. Their mockery was a good deal easier to bear than the Turk's iron collar. Nor did they believe him when he told them how he had taken up his scythe in his master's field, and struck the man off his own horse as he came riding out to beat Smith for insolence. *Let them call me a fool and a knave.* Smith could still hear the rush of his scythe through the air, the crack of it upon his master's head. Even now, five years later, he could see the Turk lying still in the furrow of his own field. He recalled how the horse had shifted and pranced when he raised his foot to the stirrup and clambered aboard. Muscovy and freedom had been but one hard ride away.

"And here we are at last, lads," Wingfield said. He spoke in his gentleman's voice, an orator's voice, the sound of it booming out across the waves as if an audience of fishes might hear him and applaud. "The New World. Each man behold it, even"—with a glance at Smith—"mutineers, and give thanks to God."

"Amen," the more pious of them murmured.

Smith kept his eyes on Wingfield, rather than casting his gaze up to Heaven. But in his heart he did thank merciful Christ. Soon they would go ashore, the locked box with sealed orders from the Virginia Company would be opened, and, by writ of their employers, Wingfield would no longer hold sway. Smith need not merely hope that Wingfield would soon deflate. He knew it would be so. God had shown him favor in the past, and He would again. Smith's days of wearing chains, whether in the Crimea or Constantinople or a ship's brig, were over.

The *Susan Constant* breasted the last high wave at the bay's mouth and sailed into gentler water. Wingfield set about ordering the men, placing them in ranks according to class. He eyed them with all the pomposity and bluster of a general. "We will send a party ashore," he declared, tugging at his wedge of copper beard.

Smith shifted; his chains rattled. "I would advise against it."

Wingfield rounded on him. "Keep your mutinous mouth closed, Smith. I will deal with you later."

"No doubt," said Smith, half-feeling the bite of a rope around his neck but unable to stop himself from speaking on. "Still, I would advise against it."

"I have no use for your advice."

"You might, if you had any sense."

Wingfield was on him in two furious strides. Smith did not cower, but he braced himself for a blow. It never came. Wingfield's face was very close to his own, and his breath was hot with anger.

"You tried to set my men against me . . ."

"I did not, and they aren't your men. You aren't even the captain of this ship. It's Newport's command, or have you forgotten?"

"Be silent! You incited mutiny. Why in God's good name you believe I should have any use for your advice, or for any part of you, is a mystery to me. Now keep your mouth well shut when your betters speak."

Matthew Scrivener cleared his throat. "Your pardon, Master Wingfield. Perhaps we ought to hear Smith's reasons."

Scrivener possessed a trait most scarce in gentlemen: intelligence. Sallow though he was from the long voyage, he still held a gleam of bright awareness in his eye.

Wingfield's eyes narrowed with anger, but Scrivener spoke on: "After all, sir, the box has not been opened. You are not the president of the colony yet."

Wingfield fairly choked on his red-faced rage. Smith lifted his manacled hands and ran his fingers through the mess of his beard, hiding his grin.

"Very well," said Wingfield. "Advise us, John Smith, you font of wisdom."

"We don't yet know the state of the naturals. Are they friends or foes? None of us can say. We ought to anchor in the bay, as near as we might come to the shore, and bide our time. The naturals will show themselves, soon or late. They know we are here already, or else I'm a virgin girl."

One of the men grabbed his cod through his stained breeches and waggled it, shouting to Smith a most indecent proposal.

"The state of the naturals?" Wingfield sputtered. "Friends or foes? Don't be a fool. You've read the reports from Spain. They're eager to trade, and once we bring them the Christ, they'll be more eager still. They're savages, Smith. They need our guidance. They're like babes in the wood, waiting for a kind hand to raise them up to civilization, to show them the light and the path."

"Truly?" said Smith. "You don't suppose they may be hostile to us—see us as invaders?" He cast a significant glance about the crowd. There were plenty in London—even in King James's court—who disparaged the very thought of colonization. Given the Virginia Company had faced such widespread opposition to the colony—resistance on the grounds that England had no right to wrest from the naturals their own God-given land—then surely at least a few of the men on this voyage felt the same.

"Don't be naïve." Wingfield pointed into the crowd. "Archer, choose five men. You'll go ashore. I'll need two sailors to row the landing boat."

He did not bother to turn back to Smith. "John Smith, allow me to offer you advice in turn: keep your useless thoughts to yourself unless *the president* requests them."

Smith stood at the rail, well back from the lines as the sailors lowered the little vessel to the waves. He watched as Gabriel Archer directed his men into the boat. A pair of oars ran out, and the silent sailors in Archer's crew began to row.

Scrivener made his way to Smith's side. "The mutiny charges are thin, Smith. We all know that, even the men who hate you.

We'll be on land soon, and they'll be in a generous mood. It will come to nothing—nothing but Wingfield's spite."

"I know it."

Scrivener looked at him steadily for a long moment. Smith could feel the intensity of the man's gaze, but he kept his eyes on the boat. It was small now, making haste for the yellow line of the shore.

At last, Scrivener said, "It's only your tongue damns you."

"My tongue, and my common birth. You're the only one who *doesn't* think the highborn cunny he slid out of on his birthday makes him the next best thing to Christ."

Scrivener sniffed at the indelicacy.

"Sorry," Smith said.

"Listen, old boy—if you'd only give over to Wingfield once in a while, be more cooperative, less . . . less haughty—"

"Less haughty, he says! It's Wingfield you want for haughtiness, not I. And I'll be hanged if I let that red popinjay strut about the colony as if he owns it."

Scrivener shifted at the rail. "He fair does. He *is* a shareholder."

"Still . . ."

"And it might come to hanging one day, Smith. Not this time, and maybe not the next. But sooner or later . . ." Scrivener trailed off. The landing boat entered the surf and grounded on the strand.

"I'd be sorry to see you hanged," Scrivener said meditatively. "Christ knows there aren't enough good men on this voyage. We can't spare a one. Not even the commoners."

Smith turned to him with a rebuke, but caught himself when he saw the humor in Scrivener's eyes. The man laid a hand on his shoulder and squeezed. Though Scrivener was slight and only a gentleman unused to real work, his grip was hard and sure.

They watched in tense silence as the landing party made its way up the embankment. The men on the shore arrayed themselves in a rough half circle, moving tentatively toward the thick stands of salt grass and wiry brush. Slowly, they poked about with the muzzles of their matchlocks, turning this way and that to stare at the high, wind-stirred landscape that now surrounded them, held them, lulled them.

"Well enough so far," Scrivener muttered.

In that very moment, Smith noted a quick blur, a black shape sliding between the trunks of two oaks.

"Merciful Christ," Smith blurted.

"Your pardon?"

"They don't see . . ." He cupped his hands around his mouth and shouted with all his might. "*Ahoy!*"

But the landing party could not hear him over the rushing of the surf. Nor could they see what Smith saw from the vantage of the *Susan Constant*'s deck: the glide of tense, muscular bodies approaching, the sinister crouch, the flick of a silent hand sign in the brush.

One of them rose up from the salt grass, a full head taller than any Englishman, the glaring face divided red and black like a devil out of a nightmare. In one rapid, unthinking movement the natural raised the black arch of a bow, drew, released. Before Smith's eyes could track the first arrow, another was on the string, and then it, too, was flying. The strand exploded in a confusion of bodies, the red and black of the naturals rising from concealment, the panicked flash of sun on armor as the men turned and cried out and blundered into one another. Somebody got off a shot; a blue ball of powder smoke expanded in slow motion; an instant later the report of the fired matchlock cracked across Smith's ears. Somebody—Archer, Smith thought—held aloft both hands in a pleading gesture, and immediately fell back on the sand, writhing.

"*Cannon,*" a hoarse voice bellowed in warning. Smith clapped his shackled hands to his ears in the same instant the cannon fired. The *Susan Constant* shuddered, a deep, bone-jarring, sickening tremor. The sulfurous stink of gunpowder burned Smith's nostrils and eyes.

The devils on the shore fled.

The landing party scrambled back to their boat and rowed frantically for the *Susan Constant*. By the time they were hauled aboard, Wingfield was shaking and pale. Whatever great oratory he'd composed to welcome the landing party back, he kept to himself.

The crew hauled Archer out of the boat and laid him carefully on the deck. He made a repetitive rasping grunt, a sound that now and then turned to a high-pitched squeal of panic before he controlled himself and resumed his gentlemanly grunting. Smith pushed through the crowd and stared down at Archer. Each hand streamed with blood, pierced clean through the palms with a pair of matching arrows. Another man, one of the sailors, clutched at his upper thigh where more arrows bristled.

"Right," Scrivener shouted, "bring whiskey to dull their wits. Russell, boil a pot of wine. We'll need to clean these wounds. Where's the ship's boy? Thomas Savage, fetch your sewing kit."

Wingfield turned to stare out at the shore. He made no move to direct the men. Smith sidled up to him.

"Unfortunate," Smith said quietly.

The glare Wingfield turned on him was sharp and dangerous, thick with loathing.

"I do think," Smith murmured, trying for Scrivener's sake to put some deference into his words, "that now would be an ideal time to open the box."

"The box," Wingfield burst out. He closed on Smith, and Smith thought for one welcome moment that Wingfield might strike him, might give him the chance to retaliate. Then the man reined himself in and seized the point of his beard in a shaking fist. "An excellent idea, John Smith."

The box was sent for, and once the men's wounds were tended, Wingfield unsheathed his dagger. With a flourish, he broke the wax sealing the lock and pried open the lid. The parchment inside was tidily rolled. It hissed as it came open in Wingfield's hands.

"By decree of the Virginia Company," Wingfield read, voice booming, "a ruling council of seven is appointed. The council shall consist of: Edward-Maria Wingfield, gentleman and shareholder . . ." He took a long and savory moment to stare into Smith's eyes. "Bartholomew Gosnold, gentleman and investor; John Ratcliffe, gentleman and investor; Christopher Newport, captain of the *Susan Constant*; George Kendall, gentleman and investor; John Martin, gentleman . . ."

Wingfield stopped short. The men on the deck shuffled, jostling one another, murmuring.

"And?" Scrivener prompted.

"And John Smith, *soldier and adventurer*," Wingfield concluded. His mouth twisted into a sour, hate-filled leer.

Smith stepped to Wingfield's side. He held out his wrists to his fellow councilman, presenting the fetters lock-side up. He had come to a new world, and John Smith would never wear chains again.

THE FIRST NAME

Amonute

POCAHONTAS

Season of Cattapeuk

The house of unmarried women was quiet for once, emptied of the usual bustle and song. The heart fire glowed with a steady, low flame, sending up a lazy tail of deep-blue smoke that dispersed into the sooty haze darkening the arch of the ceiling. The banked coals gave off just enough light to reveal the black curve of well-bent saplings, their repeating arcs as perfect and strong as drawn bows. Here and there along the dim walls new panels of pale bark showed, replacements for those the winter ice had damaged. The new bark stood out sharp and bright against years of smoke stain, the tender bare flesh of the panels still slightly damp and spiced with the odor of rising sap.

Bedsteads lined the walls, sturdy platforms of young saplings deftly interlaced, springy and soft as moss. Each bed was piled with soft mats woven of yet more bark, the strips pounded fine until they were as velvety as a moth's wing, warm and plush as the pelt of a rabbit. On one of these beds, half-covered by the drape of a deer hide, lay a girl curled in sleep. She was deep in shadow, breathing heavy and slow, following the dim blue trail of a dream. The heart fire's fitful light picked out the curve of her strong, tawny limbs, folded like the long legs of a fawn at rest. The light played over the planes of her face, the regal broadness of her cheekbones, the strength of her chin, still rounded by youth. Her lips moved silently. In the dreamworld she chanted, and her voice was as loud as thunder. A paint pot rested on the packed earthen floor of the house, its lid flung carelessly aside. The girl's hand dangled from the bed above it. Her fingertips were still shiny with the mixture of bear grease and pigment. Her arm was streaked, half-unpainted, vivid with the tracks of her wandering thoughts.

A voice called from outside the house's dark walls. "Amonute!"

One yellow finger twitched; the sleeping girl's spirit wavered on the edge of her dusky path.

"Amonute!"

The voice was at the door now, and the girl murmured, turning away from the voice in unconscious protest. Her hand trailed a smudge of ochre along the edge of the deerskin.

The house's door flap lifted. A ring of bright springtime light burned suddenly, then the room darkened again as a slender figure stooped to fill the doorway. The flap closed with a thump.

"Sleeping! I should have known."

The girl on the bed squeezed her eyes shut, gritted her teeth.

"I know you're awake now, Amonute," said the other girl. She was older by two or three years, on the verge of womanhood. Her breasts had only just begun to stand out from her bare chest, and she still wore the hairstyle that marked her as a child: shaved close at the temples and fore, the back never cut but braided prettily with the beads and copper bangles she would one day sew onto her marriage apron. She advanced on the bed. "You're lazy as a *rahacoon* with the bloat. *Hah*," she said in disgust. "You've made a mess of my yellow paint."

The girl on the bed kept very still.

"You can't fool me. You aren't asleep, so get *up*. The canoes are arriving, and if you're not there on the shore to greet the guests, you'll catch the *worst* trouble. Amonute!" She leaned closer and whispered another name, a better name, far more fitting and well earned. "Pocahontas!" *Mischief.*

Pocahontas opened her eyes. Her smile was slow, eloquent with self-satisfaction.

"You are insufferable," the older girl said. She picked up the pot of yellow paint. "You're not even properly colored. Stand up and let me fix your arm. It's nothing but streaks."

Pocahontas stood. She yawned, stretching her arms above her head, and held still for the paint.

"Our father will beat you if he sees you looking like this." The older girl smudged hastily with the paint, covering Pocahontas's skin from shoulders to wrists.

"No, he won't." It was said as a matter of fact, and the other girl bit her lip and frowned as she painted. They both knew it was true.

"Your braid is tangled and ugly."

"Stop fussing, Matachanna." Pocahontas pulled her long braid over one shoulder, running her hands along it in an attempt to make it tidy. Many black strands had worked free while she slept, and now it was wild as a patch of weeds.

"You look worse than a bear's behind in a mudhole. Father won't stand for it—not today, not even from you. Let me get my hair oil."

Matachanna pulled a leather bag from a peg driven into a nearby sapling beam. She rummaged through it until she found the clay pot that held her best oil. A few drops trickled into her hand and she rubbed her palms together. The warm herbal scent asserted itself over the ever-present sapor of smoke. She stroked Pocahontas's braid, tucking the stray locks into place among the few shell beads and copper rounds with gentle care. When she was finished, Matachanna took a long chain of pearls from her peg and looped it several times around Pocahontas's neck.

The younger girl lifted the pearls in her fingers. "They're pretty."

"I want you to wear them today, little sister, and remember you're the daughter of a *werowance.*"

Not merely a *werowance*; their father was Powhatan, the Chief of Chiefs, the *mamanatowick* who had done what no chief before had accomplished. He had united the Real People, had made them one great tribe, using every advantage the god Okeus had given him: strength, strategy, ferocity, cunning, diplomacy. The Real People were no longer the ragtag collection of widespread villages and suspicious clans they had once been. Now they were a People in truth, acting as one, fighting as one, hands interlocked in friendship. It was Powhatan, her own father, who had remade the world—her father who commanded each chief, each *werowance* of every territory for ten days' journey in any direction. It seemed to Pocahontas that his power was limitless.

She clutched the chain of pearls in her fist. Her hands suddenly trembled with anticipation. "It's an important meeting Father has called, isn't it?"

"Only the Okeus knows," Matachanna muttered, tamping the lid tightly on her pot of yellow paint. "I certainly don't."

"*Werowances* from all the territories . . ." Not a single chief would be absent. She had seen how the women of Werowocomoco worked at their cornmills and their sieves, how they heaped baskets high with round boiled dumplings and smoked fish. She had heard the impatience in their voices as they gossiped and shouted over their work. It was no ordinary feast they prepared, no mere salute to the season or routine welcome. It was many times greater than any festival Pocahontas had witnessed in her young life. Surely this meeting of the *werowances* was many times more important than any that had come before.

"There will be dancing," Pocahontas said, eagerness pushing through her thoughtful mood.

Matachanna blew through her lips, a loud, rude buzz. "When is there not dancing?"

"And," Pocahontas paused significantly, a bold, nearly mocking grin lighting her face, "I suppose the priests will come, too." Even in the dim light of the heart fire, she could see Matachanna blush.

"Come along, Sister." Matachanna hooked her own painted arm around Pocahontas's elbow and dragged her toward the door.

The midmorning light was impossibly bright. It cut unfiltered through the tops of mulberry and oak trees, where the green buds had just begun to unfurl their brilliant new foliage. The sky was well clouded, but its height and paleness promised a clear afternoon to come. The town of Werowocomoco, the largest and finest of Powhatan's villages, hummed with activity beneath the steady glare of the springtime sun. Here and there, the expanse of forest was broken by cleared garden patches, where bare black mounds of earth stood waiting for seeds and digging sticks. The arches of homes, spaced at regular intervals, peeked from between oaks and smooth-skinned maples, lifting their heads slyly through the leaves like old women straining to catch a whisper of gossip. A pall of woodsmoke hung, trapped within the tangle of branches.

In the ample space between houses, women of all ages bent to their tasks. Across one clearing, a group of girls poured water into a clay pot full of finely ground walnuts. They squeezed the rich grains in their hands, dunking their fists and splashing in time to the chanted refrain of the nut-milk song. They laughed as they worked, until an older woman emerged from the door flap of a nearby house to scold them for the wet mess they were making. A string of little boys passed, too young to draw bows but old enough to carry long skewers of smoked fish. They waved them in the air as they marched, as proud as if the fish were the feathers and bright ornaments of warriors' braids. From somewhere close by came the monotonous rasp of millstones grinding dried corn into flour.

Pocahontas and Matachanna made their way through the woodland toward the gray glimmer of the river. As they drew closer to the bank, they met more of the Real People, dressed in their most beautiful leather aprons, their faces and shoulders, arms and backs, freshly painted in colors as bright as birds' wings. A tense bustle of pleasant anticipation ran like a deer through the town, bounding and bright. Laughter and singing filled the wood. They passed the final stand of saplings at the wood's edge and dropped down onto the riverbank. The river was especially broad here, flat and blue-gray as a polished stone. Beyond the curving green margin of tall grass and muddy shore, the odd tree rose from the water itself, overtaken many years ago when the river had widened and swayed in its course. The water smelled richly of salt with a faint undercurrent of decaying vegetation, for the nearby sea's tide had turned. Soon the river's surface would ripple and eddy, seeming to slow its rush as the sea flowed ponderously inland past the great village of Werowocomoco.

Matachanna had been right: the canoes were arriving, or the first of them, at any rate. It would take all day for every *werowance* and his retinue to make their way down the cold veins of the rivers to the shore of Werowocomoco. By nightfall, when the feasting and dancing would begin, the muddy riverbank would be so thick with dugout canoes that a child could walk across them without getting the soles of her bare feet dirty. The first guests had rounded the inland bend, and now paddled steadily toward the wide, arched cove where the girls and the rest of Powhatan's family stood. Pocahontas squinted against the day's glare, but the canoes were still too far away, and the light on the water too bright, to make out any marking that might tell her which territory had responded first to Powhatan's summons.

She heard the tinkling of copper bells on the shore behind her, and turned in time to see Winganuske come through the saplings like a doe emerging from a mist. No one could deny that Winganuske was a beautiful woman. Tall and straight-backed, she moved with the flowing, supple grace of one who is entirely assured of her place in the world. Her face was as round and luminous as a summer moon, her expression always quietly amused. Beneath the fringe of her hair, black eyes gazed calmly out from her imperious mask. When she stepped among Powhatan's wives and children, they rippled around her in a quiet flow, halting their excited conversation to stare in admiration—or envy—at Winganuske's beauty. To all the natural charms the god Okeus had given, her Powhatan had added beads of white and cream and purple-black, looped about her neck in ropes as thick as vines. She wore a formal dress of doeskin tied over one shoulder, fine and soft and pale as dry sand. The smooth skin of her bared shoulder was painted red, not with cheap bloodroot dye, but with the thick, luminous crimson of valuable *puccoon*. She was hung all about with long, fluttering fringe, an ostentatious waste of valuable leather, and her ankles and wrists chimed with copper, a music as constant as birdsong. Above the vertical black bars tattooed on her chin, Winganuske's mouth curved in a fraction of a smile.

Of all the wives he possessed, Winganuske was Powhatan's favorite. Everybody knew it. Even if the *mamanatowick* hadn't covered her in fringe and *puccoon* and copper bells, her status as favorite was made obvious by the two children who toddled after her onto the shore, trailed by the cousins and aunts who served as nursemaids. *Two* children, and Winganuske was still here in Werowocomoco, at Powhatan's side!

It was customary for a wife to be sent back to her mother's village once Powhatan got her with child. There, she would bear and raise his daughter or son while the *mamanatowick* kept her in comfort from afar, plying her with fresh bark strips for her home, with the finest clay for her pots, with corn and hides and beads. When the child had seen five or six winters—old enough to be useful—he was returned to Werowocomoco to be raised at Powhatan's knee by his female relations, and the wife was free to remarry any warrior she might choose. She would even have the *mamanatowick*'s fine gifts for a dowry. In this way the Chief of Chiefs had assured the loyalty of every village in the region. Now, after many years of marrying freely and often, there was hardly a family among the Real People that was not related to Powhatan by blood.

But Winganuske had not been sent back to her mother's hearth when she grew big with the first of her children. She had borne the baby there in Werowocomoco, and then another, and soon all of the *mamanatowick*'s wives had accepted the fact that the heart of their husband was well and truly conquered.

All of Powhatan's wives were reconciled to Winganuske's irresistible power. But not all of his children.

Winganuske passed the girls, trailing a cloud of fragrant oils and the birdsong of her bells. She stood at the water's edge, gazing out at the approaching canoes. Pocahontas turned to Matachanna with a deliberate, regal slowness and a pinched frown. The girl's mocking dignity was so severe that Matachanna had to press her lips together to keep from bursting out with laughter.

"Stop!" Matachanna hissed under her breath, once she could control her merriment.

Pocahontas circled her sister, pacing out measured, stately strides, one hand pressed to her heart in a gesture of deep sincerity. A few of Powhatan's gathered wives snickered.

Matachanna kicked Pocahontas's ankle.

"Ouch!"

"It serves you right. If Winganuske catches you mocking her, she'll . . ."

"Tell Father?" Pocahontas grinned. The only person who stood anywhere near Winganuske in the *mamanatowick*'s affections was Pocahontas. But while his favorite wife had won the chief's heart with her beauty and bedside wiles, Powhatan's favorite daughter had won his heart with her jesting and humor, her pluck and strength of spirit. It never failed: when Pocahontas found herself in a pot of hot stew—as she often did; not for nothing was she called Mischief—a well-timed jest, a wry smile, and her laughing father forgave her on the spot.

"Look," Matachanna said suddenly. "I can see the paint on the warriors' shields. It's the Appamattuck!"

Across the expanse of river, wider than three felled trees laid end to end, Pocahontas could make out the hide shields hanging over the boats' sides. Each was adorned with the black image of a shambling bear. The Appamattuck would receive the honor of being the first to come to the *mamanatowick*'s call.

Pocahontas bounced on her toes. A large, blocky shape was seated in the fore of the nearest canoe. The features were as clear as the painted bears: a face severe with rough lines, thin-lipped and deep-eyed, decorated with a woman's tattoos; the hair shot with silver, cut straight across the forelock in a woman's style. Opossu-no-quonuske, the *werowansqua*, female chief of the Appamattuck. She was sister to Powhatan. Even at a distance, she shared her great brother's intensity in her dark-eyed stare.

The lead canoe beached. Opossu-no-quonuske rose. She was as tall as any man and nearly as broad-shouldered, a force of might even in old age. The sun broke through the clouds and shone on the black feather cloak tied about her shoulders. The light rippled over the cloak in bands of blue and violet iridescence. She had all the presence and majesty of a god, as if she had stepped from the words of a priest's sacred chant into the realm of mortals.

"Oh!" Pocahontas breathed.

Matachanna cut a narrow-eyed stare at her sister.

"Look at her! She looks . . ."

"Like a chief," Matachanna finished drily. "Don't plant seeds in your head that can never take root, Pocahontas."

"What do you mean?"

"You know you can't be a *werowansqua*. Your mother wasn't born of a chief's line."

Clouds closed over the swath of blue sky again. The light dulled on Opossu-no-quonuske's cloak. Dimness closed over Pocahontas's heart. What Matachanna said was true: only those born of royal women—the sisters or mothers of chiefs—could lead the Real People. Pocahontas's mother had been only a pretty maiden whose youth and spirit captured Powhatan's heart for one brief season. She was not related to even a minor *tanxwerowance*. She was a woman of no consequence. Her marriage to the *mamanatowick*, though happy by all accounts, had been a fleeting affair of the heart. It had brought no political alliance, forged no ties with a powerful family, and gained Powhatan nothing save for Pocahontas herself. And what good, after all, was a daughter who could never be given in chiefly marriage?

Matachanna, on the other hand, came from the right sort of blood. Her mother was sister to the mother of a chief. Matachanna could be useful in marriage, and could expect to be given as a first or second wife to a great husband, a man of real power and influence. All the finest things in life would be hers: beads and pearls, dresses with fine pale fringe, the most fertile plots of land for her gardens, and more copper bells and charms, Pocahontas thought sourly, than Winganuske herself could ever desire. Under the right circumstances, Matachanna might even inherit a chiefdom—might one day become a *werowansqua* of the Real People. Pocahontas's mouth turned down bitterly at the thought. She could not imagine a girl who desired prestige less than prim, quiet Matachanna—and yet one day it might be hers to inherit. Pocahontas, whose spirit was full of a chief's natural charisma, whose mind was sharp and clever and perceptive, was doomed to a life of obscurity and servility.

She watched with a dark frown as Winganuske greeted the *werowansqua*. The two great women exchanged gracious words, hooking their first fingers together in a solemn gesture of friendship. Pocahontas stamped her bare foot in the mud.

"Look there—who's that?" Matachanna seized Pocahontas's hand. They stared together at the *werowansqua*'s canoe. A small figure, painted in scarlet *puccoon* from hairline to waist, was half-crouched in the canoe. The figure wobbled as the boat rocked. One of the warriors tossed his oar into the belly of the boat and held it steady so the little one could climb ashore. It was a girl, naked and slight, the sides of her scalp freshly shaven and her braid wrapped with several chains of pearls.

"I never saw her," Pocahontas said. "She was hiding behind Opossu-no-quonuske's cloak."

"She must be one of our sisters."

Pocahontas squinted doubtfully at the red-painted figure. The girl might be the right age to be sent to Werowocomoco, if indeed she were one of the *mamanatowick*'s children. *Though she seems a bit old for it*, Pocahontas thought. *Six winters is the usual age, but this girl has seen eight or nine.*

A wrinkled hand emerged from the *werowansqua*'s feather cloak. The little girl went obediently to Opossu-no-quonuske's side and allowed her hair to be stroked. Pocahontas leaned toward the women, tugging against Matachanna's restraining grip, but she could not hear their words over the buzz of conversation among the wives and the slap of water and scrape of stone against the hulls of arriving canoes.

Winganuske turned on her heel. "Amonute!"

Pocahontas flinched and made as if to duck behind Matachanna, but her sister stepped away. Winganuske's piercing dark eyes found Pocahontas, traveling over her body. She eyed the neatness of her paint and braid, the straightness of her back, the loops of pearls at her neck. Pocahontas kept her hands still. She felt an urge to grab at her necklace, the way a priest clutches an amulet to ward away an ill spirit.

"Come here, Amonute."

Pocahontas shuffled forward.

"This one is a daughter of Powhatan," Winganuske said to the *werowansqua*, "but her mother was just a village girl of the Pamunkey."

Opossu-no-quonuske stared down at Pocahontas, hard-eyed and assessing. "Mm," the old woman grunted.

Pocahontas watched the *werowansqua*'s face carefully. Its shape was so like her father's: the square, heavy jaw; the strong nose; the intensity of the eyes. Heartened by the familiarity, she drew herself up and stared back, unblinking.

Winganuske saw how Pocahontas puffed herself up, and cuffed her sharply on the back of the head. Copper bells rang loud in Pocahontas's ear. "She can show your little one how to get along here in Werowocomoco, and since she is low-blooded, I can swear her to the task."

Pocahontas looked up at Winganuske, mouth agape with disbelief, but Winganuske just stretched out a hand to the *puccoon*-covered girl. The girl came to her call, a placid pup, and tucked herself comfortably under the favorite wife's arm.

"Amonute, this is Nonoma, the granddaughter of Opossu-no-quonuske and daughter of Powhatan. She is high blood of the Appamattuck, and you must treat her kindly. Nonoma, this is Amonute, a common girl of the Pamunkey and daughter of Powhatan. I give her to you. She will be your handmaid, and will help you learn how we get along here in Werowocomoco."

Pocahontas gasped. *Handmaid?* She must follow this red-stained chit about the town, toting her meals and shaking out her sleeping mats? And what more? Would she be required to wash Nonoma's high-blood hide at the morning bath, comb the tangles from her hair, chase the fleas from her bed with herb whisks in the middle of the night?

"Take her, Amonute," Winganuske said shortly.

Pocahontas grabbed Nonoma's hand and stomped back to Matachanna's side. Her face burned hot with rage.

Separated from her grandmother, Nonoma's eyes welled with tears.

"Don't weep," Pocahontas snapped.

"Don't be so cruel, Pocahontas." Matachanna dabbed the tears from Nonoma's eyes with her fingers, and then smudged the *puccoon* to cover their wet tracks. "You remember what it was like to leave your family and your village and come to Werowocomoco all alone. Poor Nonoma."

Pocahontas clicked her tongue in disgust. "How old are you?"

"I've seen nine winters," Nonoma said. Her voice was high and tremulous.

"Nine! You should have come to Werowocomoco years ago!"

Matachanna frowned. "Don't make her feel badly, you nasty black crow. She didn't choose when to come."

Pocahontas turned her back on the beaching canoes and led the way through the underbrush to the footpath. Nonoma followed closely. When they broke from the trees into the first great clearing, Pocahontas felt the new girl pause and stare at her first sight of the capital. Pocahontas had never been to Appamattuck-town, of course, but there was no doubt that Werowocomoco was far bigger than the village this red-painted whelp came from. In the five years since she had first arrived in her father's capital, Pocahontas had come to think of Werowocomoco as her true home, even though her mother's hearth was in Pamunkey territory, two days' journey up the river.

"It's such a big town," Nonoma said.

"Of course it is. Would you have the *mamanatowick* live in a squalid little heap like Appamattuck?"

"Appamattuck is not a squa . . . squal . . . what you say it is. It's the loveliest town in all of Tsenacomoco."

Matachanna laid an arm around Nonoma's shoulders. "Don't mind Amonute," she said. "Her tongue is sharp as a fish spear, I know, but she's good inside, once you get to know her. She's . . ."

Matachanna's mouth pressed into a thin line. Her warm, dark eyes wandered over Pocahontas's face and fell upon her chest as if Matachanna saw through flesh and bones, into her heart. Pocahontas knew she was searching for the right word—the truest word to describe her, the mantle that clothed the spirit inside. Pocahontas watched with growing dismay as Matachanna evaluated and discarded each possibility in turn. Earnest? No. Hardworking? Never. Loyal? Not even that.

At last Matachanna found what she was looking for. "She makes good jests."

Nonoma sniffled and balled her fists. Pocahontas raised an eyebrow as the younger girl drew herself up, donning haughty confidence like a cloak of feathers to disguise her trembling fear.

"Insulting Appamattuck-town is not a good jest," Nonoma said loftily. "And I shall not put up with the envious hissing of a common-born flea."

Pocahontas lunged toward the girl, her fingers like claws, grasping for the pearl-wrapped braid.

"No, no!" Matachanna stepped between them, flinging her hands out.

Matachanna missed her grab for Pocahontas's wrists, but Nonoma ducked away, and Pocahontas's tingling fingers closed on empty air.

"No fighting," Matachanna shouted. "You are to be Nonoma's handmaiden—you heard Winganuske's command. You two must get along! You have no choice but to be friends."

"*I* never got a handmaiden," Pocahontas said.

Nonoma sniffed. "You're not the blood of a *werowance*. If you're to serve me, you must learn to keep your place."

Pocahontas stepped calmly toward the girl, her face still, emotionless, serene as Winganuske's perfect mask. Her hands hung relaxed at her sides, but her palms burned with the flush of indignation. Nonoma peered up at Pocahontas, and a tentative smile appeared on the girl's round face. It was a smile of satisfaction, a sudden realization that this Amonute, this wild Pamunkey commoner, this Mischief, could be controlled with a firm word from high-blood lips.

"Well—" Nonoma began.

She didn't finish.

Pocahontas spat full in her face. There was a moment of shock, a thrilling sensation of suspended breath and heartbeat as Nonoma's eyes screwed tightly shut, as her mouth gaped round like the hollow in a tree when a dead branch falls away. Pocahontas watched her spittle run down Nonoma's cheek, clearing a sticky path through the expensive *puccoon*.

Then the moment passed, and Nonoma screamed as high and sharp as a hungry baby in a forgotten cradleboard. A roost of pigeons exploded out of the nearest tree, clattering through the branches.

"*Ama!*" the girl bawled. But of course her mother was not in Werowocomoco. The sudden reality of her isolation struck Nonoma like the blow of a war club. She crumpled to the ground, burying her face in the soft dampness of half-decayed leaves.

Pocahontas avoided Matachanna's eyes. A vicious guilt gnawed at her heart, and she could not bear her sister's reproachful stare now. The five years since she had arrived in the capital fell away from Pocahontas, peeling from her spirit like green husks stripped from an ear of corn. She was a child of six winters again, frightened and alone, thrust into a world that was much too large for her to ever find her place. She sank onto the loam beside Nonoma. The girl went on crying, keening her heartbreak to the uncaring woods. Clumsily, Pocahontas patted her back.

"I'm sorry, Nonoma. Truly. It was wicked of me. I won't do it again."

"Go away!"

A few women emerged from the door of a nearby house to stare at the scene. Pocahontas looked to Matachanna, pleading with her eyes for help, but Matachanna folded her arms across her chest and scowled.

"I won't go away," Pocahontas said. "I'm your handmaiden. So we must learn to get along. Here." She pulled her braid over her shoulder. She had tied all her favorite ornaments into her hair in anticipation of the coming feast. She was loath to part with any of them; it was not every day a common girl was given a disc of polished copper or a tassel of purple beads.

Her fingers landed on the most precious ornament of all: the dried foot of a kestrel, its delicate, jointed claws clutched tightly around a single sky-blue bead. Her uncle Opechancanough had given her the ornament last year, along with a message of love from her mother in Pamunkey-town. The blue bead was a true rarity. Her uncle said it had come from risky trade with the fearsome Massawomecks who lived beyond the rocky falls. The Massawomecks had obtained it from thick-bearded white men who hunted beaver and otter for their pelts—a strange, hairy-faced, strong-smelling tribe who called themselves the Frawh-say.

Pocahontas hesitated. A treasure like the blue bead would never come again. She pressed the kestrel's foot with her fingers, feeling the roughness of its skin, the neat, hard scales of its toes and sharpness of its claws. The bead was smooth and cool. She tugged it free of her braid.

"Look, Nonoma. See what I have."

The girl raised her face from the loam. Bits of leaf stuck to the wet red mess on her cheek. Pocahontas pressed the ornament into Nonoma's hand, then wiped the girl's face with gentle fingers.

Nonoma turned it over in her palm. She said nothing.

"It's yours." She took the kestrel's foot from Nonoma and tied it into the girl's braid among the pearls and copper bangles.

Pocahontas rose stiffly, and then offered her hand to pull Nonoma to her feet.

"We must *try* to be friends," Pocahontas said. She offered her first finger in truce. It wavered in the air between them while Nonoma sniffled. "I will teach you about Werowocomoco. But you cannot talk to me as if I'm dirt beneath your heel. Whatever you may think of my mother's blood, Powhatan is my father, just as he is yours."

Nonoma hooked her finger with Pocahontas's. "Very well."

In the *yehakin*—the longhouse Pocahontas shared with her sisters and unmarried aunts, she and Matachanna painted designs of black and yellow onto Nonoma's skin. They covered the places where spit and earth had rubbed the *puccoon* away while they taught Nonoma what she needed to know in her new life at Werowocomoco: when and where to bathe each morning, how to find the privy pits, which women made the finest corn flour and the sweetest dumplings. They told her where the best silk grass grew for weaving the softest basket straps, so soft they would never bite into her flesh no matter how heavy a burden she carried. They told her which old men in the village made good digging sticks, which grandmothers had the best remedies for cough and headache, and where to find soft moss for her belt to keep her bottom and thighs from chafing on hot summer days when she worked hard in the gardens.

After a time, Nonoma began to yawn, and Matachanna eased her down onto a heap of deerskins and covered her with a light bark mat. She and Pocahontas slid out of the house; the door flap fell into place behind them without a sound. They had talked to Nonoma for a long time. The muggy hours of afternoon were gone. The air had the feeling of impending evening, a gathering coolness and dampness. From beyond the gardens came the piping of a tiny screech owl just emerging from its hidden roost to prepare for a sunset hunt.

"You see?" said Matachanna. "She's not so bad after all."

"I still don't like being handmaiden to a high-blood sister."

"I know you don't. It isn't in your spirit to serve others. I don't know what Winganuske was thinking, giving you of all people to Nonoma. But truly, Pocahontas, *spitting* on her . . ."

"Listen!" The steady heartbeat of drums chanted through the woods. It was a sound lower than distant thunder, dark and compelling. "The last of the *werowances* has arrived. They'll be in Father's great house soon."

"And you," said Matachanna firmly, "will be here with Nonoma until the feast begins."

"Oh, come now. She's sleeping!"

"What if she wakes? She'll be frightened and alone. She needs you, Pocahontas."

"She has you."

"*I* wasn't commanded to be her handmaiden." Matachanna stared past Pocahontas's shoulder toward the river. Toward the guests. "Besides . . ."

"If Utta-ma-tomakkin has come, he will already be in the great house, and you won't see him until the feast. So you might as well stay here with Nonoma until the dancing begins."

Matachanna blushed at the sound of the priest's name. As a high-blood daughter of the *mamanatowick*, Matachanna would make a perfect wife for a man as powerful as Utta-ma-tomakkin. If only he could see how the girl followed his every movement with wide, shining eyes, as rapt as an infant staring at its mother. If he knew, he might sit with the *mamanatowick* to discuss a bride price for his prettiest and most dutiful daughter. Utta-ma-tomakkin, though, was a man of uncommon focus. He was as helpless to tear his attention from his divination bones and sacred pipe as Matachanna was to tear hers from the priest.

"If you let me go," Pocahontas said, "I will get into Father's *yehakin*. And if I see Utta-ma-tomakkin, I'll tell him you will dance for him tonight at the fire."

Matachanna gasped. "I never could! I would die of embarrassment. Anyhow, it's unkind of you to leave your work for me to do. Nonoma is your duty. You think of no one but yourself!"

"I think of you. I'll carry a message to Utta-ma-tomakkin for you. What shall I tell him?"

"You won't even get into the great house—not for a meeting like this one. Father's guards will never allow you inside."

Pocahontas narrowed her eyes to slits. "I have my ways. Well? Utta-ma-tomakkin waits!"

Matachanna scowled. "I'll stay with Nonoma. But you *must* be less selfish, Pocahontas. One day I'll grow tired of you dropping your work into my basket, and all your smiles and jests and charming ways will no longer be enough to make me like you." She did not wait for a reply, but ducked quickly back through the door and disappeared into the longhouse.

Pocahontas set off through the woodland at a run, pounding down the well-worn paths that wended between gardens and the blackened fire pits where racks of fish stood drying in columns of smoke. The sun was low and red between the trees, and the air bit at her skin with springtime chill. She passed the dance circle and the sweat lodge, and flew by the clearing where the women of the town stacked baskets of food for the feast. The pale bark siding of Powhatan's massive *yehakin* glowed a luminous crimson in the sunset. A single man ducked through the door flap; she caught the bright blur of a heavily painted apron before he vanished from sight. A *werowance*—the only one to be seen in the vicinity of the great house. All the chiefs must be inside already.

Pocahontas slowed, stopped, and braced her hands against her trembling knees as she panted on the edge of the clearing. A man with a spear followed on the heels of the *werowance*. The man took up his post outside the door, standing very straight and still. His eyes held a fierce glare, though its intensity was diminished somewhat by his ears, which stuck out from his head like a grouse's showy feather tufts.

Pocahontas strode toward the guard. As she drew closer, she could tell he was young, though she did not recognize him. This was not unusual; boys and girls kept to their own work, and Werowocomoco was a large town. Unlike Matachanna, Pocahontas had found little amusement in watching the boys' dances at the nightly fires, and so she did not know all the youth of the village on sight. She guessed the guard's age at no more than fifteen, barely old enough to shave a few wispy hairs from his chin. His arms and chest bore the remnants of bruises, not more than two weeks old by the look of them. The guard was fresh from his *huskanaw*, a months-long trial in the wilderness that ushered boys into man-hood—and killed those too weak to survive the brutal ordeal. She must be careful with this one. When the *huskanaw* was still vivid in a man's memory, his patience was short and he was quick to do violence.

"A good evening," she said politely, pressing one hand to her heart.

The guard glared.

"I have been called to serve the *werowances* bread and water. You must let me enter."

The guard snorted. "All the women who are serving went inside already. Run back to your *ama*, little girl. You have no place here."

Her spine went rigid with indignation. "My *ama* is not in Werowocomoco, for I am a daughter of Powhatan."

He gave an amused half smile. "You and half the females in Tsenacomoco. Go dig a privy pit. I'm not stupid. You want to spy on men's business so you can carry tales back to your gossip circle."

Pocahontas lifted the necklace Matachanna had given her. "Look: these aren't shell beads. They're real pearls. If I were an ordinary daughter of Powhatan, would I be wearing pearls? Now step aside! My father has called me, and I must serve his guests."

The guard said nothing. He stared into the woods, as unmoved by her words as if she were a mosquito buzzing around his big ears. Pocahontas kicked a pebble at him before remembering he was a man still aching from his *huskanaw*. He lurched at her as if he meant to grab her, and she bolted into the undergrowth, heart pounding. She kept running until the great house was well distant. Then she turned and swung wide through the trees, sliding past dark trunks, edging around the stiff branches of sapling thickets. She circled back through the gardens of Werowocomoco until she found the rear wall of Powhatan's great house.

Pocahontas crept from the brush and pressed herself against the outside wall. The smooth, well-cured bark brushed her cheek. She could smell the pungent smoke of tobacco and the animal reek of damp fur. Pocahontas moved silently along the perimeter of the great house, searching with her eyes and fingers until she found an old strip of bark whose edge curled slightly. She paused to listen to the low hum of conversation, gauging the distance between herself and the place inside where the *werowances* gathered. Then she slid her fingers beneath the edge of the strip and pried it slowly up. Several other strips came loose with it, making a gap just large enough to squeeze through. She held her breath until she was inside. The bark left stinging scrapes on her shoulders and legs. She found herself beneath the frame of a bed, well hidden in shadow and under fur. She lay flat on her belly and counted silently until the sting of her abrasions abated.

She watched several women's feet cross in front of her. They crossed and recrossed, paused, and turned. Beyond the women, in the center of the great house, the hunched figures of men were ranged in a circle around a well-fed heart fire. They were backlit, cast in stark silhouette by bright leaping flames. The chiefs passed a clay pipe among them, and as each exhaled his puff of tobacco, the black shape of his neighbor distorted and rippled through the smoke.

When the women had moved away, Pocahontas slithered from under the bed. A long-necked gourd rested beside a basket of round dumplings; she seized the gourd and hefted it to her hip. It was full of water and was heavier than she expected. She staggered a few steps before finding her balance. Water splashed over the rim and ran down her chest. Pocahontas turned quickly to brush herself against the furs piled on the bed, drying away the worst of it.

"You there," a woman's voice called, low and urgent, "bring the water. Be quick now!"

Pocahontas went where she was directed, stepping carefully between the *werowances* in their solemn circle, bending to trickle water into their oyster- or turtle-shell bowls, her face demurely downcast until she withdrew again into the shadows. "Keep a sharp eye on the chiefs, girl," one of Powhatan's wives admonished, her voice a hiss in Pocahontas's ear. "Do not let any bowl run dry."

Powhatan sat above his guests, couched on his massive platform bed. He was a man well beyond his prime, but not beyond his majesty. The years had begun to drain away some of his blocky strength, and time had blurred the edges of his tattoos, yet the firmness of his chest and shoulders was still evident. Like all men, the right side of his scalp was clean-shaven, but where the younger *werowances* had bound their left-sided locks in intricate knotted braids bristling with feathers and animal teeth, with long, ornamental copper pins that glinted in the firelight, Powhatan let his hair fall loose. It draped across his left shoulder like a curtain of misty rain. A patch of long, wiry hairs sprouted from his chin and upper lip. Powhatan had never been fond of the ordeal of the razor-shells, and now, in his old age, he reckoned he need not submit to any ritual of hygiene that disagreed with him. After all, he was the *mamanatowick*, the Chief of Chiefs, architect of the greatest unity Tsenacomoco had ever seen. He answered to no one but the Okeus, and evidently the god was willing to tolerate Powhatan's beard.

Pocahontas, half concealed by shadow, the heavy gourd pressing painfully into her hip, smiled at the sight of her father. She might have edged closer to fill his cup, but one of the pretty young wives reclining on the bed behind him uncurled her lithe body and tended to Powhatan's cup herself. Pocahontas frowned at the lost opportunity. Then Powhatan spoke, and she forgot everything but his words.

"Brothers," he said, his voice dry and deep, "most of you know already why I have summoned you to Werowocomoco. The rumors from the northern tribes are true. The *tassantassas* have returned."

It was good that the circle of chiefs hummed with murmurs, for Pocahontas could not stifle a gasp. A curious sensation knotted in her stomach, part fear, part excitement. All the children of the Real People knew of the *tassantassas*, pale-skinned men like the Frawhsay, those trappers who traded blue beads to the Massawomecks. *Tassantassas* were as small and mean-spirited as weasels. All of them, even the young ones, had beards like old men, but theirs were so thick and bushy that only their tiny blue eyes peered out above noses longer and more hooked than eagles' beaks. They smelled stronger than a deer-wallow in the rutting season. Worst of all, they took children onto their huge, white-winged boats and sailed away with them. Most of the abducted children were never seen again, though a few had found their way home, bringing stories of a white *mamanatowick* who was never seen by his subjects but demanded copious tribute of every type of shiny ore that could be dug from the earth or panned from the streams.

"We are here today," Powhatan went on, "to come to a consensus. It will please me to see all the Real People approach these white men in the same way. Let us be united, one People, as we face the *tassantassas*. Let us decide together whether we will drive them out"—a few men in the circle shouted their approval—"or make of them allies against our enemies to the west."

At the suggestion of an alliance, several men raised their voices in a cheer.

Powhatan leaned back; a deep umber shadow descended across his face. The circle of *werowances* rumbled with discussion. Pocahontas glanced from one chief's face to another, straining to catch their words. At last one man raised his palm, and the others quieted. It was Chopoke, the *werowance* of Mattaponi.

"These people are too dangerous," the chief said. "We all remember how they came before, stealing children from our villages. What kind of a people take children from their mothers? I already know the answer to that question: they are not people at all. They are demons. We should not allow them to remain. Drive them back across the sea to their homeland. We don't want them here! We have no use for them."

The next man to speak was Opechancanough, the uncle who had brought Pocahontas the kestrel-foot ornament. His great stature and bold, square face marked him as a brother of Powhatan, though he was younger by some ten or twelve years, and the slow creep of age had not yet settled on him. It had been more than a year since Pocahontas had seen her uncle last. He lifted his face to the firelight, and even at a distance Pocahontas was struck by the emotion that hung over his eyes like a ceremonial veil. She could not put a name to the strange intensity in his stare. There was something of rage in it, of loss and insecurity. There was a woundedness that was still brash and swaggering. Young though she was, Pocahontas sensed that this was a pain peculiar to a man. It put her in mind of a buck in rut, thrashing his antlers in the thicket, calling boldly to his does even while he limped with an arrow through his leg.

"Of course we remember how the *tassantassas* came before," said Opechancanough. The smoothness of his voice was at odds with the anger he wore like a bright feather mantle. "There is no doubt that they are a ruthless and unfathomable people. But they *are* people, not demons. We've killed them. We know they die when their blood is spilled. My friends, listen to me. There is much to be gained if we work with them."

"Never!" one of the men cried out.

Opechancanough raised a hand for silence. "The *tassantassas* have goods—valuable goods. Many things we can use to make our lives easier. Think of it: more copper for our trade with other tribes. Swords. Tools for your wives' gardens, and for digging *tuck-ahoe* roots out of the marshes. We can obtain these goods. We can make ourselves rich."

Chopoke's lean face hardened in a sour glare. "What have we to trade? They want nothing but our children, and all the copper in the world isn't worth that."

"We have knowledge to trade. Knowledge of the other tribes. Knowledge of trade and travel routes. They have returned seeking *something*, or else why return at all? This is our land. We will know how to get whatever it is they want. That is what we will offer in trade: the secrets of our territories. But we are smarter than they are, my friends. When we have taken all the valuable goods from their hands, we will demand their *service* in trade."

"Service?"

"They have swords. They have the terrible sticks they call *guns*, which roar like thunder and blast away flesh and bone. We will put these things to use for our own good, turn the *tassantassas* into a weapon. We will point that weapon first at the Massawomecks, take their land, and expand the domain of the Real People beyond the falls. And when we have conquered the Massawomecks, we will turn the *tassantassas* against all the rest."

Opossu-no-quonuske drained her turtle-shell bowl; Pocahontas scrambled forward to refill it. The heat of the fire struck her bare limbs and coaxed sweat from her skin. Or perhaps the sweat rose from the excitement of serving the *werowansqua*.

Opossu-no-quonuske took no notice of the girl with the water gourd. She nodded in Opechancanough's direction. "My brother is wise. We can tame these *tassantassas* to our hands. Yes, I know their weapons are terrible and their boats are swift and very large. So much the better, I say. Let us make the *tassantassas'* strengths our own. You men who quail at the thought of the white men forget one simple fact: the *tassantassas* are not Real People." She struck her chest with one tattooed fist. "In the end, they will amount to little more than dogs scrapping for bones. Like dogs, they can be trained to work for us. Do you agree with me? Or will you finally be forced to admit that a woman is braver than all the *werowances* put together?"

Pocahontas slid back into the shadows as the circle burst out with good-natured laughter. The weight of the discussion's intensity lifted for a heartbeat, and a breath of the *werowances'* relief seemed to pass across her skin.

Chopoke said, "No one doubts your bravery, Opossu-no-quonuske, nor the bravery of the Appamattuck. What we doubt is whether we can trust the *tassantassas*. I still maintain that creatures who take children away cannot ever be expected to behave like men. Or even like dogs."

Powhatan leaned forward, his sheet of silver hair glistening in the firelight. "Chopoke, I hear your words. Your concerns are well founded. Yet my brother and sister also speak wisely. What indeed has brought the *tassantassas* back to our land?" He paused. The logs on the heart fire popped; a column of sparks rose like red stars amid the smoke. At last Powhatan said slowly, "Could it be that the Okeus has brought them back?"

The gathered chiefs let out a collective sigh, a gust of awe and fear.

"Now I will tell you what I think," Powhatan said. "I think we have been granted an opportunity. The time has come to push our boundary beyond the barrier of the falls. The Okeus means for the Real People to hold all the lands, even to the distant mountains. But we need better weapons if we are to accomplish such a task. The Okeus has brought those weapons to us. He has all but placed them in our hands."

"I do not believe it," Chopoke said. His voice was nearly a shout, and several other men nodded, while others murmured in support of his dissent. "These white men are far too dangerous and ruthless to have come from our god. Our god is no fool."

"Neither is your *mamanatowick*." Powhatan stared coldly down from the height of his bed until the circle relapsed into silence. "Before we commit to taming the white dogs, we must learn more about them. How many are there? What are their habits, their strengths, their weaknesses? I know they have come ashore in the territory of Paspahegh. Wowinchopunck!"

The *werowance* of Paspahegh stiffened at the sound of his name. "I am here, Powhatan." His voice was low and tense with quiet control. The sound reminded Pocahontas of a cougar ready to spring.

"Where have they landed, exactly?"

"On the bit of mud that extends into the river—the one separated from the land by a narrow neck."

"I know the place," Powhatan said. "Barely more than a marsh."

Chopoke squinted into the firelight. "Why come ashore there? It makes no sense. There is no good land there, nowhere to plant a garden, no deer to hunt, barely any birds, except in late autumn . . . Do you not see? These beasts don't think like men. And you propose to tame them? *Hah*."

Powhatan continued as if Chopoke had not spoken. "It is your land, so you will meet with the *tassantassas*, Wowinchopunck."

The chief of the Paspahegh nodded, eager and fierce.

"Find out from them whatever you can. Count their numbers; that will be a place to start. And learn what their failings are. Learn how we can control them."

Pocahontas's arms had begun to shake from the weight of her gourd. She bent and eased it to the ground. Firelight danced in the darkness, brilliant spots of violet and blue glaring against shadow. She blinked to clear the flaring afterimage from her vision, then squeezed her eyes tightly shut. *Tassantassas.* She turned the word over in her mind, feeling the strange cold weight of it. A perfect memory of the *werowances* was burned against her eyelids. With her eyes shut, she saw them as dark voids in the shape of familiar men, sitting very still against a fire that limned them in violent colors—the colors of war paint, of spilled blood. The colors of the sky, moments after the sun has set.

SMITH

May 1607

The bundle of saplings fell from Smith's shoulder with a clatter. He stared at them where they lay shivering in the mud.

Christ have mercy, but what good are a few twigs?

Most of the men had worked industriously, expending effort and precious enthusiasm on a very civilized and very useless fence, the type one might find surrounding a proper English garden. Even some of the gentlemen had pitched in to erect this fine monument to inutility, soiling their hands alongside the rougher sort of man. The fence now stood nearly complete, more gap than barrier, encircling the tents of Jamestown like the bold black ring of a marksman's target.

Smith had suggested they build a palisade, solid and high. And because Smith suggested a palisade, Wingfield built a garden fence. For explanation, he'd made a few noises about the Virginia Company's instructions, their strict admonishment to avoid stirring up trouble with the naturals. *A fence,* Wingfield had said, *is a friendlier gesture than a palisade. A fence is neighborly. Even a savage can understand the difference between a fence and a palisade.* But whatever Wingfield might say, Smith knew the fence now stood only to mock his own caution.

Smith turned in a slow circle, staring. He was grateful to be out of the woods, where a hundred unseen eyes caused a curious pressing sensation on his skin. The tents of Jamestown squatted in orderly rows on a level expanse of grass, already trampled flat into the muddy earth. The natural clearing occupied a broad spit, thrust like a thumb into the river. The river was exceptionally wide here, and rose and fell slightly with the cycle of tides.

From a stand of trees that bristled near the spit's center came the ringing of axes. As Smith watched, one tree's great canopy slowly tilted, paused as if making up its mind, and then crashed to the earth in a rush. A flight of waterfowl rose crying from a patch of salt bog. On the flat gray face of the river, the three ships rested with sails furled. St. George's cross, crimson on a white field, flew from the mast of the *Susan Constant*. It snapped in the breeze, rolling like the shrug of a lazy man's shoulder. A little shallop, carried from England piecemeal in the hull of one of the ships, had been assembled and stood at anchor closer to shore. Two rowing flats lay beached on the muddy strand.

A crack sounded from somewhere in a bog thicket. A bird scolded, a high, repetitive call. Smith's hand fell to the short stock of his snaphaunce. The gun was a reassuring weight at his belt, and a rare sight since the expedition had disembarked. Wingfield had admonished the men to leave their firearms locked away, insisting they would not be needed. Firearms, he said, would be a temptation to do evil to the naturals. Once the first shot was fired, the savages would mistrust the English, and the expedition would fail.

Smith ignored the order. His piece would do no good packed in a crate.

Gabriel Archer's hands were healing well enough—it was a mercy the arrows that pierced his palms had not been tipped with poison—but Smith had no intention of receiving similar wounds. Archer's hands should have been enough to convince Wingfield that the naturals were not the gentle people he imagined them to be, friendly and childlike and glad to embrace civilization and the Christ, once shown the superiority of English ways. This was a harsh land, a place of dense sucking bogs and tangled forest, rushing water and changeable skies. The people who called this place home must be forged of a cold, hard metal. Only the ruthless could survive here.

And so Smith had brushed past Wingfield to retrieve his snaphaunce from its crate. Wingfield may have convinced the remainder of the council that the naturals would not look upon their fence of twigs and their unarmed condition as an invitation to be slaughtered, but not even God himself could convince John Smith that he should trust the Indians. At any rate, Wingfield had made it clear that Smith was not truly a member of the council—not yet, no matter what the instructions from the Virginia Company specified. Wingfield did not trust him. He insisted that Smith could never be trusted, and, given his attempts at mutiny, his participation in the council must be further considered and voted upon.

It was all one to John Smith. According to his calculations, if he could not be trusted with a seat on the council then he was under no obligation, official or practical, to comply with any of Wingfield's demands—including his demand that firearms remain packed away.

When Smith had tossed the lid of the crate aside and lifted his gun free of its packing, Wingfield had snarled, "If we were in England, I would scorn that any man should think you my companion."

In reply, Smith had thrust the piece through his belt and walked away.

Matthew Scrivener emerged from the cluster of tents, choosing his way through the boggy puddles and patches of muck with careful deliberation. Smith noted with grim amusement that a sidearm swung from Scrivener's belt, bouncing gently against his thigh.

Scrivener stopped at Smith's heap of saplings and stood gazing down at them in thoughtful silence. The blows of axes sounded again from the woodland. They rebounded off the opposite shore of the James River and staggered over one another, *ra-tat, ra-tat.*

"Good day," Smith said.

Scrivener said nothing. His hand was pale on the butt of his gun. His eyes scanned the thickets, squinting against the glare of midday. "Do you think they'll return?"

Two days gone, a band of Indian men had paid a visit to the spit. They came gliding across the water in their long, dark canoes, their bodies moving in unconscious accord like the limbs of a smooth-gaited horse, the paddles cutting and pulling and sliding in such unison that Smith had found himself staring at the perfection of motion, caught up in some fatal trance as the boats drew nearer. Thank God, the visit had been friendly. The men had indicated with signs—surprisingly simple to understand—that their king wished to call on the English, that he would bring a deer for a feast and all would make merry, all would be friends. They called their king Wowinchopunck.

The ease with which he comprehended the naturals' meaning had made Smith's belly quiver. He had spent two days wondering at his fear, and now, as he and Scrivener stood over the saplings that would add to the fence—their useless, flimsy protection—he understood. Never in his life had Wingfield been more wrong than he was in his assumption that the naturals were innocent, uncivilized savages. No, they were every bit as calculating and as self-interested as any Englishman—and a good deal more sophisticated than most.

"Aye," Smith said. "They'll be back."

"When, do you think?" Scrivener's voice betrayed no concern, but Smith's eye strayed again to the man's firearm. His hand was still wrapped tight around the stock.

A "halloo" rose from one of the ship's masts and Smith glanced toward the river to see one of the sailors high in the rigging making an urgent gesture upstream. There, moving swiftly toward their undefended spit with that familiar hypnotic unity, were the low black slashes of canoes.

"I should think," said Smith, "they'll return very soon."

Even before the canoes beached, it was apparent that there were at least twice as many naturals this time. The English managed to recall all their men from woodcutting duty and assemble them in a ragged crowd just as the first boats grounded. The naturals sprang from their boats with their typical alacrity, and together five or six of them bent over the largest canoe. They lifted out a deer, feet trussed up on a stout pole. It was freshly killed, judging by the steady drip of blood that fell from its nostrils. The deer's head swayed on a limp, soft neck as it was carried up the strand. The head was flung far back, dangling toward the earth, the eyes half-closed. It gave an impression of desperation so acute it was almost comical. Smith felt as if he were watching a puppet play or some fantastical masque. But the steady, sober faces of the Indian men were no fancy.

The men who did not carry the deer carried bows nearly as long as the men themselves, and the Indians towered over all but the tallest of the English. Quivers made of hides with the fur still on hung at each man's hip. The men sported leather wraps from ankle to upper thigh, and each had a flexible codpiece of pale doeskin cinched tightly to his belt, tucking his manly parts away. All else was left bare, but for sinuous black and earth-red tattoos. It was sensible costume if these men had come to make war, for they could run without chafing and sweat freely, cooling their skin, remaining spry and alert while the English roasted in their wool and steel, growing slower and more careless by the moment. Smith's palm turned damp against the butt of his gun.

What the Indians lacked in ornate clothing was made up for tenfold with their hair. Each man wore the right side of his scalp shaved down to stubble. Roached hair stood up like a hawk's crest at their crowns. The left sides of their heads were bound in looped plaits and intricate knots, bedecked as gaily as a Yuletide table. Bells of copper and iron tinkled amid discs of gleaming white shell, each as large as a man's palm. One man's knot bristled with dozens of fierce-looking quills far longer than any hedgehog's; another sported the yellow leg of an eagle with its hard scales and rictus claws; yet another seemed to house a live, bright-green snake within his hair. As the man drew near, Smith watched the serpent ripple and shudder, coiling deep within the nest of the knotted braid.

Smith also realized the function of these peculiar hairstyles: with the hair shorn from the right side of a man's body, it could never tangle in his bowstring.

Christ preserve us, everything these people do, even the way they cut their hair, is a preparation for war.

Smith glanced at Wingfield. The man was all smiles, waving his welcome, patting the other Englishmen on their backs as if to brace them up.

"He still thinks they're like children," Smith muttered to Scrivener. "A hundred of them come with bows taller than Wingfield himself, and he thinks they've come to sit at his knee and learn to take the Sacrament."

Gabriel Archer stirred uneasily at Smith's side. He held his bandaged hands stiffly away from his body. They twitched as if he longed to seize a gun. "I don't like it," Archer said, voice quaking. "Why have they brought bows? They've come to make war on us, or I'm a dog's uncle."

A rumble passed through the crowd of English, a sound tense with fear.

"Now, Archer," Smith said, laying a hand on his shoulder. "You mustn't fear. We must all remain calm. They haven't come to make war—not yet, at any rate."

"Then why are they here? What do they want?"

"They've come to learn," Smith said. "They want to see us, to know us. They want to test us, find out what we're made of. There's nothing to fear, I swear it. Not today." *Not yet.*

The procession of Indians shifted, parted, and one emerged—Wowinchopunck, their king. He carried himself with a quiet self-possession, and above his piercing dark eyes a circlet of some coarse, red-dyed animal hair bristled tall upon his brow. Wowinchopunck's stare moved calmly over the gathered English. He paused a moment on Smith's face. His mouth jerked as if he might speak, and then he found Wingfield. The Indian king nodded once and stepped toward Wingfield with a hand pressed to his heart.

"*Wingapoh,*" said the king. His voice was as deep and cold as earth.

Wingfield made some elaborate gesture; the Indian king watched in silence, and then, when he was sure Wingfield had finished, he indicated the deer on its truss. The king made a rapid rubbing motion in the air, and Smith could all but see the fire stick smoldering in his great, hard hands. Wowinchopunck's fingers danced in perfect imitation of flames.

"Er . . . ," said Wingfield.

"He wants you to make a fire," Smith said, "to roast the meat."

"Of course."

Wingfield set some of the English to the task. The collection of tents grandly known as Jamestown did have a common area with a fire pit. The men blew a handful of smoldering coals back to life and nursed them into a respectable flame, and then set about constructing a spit large enough to support the weight of the deer. Meanwhile, a few Indians bent to the job of gutting and skinning the beast. The majority of the men, English and natural alike, stood back with arms folded, eyeing one another with cautious curiosity.

Smith tried a few gestures, signs he hoped would be interpreted as friendly. At length one of the Indian men gestured back, a rather abrupt motion that set a few of his fellows to laughing. Smith gave a tentative smile. Then he presented the naturals with a gesture exceedingly rude. Some of the English gentlemen gasped; one laborer snickered. The naturals, perceiving at once that Smith had returned fire, broke into wide grins.

The Indian who had made the offensive sign nodded toward Smith's snaphaunce. His eyes were hungry on the weapon. Smith covered it with his hand and shook his head emphatically. The Indian took a few steps toward him. Smith felt his English fellows edge back, but he remained standing in place. As the Indian drew near, Smith could see that he was a young man, not quite twenty years old, with an unlined face and the barest hint of adolescent clumsiness in the long, hard-muscled arms. The Indian nodded again toward the gun, reaching out a hand in a seeking gesture. Smith held out his own hand, firm and commanding: *stop*. A flicker of anger moved across the young man's face, and then was gone again, replaced by deliberate, well-calculated calm.

Smith tapped his chest. "John Smith," he said.

The young man stared at him.

He tried again. "John Smith." Tapping.

Comprehension lit black eyes. The Indian tapped his own chest. "Naukaquawis," he said, and then, touching Smith's chest, "Chawnzmit."

Smith returned the gesture, repeating the young man's name, or what he hoped was an acceptable approximation. The lad glanced back at his fellows with a wide grin. He said something in his own tongue, a rapid, rattling sound. Soon the Indians were moving toward the crowd of trembling English, reaching out to tap chests, offering names.

Smith kept his gun well guarded, but not all the English were so careful with their tools. Young Naukaquawis, after making introductions to a few more Englishmen, managed to lift a wood-cutter's axe from a belt loop. He hefted the tool with a look of great appreciation, testing its weight and balance in his palm.

"Give it back!" cried the man who had lost it. It was Samuel Fletcher, a laborer, strong of body but rather lacking in wits.

Naukaquawis squinted at Fletcher and shuffled away, tucking the axe protectively behind his back.

"You bloody devil," one of the Englishmen snarled.

"Wait," Smith called. "Let it go."

"By God, I will not! No red devil will thieve from me!" Fletcher threw himself fists-first at Naukaquawis.

The Indian hooked a foot around Fletcher's ankle and dumped him on his backside in the mud. Fletcher roared and came up swinging. The young Indian tucked the axe into his quiver, locked his arms around Fletcher's shoulders, and heaved him headfirst across the grounds as easily as a man might sling a half-empty sack of flour.

Fletcher fell in a heap at the feet of the Englishmen. He was by no means a small man and to see a bull like Fletcher tossed about like a knotted rag fairly stole the breath from English lungs. The colonists stared down at their man in fearful silence while he slipped and struggled in the mud.

Naukaquawis tipped up onto the balls of his feet, spry as a sapling, poised to take Fletcher on again. Several of the naturals' bows snapped to the vertical. An arrow hissed as it slid from a quiver.

Smith raised his hands in a conciliatory gesture, dodging between Naukaquawis and Fletcher. He pressed his hand to his heart, struggling to remember the word their king had used. *"Wingapoh."* He hoped it meant *peace*.

Wowinchopunck, the king himself, distracted from his discourse with Wingfield, strode toward his men. He growled out a few words. Smith wasn't sure whether that harsh, guttural tone was directed at the English or at the naturals, but Wowinchopunck's men murmured and stamped.

You English are too hostile, the king seemed to say with abrupt gesture and scowling face. *Too quick to take offense.*

All at once the naturals marched away, retreating to the riverbank and hauling their half-skinned deer with them. Wowinchopunck made a few final gestures of disgust and disappointment, then gave his men one low command. They slid their canoes out onto the river, turned upstream, and paddled away as swiftly and smoothly as they had come.

"A fine day's work," Smith said. He shoved through the crowd, making for the outer edge of the encampment. His shoulder struck Fletcher's as he bulled past. Scrivener and Archer followed him.

"To be honest," said Archer, "I'm glad to see the back of them. Call me a coward if you must."

"No one questions your mettle," Scrivener told him. "The Good Lord knows you've a right to be wary of them, more than the rest of us."

"May they never return," Archer said.

Smith rounded on them. "Don't you see, we *need* them to return!"

Scrivener and Archer exchanged slow, wary glances.

"Just look at them," Smith thundered. "They're lean as greyhounds, but strong. You saw how that one threw Fletcher! Where does that strength come from? Do you suppose they eat deer year-round? Of course not. A man eats nothing but meat, he grows fat as a lord and can barely lift a tankard of ale, let alone throw a creature like Fletcher across a yard."

The others remained silent. Smith growled in frustration and threw his hands into the air. "What do they eat? Where do they find it? What do they do for food in the wintertime? We must know these things if we're to survive here."

"Steady, Smith." Scrivener laid a hand on his shoulder. "We have our supplies, with more shipments coming. Don't tell me you'd rather live on roots and berries, or whatever the naturals eat, than civilized fare."

Smith shook his head. "I thought you were wiser than that, Scrivener. What happens if the shipments are delayed? There's food all around us in this land, and yet we don't know it when we see it. Wingfield thinks the naturals are like children waiting for guidance, yet it's we who are weak in this place, we who blunder about in ignorance. We don't know a wholesome berry from a poisonous one. Come to that, we don't know a friendly Indian from a hostile one. We don't know their weaknesses, how they can be subdued. We *need* them. We must learn their ways. If we don't, we will die. Mark my words."

And so it was that Smith was the only man among the English who rejoiced to see the Indians return two days later. He was helping to raise a cabin wall when the lookout sounded again from the *Godspeed*'s mast. This time, when the canoes made landfall, Smith was waiting on the strand. Twoscore Indians carried a new deer, but their king in his bristling red-fur crown was not among them. Smith stared out across the river to the dense woodland on the opposite shore, wondering where Wowinchopunck might be hiding with the remainder of his forces. But he led the Indians toward Jamestown, talking in gestures and grunts and the few words he had gleaned of their language from their previous visit.

By the time they reached the assembled Englishmen, the naturals had made it clear that they intended to spend the night at Jamestown. Smith explained to Wingfield and the other members of the council.

"Absolutely not," said Gabriel Archer. "I've never heard of a greater folly."

Bartholomew Gosnold, square-jawed and flat-faced, shook his head. "They'll only creep about looking for things to steal."

The council was in full agreement. Even had they recognized Smith as a member, his word would have convinced no one. It fell to him to turn the Indians away. He cursed the shortsightedness of his fellows as he gestured their rejection to the naturals. The Indians grew agitated at his signs, visibly bristling with offense, and Smith cursed the council all the more.

This time they did not pause to collect their deer as they stormed toward the canoes. Smith cast about for some means of keeping them there, grasping for some small piece of knowledge he might salvage from the council's blunder. He swung his fists at his sides as if he might beat back the devil of his own helplessness, and his hand struck the butt of his snaphaunce.

"Wait," Smith cried. Though the word meant nothing to them, the desperation in his tone caused a few of the Indians to turn.

Smith drew his gun, held it casually across his chest, grinning through the tangle of his beard. The afternoon sun glinted on the wheel lock.

The Indians hesitated.

Smith aimed the gun down the length of the yard, sighted, and looked back to the naturals with an air of playful appeal.

They took a few steps toward him, arguing among themselves.

Smith beckoned to them, holding the lure of the gun in plain view, now and then sighting as if he might fire at some invisible target.

Scrivener approached. His eyes were wide and fearful beneath the brim of his steel helmet; he must have donned the thing when he heard the lookout's cry. "What in God's name are you doing?"

"Bring me a leather breastplate," Smith said. "Quickly."

"Smith . . ."

"Do it."

While the Indians milled nearby, Smith propped the breast-plate onto the highest rail of the fence. It was a well-made piece of armor, stiff and thick, near as hard as oak. By now the English had gathered, too, keeping well clear of the naturals, watching Smith's show with wary curiosity.

Smith measured forty paces from the target. At such a distance, the bullet from his gun might dent the breastplate but certainly would not penetrate it.

He aimed with exaggerated care. The Indians held their breath as one body, leaning toward him, wide-eyed and eager.

Smith allowed the moment to hang, savoring the wild thrill of anticipation. Then he dropped his arm, made a little bow with hand to heart, shaking his head in a self-deprecatory manner. *Where are my manners?* he seemed to say. He swept one arm toward the target. *Please, you must fire first.*

Naukaquawis stepped forward immediately, the dark shaft of a fire-hardened arrow already nocked to his bow. He swaggered up to Smith's side, spat a few words in his harsh tongue, and took great care in placing his feet precisely beside Smith's. The youth drew his bow, which creaked under the strain. In the heartbeat during which he aimed, the lean, hard muscles of his chest and arms sprang into sudden detail, every sinew and fiber standing in relief through his coppery skin.

The shaft thunked into the breastplate before Smith even realized Naukaquawis had fired. Smith blinked down the length of the yard. The arrow's pale-brown fletching vibrated with the force of the impact. The leather vest was knocked so badly askew that it might have fallen to the ground but for the fact that the arrow had punched straight through the leather, embedding itself deeply into the post.

The English raised their voices in a great roar of consternation.

Smith held up his hands for silence. He swept the steel helmet from Scrivener's brow, ignoring the man's squawk of indignation. The helmet crowned the post where the thoroughly slain vest hung.

Smith gestured again for Naukaquawis to take his aim. The lad was obviously pleased by the dismay his archery caused. He smirked as he pulled a new arrow from his quiver and nocked it to his string. He sighted down the shaft, his dark eyes sparking with confidence.

Then the boy loosed, and it was Smith's turn to smirk. Arrow met cold steel with a crack like lightning; a flurry of debris flashed into the air, feathers, wooden splinters, an arrowhead flipping end over end. The helmet remained resolutely in place.

The English cheered.

Naukaquawis shouted and clenched a fist in anger. His fellows clamored, stiff-backed and flushed.

Smith pressed his hand to his heart, but the Indians jeered and turned their backs. As they fled in their canoes, Smith wrenched the arrow from the post and slid the breastplate from the shaft. The hole in the center was wide enough to slip his smallest finger through.

"I can't see that we've gained anything by your display, Smith." Bartholomew Gosnold sipped spiced wine from a cracked porcelain cup, eschewing the clay jugs most of the men used. The light of the communal fire traced the cup's bottom edge, rolling like a bead as Gosnold tilted the delicate thing in his large, square hand. The four walls of Jamestown's first cabin loomed, still roofless, in the nighttime shadows beyond the fire.

"Can you not?" *How like you*, Smith did not say.

"Now the naturals are angrier than ever."

The colony had made good use of the deer the Indians left behind, gathering around the fire pit to roast and carve it. After days of gruel and dried apples, the smell of char and fat had been as sweet as the perfumes of Eden. Now, twenty or so men lounged on rough benches hewn out of logs, quiet with satiety and exhaustion.

The ship's boy, Thomas Savage, moved in and out of the fire-light like a small, pale wraith, silently gathering up bowls and knives. The boy dragged a finger through the grease at the bottom of a bowl and licked it. He watched Smith, expectant, waiting for a sharp reply to Gosnold's taunt.

Deliberately, and with great effort, Smith spoke in a neutral, almost friendly tone. "We know now that their weapons are far superior to ours."

"Superior!" Gosnold fairly barked he word. "We have *guns*, Smith. A well-aimed lead ball could tear the bow arm off an Indian. What have they got but clubs and a few sharpened sticks?"

Heat rose to Smith's face, and he abandoned his pretense of neutrality. "Aye, a lead ball could do the trick at near enough range. And while you're reloading and readying your matchlock, those Indians who haven't moved out of range will feather you with a half-dozen arrows apiece. Their accuracy is better, they're much quicker to fire, and we've found out that their sharpened sticks can pierce leather armor."

Gosnold sniffed. "But not steel."

"Am I to understand you'll be sleeping and pissing in steel from now on?"

"Smith isn't wrong," said Matthew Scrivener. "We know more about the Indians now than we knew yesterday. It was of value to us."

"Well, what are we to do with the information?" Gosnold asked.

"We ought to do as I suggested on our first day in the New World," Smith said. "Build a palisade around the fort. It would be much better protection against those arrows than whatever you call the useless contraption we've currently got."

"It is called," Wingfield said with great dignity, "a fence. And your suggestion remains as ridiculous now as it was on our arrival.

We can win their friendship if we don't take pains to humiliate them, as you've done. Building a palisade would take five times the effort we've already expended on the fence."

"If we'd put forth that effort from the start, we'd have a fifth of our palisade already," said Smith.

A few of the men nearby muttered agreement. Wingfield squinted into the darkness as if to pick out the faces of the dissenters.

"Let us be honest with one another," Smith said.

Wingfield smiled wryly. "Indeed, let's."

"The only reason you refuse to build a palisade is because it was my idea. Had any other man suggested it, the palisade would be standing by now, and we would be sheltered. God alone knows how many Indians are out there in the darkness at this very moment."

Thomas Savage dropped a bowl with a clatter. Several of the men jumped.

Smith raised his voice. "The truth is, Wingfield, that you are envious of me."

Wingfield hooted. It took Smith a moment to realize the sound was laughter. It was the first time he had ever heard Wingfield laugh. "Envious? Of you?"

Smith squared his shoulders. "Of my authority."

More voices rose in laughter. "What authority?" somebody called from the darkness. "You are no gentleman, Smith."

Stiff-backed, Smith rose from his log bench. He turned his back on the colonists with a smooth, deliberate coolness. He walked into the darkness toward his tent as though he feared nothing, certainly not the jeers of senseless men. But until he reached the concealment of his cold, damp quarters, his body was rigid as stone. He half expected the keen-eyed stare of Naukaquawis sparking like embers in the dark, and the sudden punch of an arrow through his gut.

He ducked into his tent and rolled himself in his blankets. Just as his body heat was beginning to beat back the worst of the chill, filling his bedroll with a wan, uncertain warmth, the image of the hole in the leather breastplate came to Smith's tired mind. He fought the vision away, but it persisted, until finally Smith cursed and slid from his bedroll. The wet chill assaulted his skin; he shivered violently as he bent to the box that contained all his worldly possessions. He found his steel helmet easily enough and set it beside his blankets. He tossed aside his leather breastplate in disgust. His cold, stiff fingers brushed the unmistakable roughness of chain mail and Smith pulled the shirt from his box and laid it out on the ground. It needed cleaning and oiling; he could smell the tang of rust. But in a pinch, it would do.

Sleep was a very long time in coming. Even Constantinople wasn't enough to take him away from the hard, unfriendly bed. Antonia's voice crying out in ecstasy could not drown out the jeers of the men in the firelight. *You are no gentleman.* When at last he fell into a shallow, fitful slumber, he dreamed of Antonia with a razor in her hand, shaving away all the lovely, dark hair from one side of her scalp. Smith caught the locks as they fell, thick black coils that turned to snakes in his hands. They writhed in slow loops and struck him with their fangs. The venom coursed cold through his flesh, burning along his veins.

The chill woke him. In the throes of his nightmare he had kicked the bedroll apart, and now he was wracked with cold. He groped for the ends of the blankets. A faint sound halted his movement, a whisper so slight he was not at all certain he'd heard anything. Smith froze like a rabbit in the brush, listening, splayed helpless on his back in the impenetrable darkness of the tent. His pulse beat furiously in his tight, dry throat; serpents writhed in his gut.

The whisper came again. And in another moment he heard a crackling: the sudden rush of flames. A man screamed in terror. A chorus of voices answered in piercing, yowling whoops, crying in frantic excitement, baying like hounds on the scent.

Smith rolled to his knees, seized the mail shirt, and jerked it over his head. The cold of it was a fire on his skin. He crammed the helmet onto his head, realized it was backward, and righted it with a calm so at odds to his panic that it startled him. He found his snaphaunce in the darkness and eased it into his palm.

He crept carefully from the tent, staying low. The yard was in chaos. Men staggered from their tents, some of them reflecting starlight from steel, others armored with nothing more substantial than leather, or, more foolish still, their own skins. A nearby man raised the long, lean arm of a matchlock and aimed. Smith heard the iron click of the serpentine and tensed for the blast of the gun, but none came. The man cursed extravagantly; the wick of his match had snuffed itself out in the damp night. He ducked behind his tent to relight the wick just as the pale streak of an arrow hissed by, burying itself in the mud.

The peaked roof of a tent smoldered and one wall of the cabin was ablaze. As Smith watched, a thin line of fire spread around the perimeter of the camp: the naturals had set the fence alight.

A pack of great, lean Indians went loping by. Smith pressed himself into the mud, hardly daring to breathe, still as a stone in the deep-indigo shadow of his tent. When the Indians had passed, Smith steadied his snaphaunce and fired after them. A gust of sparks hissed from the wheel lock. An instant later the gun kicked in Smith's hand. The pop of the lead ball cracked into the night. Smith blinked, blinded by the flare of sparks. He could not tell whether his bullet had found its mark.

From somewhere in the darkness he heard English voices cursing, and then screaming. Smith edged from tent to tent, making his way toward the river. He sprinted past the cabin, choking on the thick smoke, his eyes hot and streaming with tears. Beyond stood the supply tent. A row of barrels crouched sepia red in the light of the burning building. Smith made straight for them, never slowing. He hoisted his gun high as he planted his free hand atop one keg, hurled his body up and over, and landed hard on the other side. The whistle and impact of arrows on wood reverberated along the ranks of barrels.

"Master Smith!"

The ship's boy, Thomas Savage, huddled against one keg, pressing his thin, frail body against the slats as if he might find some admittance and conceal himself within it.

Smith reloaded his gun, and then peered cautiously through a gap in their wall of flour and beans. The fierce orange light was sliced by flickering shadows. The flash of strong running legs. The fluidity of a body pausing, raising a bow, drawing. Smith poked the muzzle of his gun through the gap but could not find a clear enough view to justify a shot.

The glow of the flames illuminated the bellies of the three ships anchored in the river. The ships were not far. Perhaps . . .

He caught sight of one of the little rowing skiffs resting on the muddy shore.

"Thomas, listen well. Get out to that skiff and row for the *Discovery*."

"I?" the boy squeaked.

Smith eyed the lad's skinny arms, the pigeon breast showing through the wool of his sleep shirt. "You'll have to do; there's nobody else."

"But they'll shoot me, Master Smith!"

"I'll keep them off you." Smith showed him the gun.

A scream ripped the night. Thomas gasped.

"We must stop them, boy. The sailors still aboard the ship can do it. But you must carry them a message from me. Brace up; if I see any Indian aim a bow your way, I'll shoot him. Now here is what you're to tell the sailors."

In a moment more, Thomas Savage was skittering through the darkness, half-crouched, his spindle legs carrying him across the open ground and to the skiff as quick as a loosed colt. Smith glanced around for Indians, and then watched as the boy threw his weight against the skiff. It held fast in the mud. He jerked again, and it slid toward the river with agonizing slowness. Smith heard a whoop from nearby, and trained his gun in the direction of the sound, ready to fire should he catch sight of an Indian. Thomas was ankle deep in the river now, the skiff rising free of the mud, skimming along the surface. The boy leaped into the boat and ran out the oars. His thin arms looked frail in the moonlight, but he rowed for the *Discovery* with all his strength.

Smith heard the harsh, strange tongue of the Indians, shouting from the direction of the burning cabin. He peered through his gap and found his target standing in perfect range, framed by the sides of the barrels, backlit by the blaze. There was something familiar about the whiplike strength of the limbs, the arrogant square of the shoulders. *Naukaquawis.* If he fired now, the naturals would be upon him before he could reload. He must wait until he had no choice: shoot or die. Smith gritted his teeth as Naukaquawis swaggered away.

He spared another glance at the ships. The skiff had reached them and Thomas was bobbing in the little boat, cupping his hands at his mouth, shouting. The sailors burst into action. Smith saw the tiny red eye of a lit match twinkle at the *Discovery*'s rail. Thomas Savage ducked into the hull of the skiff, clapping his hands to his ears, and Smith dropped to his belly in the cold slime.

The terrible, hollow roar of the cannon shook the earth. An instant later it rebounded from the opposite shore. Another blast followed seconds after.

The naturals set up a high-pitched cry of alarm. There were a few shouted words in their language and the thud of a final arrow smacked into the keg near Smith's head. Then the camp was quiet, save for the crackle and snap of the flames.

Smith held very still while the distant echo of cannon fire died, a spreading sonic ripple like the rings that expand and fade when a stone is tossed into a pond. He heard nothing but the sound of burning, not even the voices of frightened Englishmen. He raised his head, then his trembling shoulders above the tops of the barrels. The flames from the cabin twisted in a cold wind, tugging toward the woodland where the naturals had retreated. The forest was still.

Smith slipped around the edge of the barrels. He walked into the firelight, tense and afraid, expecting arrows that never came. After several long moments, furtive movement came from tents and thickets, from stacks of felled logs. *By Christ*, somebody muttered in the darkness.

Smith watched the men emerge from hiding like mice venturing from their holes.

"At first light," he shouted, "we cut trees for a palisade. Does any man say nay?"

Not even Wingfield protested.

OPECHANCANOUGH

Season of Cohattayough

The journey from Pamunkey-town was long, and Opechancanough had made the trek twice in half a moon. Nevertheless, he paddled his canoe with dogged focus, driving his men on with shouts and chants when their strength flagged. This time the Pamunkeys would be first to respond to Powhatan's summons. And Opechancanough would be first to know how the meeting with the *tassantassas* had gone. As his canoe cut the broad silver waters of the Pamunkey River, his river, he pictured the wealth that would come to the Real People through the *tassantassas'* hands: the precious copper, the hard iron, and, best of all, the guns that would subdue their enemies and expand the boundary of Tsenacomoco—the Tidewater—well beyond the natural barrier of the fall line.

The falls were impassable to canoes, of course. The few times the Real People had carried their canoes overland, beyond the froth and noise of the rocky falls, they had met disaster. The Massawomecks and Monacans who dwelt in that wilderness had canoes made of light birch bark, far faster and more maneuverable than the cumbersome dugouts of the Real People. But with guns, the Real People would not need canoes at all. Their enemies beyond the fall line would drop like leaves in autumn. New territories would be ripe for the harvest.

Early on the second day of paddling, Opechancanough passed into a forest of long, straight, water-blackened poles: high posts that marked the locations of fish traps. A team of men in a large, broad-bellied canoe worked on one trap, some paddling against the slow but steady current to hold the boat in place while two others hauled the trap to the surface. It broke the water with a rush, the fish inside thrashing furiously. One of the fishermen nodded in respect as Opechancanough passed. The *werowance* raised a hand in acknowledgment. The men working the fish trap bore the tattoos of Werowocomoco. He had nearly arrived at his brother's capital.

Soon the town of Werowocomoco itself came into view through its veil of trees. The pale patchwork of bark-covered houses showed here and there beside cleared green circles of garden space. For the fifth year running, the rain had been scant, and the gardens were not as lush as they might have been. A pale, thick cloud of woodsmoke hung among the treetops, white amid the clear green of new leaves, a drifting shroud like clots of old spiderweb.

One of Opechancanough's men called from a nearby canoe. "Ho! Who's that?"

Another group of dugouts came gliding from the mouth of a narrow tributary. Opechancanough recognized at once the sinuous curve painted on the men's shields: the snake of Quiyo-cohannock. His stomach went tense and sour. Their *tanx-werowance*, Pepiscunimah, paddled at the head of the lead canoe. Even at a distance, Opechancanough recognized him. He would have known that overly large, beak-sharp nose and tiny, crow-black eyes at a thousand paces. He spat over the side of his canoe.

He nearly spat twice when he recognized the figure seated behind Pepiscunimah. She did not paddle, but sat regally still, the *puccoon* adorning her fine, haughty face glowing crimson in the morning light. A cloak of dun and russet feathers was draped over her shoulders. She did not turn in the direction of the Pamunkey fleet, though Opechancanough felt certain she knew he was there, knew he was watching her.

Tsena-no-ha.

He struck the water hard with his paddle. He had not seen Tsena-no-ha since the day she left him, walking from his house straight-backed and silent, unflappable as a *werowansqua* with all her possessions in a fine basket strapped to her back. No words could make her stay, no gesture. Her mind was made up.

What more could the cursed woman want? I am the werowance *of Pamunkey. What greater honor can a woman aspire to, than to be the wife of a powerful chief?*

There was no greater honor, Opechancanough told himself. His paddle cut deep into the river, and a bitter taste rose in his throat. The only better station she could hope to reach was as a wife of Powhatan. *And yet look at her, proud as a he-grouse in Pepiscunimah's canoe, as if marriage to that squirrel-faced fool is something to boast of.*

Hard as he might paddle, Opechancanough could see he would not reach the shore before the Quiyo-co-hannocks. Pepiscunimah's dugout reached the bank of Werowocomoco, and the women and children waiting on the shore set up a welcoming cheer. Opechancanough's jaw clenched in rage.

He watched as a handful of Pepiscunimah's men leaped from their boats and made their way to the lead canoe, splashing in the shallows. Two of them bent over Tsena-no-ha's immobile figure. Opechancanough's brow furrowed as the men lifted her in their arms, carried her well up the shoreline, and deposited her on the driest part of the strand.

"*Hah,*" he spat in disgust.

He dug in with his paddle; his men followed the lead, bringing the Pamunkey canoes up to a terrible speed, the rush of a war party going boldly into battle. "Ho!" one of the men shouted in warning as they sped into the shallows. Opechancanough only paddled all the harder. His canoe launched itself onto land with a tremendous scrape, grating as loud as springtime thunder against the mud and rock of the shore. Powhatan's women and children leaped back, shouting in surprise, and then subsided into uneasy laughter, sensing Opechancanough's dark mood. He did not care.

Pepiscunimah, towing his boat sedately onto land, cast a tentative smile in Opechancanough's direction. The man's look was half-apologetic and more than a little humble, yet Opechancanough still saw the smallest spark of triumph in the close-set eyes.

"Pamunkey always makes a dramatic arrival," said Pepiscunimah good-naturedly.

"Not nearly as dramatic as your *wife's* arrival," Opechancanough shot back. "Ho, Tsena-no-ha! Have you shattered your ankles? Can you not walk? Shall we fetch you a cradleboard to ride in?"

Dutifully, the Pamunkey men laughed.

Tsena-no-ha pretended her ears were as broken as her legs. She never flinched from her easy conversation with Powhatan's favorite wife, as unconcerned as if Opechancanough's taunt had been the yips of a lone coyote in the brush.

But Pepiscunimah did not hide his scowl. "Do not presume to speak to my wife, Opechancanough. Even if she was once yours."

"Do not presume," Opechancanough rejoined, "to speak to a chief, *tanx-werowance*." He brushed past Pepiscunimah, trailing his warriors in a restless, bristling pack. Before he strode away, he caught a look of helpless anger and a red flush of shame on Pepiscunimah's narrow face. The sight was as delicious as cool nut milk on a hot day.

But almost as soon as the victory came, it vanished again. Opechancanough recalled the message he had received from Powhatan just a few days after Tsena-no-ha had walked away forever. *Brother*, the messenger had quoted, *be assured that Pepiscunimah's audacity in taking what was yours will not go unpunished. From this day forward, he is no longer a full chief, but only a* tanx-werowance, *and his territory and people are subject to my primary rule.*

Opechancanough still did not know whether he felt grateful to Powhatan for demoting the wife-stealing louse or angry over the gesture. *I should have been the one to dole out what Pepiscunimah deserved, not my brother.* And yet, what could he do? Powhatan was the chief of chiefs. The *mamanatowick* did not choose to wield absolute authority often, but when he did, not even a dear brother would contradict him.

The Pamunkeys reached the *mamanatowick's* great house while the Quiyo-co-hannock were still beaching their canoes. If he could not arrive at Werowocomoco first, Opechancanough would at least be the first man to greet the chief of chiefs. The young man guarding Powhatan's door nodded his acknowledgment, and Opechancanough ducked through the door flap and entered his brother's longhouse.

The rough, homey odors of pine smoke and burnt cornmeal surrounded him. The curved black bones of the house's interior stretched down the length of a long, smoke-darkened hall, lit by the heart fire and by pillars of light streaming down from smoke holes in the arch of the roof. Thick eddies of motes swirled and glimmered in the shafts of white light. Past the neat rows of bedsteads for the chief's many wives, beyond the stacked baskets of tribute from his many territories, still to be sorted and approved, was the stooped form of Powhatan himself, sitting on his high bed, leaning forward as if to listen to an unseen speaker. As Opechancanough watched, Powhatan threw back his head, sending long silver hair swinging across his shoulder. The boom of the old man's laughter traveled down the length of the hall.

Opechancanough made his way toward his brother. One of the wives was there in the shadows of the great bed, daubing *puccoon* onto the old man's leathery hide. The woman was young and alluring, with enchanting, wide-set eyes and large breasts still round and high. Opechancanough could tell from her graceful, gentle movements that she must have a singularly seductive touch. Yet Powhatan ignored his wife. It was the figure who stood beside the heart fire who held the Great Chief's attention.

Even with her back to him, Opechancanough recognized his niece at once. Only Amonute would stand so before Powhatan, straight and unshakable, square-shouldered, a little she-bear on its hind legs, roaring. He saw with a hot ripple of pride that the girl had acquired her first tattoo: the crossed bows of her home tribe, Pamunkey. The mark stood out blue-black on the sparse meat of her wiry shoulder.

"But you *must* let me serve at the meeting, Father!"

At her audacious words, Opechancanough heard a gasp of disbelief. Another girl, younger than Amonute, crouched near a bed, shrinking against a stack of furs as if she wished to disappear inside them.

"*Bah,*" said Powhatan. He waved away Amonute's insistence, though his eyes shone with appreciation for the girl's display of courage. "You won't be needed here, child. The women can use you at the ovens, baking cakes for the feast."

"Oh, yes," said Amonute airily. "I shall bake all the cakes for the feast, and won't your *werowances* be impressed! 'Mighty *mamana-towick,*' they'll say, 'truly you sow the strongest seeds of us all. Why, this girl you sired is so strong, she's baked her toughness right into this bread, and we've all broken our teeth off on the crust. Now we look as fearsome as bass.'"

Opechancanough stepped into the firelight beside Amonute in time to see the girl pull her lips over her teeth. She flapped her mouth open and closed in imitation of a landed fish, eyes rolling wildly.

"Won't the Massawomecks be terrified of your fearsome bass warriors," she said. "Let us all paint minnows onto our shields!"

Powhatan bellowed with laughter. He beat his knee with one red-painted fist. "My Mischief," he said warmly.

"So you see, it would mean the tragic downfall of the Real People if you were to force me to bake cakes. Better I should pour water in your great house, where I could do no harm to your influence."

"No," Powhatan said, still chuckling, "this meeting is no place for one as young as you."

Opechancanough laid a hand on the girl's shoulder. Amonute looked up at him, startlement flushing her wide, high cheeks. "Now, Amonute," he said, "you know it won't impress your father's guests to see a common girl serving, and one not even old enough to wear an apron at that. Leave serving for the royal-born women. You have your place at the cook fires."

Amonute frowned; the beguiling little cleft in her chin deepened.

"Besides," Opechancanough went on, nodding toward the other girl, the one huddled shyly against the sleeping furs, "you already have another duty of great import, do you not? Unless I'm a fool, I'd say this child is yours to care for. You cannot leave her alone while the *werowances* meet."

Amonute's frown soured into an open scowl. She turned away abruptly, snatched up the shy girl's hand, and hauled her to her feet. "Come, Nonoma."

When they had disappeared down the length of the dim hall, Powhatan pounded his knee again. "That Pocahontas of mine. She is a sight to warm an old man's heart."

"You give her too much leeway. She is too stubborn by half, Brother."

Powhatan tilted his head in gracious acknowledgment of the criticism. "I blame her Pamunkey blood."

"You ought to get control of that one before she causes trouble. Okeus save you if she inspires all your women and daughters to clamor that way, to make demands."

"Oh? And how ought I to bring her under control, eh?"

"Marry her off."

"She's not old enough for marriage," said Powhatan soberly.

Opechancanough sensed in his brother's sudden gravity a real attachment to the child. She was valuable to him: her antics cheered him, lifting the weight of the mantle of power if only for brief moments. One day the Chief of Chiefs would grieve to send this common-born daughter away, as he grieved over parting with none of his more valuable daughters.

"It will not be many more seasons before she is old enough to marry," Opechancanough said gently. "You must consider this soon."

"Ah!" The fond grin returned, the fist pounding the knee. "Perhaps you want her, is that it? You are in need of a new wife, I know. When she comes of age, perhaps I'll give her to you."

It was a bluff, of course. The girl's low birth made her no fit consort for even a *tanx-werowance*, let alone the chief of a territory as great as Pamunkey. But even knowing Powhatan's offer was made in jest, Opechancanough cringed.

"And strap me to a wildcat like that one? Okeus save me! No, settle her down with a good hunter in some distant town, far on the fringes of Tsenacomoco, where she can stir no trouble into anybody's stewpot."

Powhatan sighed. "I suppose it will come to that someday. May the god grant it's not too soon."

One after another, *werowances* filed into the great house, made their shows of respect to Powhatan, and settled onto mats around the fire. Wowinchopunck, chief of the Paspaheghs, was nearly the last to arrive. He wore a quiet intensity about him like a winter cape, heavy and enshrouding. Opechancanough clenched his fists in sudden apprehension. Although he sampled nut milk and smoked fish on dumplings as the *werowances* gathered, he tasted nothing of the delicacies. His thoughts were all on Wowinchopunck and the tale of the visitors. When the meeting was opened with prayer and tobacco, Opechancanough puffed at the pipe too quickly in his state of distraction. He coughed and sputtered, and a few of the other *werowances* fired disapproving glances his way.

At last, with Opechancanough fidgeting like an undisciplined child, Wowinchopunck began his recitation.

He told of the first meeting with the *tassantassas*, of the strange structures they built, and of the way they displayed fine tools openly but refused to trade. He told of the altercation over the hatchet, and of how he had deemed it better to withdraw to safety than to remain and feast with a people as unpredictable and touchy as the *tassantassas*.

Wowinchopunck told of the next visit, when he sent a small but elite troop of warriors in his place. He related that the *tassantassas* refused to host the Paspahegh men as overnight guests—the very pinnacle of rudeness. Then the visitors doubled their offense when one of their number, a short man covered in wiry yellow hair, lured them into a shooting contest.

"The arrow shattered on their metal clothing," Wowinchopunck said.

"Shattered?" said Powhatan. "You cannot mean it."

"Like a dropped pot. I spoke with men who saw it with their own eyes. They are serious men, not given to exaggeration. These *tassantassas* have clothing that arrows cannot pierce."

"Iron?" said Opechancanough. "It's so heavy. How could any man wear iron, let alone men as small as these?"

"No, not iron. Something new. I have seen a little iron myself. It is black, but this metal is bluish, or pale gray like a sky after rain—like the *mamanatowick*'s hair. And it was shiny where it was scuffed or polished. Not iron."

"And you say they refused to host your men for a night's sleep?" Powhatan's voice was low and dark, meditative.

"They were obviously very strongly opposed." Wowinchopunck shook his head. "My men say they sneered at the idea, and some of them spat on the ground. They shouted at one another over the very suggestion. They clamored like crows over a carcass.

"But what is worse than their rudeness is the magic they have. We fell on them in the night, so angry were we over their poor manners. They had . . . *something*, some gun, I think, larger than any gun that can be imagined."

Powhatan frowned. "Did you see it?"

"No. But we heard it. It split the air like a hundred claps of thunder and it made our ears ring for hours afterward. The Okeus knows what kind of a weapon it might be. It's terrible, whatever it is. Of that I am certain."

Opechancanough raised his eyes across the flames of the heart fire. The bright, bead-small eyes of Pepiscunimah stared levelly back at him. A knot twisted and swelled in his gut. *The disrespect of it all. No one knows how to properly respect a man anymore, not that* tanx, *and certainly not the* tassantassas . . . "If these strangers can show no respect for the Real People," Opechancanough said loudly, almost a shout, "then let us rid ourselves of them now. Pick them off like lice from a hide, before they dig in and make themselves impossible to rout."

Wowinchopunck raised a hand. "I agree."

Pepiscunimah cast a casual glance toward Powhatan. "*Mamanatowick*, I am only a *tanx*, but I recall our first meeting about these visitors. I remember how Opechancanough agitated for peace with the white men. Did he not say that we could use them, could trade with them for goods that would make us powerful? Why does he change his song now, I wonder?"

"If I fail to alter my song when the drumbeat changes," said Opechancanough, "then I am nearly as great a fool as Pepiscunimah."

Pepiscunimah's mouth twisted in a sour smile. "Women love fools, or so I hear."

"All right," Powhatan broke in. "Enough of this feud. Our purpose is serious, and much larger than any conflict between the two of you. Now, tell me, all of you, what are your thoughts?"

Each *werowance* offered his opinion in turn, and the knot in Opechancanough's gut tightened more with each successive comment. Far more chiefs raised their hands in favor of pursuing trade than killing the *tassantassas*, or even driving them back across the sea to the distant land from which they'd come.

"This is short-sighted," Opechancanough said with a growl. "Men who don't understand basic respect can never be trusted." He flicked his eyes toward Pepiscunimah. "I now regret my words from our previous meeting. I regret that it was I who put this idea into your minds."

They went on debating for several hours. It was a futile exercise; Opechancanough could see that none of the men who wanted trade could be convinced by Wowinchopunck's account that the *tassantassas* were too dangerous to bother with. And he could not be convinced of their benefit. He felt Powhatan's eyes upon him many times, and wondered whether with this debate the *mamanatowick* hoped to reason his brother into consensus. *Why? He can act without my blessing, can pass down any edict he pleases. All my life my brother has been the strongest man I've ever known. Does he feel the need for my approval now that he finds himself at the tail end of life?* The thought fanned the flame of Opechancanough's rage. He glared up at his brother.

Powhatan raised his hands. The debate settled into murmurs, and then silence. "We have been at this discussion a long time. Let us eat now, and rest. Tonight we will have dancing and games.

These *tassantassas* are not reason to miss a feast, eh? We will speak of this again in the morning, when our heads are steady."

The chiefs rose from their mats, stretching, and shaking cramps out of hard-muscled limbs.

"You will remain with me a while, Opechancanough."

Opechancanough held his brother's eyes for a long moment, tense with a roiling, choking anger whose exact source he could not name.

At last he nodded.

When the other chiefs had gone, Powhatan sent his women away, too. The brothers were alone with the heart fire. It had burned down to one charred log laced with the intricate white patterns of hot ash, its underside pulsing ember red with heat. Opechancanough stared at it. The hot air rose in ripples, distorting his vision.

"You are so angry, Opechancanough." There was sadness in Powhatan's voice. Grief and resignation.

"You aren't angry enough."

"Your rage over your wife controls you. It clouds your judgment."

"The *tassantassas* have no respect for us. If they do not respect us, even as honorable enemies, then I shudder to think what they may do to us. Don't you see what a threat these people are, Wahunse-na-cawh?" He used the old name, the name Powhatan had worn before he was Powhatan. He hoped the sound of it would recall to his brother those traits Powhatan had once possessed: the shrewd, quiet cunning, the assured bravery.

"I ask you to consider," Powhatan said slowly, almost gingerly, "whether you are seeing threats and disrespect where none are intended. Are your feelings over Tsena-no-ha's betrayal unmanning you?"

That unfamiliar hesitation in his words . . . *How unlike you, Brother.* Opechancanough wanted to lay a hand on the tattooed shoulder, transmit some strength into the old man's spirit and bones. Instead he said quietly, "Don't be insulting."

"I only ask you to consider what I say."

"If you won't allow us to drive them out, then we must learn more about them. We must discover their weaknesses. The *tassantassas* have blue metal that shatters arrows; they have the great gun that booms like thunder—you heard Wowinchopunck. What is it? How is it used? Can it kill, or does it merely make a terrible sound? We must know these things, if we are to have any hope of keeping them under our control."

"You are right. We do need this knowledge, at least as badly as we need their trade goods. Listen: this is what we will do."

Opechancanough held his breath. He found himself praying, *Please, please . . .* He didn't even know what it was he asked for, only that he begged the stern, silent god for something. He stared into his brother's face, watching the old eyes flicker in thought, and in a rush the desperate pleading turned to a clear, emphatic wish: *Let him present some real strategy. Let him be wise. Let him be the brilliant tactician he once was, the man who united the tribes. Let him not be a tired, frightened old man, Oh, great Okeus, please.*

Powhatan's back straightened. His eyes sharpened to their old familiar keenness. "We will tell the Paspaheghs and the Quiyo-co-hannocks to increase their assaults on the *tassantassas*. They must keep the white men under great pressure, always on their guard, always afraid. And then you and I will go to them, and with a word I will stop the attacks, bring them the respite they will be hungry for. We will show them that Powhatan holds sway over all this land and can give them life or death at his whim. They will see that it is to their benefit to show us some respect, to work with us as partners, not to insult us and make enemies of the Real People."

It might work. It was the kind of plot that would never fool a tribe of the Real People, but these *tassantassas* might be susceptible to the deception. *Perhaps the true Powhatan is not as long gone as I'd feared.*

Powhatan held out a finger. Opechancanough hooked it with his own, and for a moment they were youths again, smiling at one another over a basket full of stolen dumplings, happy in brotherly conspiracy.

"Very well," said Opechancanough. "Let it be so."

SMITH

June 1607

Smith's arms trembled as he strained against the rope. The coarse fibers bit into his hands. The men hauled together, and the wall of the cabin inched upward, wavered, sagged back toward the ground.

"Heave, men!"

Smith cursed, leaning against the impossible weight of the log wall, against the pain in his chafed, raw hands and the cramping in his legs. The wall made a valiant surge and came to rest upright against the posts with a solid smack that reverberated through the ground into Smith's bones.

The men were so exhausted they could not even muster a cheer. Smith dropped the rope and pressed his stinging palms against his thighs. His heart beat at an alarming pace, pounding in his neck and shaking his limbs. It strained against its cage, those weak and brittle bars, as if it might break free of him and rise into the sky on frantic, fluttering wings.

The work crew passed a jug of water. It tasted bitter, sharp with salt. Smith rinsed his mouth and spat into the mud.

From the direction of the supply tent, Thomas Savage pushed a barrow toward the drooping crew. Inside was a squat black cooking kettle, accompanied by a stack of wooden bowls. A wisp of steam trailed over the boy's thin shoulder as he brought his barrow to a careful halt and began ladling up the midday meal.

Smith stared into his bowl with leaden dismay. Porridge. Every meal was porridge, sometimes flavored with a few bones from a duck or a pigeon, when one could be shot. More often it was peppered with black flecks of weevil. The weevils were almost welcome. They crunched in the teeth, which added a dimension of excitement to meals that porridge could not otherwise aspire to.

Smith raised a lump of the pale, pasty stuff on his eating knife. He shut his eyes tightly as he forced it down, longing for the taste of pork, roasted and charred, or stewed, or fried in its own sweet fat. It had been weeks since they'd butchered a hog. They had found the half-feral beasts on an island in the hot, languid south, where they had stopped to replenish the ships' freshwater stores on the long way from England. They'd taken the hogs onboard and, when they made landfall in the New World, set them loose to fatten and breed.

Were it not for the naturals, the hogs would have made a glorious store of meat. Nearly the moment the palisade was finished, though, the naturals had returned with their arrows and their knives of flint and bone. They shot whatever hogs they could find, leaving them to lie and rot in the sun. When the English ventured from their protective walls to retrieve the precious carcasses, the naturals shot at them as if they, too, were swine to be killed for sport. One man was even killed trying to fetch a plump fallen sow.

As spring gave way to the hot blue haze of early summer, the grass around the palisade grew well above knee height: cover aplenty for the Indians. They slunk about unseen, and then rose up like devils out of Hell where a body least expected to find them, their skin shiny with the crimson and black greasepaint they favored. They drew their long bows with as little effort as a child might tug a sprouting weed from a flower bed. The English, weakening by the day on their rations of weevils and gruel, could scarcely swing a hand axe. Leaving the palisade—entering that treacherous tangle of grass—could be deadly. It was certainly foolish. The Indians had penned the English in like fattened lambs awaiting slaughter.

Jamestown fare was poor for belly and spirit alike. A man could derive no strength from such conditions. Smith trembled constantly when he was not lying in his bedroll. His arms and legs moved too slowly; his steps were untrustworthy and his knees prone to buckling. After a day spent building and digging and trying in vain to bring down the waterfowl that sometimes passed overhead, by evening he was as weak and useless as a babe.

At least—thank Christ for small mercies, he reflected with cruel satisfaction—Smith was not the only one whose spirit and strength had drained away. The men of the colony often dropped into exhaustion or apathy after only a few hours' work. The progress of erecting a respectable fort crept by at a lethargic pace. They needed solid buildings, watchtowers of sufficient height to spot the Indians at a distance, storerooms large and hopeful to receive the wealth of the supply ships that *were* coming from England, by God, any day—and yet their efforts flagged.

They must continue to build, Smith knew. Proper roofs and walls would raise spirits, and cheer might be enough to combat the weakness that had crept into their bones, might be the lucky token they needed to formulate some counteroffensive that would free them from the terror of the Indians outside their gate. He scraped the last dregs of his porridge from the bowl with a dirty thumb. The gentlemen did the same, sucking their fingers. That would have filled Smith with wry amusement, had he any strength left for humor.

The palisade surrounding Jamestown was a great triangle enclosing a trampled morass of yard. Spindly scaffolds, the beginnings of watchtowers, rose at each corner. Men in steel breastplates and helmets wedged themselves atop each scaffold, backs or legs braced against the rough bark of the palisade wall, roasting in their armor.

One of the lookouts gave a shout and gestured urgently toward the river.

Smith, Scrivener, and Wingfield dropped their bowls and rushed to the scaffold. Smith pulled himself carefully up the framework, the thin poles vibrating and wavering beneath his weight. He raised his unprotected head clear of the wall and wrapped one arm about a scaffold pole while his free hand rested on the comforting, solid coolness of his gun.

A single canoe slipped toward the bank. It moved with a sinister grace, low and swift and certain, like the temperamental brown snakes that often crossed inland tracts of brackish water. Three men rode in the craft, though only two manned the paddles. As Smith watched, his mind moving slowly, fogged by exhaustion and hunger, the canoe beached and its passengers disembarked. The man who had not paddled wore a mantle of white so pure it stung Smith's eyes in the midday sun.

"What is it?" Wingfield called.

"A party of naturals. They look important."

"Important?"

"One of their kings, unless I miss my guess."

"Come for some royal sport," Scrivener muttered, "shooting at tethered goats."

"I don't see any bows," said Smith.

One of the men made a broad gesture, sweeping his arm in a great arc, bringing hand to heart. "*Wingapoh,*" the man called.

Smith held very still on his rickety perch.

The Indians turned to one another, made a brief conference. Then the man tried again: the wide swing of the arm, the hand on the breast. "*Wingapoh!*"

"What are they saying?" Wingfield whispered it, as if the Indians would understand his words if they heard.

"Their word for *peace*."

"It can't be," said Scrivener. "They have proven their intentions; they mean us no goodwill. You misunderstand, Smith."

The Indian made his gesture again. "*Wingapoh!*" The man had the familiar lankiness and youthful arrogance Smith had seen before.

"I recognize that one—the one calling out to us. He's the one who shot at your helmet, Scrivener."

"Excellent," said Scrivener. "No doubt he's come back to finish the job, this time with something that will punch through steel."

Wingfield's face was flushed red as an apple; he stared up at Smith with a curious intensity in his pale eyes. "If you are certain they mean peace, then you ought to go out to them."

"That's madness," Scrivener said quietly. "He'll be killed, and we cannot spare a single man. You know that."

From his superior perch, Smith watched Wingfield steadily for a long moment. His attempt to pin mutiny on Smith had failed and now the great dandy thought to send him into the enemy's hands to be brought down like a squealing pig. Smith imagined the man's satisfaction, watching through a chink in the wall as Smith buckled, feathered like a half-plucked goose, all his certainty and power draining away with his life's blood into the grass while the Indians and Wingfield alike danced over his corpse, each on their respective sides of the palisade.

Naukaquawis called again into the tense quiet.

Not today, Smith promised Wingfield silently.

He was certain the Indians' word meant *peace*. And though they were violent and terrible, though they were fitter by far than any Englishman and more cunning than foxes, Smith detected in the Indians a certain forceful earnestness, a code of honor that bound them and held them fast. If they came under the banner of peace, they would not violate that sacred oath.

He prayed to Christ he was right.

Smith loosed one arm tentatively from the scaffolding. It wobbled beneath him as he made an arc through the air and brought his hand to his heart.

"*Wingapoh.*"

The palisade gate screeched on its wooden hinge. Smith felt the anxious, coil-tight rustle of armed men at his back, smelled the fresh sulfur of gunpowder and singed-air heat of lit matches. The men were ready to fire should any of the naturals attempt to enter the fort, but Smith stepped through the gate and it swung shut behind him, closing with a clatter as the stout lock bars fell back into place. He would face the three naturals alone, with only his snaphaunce for protection—the gun and his steel, which suddenly felt thin as parchment.

The Indians stood some twenty or thirty paces away, immobile and fierce-eyed. All about them the waist-high grass moved in waves of shifting silver. Smith stepped into the grass. It hissed against his breeches, sliding like a woman's touch over the lower rim of his breastplate while seed heads caught and broke off in the joints of his mail shirt. He had the sensation of wading into deep, murky water, the ripple of skin creep, the brief clutch of nausea when one realizes that anything—*anything*—might be hiding below the surface, waiting to reach out and seize one's leg with sharp teeth or a strong, cold hand. He recalled with a thump of blunt, heavy panic what another slave had told him in the Turk's field as they labored with their scythes. There were tigers in the slave's homeland, cats the size of ponies. They sprang from the cover of tall grass to take victims in their jaws, biting the back of the neck, carrying grown men away into the shadows of the jungle. The men dragged like knotted rags.

Smith raised a hand to the nape of his neck. His own touch was cold with fear.

And yet he crossed the ground to the Indians alive and unharmed. Even his breeches remained dry. He counted that a victory.

Smith nodded a cautious, straight-faced greeting to Naukaquawis. The youth's arms were crossed over his chest; the hint of an ink-black tattoo, a sinuous curve, showed on one arm where a patch of red paint had rubbed away. Naukaquawis solemnly returned the nod.

Beside him stood a very tall man with a stern, almost bitter mien. The face was sharp with a strong, aquiline nose, and thin lips tightly pressed. The man's eyes were deep-set and dark, and carried in them the spark of a hot fire, a force of charisma and potency that Smith imagined he could feel emanating from the tall man's presence, a physical vibration like the stamp of a great horse's hoof shuddering through the earth. The tall one was nearing old age but had not yet reached it. His face was lined, the cheeks barely hinting at a jowliness to come, but the man's body was as hard and capable as that of his young companion's. The braid knotted at his left side was adorned with a collection of feathers. They twirled and fluttered in the wind, a counterpoint to the man's stillness that might have been comical if not for his predatory air.

The third man was the one Smith judged to be their king. He was old; silver hair fell loose across the overlapping feathers of a white cloak. Above a face like well-worn leather, deep-creased and burnished with time, rose a bristling crown of deer's hair dyed red. It was like the crown the other Indian king had sported when Smith had goaded his men into the shooting match, but its bristles were darkened with age, and seemed to convey a more regal air. Even had the old man not been wearing a crown, Smith would have known him for a king. Despite his advanced age, he carried himself with a particular brand of dignity. His eyes were pink-rimmed and rheumy, but his unblinking gaze was thoughtful, possessed of a quiet self-assurance found only in the most natural of leaders.

"Wingapoh," Smith said again.

The king began speaking in a resonant voice, as deep and hollow as the sound of a large drum. Smith, of course, could not follow his words, but the tone of voice was not threatening. It was both confident and explanatory, the tone a parent takes when instructing a child. The king indicated the tall, sober man, and through gestures and tone Smith gathered that he was a person near to the chief's heart—a brother or a close associate. Naukaquawis, Smith learned to no small surprise, was the king's son.

Smith tried his gesture as before, tapping his chest, giving his name. He correctly named Naukaquawis, and indicated with smiles and nods that he and the young man had met before. *Better to leave out*, Smith thought, *the fact that I very nearly shot him the night of the attack.*

The king tried his name, and to Smith's carefully concealed amusement, gave it in the same harsh burr as his son had done. "Chawnzmit." Then he offered up his own name with a hand to his heart. "Wahunse-na-cawh."

The tall, sour one flashed a quick glare at his king, placed a protective hand on the old man's shoulder. "Powhatan," he insisted.

Smith took it to be a title of respect. He bowed his head slightly and repeated, "Powhatan."

And you? Smith gave the tall one a questing look.

The man stared levelly back and did not reply.

Powhatan went on, through elaborate hand signs and a soft, almost lilting tone, to indicate that his people desired peace and friendship with the English. Smith raised his brows, offering an openly skeptical look.

At that moment, with a sinister rustle of parting grasses, a fourth man erupted from hiding. Smith had only a heartbeat to step back, his hand groping wildly for the butt of his gun. The interloper drew his bow. The arrow hissed along the skin of his knuckle; he was so close that Smith could see the tiny red veins in the man's eyes, the bead of sweat shining on his lip.

Just as Smith found his gun, Powhatan held up a peremptory hand and barked a few quick words. At once the man with the bow subsided, head and shoulders stooping minutely in an obedient shrug. He vanished back into the grasses, melting from view like fog before the sun.

"Sweet Christ preserve me," Smith whispered.

The three visitors had never flinched, and the bowman had given in too readily. Even through the rush of blood pounding in his ears, Smith could see the scene had been staged. *Clever. How do you make a man who cannot speak your language believe that you hold absolute control over your people? You demonstrate that it is so.*

Smith did what came naturally to any Englishman in the face of great power—even an Englishman as cantankerous as he. He dropped his eyes and bowed deeply to Powhatan.

The tall, unnamed Indian grunted his approval.

"*Wingapoh,*" Smith said emphatically, slapping his hand against his pounding heart. He bowed again, nodded vigorously. "Peace."

Powhatan extended one wrinkled hand, all his fingers clenched in a fist but the first. Smith turned slightly, trying to identify whatever the chief pointed to. There was nothing behind him but the palisade wall and a few men's heads peering fearfully from the tower scaffolds. Smith turned back to Powhatan, shaking his head in apologetic bewilderment. Naukaquawis pointed as well, and at last Smith extended his own hand in a similar gesture.

The king stepped forward and hooked his finger with Smith's. The skin of his hand was rough and warm. The old king said nothing more, but when Smith looked up into his eyes, the returned stare was rich with mistrust.

Two days after Smith met with Powhatan, Captain Newport raised anchor on the *Susan Constant*, turned her east, and sailed for England. John Smith was not sorry to watch the ship vanish into the distant blue horizon. He had no fond memories of her cramped, stinking brig, but quite aside from his personal ire, the *Susan Constant* would soon return bearing supplies: fresh and varied food stores, tools to work the land, copper and glass for trading with the naturals. She would come back laden with men, too: eager new colonists, young and strong and, Smith prayed, commoners well versed in the practicalities of labor.

At least, Smith hoped Newport would soon return. The supply ships the Virginia Company had promised still had not arrived, and the storehouse grew emptier by the day.

A week after Newport's departure, the men of the colony cast their votes and declared Edward-Maria Wingfield their new president. In the immediate wake of Wingfield's appointment, the work of the fort's construction all but ceased. Oh, a chink in the palisade wall might be patched with a sloppy handful of mud, and here and there a hammer lazily tapped at a nail, but Jamestown's growth had stalled, just as Smith had feared it would.

In truth, Wingfield was only partly to blame, and the weakness induced by a steady diet of gruel was scarcely much more the cause. Ever since Powhatan's declaration of peace, all sense of urgency had drained from the men. Most of the men couldn't even be motivated to hunt. All their hogs were dead or driven away, but Smith and his few allies could find no words to urge the men beyond the palisade walls. "Why bother?" they said. "The supply ships will be back soon."

At least one small blessing came of these days. Smith found his friends, a pack of true men with strong backs and iron constitutions. Save for Scrivener, they were to a man common born. They went on about the business of construction while the well-bred took their ease, retiring to the shade of roofed cabins to write letters and journals or shooting at stationary targets, a fruitless sport that added nothing to the supper kettle. Smith's lot came to look on him as a fine leader, and some of them absorbed a touch of his resentment toward the strutting coxcombs who lorded over Jamestown. The gentlemen, however, far outnumbered the commoners, and, in the end, the pack of good, gritty workers could do nothing to motivate the gentlemen into honest labor.

Deep summer arrived with a pale, hot sky. At sunrise and sunset great clouds of insects rose from the marshes of the spit, driving men into cabins or tents where they huddled to wait out the worst of the plague. At times the clouds of gnats did not disperse at midday, and the barrage simply had to be endured. The tiny black bodies were a constant bombardment, their gripping legs like starched threads, wings like veined slivers of glass. The dreadful itch of their stings could only be assuaged with packs of cool, salt-laden mud. But the scant hour or two of relief was hardly worth the stench.

Smith would have given much for the secret of the Indians' body paint. They often visited the fort now to trade, and he had observed on more than one occasion how the gnats avoided the Indians' skin. It must have had something to do with the colorful paint they wore, but Smith could not convince them to bring any for trading.

They did, however, bring food. Smith traded eagerly for it, and soon had laid in the supply house a small but precious store of smoke-cured fish, dried clams strung like beads on looped leather thongs, and a few baskets of corn. In return he gave the simplest trinkets, glass beads and copper bells, and here and there a digging hoe for particularly sweet corn or a quality selection of fish. The cheapest and most insignificant items seemed to delight the Indians the most. They paid especially well for beads of bright, showy colors.

The naturals preferred trading with Smith to any other Englishman. He suspected their preference was due to his earnest effort to learn their tongue. The task came with great difficulty, but Smith worked at it tirelessly. By the height of summer he had picked up enough of the local language to understand the fort's precarious situation.

One evening as Smith crouched on his haunches, eyeing the spread of goods brought by a lone Indian of the Paspahegh clan, he remarked on the rather meager quantity of corn.

"There will be much less corn soon," the man said, a faint twinkle of guarded amusement in his eyes. His name was Taka-way-wemps, not a newcomer to fort trade, and one whom Smith knew to be as honest as any natural ever was.

"What do you mean?"

"Now is the season of *nepinough*, when the corn ripens. But soon comes the season of *taquitock*, Chawnzmit, when the gardens cease to bear. Then we go out and hunt." Seeing Smith's hesitancy over the rush of words, Taka-way-wemps mimed drawing and firing a bow into the distant trees.

One of the Englishmen staggered past, groaning, clutching at his belly with one hand while he fumbled at his belt with the other. Taka-way-wemps gave a grunt, somewhere between sympathy and wry smugness, as he watched the man duck behind the barrels that blocked the privy pits from view.

"Slow water," Taka-way-wemps said knowingly.

"What is this *slow water*? I don't understand."

"Now, when the days have been hot for long, the river slows. It runs lower." He held out a hand like a hard slab of wood, parallel to the earth. It sank toward the ground. "The good water goes, but the bad water from the ocean comes to replace it." Taka-way-wemps's hand rose again. "Makes men sick. Better not to drink it until the hunting season is done."

Smith shook his head in bewilderment. What fresher water could they hope to find than the great James River? To be sure, there were ponds and puddles in abundance on the muddy spit, but they were stagnant and full of frog spawn. Smith could not be induced to drink from them unless he was dying of thirst.

"Where do you find good water in"—he struggled to recall the naturals' word for late summer—"in *nepinough*?"

"From small, fast-moving creeks and from springs."

"There are no creeks or springs on this bit of land."

Taka-way-wemps broke into hoarse laughter. "I know!"

In the weeks that followed, Smith comforted himself with the knowledge that at least Taka-way-wemps had provided him with some warning of the crisis to come. Not that the warning was much use. Even had he been able to rouse the majority of Jamestown into action, the English could not lift the fort by its roots and transport it to a more favorable location.

It was clear now why the Paspaheghs, the clan who claimed ownership of the spit where Jamestown stood, had never built upon this land. Aside from the marshy ground and the plagues of gnats in the summer, there was no convenient freshwater source. The river had grown so sluggish and salty that it was nearly undrinkable. A few of Smith's industrious band scouted out a trickling spring that could be reached by trudging through the bogs and wading across a brackish stream that cut across the spit, but it was a long, difficult journey through sucking mud and stinging flies. The few skins of freshwater that could be hauled to the fort each day were almost not worth the effort, yet it was better than drinking the James River's foul brine.

Smith shuddered to think what would have become of the settlement if he had not brokered a peace with Powhatan. He was sharply aware that no man made it through the marshes and across the creek to the meager spring except by the Indians' permission. It was not so long ago that they had watched through the chinks of their palisade as their pigs were shot for sport.

Under the onslaught of hot sun and winged pestilence, laboring just to secure a few mouthfuls of potable water each day, the English fell ill one by one. Those who were not seized by the flux contended with bouts of wretched vomiting, and even those who did not gag and gasp on hands and knees were nearly too weak to walk. Day by day, hope for the first supply ship waned. Smith's cache of traded Indian foods was the only surety against malnutrition. But it was a small store and would soon be gone, as would the closest Indians, who in the autumn would pack up hearth and home to pursue the deer and migratory birds deep into the western woodlands.

Soon even Smith succumbed to the sickness. His bowels and his joints turned to water, so that each step was a wavering agony. Each hand sign he made during trading sessions trembled; the effort of remaining upright and stoic was nearly too much for him. When he realized he could no longer keep his weakness concealed from the naturals, he closed the fort to all trade. It was a bitter decision to forgo the final stores of food, the last the Indians were willing to part with before their season of *taquitock* set in. God alone knew when they would return, or whether they would bring meat from their hunts to trade for copper and beads.

Smith prayed that they would. He could do little else but pray.

OPECHANCANOUGH

Season of Nepinough

The Pamunkey canoes were so heavily laden that the river nearly spilled over their sides. Opechancanough scowled at the brace of turkeys and the many baskets of corn packed into his vessel. They were not from Pamunkey-town; Opechancanough would not ask Pamunkey women to deplete their precious caches. Not during yet another drought year—not for the sake of the *tassantassas*. And yet by the order of Powhatan, it was Opechancanough who conveyed the *mamanatowick*'s gift to the fort.

The tribes nearest to the white men's strange, squalid, log-built town reported favorable trades and largely pleasant interactions with the *tassantassas*—pleasant enough, if one overlooked their naturally brusque and rude dispositions. But Opechancanough recalled Wowinchopunck's relation of his early interactions with the fort. They might mask their true intentions with friendly trade, but first impressions said much of a man's real spirit. These *tassantassas* were touchy, stingy with their best trade goods, and quick to turn aggressive. Their lack of manners said much about their intentions. They certainly could not be trusted.

And quite apart from their poor behavior, they possessed the great, terrible gun, the one Wowinchopunck had heard cracking like a thunderstorm. Only the Okeus knew what such a weapon was capable of, the scale of death and destruction it might inflict. Powhatan might harbor hopes of turning that weapon against the western tribes, but Opechancanough was no fool. The great gun would be trained on the Real People if it would be aimed at anyone. No matter how many exotic beads they dangled before his eyes, Opechancanough would not be lulled into trusting the *tassantassas*.

The Pamunkey delegation beached their canoes carefully. At Opechancanough's order, the warriors remained in their boats, paddles at the ready, prepared to make a hasty retreat if he gave the word. Opechancanough set out alone across the muddy shore.

The fort had grown since the last time he'd seen it. The high wall was the same, its logs hacked into sharp points, biting into the sky like a wolf's ravening fangs. Where the corners of the walls met, mounds of earth lifted drum-shaped towers high; the drum towers extended forked projections like the tail fin of a fish, platforms from which a pair of armed men could see clearly in any direction. *An elegant design*, Opechancanough was forced to admit. *The entire town can be defended from those towers by only a handful of men.* They may be unconscionably disrespectful and unable to recognize Real People when they met them, but the *tassantassas* clearly possessed some measure of intelligence. It would be a challenge to break them.

"*Ho!*" a voice called from one of the drum towers.

Opechancanough halted in the bare ground outside the fort and waited. He noted with wry amusement that the *tassantassas* had finally cut the grass down to ankle height.

After a moment, a familiar face peered over the edge of the nearest tower's fin. His thick yellow beard was as tangled and unkempt as moss, the skin around his eyes and along the bridge of his nose stained bright pink. He'd heard from Paspahegh traders that this was a curious feature the *tassantassas* displayed after too much exposure to the sun.

Opechancanough raised a hand. "Chawnzmit."

The man returned the greeting, his pale palm rising over the edge of the wall.

Opechancanough made the hand signs to indicate he wished to make a trade. Chawnzmit turned to confer with a few of his companions. Opechancanough held his breath; word had circulated through the towns of the Real People that the *tassantassas* had refused trade for weeks. Just when he thought they would turn him away, Chawnzmit shouted something in his odd, singsong tongue. There was a thump and a scrape, and the log gateway swung open with a piercing, high-pitched whine.

At Opechancanough's word, the gifts from Powhatan were carried into the white men's town. There was no mistaking the wide-eyed desperation with which the *tassantassas* stared at the offerings: several turkeys strung up by their feet; twenty squirrels bundled by their tails, fat enough for a rich stew; a dozen baskets of well-dried corn that would keep in a dry cache for months to come; woven grass bags full of smoke-preserved fillets from the river's huge, long-nosed sturgeon.

There was no mystery to the men's thin, shaky condition, to the dark-violet rings beneath their eyes. In the middle of their town, Opechancanough displayed the wealth of Powhatan. He looked at the ring of *tassantassas*, observing their frail weakness with satisfaction. As more white men gathered to stare at the food, he felt the calm assurance of one who has the undisputed upper hand. Opechancanough smiled.

Chawnzmit approached, a man as squat and ill-proportioned as a child just learning to take its first steps. He tottered like a child, too, weak and wan, still feeling the effects of the illness that had swept through the town. Chawnzmit issued a command to his men, a harsh, raspy bark, and they dispersed with reluctant, sullen faces, leaving their leader to bargain with Opechancanough alone.

Wise. Hungry men in a desperate crowd were apt to trade poorly. Chawnzmit clearly wished to retain control of the situation, to broker the most favorable terms he could. *He will find me just as canny a trader, though. And anyhow, I've already received what I desired most: knowledge of your men's condition, Chawnzmit. That is more valuable by far than your copper and your pretty beads.*

"I know you," said Chawnzmit, "but I do not know your name."

Opechancanough's smile faded in the wake of his shock. He had thought to deal in hand signs; he had not thought to encounter his own language in the mouth of a *tassantassa.* The accent was thick and rough, but the meaning was clear.

Chawnzmit sank onto his haunches across from Opechancanough, the posture of open trade. "You came here before, with Powhatan and Naukaquawis."

"Yes," Opechancanough admitted.

"You are Powhatan's . . . brother?"

Opechancanough nodded.

"Do I surprise you?" Chawnzmit gestured toward his own mouth.

"You have learned well."

"I am a swift learner."

Opechancanough studied the man. His squat body and bushy hair, yellow as a deer's hide, gave him a bestial appearance; the blue eyes were disconcerting in their paleness. A strong, sour smell rose from him, the same pungent reek that trailed all the *tassantassas.* Opechancanough had heard of it from the Paspaheghs, but had not experienced it himself until now. The smell pinched at his nostrils, which twitched as if to close themselves off against the assault. *How can a creature be so like an animal, and yet learn so quickly?* And if the *tassantassas* were capable of learning the Real People's tongue, why could they not learn simple respect?

Still, the man had learned, had made an effort to build a bridge between the Real People and his own kind. Opechancanough felt the stirrings of a slow, grudging respect.

"What is your name?" Chawnzmit asked.

"Opechancanough. *Werowance* of Pamunkey."

The yellow-bearded man placed a hand to his heart. "I am honored to trade with you, chief."

They set about their business. Opechancanough made it clear that the goods came courtesy of Powhatan, and that items offered in return should be suitable to his lofty station. He had seen the hunger and eagerness in the other *tassantassas'* eyes, yet Chawnzmit bargained coolly, considering and rejecting suggested terms with an offhanded casualness that astonished Opechancanough. Surely Chawnzmit was intelligent enough to know how dire his situation was. He and his men were depleted by illness, deprived of fresh water, and obviously on the verge of starvation. Yet in the end, Opechancanough was not able to secure the guns he longed for. He loaded his canoes with an assortment of tools, a few hatchets, and a fair sum of copper to bring to Powhatan. In truth, it was a treasure that should please any man, even the wealthy *mamanato-wick*. And yet Opechancanough could not rid himself of a creeping suspicion that he had come out the poorer in the deal.

Opechancanough arrived at Werowocomoco as the sun was setting. His men unloaded the trade goods while a crowd of women and children gathered, eyeing the chains of copper and exclaiming over the tools. He made his way through the press and found the footpath that led through the dense thicket windbreak and into the town of Werowocomoco. The few women who were not gathered on the strand to examine the *tassantassas'* wares were busy in their little yards making early preparations for the trek to come, shaking out grass mats and rolling them tightly, and nestling pots within pots within carrying baskets. The days were still hot—hotter than anyone liked in this maddeningly dry year—but the slow turn of seasons was still evident in the tinge of gold in the treetops and the dry curling at the edges of corn husks, the last ears' tassels hanging limp and brown in the heat. The harsh rhythm of the digging song rose from an unseen garden in the distance. The sound of women's voices was sweet. A pang of homesickness gripped Opechancanough, a deep, raw longing for the way things had been, for the days when Tsena-no-ha still smiled to see him.

Powhatan waited, as ever, in the depths of his great house. A certain sallowness hung about his well-worn features. In a painful rush of bright, sharp memory Opechancanough saw his brother as a youth, leading him on a race through the trees, a bag slung over one shoulder. *Come back*, Opechancanough had shouted. *Mother will beat you for stealing the sweet cakes!* But his eldest brother was as strong and fleet as a buck. He recalled the soles of Wahunse-na-cawh's feet flashing as he ran, the bag bouncing on his broad back with its tracery of new tattoos, the dappled light and shade of the forest flickering over his skin and the solid muscles of his legs.

No, Opechancanough mused, *not Wahunse-na-cawh*. Those were the days long before his brother was called Powhatan, even before he had taken the name Wahunse-na-cawh to celebrate his accession to chief. The days before he himself was called Opechancanough. For one moment of panic and bitter self-loathing, Opechancanough could not recall their oldest names, their childhood names. *This is what it means to grow old. You forget who you were. You forget who you are. You stay hidden away in a dark lodge while outside the seasons change and the women sing and the world goes on eternally while you forget everything.*

Then the names came back to him in a flood of relief. He had caught up to his brother at last, tackled him; they had rolled over and over, crushing the bag of stolen cakes, and laughing, gasping, shared the sweet crumbs between them.

Opechancanough blinked; the smoke inside the great house stung his eyes.

"Brother," said Powhatan. "How did they take my gifts?"

"I suspect I could have worked a gun or two out of them if I'd had more time. Still, I think you will be pleased with the goods we secured."

Powhatan nodded silently.

"I noted, *mamanatowick*, that they were weak."

"Weak?"

"They seemed to be suffering from an illness."

"Probably due to bad water. There are no good springs on the land where they settled."

"Possibly."

Opechancanough lapsed into a tentative, thoughtful silence. Powhatan watched him expectantly, waiting for the words they both knew would come.

"Now is the time," Opechancanough ventured at last, "to finish them, while they are sick and weak."

"Finish them?"

"I keep thinking, Brother, about their guns—about the great gun Wowinchopunck heard."

"You fear it?"

He bristled. "You know I fear nothing."

Powhatan raised a placating hand. "You are no coward. I know that well. But this gun concerns you."

"Of course it does."

"I would use it—"

"Against your enemies," Opechancanough said impatiently. "I know."

Powhatan fell icily silent.

Opechancanough's face flushed, and he cursed himself for his cringing shame. "I apologize, Brother. I know better than to interrupt you."

"The *tassantassas* are here now. We may as well make use of them."

"*Why* are they here? Have you not asked yourself?"

"Of course I have."

"This isn't like the times before, when the *tassantassas* came on their boats, took a few children, and left again. They have built a town—a strange town, I grant you, and one without women to tend gardens or raise children. But it is a town. There is no doubt of it."

"What do you think they mean by it? You saw them today. What is your impression?"

Opechancanough drew a deep breath. He hadn't actually put any thought into what the *tassantassas* might intend, why they haunted Paspahegh territory like pale, malevolent ghosts. But the moment Powhatan asked the question, Opechancanough knew the answer.

"They want our land. All of it, not just that miserable boggy spit. Their town will grow. Its walls will spread. They will take every territory for their own. They want the whole of Tsenacomoco."

Powhatan scoffed. "Be reasonable. There are hundreds of us—thousands. Not even a hundred of the *tassantassas* are left alive. I have heard of the ones who were killed and our scouts have seen them bury more dead in recent days. It must be the sickness that did them in. How can so few men defeat the Real People? Talk sense, Brother."

Opechancanough shrugged helplessly, and hated himself for the weakness of the gesture. "I know I speak the truth. Maybe the Okeus puts these words into my mouth."

"So you are a priest now?"

"Of course not."

"Again, I say, be sensible. Think of all we can gain from them, if only we can make them our allies. We are halfway there. They trade with us eagerly. You said they have no gardens. Therefore they have no sufficient stores to see them through the winter. They will be reliant on us. They will come to know how I control this land, the people, even the food they eat."

Opechancanough's jaw tightened. He fought back harsh words, shielding his eyes to his brother's advancing age and the weakness that encroached like a killing frost. He schooled his voice to a calm, reasonable tone. "They will do us no good in the end. In a dry year like this one—five dry years in a row, Wahunse-na-cawh, my wise brother—how can we take food from our women and children to keep these beasts alive? They are not Real People. You must see that."

"What would you have me do, then? Allow them to starve when *taquitock* sets in?"

"Let me take three bands: Paspahegh, Quiyo-co-hannock, and my Pamunkey. Let me put an end to them. It will be quick. Efficient. Thorough."

Amusement lit Powhatan's hooded eyes. "Quiyo-co-hannock, eh? You would fight beside Pepiscunimah?"

"I will do what I must do. Quiyo-co-hannock is near to the white men's fort. Together we could make short work of it. It would be clean, and over with swiftly."

Powhatan gazed off into the shadowed depths of his great house, weighing the proposal, tasting it. Opechancanough allowed himself to feel a swell of hope, a thrill rising high and hot along his spine. But in the next moment Powhatan spat it out, and his words were bitter.

"No, Brother. I will not allow this. You will continue to support the *tassantassas'* fort. You will bring them more gifts when I direct you."

His fists clenched hard at his sides. "I will not. You are the *mamanatowick*, but I am a chief in my own right, and in this I cannot obey."

"You will," Powhatan said quietly. "Because you are my brother."

"I will not, because I am a chief of the Real People."

Their eyes met and held over the heart fire, locked like the antlers of two great bucks in dire contest.

"This anger, Opechancanough, the way you lash out. It is not becoming of a man."

"Your indecision is not becoming of a man. You are weak and wavering, like a woman fretting over village gossip."

Powhatan's eyes narrowed. Opechancanough saw the threat in his brother's dangerously still face. *I can take away your power*, the old man's eyes said. *I can make you* tanx, *or less.* He braced himself when Powhatan's mouth opened, prepared for the axe blow that would un-man him. But Powhatan said only, "I wonder who is the weaker of us, after all."

Opechancanough clapped his hand to his chest in a terse salute and spun on his heel. He was at the door flap before he knew it, with no sense of traveling the dark length of the great house, no memory of his own footsteps. One moment he was in Powhatan's *yehakin*, and the next he was outside, beyond, breathing air that was warm with the promise of change, bitter with the promise of frost.

He would find another way to bring the *tassantassas* under control, or crush them altogether. He swore it silently, made an oath to the season with every beat of his heart. He swore it to the women who still chanted innocently over their work, their voices rising in concert as the last rays of the sun bled crimson from the sky.

It would come to pass. He was a *werowance* of the Real People; he would make good on his vow.

SMITH

August 1607

John Smith watched in wary anticipation as the final spadeful of earth fell onto Bartholomew Gosnold's grave with a hiss and a wet smack. The men who were strong enough to stand bowed their heads for prayer. The rest huddled on the ground, dull and listless, while Edward-Maria Wingfield stood over the grave with Bible in hand.

Wingfield met Smith's eye. The president's stare was hard and cold as winter ice.

Fourteen men dead since the flux swept through our ranks. Smith glared his accusation at Wingfield. *All of us fell ill—all but you.*

Wingfield looked resolutely away, breaking the grip of Smith's stare with a ponderous dignity that seemed almost resigned.

He knows what is coming. He knows there is no stopping it. No way to stop it, no way to repent—not with Gosnold, Wingfield's most powerful friend, sleeping under a blanket of salt-black mud.

As credit to his bravery, Wingfield remained focused on the work at hand. He gave a respectful elegy in a voice that never wavered, expounding on the mystery of God's workings, declaring what an inspiration Gosnold was, that he should not only found the Virginia Company but be willing to die in its service, far from home on a savage shore. When he finished the closing prayer in his ringing orator's baritone, when the gathered men had delivered a ragged "Amen," Wingfield gave one small, keen-eyed nod to Smith and turned on his heel. He strode toward the open palisade gate, the Holy Book swinging like a pendulum at his side, arms stiff, legs stiff, neck stiff, but never deigning to glance right or left.

"Come on, then," Smith muttered. The men helped one another to their feet and followed, wobbly, leaning on shoulders and backs that were no more stable than their own.

When they reached the cabins, Wingfield paused outside his private quarters. He said nothing, only stood aside and watched Smith enter. The room was fastidiously neat. The men drew up in a half circle around the cabin door while Smith went about his business, shaking out the blankets, flipping the cot, upending the wooden crate that served as a foot trunk . . . and *there*. A package of oilcloth tied with a worn length of leather thong tumbled onto the packed-earth floor.

Smith looked up at Wingfield. The man's eyes were very nearly sorrowful.

Smith opened the bundle with trembling hands. He folded back the cloth from the evidence that would damn Wingfield to the brig, the evidence he knew he would find: dried fruit, dried meat, and a small brown bottle of nourishing olive oil. There must have been two pounds of the stuff remaining. The cache Wingfield had kept since their landing had surely been rich and plentiful.

A roar of indignation went up from the gathered men.

"You see," Smith shouted. "Now you know why he never fell ill like the rest of us. He has been keeping a private store to fortify himself. He has hoarded wellness for his own while we suffered and died. I would have discovered it sooner, but I was too weak from the flux myself."

Wingfield stepped backward. It was not a retreat; he did not recoil from Smith's words or from his bold eyes. It was a quiet surrender. He gave himself gently but firmly into the hands of the men.

"Put him in the brig!" somebody shouted.

"Aye, the brig, where he kept John Smith!"

Smith moved toward Wingfield, toward the shouting men who surrounded him. This time the tremor in his knees was the blood rush of victory, not the residual quaking of his illness.

Wingfield's shoulders jerked; he might have swept an ironic bow, had so many hands not held him upright. "I leave you to it, Smith—you and whatever council you can raise from this depraved lot. You ease me of a great deal of trouble. I am at your pleasure; dispose of me as you will without further theatrics."

Smith hefted the bundle in his hands as if testing the weight of Wingfield's sins. "Send him to the brig," he said at last.

The men cheered.

The woodland canopy had turned to shades of fire. Gold and orange, russet and blood red moved in a small but ceaseless wind, speaking in a constant whisper across the grassy brake of the spit. Smith paced the watchtower. His eyes never left the deep-blue shadows beneath the canopy, the veiled shade of the forest floor. He hoped to see Indians moving there, bearing baskets full of corn and sacks of dried fish as they once had. It had been more than a week since their last trading visitors, and already Smith feared that Jamestown's stores would soon be empty.

He shifted his gaze to the *Discovery*. It stood still and dignified, unmoved by the river's current, as stoic as the prisoner who dwelt in its cramped brig. The knowledge of Wingfield's defeat brought Smith less satisfaction by the day. The council had voted a new president into office immediately upon securing Wingfield aboard the *Discovery*. Smith had not dared to hope the vote would fall in his favor, and indeed it had not. John Ratcliffe was the new president of the council, a bright man, but one of intense and varied moods with a history he was strangely reluctant to discuss. He was, of course, a gentleman, and he had no disinclination to trumpet his fine pedigree.

Smith heard the scrape of boots on the ladder. He turned in time to see Ratcliffe rise up onto the watchtower. The steel of his breastplate and helmet shone in the clear, warm air of early autumn.

"Good day, Smith."

Smith nodded.

"I hope you don't mind my coming to speak with you. I have been meaning to ever since the vote." Ratcliffe's eyes had a mild squint even in dim light, and now, with the sun bright on the nearby river, they were two thin black creases in the man's face, eerily unreadable. "I understand you donated Wingfield's . . . the supply of food to the fort's storehouse."

That particular vote *had* gone in Smith's favor. The fact that he was unanimously awarded the secret store of fruit and meat was a small sop to his lack of presidency. "The men would have torn me apart if I'd kept it for myself," he said. But he would have donated it to the storehouse even had the men not been wild with hunger and power.

Ratcliffe squinted for a long moment, first at Smith, then out at the *Discovery*, which was ringed by a dazzling halo of sun on water. "You don't like me, Smith. I can see that."

"You don't like me, either."

Ratcliffe did not deny it. "But I do respect you. I know of your skills, not only among our own but with the naturals. I have noted the work you do with them, learning their tongue and their customs."

Smith felt his spine straighten, his chin raise. *Like a damned dog perking up when its master calls.* "I have been gaining whatever I can from them—not only food for our storehouse, but knowledge, too."

"I see that as well."

"We need to know whatever they can teach us." Smith waved toward the fiery treetops, the endless rustling. The gentle breeze tugged a few leaves free, and they skittered, bright and airy as feathers, out into the marsh. "Winter is not far off. It will go hard on us if we don't know what to expect."

Ratcliffe nodded slowly. "I believe you are right. That's why I've come to you today, Smith. I've a task for you."

Smith eyed the president warily, measuring him, searching for mockery or lie. But Ratcliffe was inscrutable. At last Smith said, "Well?"

"I would set you in charge of our relations with the naturals."

Smith exhaled roughly. "I nigh am already."

"Good. Then it won't be any trouble for you. Listen, Smith. Skilled as you are with the locals, I must ask you: Do you know why they've stopped coming to trade with us?"

They both looked down from the watchtower to the dark roof of the storehouse. The casks of meal were infested and near empty; the Indian corn had long since been eaten.

"It is their hunting season," Smith said. "They've gone west, upriver, following the deer."

"And when will they return?"

"I don't know," Smith admitted reluctantly. Not until the spring, for all he could tell. His skill with the language was not great enough that he had learned what the naturals did in the wintertime, where they went or how they survived. Through the autumn warmth he felt the bitter cold of snow and sleet creep into his bones. He shivered.

"Find out," Ratcliffe said. "As quickly as you can. Learn how we're to make it through this winter."

"The men believe Captain Newport will return by then, with plenty of supplies."

The dark slashes of Ratcliffe's eyes turned on him again, held him for a long moment. "You don't believe that any more than I. You say the Indians have gone upriver. Then that is where you must go. Tomorrow you will select your men and take the shallop inland."

"Aye."

"If any man can learn how to survive the winter, John Smith, it is you."

So began months of trade and exploration. As the autumn advanced and cold crept deep into the woodlands, Smith, together with a crew of five, sailed the little shallop up the James River into the heart of Indian territory.

He quickly became adept at spotting the identifying marks of a village: the low-cut riverbank, the bare-scraped earth and dark paths through bands of gravel where they had dragged their canoes. The villages near the fort, however, were thoroughly abandoned. A time or two he went ashore and inspected the remains of their towns; charred rings of fire pits were like bruises in the earth, the skeletal black frames of houses, bent into high arches but stripped of their coverings, half-concealed among the tangle of oak and willow.

As the shallop progressed inland, the river narrowing by the day, Smith encountered his first tribe. The Chickahominy were still making their preparations for the hunt. Smith watched with interest as a group of women and young boys removed long strips of bark from the sides of a domed house. The strips were rolled and packed into bags for transportation to some distant autumn residence, to shelter a family beneath a new arched framework while the men of the household hunted the winter's supply of meat.

Smith's guide, a man of middle age with a pronounced limp, explained with obvious pride that the Chickahominy were *not* members of Powhatan's group—they had not capitulated, had not thrown away their identity for the privilege of paying tribute to that fat old grubber.

"Let him keep his hundreds of wives furnished with shells and *puccoon* by his own sweat, not by ours!"

Smith was left with the impression that these Chickahominy must settle for the less desirable hunting territories, whiling away their autumn in distant seclusion while the lands rich with migrating game went to Powhatan's lot. The guide certainly kept up a brave face about their predicament. Indeed, he blustered near as much as an English gentleman.

With prospects for the autumn hunt rather poor, the Chickahominy were overeager to trade. They had not dared approach Jamestown for fear of Powhatan's retribution and were as hungry for Smith's goods as he was for their dried corn. He used their desperation to his advantage, drawing them into long conversations about local weather, resources, game, and food plants. In the end he offered just a few trinkets. The English goods were so new to these isolated men that he reaped an exchange of preserved foods far out of proportion to his handful of beads. Smith almost felt guilty for it.

Within a few weeks, the novelty of his items lost some of its luster. The Chickahominy began to bargain in earnest, and Smith coolly walked away from their offers, dropping chains of copper links and strings of coveted gaudy-colored beads around the necks of the village children. The largesse was too much for the men to ignore. The next time he appeared in his shallop, the Chickahominy were prepared to offer him a load of dried beans so extravagant the boat's ballast had to be redistributed to accommodate the weight.

It was a lucky strike. When Smith returned to Chickahominy territory the following day, the village was gone, its inhabitants vanished to their autumnal hunting grounds with barely a trace left behind.

He did his utmost to share with the men of Jamestown the knowledge he had gleaned from the Indians. He told them of the marsh root called *tuckahoe*, bland and tough and difficult to dig from the mud but nourishing enough to keep up the strength of entire villages through famine. The men were not interested in digging *tuckahoe*; they kept their eyes fastened downstream, where the wide mouth of the James opened on the sea. They were certain Newport or the first supply ship—the one that had been due for months—would arrive any day now. *Tuckahoe* was no kind of substitute for familiar English foods, English goods, English life.

But the prismatic, blue-skied chill of October gave way to a dreary November, heavy with rain and sleet and soaking with cold. At last even the most optimistic of the men were forced to admit that Newport would not be returning.

The beans and corn obtained from the Chickahominy were running low. The stores of weevil-black meal were a memory now, but an experience Smith would gladly live through again if it meant a reliable source of food. There were only so many *tuckahoe* roots one man could dig, and Smith was not inclined to share the coarse, tasteless things with any man who did not put his own back to the task.

"I can move farther inland," he said to Ratcliffe one miserable morning as they took their turn at the watch. Rain drummed on their helmets and drifted in white veils across the river. "They travel by canoe. There is a barrier of some sort, they've told me, impassable to their vessels: rocks or falls, I'm not certain which. But I am certain they can't move past it—not with so many women and children in tow. They must be somewhere nearby, somewhere within our reach."

Ratcliffe nodded thoughtfully. "We must do something, and soon. Day by day I watch those baskets and barrels of corn growing lighter." He sighed. "It's a terrible place we've come to, John

Smith. This is nothing like the Virginia Company said it would be—nothing like I expected."

Smith kept his words to himself, but he watched Ratcliffe's emotionless face with interest. *What did you expect then, man?*

The president was probably not among the few who believed Smith's tales of past adventures, his mercenary days, his time in Constantinople and his toil in the Turk's fields. Smith could have told Ratcliffe—could have told any of them—how it would be, had they only cared to listen. At least no one left alive still believed the Indians to be innocents. Too many of the Virginia Company, never having gone farther from London than their country estates, expected the naturals would be childlike and eager for the improvements the English would bring to their lives, glad to be shown more efficient and civilized ways, hungering for the salvation of Christ. They'd assumed that in their gratitude the naturals would be quick to take the colony under their wings, and the adventurers would want for nothing.

You pitiful, mad, mad fools.

"I know enough of their ways now," Smith said, "what they value, how they think. I can . . . trade more *assertively*, if need be."

Ratcliffe stroked his beard. It was wet from the rain, and tiny crystalline beads of ice had formed at its end. "Yes. I suppose it has come to that. Or it will very soon."

"And yet, we must be careful," Smith said. "The naturals are our only help in this land, unless Newport finally does return. We mustn't destroy what we've built. We mustn't let it return to . . . what it was early on."

"No—no, never that. It will be a fine line to walk. But we mustn't allow ourselves to fall again. We've lost too many men—nearly half our number. We cannot lose more."

But we will. The winter would go hard on them. Smith knew it, without understanding how he knew it. Perhaps it was something in the eyes of the Indians he'd met in trade, some wariness, some resignation. He watched droplets of rain bead and fall from the rim of his helmet. Soon those drops would turn to snow. Perhaps this river would ice over—who could say?—and then all hope of trade would be lost, even if he could find the hunting villages, even if he could extract food from them by trade or by extortion.

Faced with so many terrible possibilities, John Smith was certain of only one thing: he would not see the men of Jamestown starve.

POCAHONTAS

Season of Taquitock

A cascade of chestnuts poured from the girls' foraging bags. The shiny red spheres clattered as they fell; a few escaped the wide sorting basket and rolled across the floor of the house. Small children scampered after them, making a game of it, scooping the runaway nuts from under beds or behind stacks of sleeping mats and returning them to the sorting basket with wild giggles.

Pocahontas and Matachanna grinned at each other over their task. Sorting chestnuts was a favorite chore, more play than work. It was pleasant to sit by a warm heart fire on a chilly day, with plenty of breath for gossiping. The chestnuts were as smooth and cool as precious *roanoke* shell in the hand, and there was the anticipation of delights to come: roasted chestnuts hot and steaming, or the raw meat of the little red globes ground to flour and baked into chewy cakes. Pocahontas put a nut between her teeth and bit down gently until its thin shell gave way. She peeled it and savored its sweet earthiness and grainy texture.

"Don't eat them all," Matachanna scolded. "And if you keep cracking nuts with your teeth you're bound to break them."

Pocahontas shrugged. She lifted a handful of chestnuts and thumbed through them expertly, flicking the rotten and shriveled ones into her discard basket and dropping the rest into the tall woven-bark canister that sat between her and Matachanna.

Her half sister picked up a string of chatter as if she had never dropped it to scold. The topic, as it so often was these days, was the handsome priest Utta-ma-tomakkin. "Three days ago when he came to Werowocomoco to bless the hunt, he *looked* at me. For the *longest* time."

"Surely he intends to marry you, then," Pocahontas said drily.

"Don't tease! Oh, I'd burst if he asked me to marry him!"

"Just like a rotten chestnut."

Matachanna's braid had crept forward to dangle in the pile of nuts, and she scowled at Pocahontas as she flipped it back over her shoulder. In the sudden movement, Pocahontas saw that her sister's chest was beginning to swell into a woman's breasts. Why had she not noticed before? *She truly will be marrying soon.*

The sudden realization made Pocahontas burn with a poignant loneliness, like a wind moaning through a desolate wood. She had no man of her own to giggle over, no handsome priest or young warrior destined to become a great *werowance*. She still found men and boys to be uninteresting at best and infuriating at worst, forever puffed up with their boasts, strutting about town displaying the deer they'd shot or the muscles they'd made by endlessly drawing their precious bows.

Worst of all men was Naukaquawis. At the opening feast of *taquitock*, Powhatan had announced that soon Naukaquawis would be promoted to *werowance*. Her heart still sank when she recalled the scene. Envy and a desperate, futile desire had stabbed at her with twin knives as she watched her half brother accept the acclaim of the tribe, their father beaming as he draped a feather cloak around Naukaquawis's shoulders. Pocahontas had had no choice but to shout her approval along with everybody else, while inside she felt as hollow and sour as last winter's gourds.

Matachanna noted the sudden sorrow on Pocahontas's face. "What is it?"

"Toothache," she said quickly.

"I warned you about cracking nuts."

"I will never disregard the advice of wise Matachanna again. But tell me . . . doesn't Utta-ma-tomakkin love Chiskinute?"

Matachanna blinked at her. "Chiskinute?"

The girl was homely and simple, though friendly enough. The very idea of a man like Utta-ma-tomakkin losing his heart to the empty-headed muskrat Chiskinute was more than Pocahontas could bear. She pressed her lips tight to hold back her laughter, but it forced its way out in an explosive snort.

"You are cruel to torment me!" Matachanna grew serious. "You shouldn't mock Chiskinute, though. She has a good spirit."

"She has a dull spirit."

"Chiskinute looks up to you. She would be your friend, if you'd have her."

Pocahontas fluttered her eyelids. "I have no need of more friends."

"As far as I'm concerned," Matachanna muttered, "you don't have so many to spare."

"What?"

"Oh, come now, Pocahontas. Don't play the fool. You're smart enough to see how many girls dislike you."

Pocahontas gaped at her sister. "Why should anyone dislike me?"

"You truly don't see it?" Matachanna dropped her chestnuts to study Pocahontas's face, eyes wide with surprise. "Then I'm sorry I teased you over it. I didn't mean to wound you."

"Who dislikes me?"

Matachanna blushed. "You must admit, you can be . . . abrasive."

"Abrasive! Is that what you think of me?"

"Not me," Matachanna said weakly, in a hesitant, halting manner that revealed her lie. "Others. And it's only your ambition that makes you so . . . so *rough* with other girls."

"My ambition?" Pocahontas folded her arms across her chest and glowered. "What are you talking about?"

Matachanna sighed. "Oh, Pocahontas. I'm not trying to wound you, truly. You must believe me. But the way you desire . . . whatever it is you desire. Status? Influence? I don't know what to call it. I only know the longing I see in your eyes whenever we're around our father, or another chief."

"I long for nothing."

Matachanna went on as if Pocahontas had never spoken. "But you know what you are, what your place in life will be."

Pocahontas tensed, offended by the stark truth of her sister's words.

"You must accept it, Pocahontas. You'll be happier if you accept it, if you acknowledge your true place among the Real People rather than striving for what can never be. It will make you kinder to others, more generous, more giving."

Pocahontas rose stiffly. "Maybe I see no reason to be kind or generous or giving to those who are not kind to me."

Matachanna scowled. "Who is not kind to you? You, who can get away with any kind of foolishness in Powhatan's sight? Who doesn't treat you better than you deserve to be treated? It's time you returned the kindnesses you've been granted."

Pocahontas stalked to her bed and rummaged through her baskets. She found a pair of doeskin leggings and yanked them over her bare legs, jerking the laces so tight they bit into her thighs. It was too cold outside to go about naked; she wound a soft silk-grass cloth between her legs and knotted it about her waist.

"Where are you going?" Matachanna shrilled. "We still have chestnuts to sort!"

Pocahontas made no reply. She took her cloak down from its peg and flung it across her shoulders, slid her feet into her warm winter moccasins, and tied the strings at her ankles. Then she stomped past her sister, who still crouched wide-eyed on the fireside mat.

"Be careful," Matachanna called crossly as Pocahontas lifted the door flap. "I won't continue to pick up your dropped oars and paddle your canoe forever. One day even I will grow tired of your selfishness, Pocahontas, and then you'll be all alone!"

Taquitock had set in—cold, bitter, and grudging, a sudden, dramatic counter to the unrelieving heat and dryness of summer. The slap of the late-autumn air left Pocahontas gasping. The exposed skin of her stomach and face prickled like nettle-burn and her eyes watered in the cold. Here in Werowocomoco, where Powhatan received the wealth of his tribute, there was no need to move for the winter. An early sunset was falling beyond the most distant cornfields, and a rose-soft glow tinted the rounded roofs of the village. The warmth of the light played cruelly against the biting chill.

From a far garden she heard the rising whoop of children perched in a crow tower. They were crying and leaping, slinging stones, frightening the evening roost away from the season's last ears of corn. The women all said that in a normal year, such small and withered ears could be left for the winged pests; late *taquitock* corn was hardly worth gathering when the rains were steady and the summers damp. Pocahontas could recall neither damp summers nor rich crops. Plentiful harvests with more baskets of corn than any family could store seemed to belong to a distant time, so long gone it might as well be the time of legends, when gods and spirits walked freely among men. Now, even these small, dry ears were precious, and crows were more than ill-luck spirits to be spat at and killed, they were an open threat. Every bit they consumed meant less food for already-thin caches; each ear lost to the crows meant a night of hunger for one of the Real People. This winter would be brutal, the food stores sparse, and the crows wary and sly.

Pocahontas headed for the nearest crow tower. After Matachanna's harsh words, she would welcome the task of hurling stones at the roosting birds; it sounded splendid to shout until her throat was raw and her lungs burning. But halfway across town she drifted to a halt.

Is it true what Matachanna said? Do the other girls hate me?

If so, they would not welcome her at the crow towers. She paused, listening to the laughter and the happy cries mingling with the loud, repetitive pop of stones beating against old bark sheets. A flight of crows lifted from the cornfields with a great rush of black feathers. Their raucous cries erupted in the treetops, fading to a rolling echo as they crossed the river to seek out a friendlier evening roost. The chorus was thin with distance, yet the crows' ominous calls still shivered the bones of her head, trembling behind her eyes, running through her veins like the sound of a copper bell struck by a mallet. She turned to follow the path of the crows, down toward the low bank of the river.

Before she had even passed the outer ring of houses, Pocahontas became aware of a commotion on the river track. The sound filled her with a slow, wary dread, a pinch in her stomach that was halfway between curiosity and fear. She slunk behind the planks of the nearest drying rack and peered between slats rank with the odor of fish scales and hardwood smoke. There were footsteps coming up the track from the direction of the shore—the heavy steps of men—several men. There was nothing unusual in that. Likely a band of hunters had returned from one of the nearby meat camps, bearing deer and fowl for the *mamanatowick* and his relations.

Then why this pressing, instinctive worry?

A moment before the men rounded a bend in the path, Pocahontas realized what it was she feared. Unfamiliar voices rose in a strange, round-soft, songlike tongue, speaking words she did not know. The timbre of their words was pleading. They were afraid, that much she could tell. Half a heartbeat before they marched into view, she smelled them: pungent, salty, and sharp, musky like an animal hide, not at all pleasant. The odor was strong enough to cut through the smell of the drying rack.

Tassantassas.

There were two of them, hemmed in by a guard of Real People, warriors who walked with knives and hatchets ready in case the white men should try to escape—or attack. They didn't look capable of an attack, though. They were thin. Through their bushy beards she could see how the bones of their faces pressed sharp as broken flint against thin, pale skin. They moved with a defeated hunch, a stumbling weakness that spoke of ill health, and their eyes were dull with long hunger.

With a start, Pocahontas realized that the man who led the *tassantassas*, who directed them with prods and pokes from his bow, was her half brother Naukaquawis.

He will take them to Powhatan.

Pocahontas waited until the bedraggled white men shambled past. Then she slipped from her hiding place and followed them silently through the lanes of Werowocomoco, to the great house of the Chief of Chiefs.

By the time the party arrived at Powhatan's *yehakin*, word had spread through the town that the young warrior Naukaquawis had apprehended a pair of white men. Women dropped their work and thronged on either side of the wide central lane that ran past the communal fire pit, drawing into clusters of three or four, whispering and staring. Children bounced and sidled to within a few paces of the bewildered *tassantassas*, daring one another to touch the pale, hairy creatures before the warriors drove them off with lazy flicks of their bows.

Pocahontas threaded her way through the watching crowd, struggling to reach Powhatan's lodge before the *tassantassas* did. Powhatan's wives made a frantic commotion, scrambling into the great house to scrape together a suitably impressive array of foods and fineries to impress and intimidate the strangers. They cursed as they ran, clicking their tongues as they brushed dirt from one another's faces and tucked ornaments into glossy black hair.

Pocahontas hesitated in the clearing outside the great house. The clearing was as lively as an ant heap, and the *tassantassas* were only a few steps behind. She glanced quickly about; the guard was at the door, the same young warrior who had chided and mocked her the time she'd sought admittance at Powhatan's council. The guard's smooth brown skin was unmarred, the bruises from his *huskanaw* long gone, but his eyes were as keen as ever. She had no illusions that he would be friendlier today.

A young wife, nearly wailing with anxiety, rushed past clutching a long-necked gourd full of nut milk. Pocahontas snatched the gourd from the wife, who let out a piercing shriek, and then ran full tilt toward the door flap.

The guard's eyes widened. She gritted her teeth as she ran, silently daring him to remain where he was. A heartbeat before she would have collided with him, cracking the gourd and sending nut milk spewing across the clearing, he stepped to the side. Pocahontas's body punched against the door flap. It held just long enough for her feet to lift from the earth and paddle helplessly in the air. Then it collapsed inward and she skidded on her knees into Powhatan's great house. The guard shouted a curse from the doorway. Nut milk had sloshed from the gourd onto her face and she wiped herself clean with a corner of her cloak. Then she turned to grin up at him.

"You ought to be beaten for this," he snarled.

"I won't be. Don't you know who I am?"

"Some Pamunkey whelp with no manners." He scowled at her from the other side of the doorway, tugging at the flap until the thick hide lay straight again on its wooden frame. "And you nearly broke Powhatan's door."

"I'm Amonute, the *mamanatowick*'s favorite daughter."

He squinted at her. "The one they call Mischief—is that you? I can see you're well named, you wicked crow of a girl."

She stood, then brushed the dirt from the knees of her leggings. "And who are you, to speak to me in such a manner?"

"Don't put on airs," he said harshly. "I know you're no high-blood daughter. My name is Kocoum, not that it's any concern of yours."

The flap closed briefly, dimming the evening glow. Then Kocoum's head and shoulders appeared again, quick as a mole peeking from its burrow. "The *tassantassas* are here! Move aside!"

She pressed herself against the wall, hiding in the shadow and the folds of her cloak.

She could hear the *tassantassas* pausing and shuffling before ducking through the doorway. She sensed fear in their hesitation. Then the smell of them filled the hall, forceful and thick. They stood blinking in the interior gloom, their eyes pale as autumn leaves and stained by dark-purple pits.

Naukaquawis laid a hand on one man's shoulder and he shied like an ambushed deer, his feet drumming like panicked hooves, his body heaving. He would have run, had he not been hemmed in by the walls of Powhatan's great house. Naukaquawis made soothing gestures and motioned down the length of the hall, indicating that they should walk. The heart fire pulsed in the depths of the lodge like a brooding heart. When they had moved down the great central aisle in their shuffling, sick-bear gait, Pocahontas slid from her cover of shadows to follow.

Powhatan was waiting like a dark god on his high bedstead, mantled in firelight and silence. The hot glow intensified the hardness of his face and sharpened his features, exaggerating him so that his fierce countenance seemed to leap from his surroundings, stark and forceful as a ceremony mask. Even Pocahontas, for whom Powhatan always had a smile and a fond word, felt a twinge of awe. The *tassantassas* shook where they stood beside the fire.

"What did you bring me?" he asked of Naukaquawis.

"I found these two near the river. Or rather, they found me."

Powhatan stared at the white men. His eyes were two glimmers of black in a copper sky, like stars reversed; and like stars, they were distant and inscrutable.

"What do you want?" he asked the *tassantassas*. "Why are you here?"

They seemed to know that the Great Chief spoke to them, for they glanced uneasily at one another and shifted on the stiff soles of their worn, dark moccasins. But they made no reply.

"They don't understand you, Father," said Naukaquawis.

"I have heard that the *tassantassas* can speak the Real Tongue in trade."

"Only the one with the yellow beard—Chawnzmit."

Powhatan grunted.

Naukaquawis made a few hand signs, palm open, head tilted quizzically, brows raised. One of the *tassantassas*, the taller of the two, seemed to draw himself up. His eyes sparked with sudden understanding. He gestured back: first touching his own chest and his companion's, then the thin hand arcing through the air, a simulation of tossing something away. He pressed a hand to his middle, and his face looked haunted, desperate—sad.

Powhatan and Naukaquawis exchanged uncertain glances.

The *tassantassa* lifted one hand as if it cupped water and raised the other perpendicular, spread wide; the pale hands traveled together, moving away from his body, pressing onward until his arms reached to their fullest extent. Then the fingers spread, separated; the palms turned outward, drifting away.

Naukaquawis shook his head. "I don't know . . ."

Pocahontas rushed into the ring of firelight before she quite knew what she was doing, or why. She still held the gourd full of nut milk. Powhatan looked down at her, surprise cracking the stern lines of his mask.

"They ran from their town," she blurted.

"Get out, Amonute." Naukaquawis scuffed his moccasin in the earth, kicking an invisible stone at his lowborn little sister.

She set the gourd on the earthen floor and repeated the *tassantassa*'s gesture, the arcing toss. "Away," she said. "They ran far away."

"Go on," Powhatan said slowly. His eyes were on the *tassantassas*.

She squinted up at the tall one, trying to recall every movement, the placement of each bony bird-claw finger. She mimicked the cupping of his hands, the pressing out and away.

What does it mean?

Her arms extended fully, and like the white man, she allowed her fingers to spread, her palms to separate . . . allowed the unseen object she had held to disappear into the air.

Disappear. Of course. The cupped hands were like a boat, moving swiftly across the vast ocean.

"Some of them took a boat and went across the sea," she said. "But they never came back." She pressed a hand to her stomach. "And now . . . they are starving."

"Anyone can see they are starving," Naukaquawis muttered.

"But some have gone back over the sea," Powhatan said in a low, musing tone. "You are sure that's what he meant, Amonute?"

She was sure of nothing, but standing in the light of her father's approval, a thrill of triumph warm as licking flames filled her chest. She nodded.

The tall one made his hand signs again. He made imploring motions toward Powhatan, mimed eating, made curious bows from the waist, and touched his forehead. Again the signs for eating, and again the bows.

"He is begging," Naukaquawis said, disgust tinting his voice.

"No," said Pocahontas. There was nothing pleading in the man's manner. It was respect he showed, and something akin to thanks. "He knows it was you who gave the *tassantassas* food, Father, in the summertime. He thanks you for it."

Powhatan leaned back slightly, eyes narrowing, a dignified acceptance.

Now the white man made fearsome motions, the drawing of a bow, the grimace of a warrior's face. He held up a hand as if halting his own aggression. And again, the strange, vehement bowing.

Pocahontas saw the meaning at once. "He thanks you for stopping the Real People from attacking the fort."

Powhatan chuckled deep in his chest. "Our trick with the Paspaheghs and the Quiyo-co-hannocks," he said to Naukaquawis. "I told Opechancanough it was a good plan."

The *tassantassa* went on gesturing and bowing. Pocahontas watched carefully, feeling the man's movements in her own small frame, sensing his desperation in her spirit, *understanding*.

"He throws himself on your mercy. He begs help from the *mamanatowick*, for without your assistance, all of the white men will die."

Naukaquawis and Powhatan locked eyes for a long moment. The heart fire snapped and muttered in the silence. At last the *mamanatowick* seemed to come to a decision. He nodded slowly, thoughtfully, his eyes staring into the deep, swift current of his own thoughts. He called for one of his wives, who came at once, smoothing her painted apron over bare thighs.

"Bring food for these men. Naukaquawis, find me a man who has traded often with the *tassantassas*."

"That will be difficult, with so many off at the hunt."

"But there must be someone still in Werowocomoco. Find him and bring him to me. I need a man who has enough of their language to make my intentions clear—to make my offer clear."

"Offer, Father?"

"An offer I am certain starving men will not refuse: I will give these two food if they will give me information. I want information about their kind. Why they are here, what they intend, how many died, how weak they are."

Naukaquawis crossed his arms over his broad chest. "I suppose they will give what you seek, and willingly. I've seen squirrel carcasses picked clean by crows with more meat on their bones than these two have between them."

"But I want more knowledge from them than what we can gather in a few days' time, my son. The other *tassantassas* will come looking for these men, starving or not. They are a suspicious, untrusting people. We need more than hand signs. We must learn their tongue."

Naukaquawis shrugged. "I suppose I can . . ."

"Not you," Powhatan said, raising a hand to stop him. "You are needed on the hunt. Our winter caches are too low already. This winter we can't spare a hunter as skilled as you."

Naukaquawis's chest swelled with pride. "When the hunt is finished, then."

"They will come looking for their runaways long before then. We have perhaps two weeks' time to learn all we can. After that, I shall move them to a distant town to keep them out of the way of their own people. In the meantime, the task of learning will be yours, Amonute."

A jolt of excitement ran through her body, stiffening her spine so suddenly that her neck twinged with pain. "Mine?"

"You have shown aptitude for it this day. In truth, I never thought to see such focus and wisdom in you. I am pleased."

Pocahontas felt as though her welling spirit would burst right through her skin. "Thank you, Father," she said as humbly as she could manage.

"You must be aware of how important this task is, child. Much depends on it."

"I won't disappoint you."

Naukaquawis snorted. "Why entrust work so crucial to a girl?"

"The *tassantassas* will not fear her, for one thing," Powhatan said. "They will open up to her, answer any question she asks. They are not Real People, but they are not stupid, either. Do you suppose they will spill their secrets to a warrior?"

Reluctantly, Naukaquawis subsided, and shook his braided knot. "Do as you think best, if you believe you can trust men like these with your precious daughter."

"I will give her a guard."

"Not I. I am needed on the hunt," Naukaquawis said with a petulant twist of his mouth.

"My door guard, Kocoum. He has sworn to my service until *cattapeuk*. He was to remain in Werowocomoco during the hunt. He will do nicely."

Pocahontas stifled a groan.

A handful of wives brought baskets of dumplings and turtle shells brimming with hot mix-pot stew. The *tassantassas* descended on the food like feral dogs, stuffing their mouths with both hands, not even pausing to clean the thick dribbles of stew from their wiry beards. Pocahontas watched them with raised eyebrows. These white men were creatures apart; there was no mistaking it. But the fast throb of triumph still raced through her limbs. Powhatan had given her a task—an important task, one for a trusted and respected daughter. It was more than sorting chestnuts, more than baking bread or weaving mats. It was work fit for a girl of high blood.

If she did the job well, she would make herself indispensable to Powhatan. She would gain a permanent place at the *mamana-towick*'s side. She would have influence. She would be more than a lowborn castoff.

And then it wouldn't matter one bit whether Matachanna or anyone else disliked her.

She was so eager for the task, she didn't even mind the prospect of spending her days in Kocoum's company.

The next morning, while the sunlight still played among the fiery leaves of the canopy, Pocahontas led the *tassantassas* to their lessons. They followed her meekly as she strode through the lanes of Werowocomoco, as confident as any chief. Behind the *tassantassas*, Kocoum stalked like a hunting wolf, silent and alert. His hand never strayed far from his knife, and his face was so full of stern mistrust that his large ears almost lost their comical appearance.

Pocahontas chose the yard of her own *yehakin* to teach the men. There were so many more things to see outdoors, more words to test and exchange. And she relished the look of shock on Matachanna's face when she emerged from the longhouse with her nut-gathering basket, gaping at the two white men who crouched beside the fire pit.

"What is the meaning of this?" Matachanna cried, shrinking back against the longhouse wall and clutching her basket to her chest like a warrior's shield.

"My task," Pocahontas said loftily. "Father gave it to me alone. I'm to learn the *tassantassa* tongue."

Matachanna tore her eyes from the white men to glance at Kocoum. Kocoum returned her disbelieving look with a slow shrug and a wry twist of his mouth.

"Must you do it here? What if they try to steal from our *yehakin*?"

"Kocoum is to be my guard. He won't allow anything to happen to our longhouse—or to me, and thank you for your concern for *my* well-being." Pocahontas couldn't resist driving the thorn into Matachanna's flesh. "That's right—I have a guard. I, who was once given as handmaid to another girl!"

Matachanna leveled a dry look at Pocahontas. She never had learned to get along with Nonoma, and eventually Winganuske had entrusted the younger girl to a different child's care. Pocahontas was pleased to be rid of the chore, but she never had gotten over the sting of being given as a servant to another.

Kocoum stepped forward and tugged sharply on Pocahontas's braid. Her face heated with fury.

"Don't swell up to the size of a sturgeon," he warned. "You're still a low-blood child. And I only have to protect you—I'm not your handmaid. *Mischief.*"

Matachanna frowned. "Don't let these crows into the longhouse, Kocoum. Please."

"I won't let them in," Pocahontas insisted. "Now leave us be, Sister. You have nuts to gather, and I have a great duty to the *mamanatowick*. We both have work to do."

When Matachanna had stamped away, muttering about girls with too much ambition, Pocahontas turned to the *tassantassas.* They had been well fed throughout the night, and now that they understood they would not be killed, much of the fear and strain had left their eyes. They looked around, peering curiously at the *yehakin* that clustered beneath shady mulberry trees and the women and children who gathered at the edges of yards to stare back with equal curiosity.

It was simple enough to learn the men's names. The taller was called Will-yum, and the smaller one, whose hair and beard were the same bright orange of a maple in *taquitock*, was named Tom-mass. She tried to correct their way of saying her own name—Poca*hunt*as—to no avail. She finally broke into gales of laughter, clutching at her sides.

Her laughter seemed to build their confidence, and they chuckled tentatively at first, and then more openly. Soon the smiles never left their faces. They took to the lesson playfully, like boys splashing in shallow water, and Pocahontas saw that her father had been right: the white men were comfortable with a child, and they opened to her prying in ways they never would have done with a sober-faced young man like Kocoum or Naukaquawis.

As the two weeks progressed, Pocahontas stripped away the mystery of the *tassantassas* while Kocoum watched, whittling new shafts for his arrows with one hard, wary eye always on the white men. She learned that their moccasins were called *boots*, and the scratchy, sour-smelling cloth they wore was *wool*. The pale-blue metal of their knives was *steel*, and it was harder and sharper than any copper. Also made of *steel* were their many strange weapons: *snaphaunce* and *matchlock*, *musket* and *piece*. The fearsome bits the guns fired were *bullets*, hard and black as seeds, but with the terrible power to destroy flesh and drain the blood from a man's body in an instant.

She learned that the territory they came from, far across the sea, was called *Iing-land*. It was, they told her, a place of many wonders, where people did not walk or paddle in canoes but went from place to place mounted upon animals they called *horses*. The wealthiest *tassantassas* tied their horses to *carriages*, which were, she understood, rather like canoes that went about the land balanced upon rolling hoops. Will-yum scratched a drawing of a horse in the ash of the fire pit. It was somewhat like a deer, with a hairy tail, long face, and tiny ears.

With practice, they moved beyond hand signs and scrawling pictures in the dust. Pocahontas grew more skilled in the *tassantassa* tongue, and she coaxed admissions from the white men with her winning smiles and playful ways. They told her that many of their kind had died at the fort they called Jamestown. The water was poor, the food infested by insects and a type of naked-tailed squirrel they called *rats*, a creature they had brought with them from *Iing-land*. They often quarreled about which of them should be chief, and at times leadership of their village broke down altogether.

Each evening, after returning the *tassantassas* to the warriors who watched over them at night, she followed Kocoum back to her father's longhouse, where she told Powhatan everything she had gleaned from the white men.

Her father nodded, smiling his approval. "You are doing well, Amonute. I am pleased."

If only I could keep the tassantassas *near me longer. I am important to Powhatan now—I am the only one who can learn about the* Iing-lish. *I must keep my grip on them for as long as I am able.* "Father, wouldn't it be wise to keep the *tassantassas* here, and not send them to some distant village where they will do you no good?"

Powhatan shook his head. "No, child. Recall what I said to Naukaquawis. Their fellows will come hunting them. If we want to keep them alive, so that we may learn more from them, they must go into hiding. And soon."

Pocahontas balled her fists in frustration, but she did not allow the emotion to show on her face. "How much longer do I have with the *tassantassas*?"

"Three days more. Then I will move them. Make the time count, Pocahontas."

"I will. But when they are gone . . ."

"Perhaps then," Powhatan said lightly, "we will find another *tassantassa* for you to learn from."

SMITH

December 1607

The shallop crept against the current, oarlocks whistling faintly with the rhythm of the silent rowers. The two sails lay bundled like discarded rags along the boom's length. Not the faintest wind rose to stir the bare branches of the forest. God had not seen fit to send the breath of a breeze for days, and the shallop moved sluggishly under the power of men who grew wearier by the hour.

At least they were no longer starving. Neither of the two expected supply ships had arrived and rations had been pared from paltry to meager. Just as Smith began to fear that they would have to resort to boiling shoe leather, the skies came alive with food. Migratory birds clattered overheard at dawn and dusk, filling the air with streams of black bodies and a chorus of wild, harsh cries. Attracted by the still waters of the marshy spit, they were easy hunting. Soon the men were eating their fill for the first time in far too many weeks.

Smith's forays to nearby tribes had reaped only small returns, but coupled with the blessing of the birds, it was enough to restore most of the men to health. Their salvation had come late, however. Throughout the autumn, more colonists had succumbed to privation and the palisade of Jamestown was ringed by marshy graves. Other men were lost to fear. They ran off in the night in twos and threes, likely hoping to find succor with a friendly tribe. Smith watched the faces of the Indians he traded with and he saw suspicion and distaste moving like twin shadows behind their eagerness for beads. He doubted whether the runaways found the refuge they hoped for. It wasn't worth risking live men to search for their corpses.

Let them rot with their empty guts full of arrows. A fitting end for cowards and deserters.

With starvation averted for the time being, Jamestown finally turned to its primary directives. A handful of men moved up tributary streams to pan for gold, seeking evidence of the rich treasure the New World was certainly concealing beneath its boggy black hide. Others felled trees and split clapboard, laying by a stock of lumber to send home to England when the supply ships returned. One cold November morning when the night's frost made laces of hoar on the logs of the palisade, Ratcliffe took John Smith aside.

"It is time to find the passage to the Pacific," Ratcliffe said, his eyes as direct and emotionless as ever. "You've done well with the trading, commanded the shallop with great skill. It's yours again, Smith. Take it upstream. Get the naturals to talk. They must know which of these blasted rivers leads to the Pacific Ocean. Secure England's trade route to India before the Spanish can get there first, and you'll be a hero back home, old boy. King James himself will knight you, I'd wager."

But it wasn't the prospect of knighthood that drove Smith back aboard his shallop with a crew of reliable workmen. Knighthood was nothing but a life of unwarranted respect and unearned ease. Discovery, though—that was a different matter. The Spanish had beaten up and down the coast of the New World for years, had sailed up these same rivers dozens of times, trading with and terrorizing the naturals. In all that time, the Indians had kept the secret of the Pacific passage. It was certain that the Spanish had failed to find it; if they had located the passage, that Habsburg lout

Philip III would have trumpeted it across the whole of Europe. No, Spain would not claim that particular victory. Only the Indians knew the route. The Spanish worked by sword and fist, and the naturals were resentful of such uncouth tactics. John Smith preferred finesse.

Some two miles beyond the town of Chickahominy, emptied now of occupants, Smith and his men came upon a village that showed a few signs of life. The lanes between the houses were largely still, stripped of the usual mob of naked children running in play or hauling baskets of corn or *tuckahoe* roots. But here and there a body ducked through a doorway, a hide flap swung closed, a line of thin smoke coiled and eddied in a slow haze above a pale domed rooftop. Smith had visited this village before. It was called Apocant, a minor tribe sworn, unlike their stubborn Chickahominy neighbors, to Powhatan's confederation. Smith had found the Apocants no more reluctant or hostile than any other group. Better still, it had been some time since he had paid a visit. They should be willing to assist, eager for the trinkets he would offer in payment.

But as he stood gazing over the shallop's rail at the silent village, a finger of doubt traced lightly along Smith's flesh. An early winter dusk had begun to fall in shades of pale violet. Through the darkening trees he saw a strange glow, carmine red, stretching through the maze of forest. It lingered like a half-remembered image from an unsettling dream. A crow scolded, raucous and sharp. From somewhere in the far twilight a voice cried, a rising pitch, thinned and distorted by distance, wavering like a reflection in a pool. Smith could not say whether it was the call of a man or beast.

"Drop anchor," he said.

A few Apocants began to cluster on the riverbank. They were mostly women, though a small complement of armed men stalked warily among them. Men and women alike wore leather aprons painted with bold designs: snakes and blooming flowers, char-black bears and slinking red coyotes, birds with wings spread wide. Though the day was windless, it was quite cold. Jagged shards of ice rimmed the puddles on the shore and clustered in fat frozen drops along the sides of beached canoes. The Apocants were dressed against the chill of winter, with long leggings of furred hide and hooded cloaks that covered their bodies from bare shoulders to equally bare haunches. Their breath rose in soft clouds.

Smith took three men ashore with him, the three he knew to be the steadiest and most obedient. He would need men with blank faces and tight-shut mouths for this task, men he could count on to do as he said quickly and without fuss—men who would not interfere with Smith's finesse. Thomas Emry and Jehu Robinson rowed the tiny landing boat while Smith and William Baker crowded on its flat bow. Smith was over the side and splashing through ankle-deep, icy water before the rowers had even shipped their oars.

"*Wingapoh*," he called in greeting.

After so many weeks of trade, Smith was confident in the naturals' tongue, and though there were dialectic differences so far upriver, he had no difficulty in making himself understood. Soon he had attracted the few Apocant men with his easy smile and friendly words.

One of the men, somewhere near Smith's twenty-eight years, with a pale scar slashing through his left brow, indicated a line of flickering fire with a jerk of his head. It was the distant snake of hunters' torches twisting through the wood. "The hunt is on, Chawnzmit. Last of the season. There is not much to trade; you will be disappointed."

"What we most desire," said Smith, "is a hunting guide."

The man shook his head. He was called Mahocks, and he watched Smith's tiniest movements with a darting, keen-eyed attention that put Smith in mind of a kingfisher ready to dive on its prey. "All the game is gone for the winter," he said. "All the deer and turkeys have been hunted, and what wasn't killed ran away. This is the last; after tonight, no more animals for the shooting. No more until *cattapeuk* comes again."

"We don't want deer," Smith said quickly. "Birds. Ducks, geese. We have seen many ducks downriver, but everybody knows that the ducks are best in your territory."

A curious light kindled in Mahocks's eye, a sly, glinting amusement. He nodded slowly.

"We want the best birds, the most delicious and fattest. We will need a guide who knows the rivers very well."

Mahocks tossed his head. The loops of his braid flashed like the sheen on a snake's skin. "We all know the rivers very well, Chawnzmit."

"But I want the man who knows them best. And I will pay him well." He knew how bargaining with these people worked. Never open with your best goods, but keep the offers small. They would wave their hands and throw out insults, turn their heads away, but soon or late they would cave to an extra chain of copper, a few more strands of blue or yellow beads. Smith had one particular bauble in his leather pouch, a wide cuff of copper beaten so that it was nearly as faceted as a diamond. It was an ornament even Powhatan would be proud to display. In a village as poor and remote as Apocant, the copper cuff would be a treasure almost beyond price. He left it in the pouch in case the bargaining grew truly difficult, and instead lifted out a string of common white glass beads.

Mahocks fingered his sharp chin in sober deliberation. Then he reached out and took the beads. "Very well, Chawnzmit. If you wish to hunt fat birds, we will hunt the fattest."

Smith gave a wide grin, but his breath caught with sudden uneasiness. The price was too cheap, and the bargaining far too easy. Something was afoot, but Mahocks's wide, hard-edged face was impossible to read.

"Fetch my canoe paddles," he said to one of the women, and he clapped John Smith on the shoulder with a rough, heavy hand.

Four men traveled upriver in the long dugout canoe: Mahocks, Smith, Thomas Emry, and Jehu Robinson. William Baker had returned to the shallop in the rowboat, with Smith's strict orders for the remaining crew to stay aboard the ship and at anchor until he returned. No man was to go ashore for any reason; they had plenty of food and fresh water, and enough sturdy sleeping mats, obtained in trade with the naturals, to create sufficient shelter if foul weather overtook them. The mats were patterned with strips of contrasting bark, tight-woven and as water-repellent as good oilcloth. Some of the colonists had jeered at Smith when he'd returned from a trading visit with a load of mats and little food, but they had seen the utility of the mats quickly enough. They had balked, however, at the idea of learning to make mats of their own. Weaving was not fit work for men, though apparently shivering in a rainstorm or turning to ice in one's sleep were respectably masculine pastimes.

Mahocks's canoe had a complement of mats, too, as well as the man's hunting bow and a quiver of long, light bird arrows. The inside of the dugout was shiny and smooth, darkened from many years of use. It was difficult to paddle at first, and Mahocks laughed and mocked good-naturedly while the men accustomed themselves to the alien motion, driving the paddles downward like stakes into the earth, pulling and lifting and crossing, driving down again. When they had learned the motion to Mahocks's satisfaction, Smith was startled at how smoothly the great lumbering canoe pulled through the water, and he fell into the rhythm of paddling with an easy pleasure, as one falls into the rhythm of an idle stroll. He even warmed with the steady toil, until faint wisps of vapor rose from his body into the cold evening air.

Before long, though, the darkness had grown too thick to continue. Well out of sight of the village of Apocant—and the shallop—Mahocks directed them to turn up the fork of a tributary stream. Black draperies of bramble hung over its banks; wet clots of dead leaves were evident in the moonlight, still clinging to the thorny canes. Their paddling slowed, and the night's fierce cold began to cool Smith's overworked muscles. His back and shoulders ached.

Mahocks found a low bank where they could beach the canoe. Once ashore, the Englishmen stood hugging themselves and shivering while their guide built a fire in a wide, flat clearing. It was a well-used campsite; even in moonlight Smith could see the circle of char that ringed the existing fire pit. Beyond their campfire's ruddy glow, an incarnadine trail of distant torches flickered in the night. The forest air burned with the scents of smoke and cold.

Mahocks settled onto one of his mats near the fire. "Tomorrow," he said, "I will show you where the best birds are. They come in at dawn."

"Good," said Smith. He and his men hunched close to the flames. The welcome heat coaxed steam from their damp clothes.

Smith eyed Mahocks surreptitiously. The man seemed pleasantly lost in thought as he removed dried meat from a traveling basket and unwrapped flat corn cakes from their covering of woven grasses. The guide had an air of contentment about him that Smith found puzzling . . . and worrisome.

"Do you know," Smith said airily, choosing words in the unfamiliar language with care, "I believe this place is near where the Iroquois did their ill deed some years ago."

Mahocks looked up sharply. "What do you know of the Iroquois? They were never in this place. They stay far to the west; they never come here."

"I may be wrong," Smith said. "I have only heard . . . I did not see the deed myself."

Mahocks passed him the basket of food. "What deed?"

"We have a *mamanatowick* of our own, across the sea. King James is his name. He sent his most beloved son here to trade and make friends. But a party of Iroquoians captured him. They took him far away, and the *mamanatowick's* son never returned. We believe he is dead."

Mahocks stared at Smith with an expression of disbelief and annoyance, as if he were a simpleminded child shouting during church. "It never happened here," Mahocks said.

Smith shrugged. "As you say. I may well be wrong. But my *mamanatowick* wishes me to find a way to get to the Iroquoians, so that we might bring justice to the men who killed our *mamanatowick's* son." He indicated Thomas and Jehu, who now dug hungrily into the basket, oblivious to the nature of Smith's tale. "Perhaps when we have hunted our fowl, you might show us a passage."

Mahocks grunted a short laugh. "There is no passage, *Tassantassa.*"

"A way to move farther inland, toward the mountains where the Iroquoians dwell . . ."

"Your feet. That's the only way. Through Massawomeck territory, or Monacan territory." Mahocks grinned. "Good luck to you, if you're foolish enough to attempt walking through Massawomeck territory."

The grin faded from Mahocks's face. He turned his head fractionally, as if catching some faint sound or scent that Smith could not isolate. In the brief moment Mahocks's eyes shifted, a dark veil fell over his friendly countenance. He seemed to gaze inward with amused satisfaction. In the firelight his features turned fox-sharp, an animal mask.

Smith looked about tensely. "What do you . . . ?"

And then he caught the movement in the trees. A shadow slid between the black boles of two oaks, silhouetted for a heartbeat against the far-off fires. Smith's hand fell to the butt of his gun. In a flash, Jehu and Thomas were on their feet and shouting, grappling arms from their belts. Smith stayed low. His stare locked with Mahocks's, whose sharp eyeteeth appeared in a chilling smile.

"Ambush," Smith shouted in English. "Get down!"

The near-silent zip of arrows in flight rushed above his head. Two thick, percussive punches of sound, and then an agonized cry, the shuffle and thud of a man hitting the ground.

Smith thrashed forward, scuttling like a crab around the edge of the fire, and caught Mahocks by the ankle as he was rising with bow in hand. Smith seized the quiver at the man's hip and tore at it; arrows spilled into the fire, and Smith saw that not all of them were the delicate arrows used for hunting birds. Thicker, shorter shafts tumbled into the flames, the kind that could pierce hardened leather.

Another flight of bolts sped from the trees. Emry screamed.

Mahocks cursed and kicked viciously at Smith's hand. Smith let go of the man's ankle just long enough to lurch to his feet and take him by one arm. The man's muscles were as tense and rippling as a serpent's body. Mahocks reeled and jerked, striking at Smith's face and clawing at his eyes with talon fingers. Smith pressed his face against the man's shoulder to protect himself, and then bit hard until Mahocks yelled hoarsely. Smith held on like a bulldog; Mahocks, panting, said, "Run, Chawnzmit. It would be better for you to run than to try to fight."

Zip.

Smith released his mouthful of Mahocks to cry out in pain. At first he did not know where he had been hit; the pain was loud and bright and everywhere. Then the sensation shrank in upon itself, concentrated to a fast throb in his right thigh. He glanced down. The arrow was still vibrating from the force of the impact, the fletching a white blur in the moonlight.

"Okeus!" Mahocks shouted, as angry at the arrow in Smith's leg as Smith was himself. "Don't shoot, you fools! The *tassantassa* has me!"

In answer, another volley of arrows sped past them and skittered in the earth a hand's breadth from where their feet danced and stamped, as Mahocks struggled to get to safety and Smith fought to hold on. They grunted and roared at one another, all the while braced for the slam of arrow meeting flesh. Then Smith managed a lucky twist, twining his leg with Mahocks's, nearly throwing the man to the ground. But he didn't want him on the ground. Smith jerked Mahocks across his body, braced him against his chest, and spun so that the man's naked back was between Smith and the unseen ambush.

"You crow," Mahocks spat.

"Call them off."

For one heartbeat Mahocks hesitated, clinging precariously to Smith's woolen tunic, dragging at him with his full weight. Smith's injured leg tremored. He could not even reach for his gun; both arms were locked around Mahocks, and Mahocks was his only shield.

"Call them off."

Mahocks sucked in a cold breath. "He's a *werowance*," he shouted into the darkness. His words were pale mist in the night. "You cannot shoot this one. He is a chief of his people."

Voices in the darkness. Smith strained to make out words, but they were speaking too fast, speaking over one another, and his heart was pounding in his thigh, his senses running hot and red and fast down his quivering leg. It was all he could do to stay on his feet, to hold Mahocks off-kilter and vulnerable, their ankles twisted together, ready to fall into a heap on the black earth.

At last he heard low laughter in the trees, a voice as smoky and cold as the night itself. A shadow approached, towering, moving with silky confidence through the forest. The shadow stood over him, and although he could not see the man's face, he felt arrogant triumph roll from him in palpable waves.

"Chawnzmit," said the shadow.

Smith recalled the days just after his illness, when he had reopened Jamestown to trade. He remembered the fierce, wounded-animal stare of the man who came bearing the gifts of Powhatan. *Do I surprise you?* Smith had said, gesturing smugly toward his mouth, pleased at his own wits.

He recognized the rich, chill timbre of the shadow's voice.

"Opechancanough."

OPECHANCANOUGH

Season of Popanow

Chawnzmit was strong for a *tassantassa*; Opechancanough was willing to admit that much. After months of starvation and illness, after padding upstream from Apocant in darkness and winter cold—to say nothing of his admirably fierce wrestling match with the warrior Mahocks—the little yellow-bearded man still had the stamina to make the brisk march through the forest without stumbling or falling behind. The stout, broad chest puffed like a courting grouse. It seemed a point of pride with this Chawnzmit to keep pace with the Real People, even as his fear, well controlled but still evident in his blue eyes, grew.

As the last night of the hunt deepened, the long line of fires slowly extinguished, contracting toward the central camp, where women and children waited to dress and skin the deer. The beasts had been driven into the clever traps of the hunters, fleeing the slow advance of the fire line, which drew into a great ring throughout the woods. In the center of the ring hunters lurked, draped in deer pelts and crowned by their solemn, slender heads. The hunters played their roles well, cajoling the deer with careful movements, soothing their terror of the flames, until at last the deer came within range of bowshot and the pelts were flung away.

A satisfied chuckle rumbled in Opechancanough's chest. Fitting, that he should draw *tassantassas* into his trap on the last night of the hunt. These small white men were obviously as simpleminded as deer, to be taken in by Mahocks's false pelt and soothing words. When he had understood himself to be a captive, Chawnzmit had taken a copper bracelet from his pouch and offered it to Opechancanough, making noise about buying his freedom. Opechancanough swiped the thing from Chawnzmit's hand and tossed it to Mahocks in one quick motion. Suitable payment for an effective lure. Mahocks had certainly earned it, and had nearly been shot in the process.

The sounds of the hunting camp bubbled faintly through the wood. Opechancanough heard the echo and whoop of laughter, the occasional high note of a woman crying out in delight at the success of the hunt or at something else a man brought her. A good hunt always made a man hungry for more activity and put the women into a festive mood, free with their affections and glad to oblige. The sounds and the glow of the fire line seemed to heighten Chawnzmit's dread. But it only showed in his tense, wide stare. Chawnzmit's gait never faltered, nor did he wheedle or plead. He moved with a brave acceptance, striding toward captivity with a dignity that was nearly worthy of one of the Real People.

This, of course, only after his attempt at escape.

Shortly after Opechancanough had tossed the copper bracelet to Mahocks, Chawnzmit had made a break for freedom. His crashing sprint was easy enough to follow through the dark woodlands. Opechancanough's party would have apprehended him easily as he lumbered off toward the river, even if he had not fallen into a quagmire. Chawnzmit's howl of dismay as he plunged into the half-frozen bog was a sound more animal than human. He was stuck fast in the thick mud, and though he bared his teeth like a harried wolf, he allowed the party to pull him free of the quagmire meekly enough. Opechancanough did not begrudge the *tassantassa* his attempted flight. It was the man's only undignified moment, and no one could expect a white man to be unfailingly brave.

Smoke was thick in the air, sharp in the eyes. Up ahead, the hunting camp bustled through the trees. Rhythmic, panting cries rose from somewhere nearby; in the deep shadow of night Opechancanough caught the shape of a woman, arms braced against an oak bole, a hunter rutting her from behind with his apron twisted to the side. Opechancanough turned an amused eye to Chawnzmit. The white man stared in obvious bewilderment. The honest lust of a good hunt only seemed to deepen his fear. Perhaps it was because he now knew himself to be prey, just as the deer were prey, manipulated and conquered by a force much greater than he.

The hunting camp was lit by a high, pale moon and the red glow of one great central fire. As the last of the hunters returned, they tossed their torches into the fire and stretched sore muscles, slapped the backs of friends, and pulled women against their bodies. A row of slain deer stretched along the ground; a group of women laughed as they hauled one by its forelegs into the firelight to be skinned and cleaned. A viscous trickle dripped from its nostrils, tracing a black snake track through the earth. The salt odor of blood and offal moved in a slow current beneath the friendlier smell of the great fire.

As Opechancanough passed with his captive, a cluster of Pamunkey women set up a trilling victory cry. Their eyes were full of firelight, shining with an inner heat; their spirits were intoxicated by the power of the hunt. One of them seized his hand.

"Lie with me tonight, *werowance*," she said in a voice dark as smoke. Her skin was smooth between its small, hard calluses, and the heat of her spirit flowed into his own veins, crackling like red sparks against a nighttime sky. She did not even seem to see the *tassantassa* who trudged along at his side, so overcome was she by the pleasures of the night.

Opechancanough shook off her touch. He could hardly make out her face, didn't even know the woman's name, though the crossed bows of Pamunkey tattooed on her lithe arm told him she was one of his own. It had been far too long since he had locked a woman tight in his arms, felt her writhe and press against him, heard a female voice whisper against his neck. The heat of triumph was high in his blood; he was as hungry as any man tonight. But Chawnzmit must be tended to. Opechancanough would see to the man himself. A *werowance* of the white men—if indeed Chawnzmit were a *werowance*—was not the sort of treasure one could entrust to any other man's care.

Temporary houses had been erected for the hunt, built of thin boughs rather than the sturdy saplings of springtime, and covered by well-used bark sheets. Opechancanough found his beyond the line of slaughtered deer. Chawnzmit's pale eyes dropped to the carcasses and flashed away again with a flicker of fear. Opechancanough held the door flap open. Chawnzmit paused, staring up at his captor with a wily defiance, then ducked his head and went inside.

Some woman had kindled a small heart fire. Opechancanough stoked it, called for blankets for the *tassantassa*, and dismissed his men to the festivities. When the fire was well fed, Opechancanough jerked his head toward Chawnzmit.

"Take off those wet clothes." He tossed the bundled blankets to the white man. "Hang them from the walls to dry."

Chawnzmit moved slowly, carefully, his eyes always on Opechancanough. He dropped a leather belt, weighted by the intricate metal parts of a gun, onto the ground behind him.

"I'm cleverer than to steal your weapon inside a house, *Tassantassa*. I saw how you fought Mahocks. I am not foolish enough to try it here, alone with you."

Chawnzmit's thick beard moved with his slow smile.

He undressed faster, stripping away many layers of leather, rattling metal, and the sour-smelling cloth the white men favored. His small body was furred with a mouse-brown pelt, the hair spreading up an abdomen light as a fish's belly, marking Chawnzmit's chest with a pattern not unlike a bird's spread wings. The man peeled off two layers of his odd one-piece leggings and tucked the dry blankets around himself. He sank onto a mat by the fire and looked at Opechancanough expectantly. His fear seemed gone, replaced by a curious, questing wariness.

"And so," Opechancanough said, "I have you."

Chawnzmit nodded without a trace of confusion. He had grown even more skilled with the Real Tongue since Opechancanough had last seen him at the white men's fort.

"What were you doing as far west as Apocant?"

"Trading."

"In the hunting season?" Opechancanough leveled a skeptical stare at his captive.

"And seeking," Chawnzmit confessed.

"Seeking what?"

"A river passage west."

Opechancanough frowned. "For what purpose?"

Chawnzmit leaned back in his blankets, appraising Opechancanough with those unsettling blue eyes. Instead of answering, Chawnzmit reached for his leather carrying pouch with a slow, careful hand. He withdrew a small bauble, a metal disc that fit in the palm of his hand. Chawnzmit passed it to Opechancanough with a look of great significance.

He took the disc, feeling its cool weight, and tapped its hard transparent cover with one finger. A series of black tick-marks decorated the circumference; a few bold symbols were spaced at regular intervals around the edge. A slender dark stick balanced in the center, vibrating faintly with the rhythm of Opechancanough's pulse. He tilted his hand, and the stick remained oriented toward one of the symbols. He rotated the disc in his palm, yet the stick maintained its position, floating above the indecipherable markings, pointing always in one direction no matter how he turned or tilted the thing, no matter which markings he attempted to align with the stick's arrow-sharp point.

"What is this?"

"A thing my people use," Chawnzmit said mysteriously.

"For what?" It was a good trick, keeping the little arrow pointing always in one direction, but Opechancanough could not fathom a *use* for the disc, other than amusement.

"It tells our boats where to go. It guided us across the sea to this land."

Opechancanough tilted the disc again. The arrow trembled, then swung to point again in its accustomed direction. He handed it back to Chawnzmit. "Your boats—tell me more about them. Are there more?"

"So now we arrive at your purpose," Chawnzmit said. His eyes and mouth were tight with smugness.

"Well?" said Opechancanough, impatient.

The *tassantassa* shrugged. "More? Many more. An uncountable number more."

Opechancanough felt his heart still. "Are all of your people coming to Tsenacomoco?"

Chawnzmit shook his head at the unfamiliar word.

"This land," Opechancanough snapped.

"All of us? I don't know."

It was an evasive answer, one that made Opechancanough's jaw clench at the man's arrogance. Here he was, a captive shivering in a blanket, two of his men slain, and still his spirit was undaunted, even supercilious.

"You are a chief of your people," Opechancanough said. Not a question.

Chawnzmit's bushy head jerked on his shoulders. "Yes," he said after a pause that was just a moment too long.

"That is well for you. We would have killed you if you were not." Even in the firelight, he could see the man's face blanch. Opechancanough concealed his amusement behind a scowl. Chawnzmit's fear was a useful tool, and Opechancanough would offer no hint that his threats might not be real. "Of course," he went on, "*werowances* are only kept as captives so that they may have a fair chance to demonstrate their bravery before they are put to death."

He could have laughed aloud at the white man's reaction, another of those uncaring shrugs. It would have been more convincing without the sudden tension around the sharp eyes.

"But then, I do not believe you are a *werowance*, Chawnzmit."

"Do you not?"

"I don't think the other *tassantassas* do as you say. You do not command them. I am a *werowance* myself. I know the look in other men. I can recognize one of my own, even through white skin and a beard thick as a bear's fur."

"Well, then." Chawnzmit lifted his carrying pouch again. "I shall demonstrate my own command to you, *werowance*." He took another strange object from the pouch, a small folded packet of what looked like very thin bark. Chawnzmit laid it before the fire. "In the morning, when this has dried, I shall use it to send a message to my men."

"You will not be allowed to speak to your men."

"I will not need to speak to them: such is the power of my command. We shall send a messenger, one who has never traded with the fort, who knows nothing of our tongue. And yet my men will do as I say; you shall see."

Opechancanough could not help but laugh. "A messenger who doesn't speak your tongue? Very well, Chawnzmit. Show me the power of your command."

The thin bark-like stuff was dry by the following morning, and Chawnzmit used a slender stick to make a few black marks on one sheet.

"I will tell them," the *tassantassa* declared, "that I am well, so they will not come looking to avenge my death. I wouldn't want you harmed, Opechancanough."

"Very kind of you," Opechancanough said wryly.

"I will also instruct them to send gifts for you. What do you desire?"

Opechancanough's gaze traveled to the gun hanging from Chawnzmit's side. Its end brushed the mud stains on the man's leggings.

"Other than a gun," Chawnzmit said. "My *mamanatowick* has instructed us not to part with any of our guns."

"An axe, then. A good one, suitable for throwing."

Chawnzmit nodded and added a few more marks to his message. Then he folded it carefully and handed it to the chosen messenger, a very young warrior who had never been near the white men's fort. The youth was eager to prove himself worthy of the task, but he took the message from Chawnzmit's fingers with the wariness of a man handling a snake.

Opechancanough kept the *tassantassa* confined in his own house while they waited. Daily he pried at Chawnzmit for more information, seeking to discover whatever weaknesses the white men had. His captive was cautious, though, and more clever than Opechancanough cared to admit. Always Opechancanough's questions were met with meticulous evasion, or worse, sly counterattacks designed to make the *werowance* give up his own people's secrets. The thought of an uncountable number of the white men's boats gnawed at Opechancanough's spirit, though reason told him that Chawnzmit must have lied about that, just another bluff to throw his captor off balance and put the white man at some advantage.

He worked steadily at his task, patiently approaching Chawnzmit from novel angles as the days sped by and winter closed an ever-tightening fist around the land. Whatever information he might coax out of the *tassantassa* was valuable beyond price, for Opechancanough's declaration that he did not believe the man to be a chief was no bluff. In spite of his bold confidence, there also ran in Chawnzmit a truer current of defensiveness. He may have been born to rule—his sharp mind was certainly as capable as any chief's—but no *werowance* ever felt such an obvious need to prove his own worth to others. Opechancanough had no doubt that among his kind, Chawnzmit was as common as a flea, and the fact of it gnawed at his spirit day and night. If he was no chief, if the white men did not follow his commands, then Chawnzmit served no purpose as a captive. Once Opechancanough had gleaned whatever knowledge he could from Chawnzmit's clever half answers and vague equivocations, he could safely be put to death without fear of reprisal. Of course, once Chawnzmit was disposed of, the Real People would lose this opportunity to learn about the white invaders.

Three days after he left, the messenger returned, wide-eyed and bedraggled from the harrowing experience. Opechancanough left a guard with Chawnzmit and ran through the hunting camp, its colors subdued by a thick blanket of frost, to the riverbank. A few young men helped the messenger tow his canoe out of the icy water. One handed the youth a corn cake, which he tore into hungrily, nodding his thanks. When he saw Opechancanough, the messenger swallowed hard and clapped his hand to his breast in salute.

"What news?" Opechancanough said. It was a struggle to keep his voice casual. The young man's expression was serious, nearly dire, and Opechancanough wanted to seize him by the shoulders and shake him until the story fell out of his mouth.

"I gave the message to the first white man I saw," the youth said, "without speaking a word, as you instructed. The white men gathered and looked at it for a long time, then they shouted among themselves. Finally one gave the gift you demanded, and then"— he dropped his eyes, ashamed of the fright that still harried him— "and then they fired a huge gun at me. The sound was so loud it felt like it split my bones. I saw a tree covered in ice burst as the great gun fired. It just shattered, like it was nothing more than an old pot thrown against a boulder."

Opechancanough stared downriver. So the *tassantassas'* great gun could shatter a tree. How many of the Real People would fall before a single blast of that terrible weapon?

"How many boats do you have?" Opechancanough murmured, unaware that he spoke aloud. He watched a bank of mist move like a sorrowful ghost across a distant bend in the river.

Inside his head, he heard Chawnzmit's haughty reply. *An uncountable number.*

"I am sorry, *werowance*," the young messenger said. "I didn't hear you."

Opechancanough shook his head.

"The white men sent this gift for you, *werowance*." He reached behind himself and drew an object from the belt that held his wrapping cloth.

It was the axe Opechancanough had requested. He took it in his hand, testing the weight of it. Good for throwing. The blade was crafted of that strange blue metal, pale as winter, pale as Chawnzmit's skin. Its sheen revealed a vague reflection of Opechancanough's face, a distorted blur from which he could discern no features. *They obeyed your command*, he conceded silently to Chawnzmit. And although the white man could not hear the words, still Opechancanough felt Chawnzmit laughing.

Opechancanough dismissed the guard and slunk inside his house. Chawnzmit was bending over the fire, adding a bit of wood.

He straightened at Opechancanough's arrival and looked at him solemnly. For once, all the accustomed bravado was stripped from his face.

Opechancanough held up the axe in the space between them. Though he felt the weight of it in his hand, the thing seemed to float of its own accord, orienting itself between the *werowance* and his captive with the same strange, unbreakable persistence of the arrow in Chawnzmit's disc.

"Gather your carrying pouch," Opechancanough said. "I will find a cloak for you."

"Where are you taking me?" This time Chawnzmit's voice betrayed no fear. Opechancanough studied his face for a long moment, but he could read nothing of the *tassantassa's* emotions.

Opechancanough ducked back through his door without replying, leaving Chawnzmit alone with his inscrutable thoughts.

So began the captive's tour of the tribes of the Real People.

They marched on foot from one town to the next, the entire hunting camp following Opechancanough in a parade of boastful triumph. The women carried the bark strips of their houses and the many baskets of dried deer meat; the men toted hides and tools, and all of them set up a cry as they approached each successive settlement.

Come and see! Come and see what the chief of Pamunkey has taken!

Chawnzmit bore it stoically, moving with his head held high, his keen eyes watching straight ahead while women and children, warriors and old men, clustered around him in groups, singing chants about his capture, dancing in honor of the Pamunkeys' bravery.

The white man's unflappable calm only heightened Opechancanough's private distress. Although the fort of the *tassantassas* had certainly responded to Chawnzmit's command—

responded out of all proportion with their display of tree-shattering might—Opechancanough still could not reconcile himself to the fact that this man might be a chief. He was not wrong about Chawnzmit; he was certain of that. The appearance of the axe had bolstered Chawnzmit's confidence, but Opechancanough still sensed that quiet pulse of defensive ire in the white man. Worse, he felt in his own spirit the same deficiency. It grew steadily from the place where Tsena-no-ha's wound still festered, spreading over him like a suffocating mantle. He glanced at his Pamunkey warriors as they led Chawnzmit through town after town, wondering how long it would be until his men finally saw the self-doubt occluding his chiefly bearing.

They came at last to Pamunkey-town, and those few people who had not joined the hunting camp set up wild cries of welcome. Normally the homecoming after a successful hunt filled Opechancanough with pleasant warmth. Now the sight of his own people made him wary. They knew him better here than in any of the towns they'd passed through. *How long until they see me for what I am?* He felt Pamunkey eyes upon him and heard their approving shouts, but Opechancanough's spirit quailed. *I am a fallen man, despised by his wife, wrong in judgment, stripped of confidence.* He drew himself up to his full height, pushed out his chest, and swaggered beside his captive like a cocky boy strutting in a contest of boasts. *If this Chawnzmit can conceal his true nature, so can I.*

It did not take long for the women to restore the bark strips to Opechancanough's house. He ushered Chawnzmit inside and snapped a few orders to the town's women. Soon a blaze roared in the fire pit, banishing winter's chill from the newly covered dwelling. A woman laid freshly cleaned mats on Opechancanough's bed, peering shyly at the *tassantassa*. Opechancanough sent her scuttling away with orders for a lavish supper.

When it arrived—two kinds of stew, baskets of cakes and dumplings, a platter with an array of dried fish, and a whole shoulder of fresh roasted deer meat—Chawnzmit's face fell into sorrow for the first time since Opechancanough had marched him from the hunting camp.

"What is it, *Tassantassa*?" Opechancanough narrowed his eyes at Chawnzmit and drew a twig of seasoning stick from one of the breadbaskets. He held the end of the twig in the fire. When it was well charred, he pinched it between thumb and finger, crumbling the salty ash over a hunk of deer meat.

"You have fed me very well at each town," Chawnzmit said quietly.

Opechancanough bit into the deer. It was perfectly roasted, seared on the outside, still juicy and rich inside. The fresh meat would last only a week or two, and then it would be nothing but dried venison and leathery fish and cached corn and beans until *cattapeuk* came again with its abundance of lively fish runs, filling bellies with fresh food and spirits with cheer.

"Don't waste this meat," Opechancanough advised. "Eat all you can."

Chawnzmit looked up at him with a stare that was suddenly hard and fierce, quite unlike the cool self-possession he had shown through the many days of his captivity. "You are fattening me up, aren't you?"

Opechancanough snorted around his mouthful of meat. "Fattening you up? For what purpose?" Did the man think Opechancanough would make him as plump as a woman, and then slide into his blankets for a tumble?

"To eat me," Chawnzmit spat. His eyes burned with hatred and a desperate fear that took Opechancanough aback.

Opechancanough's brows rose before he could still his own face. The Real People seemed convinced that Chawnzmit was a *werowance*, even if Opechancanough still harbored doubts. A captive chief could not be starved like a disobedient dog. The lavish feasting was a customary mark of respect, though Chawnzmit's certainty that it was intended to fatten him up like a ripe ear of corn could only mean that the *tassantassas* engaged in the grisly practice themselves.

Opechancanough swallowed his venison in a painful lump. He schooled his face carefully. Then he met Chawnzmit's frightened eyes with a slow, deliberate smile.

Chawnzmit turned his face away from the food with a gasp that was nearly a sob.

Perhaps this man could be worn down after all, and made to cooperate. Made to give up his secrets.

Opechancanough dipped his oyster-shell bowl into one of the stewpots, watching Chawnzmit with a steady glare. Before he could bring the shell to his mouth, though, a voice called through the door flap.

"*Werowance!*" It was one of the town's women. There was a distinct note of urgency in her cry.

Opechancanough slipped outside.

The woman gestured toward the town's central fire pit, the location of all ceremonies and public meetings. "There is a message from Powhatan, *werowance*. A message . . . and a priest."

Opechancanough cursed under his breath. Two of his best warriors loitered nearby, exchanging tales from the hunt. Their faces were relaxed, flush with the pleasure of being home at last, after a long and arduous *taquitock*. He envied them their ease. A few young women watched them from the yard of a nearby home, giggling and whispering behind the folds of their winter cloaks. Opechancanough pulled the men aside, gave them their instructions, and left them guarding his door while Chawnzmit remained within, chewing on nothing but his own fear.

He ground his teeth when he saw who was waiting at the communal fire. Utta-ma-tomakkin was young for a priest of his esteem, smooth-faced and slender-limbed. He had surely seen no more than twenty-two or -three winters, if that. But for his recent youth, he carried himself with the gravity, the slow-moving, ponderous dignity, of one well aged in the temples. A long cloak of bearskin hung from his shoulders, fur side in, the deep black shag resting against unscarred copper skin. The flesh side of the pelt was adorned with the symbols of ceremony. Dark *roanoke* beads were stitched into the shapes of a rearing cougar and deer, facing each other, locked in their opposing postures of violence and flight, dancing on the edge of that strange, dark realm only the priests could occupy, the place between knowing and feeling, dreaming and waking, living and dying. Below the cougar and deer, scores of white shell discs clattered as the priest shifted his weight at Opechancanough's approach. Utta-ma-tomakkin's deep-set eyes, black as a wood buffalo's horn, stared out from behind the fringe that dropped from the front of his headdress, a heavy, swaying curtain of white weasel tails and iridescent strips of discarded snakeskins.

The boy-priest, the prodigy of Uttamussak in the flesh, Opechancanough thought viciously, sensing that his prize was about to be snatched away by the Okeus's cruel caprice. As he gazed into the solemn eyes of the young priest, his inner bravado melted like a shard of ice dropped into a heart fire. It was whispered that this Utta-ma-tomakkin was touched by the gods themselves, that when the Okeus's hand fell upon him he shook and frothed at the mouth and made sounds like a beast in the forest. It was said that the things he saw during these sacred fits were truer than the things normal men saw—truer than the things other priests saw. Young as he was, Utta-ma-tomakkin was a force in the world, and he knew it, silent and satisfied with his own great import.

Even if he still looked like a boy ready for the *huskanaw*.

By sending the most revered priest from the greatest temple in Tsenacomoco, Powhatan had certainly communicated the gravity of his message. Opechancanough must tread with care if he wished to retain his grip on Chawnzmit.

He greeted the priest with humble formality.

"Powhatan sends me," said Utta-ma-tomakkin, "to conjure the white man."

Opechancanough said nothing, hoping his face imparted none of the helpless rage he felt.

If the priest detected his anger, he did not deign to show it. "I will require seven priests from your own temple, tobacco, and corn."

Opechancanough nodded brusquely.

"Once the spirits have spoken," the young priest said, a touch of severity in his tone, "I am to decide what to do with the man."

Opechancanough steadied himself with a long, slow breath. "This is my territory, my town. He is my captive."

"I move on the orders of the *mamanatowick*."

"Even my brother may not tell a *werowance* how to run his own affairs."

Utta-ma-tomakkin shrugged, an infuriating gesture from one so young. "And yet *werowances* rise and fall at your brother's word. You would be wise to cooperate, Opechancanough." The priest suddenly smiled, his flashing teeth as white as his weasel-tail fringe. "Cheer up. The Okeus might declare him a dead man. In that case, I shall give you the honor of carrying out the death rites yourself."

In the end, it was Opechancanough who presented Chawnzmit to the temple, leading him past the spirit posts with their terrible carved heads, the leering wolf, the ravening cougar, the brutal, howling man. He stood side by side with his captive on the threshold of darkness, facing the void where the great cat and the fleet, delicate deer remained eternally poised, suspended in the moment before claws raked flesh, before hooves sprang from the earth, the moment of one held breath stretching on forever.

Opechancanough felt a certain loosening within, the opening up he always felt whenever he stepped into the presence of the god. In the doorway of the temple, his spirit bowed to the inevitable. Chawnzmit similarly shifted, his body seeming both lighter and heavier in the space of the same heartbeat, as if he, too, caved to his fate. The *tassantassa* released the weight of his fear, replacing it with the bold curiosity that was his native state of being. But he also took up the burden of acceptance, surrendering himself to whatever lay within the temple walls.

As they stepped through the doorway, Opechancanough felt a fleeting sense of brotherhood with Chawnzmit, though he knew that brotherhood with this man could never be. The certainty of that knowledge nearly brought sorrow to his spirit.

It was not long before their eyes adjusted to the temple's dimness. Chawnzmit blinked his watery blue eyes as he stared about. Opechancanough watched silently as the *tassantassa* goggled at the shaggy shadows of draped wolf pelts, the racks of baskets full of tribute to the god and his attendant spirits. The baskets squatted row upon row along the walls like malign dwarf demons waiting for the unwary to draw too near. Deep in the heart of the temple, the pop of a heart fire kindling to life rose up with the rhythmic chant of men's voices. Chawnzmit stepped toward the sound. The claws of fate were well hooked into his hide, and they drew him on with a steady, undeniable hand.

They reached the central fire pit. The seven priests, each with a headdress of a different creature's hide, sang low as they went about their tasks. The stooped as they moved around the fire, delineating five concentric circles, one for each season: corn seed, finely ground nut husks, black soil, pale dry ash. The fifth circle, smallest and nearest to the flames, was a ring of dried tobacco leaf. One by one the priests straightened their backs. Below their concealing headdresses, the fire now and again illuminated the sloping plane of a cheekbone or a chin, and the bright colors of ceremonial paint flickered against the darkness.

Opechancanough whispered his instructions to Chawnzmit. The man did not hesitate, but walked through the five rings, his small feet tracking a little of each substance as he went. He stepped within the circle of tobacco and turned to face Utta-ma-tomakkin, placid as a deer at midday.

The young priest gave a wild howl. He raised a turtle-shell rattle above his head, crying to the four directions, shouting to the four winds. He shook the corn seeds within the shells until they thundered like a spring deluge. The seven priests began to whirl, stamping and beating at their own skin with hands and twig switches until their skin ran with sweat.

"Okeus," Utta-ma-tomakkin cried, "judge this man. Oh, great god, most powerful spirit, you of the holy hair and the righteous way, shining man of the bow! I call upon you, Okeus. I beseech with corn, I beseech with smoke, I beseech with tobacco! Show me, instruct me in your will. Put the fate of this man into my hands!"

They danced, they shouted, they beat upon themselves until even Opechancanough lost himself in the wild power and the heat. Sweat stung his eyes and slid down his back. He swayed, and the chattering voice of the rattle ran like lightning along his blood, flashing and hot, inciting his spirit like war, like a woman's touch. He did not know how long they danced, how many times the young priest called upon the god. It may have been a dozen times or a hundred. But at last Utta-ma-tomakkin gave a piercing scream, and the priests staggered to a halt.

The only sounds were the heart fire, and the ragged rasp of Chawnzmit's breath.

Opechancanough's hands worked into fists behind his back. Slowly he raised his eyes from Chawnzmit's thick-bearded face to the still specter of Utta-ma-tomakkin, tense as a sky laden with thunder.

"This man means no harm. Nor do his people." Utta-ma-tomakkin pronounced the judgment in short, clipped tones. "He stays. He lives."

Opechancanough blinked, gaped, and shut his mouth again quickly. *It can't be so.* None of these *tassantassas* displayed so much as basic courtesy. Their hostility was plain for even a blind man to see. And this Chawnzmit, brave though he was, held more arrogance in one sly, blue glance than Utta-ma-tomakkin could ever hope to dole out in a lifetime of serving the god. Arrogance was not a habit of the benign. Chawnzmit and his kind meant nothing but harm. Opechancanough was certain.

Utta-ma-tomakkin turned to regard Opechancanough. "You have heard the god's word, *werowance.*"

Opechancanough bowed his head in the smallest and most grudging nod. "And what does my brother wish for me to do with my captive?"

"Take him to Werowocomoco."

Indeed I will. Opechancanough would cast this pale creature at Powhatan's very feet, and pray that the *mamanatowick* would come to his senses. Conjuring or no, the fire in this *tassantassa*'s eyes smoldered with danger, with a fierce cunning that must be snuffed like an errant spark before it caught the whole world ablaze.

Okeus, Opechancanough prayed, still feeling the thrum of the rattle in his veins, *make my brother see the truth of it. Make him kill this man. Kill him, and then fall on the rest of his kind, and wipe their stain from the land.*

POCAHONTAS

Season of Popanow

She ran from the cache pits, panting under the weight of a basket heaped with shelled corn. The grains shifted in the basket like flowing water, hissing like rain. She ran to the smokehouses, shouting for more sturgeon and bass. She ran for nuts, for fresh hare, for stacks of turtle-shell bowls. She *ran*, crossing and recrossing the length of Werowocomoco, and her legs burned with the effort as her spirit burned with excitement.

Crisp winter air bit at her nostrils, clamoring with scents from dozens of cook fires: the warm, meaty earthiness of the summer's beans growing plump in boiling water; corn dumplings, sticky and sweet; dried fish yielding their salty oils as they were shredded by the busy fingers of so many women. Sun-dried mulberries added their pleasant tartness to the flat, bland smell of roasted squash, and from a distant fire there drifted the enticing seared-fat aroma of spitted venison, the last of the hunters' fresh meat.

Pocahontas lifted the flat stone from her house's cache and lowered herself into the chest-deep pit. The earth inside was fiercely cold, the walls tattooed with white twists of frost. She puffed, enjoying the sensation of the cold working its way beneath her cloak and leggings to soothe skin flushed from running. As she caught her breath, she peeked beneath the tight lids of baskets and clay jars until she found the store of pale groundnuts, wound into neat coils and still connected by their fibrous root strings. She grunted as she lifted the jar from the pit, and then lifted herself out, frozen soil biting into her hands. Time enough to mind her scrapes later. Powhatan had called for a great feast, and the flurry and joy of its preparation was not something she wanted to miss, even for a moment.

"Amonute!" Matachanna called. She straightened her back, still kneeling beside her troublesome cook fire; it lifted a banner of white smoke and the pale-yellow flames staggered. "Be quick with those groundnuts!"

Pocahontas hoisted the heavy jar to one hip and ran.

At the fire, she crawled on hands and knees with Matachanna, giggling and shrieking as they blew strong gusts of breath into the coals. Fountains of ash floated on the breeze.

"I swear, there is more ash in the sky than in all the fire pits in Werowocomoco." Koleopatchika, a young sister of Powhatan and the girls' favorite unmarried aunt, sauntered out of their shared longhouse, a string of dried fish looped around one shoulder. She laughed over the mess of ash in the yard. She was still young enough to find humor in their struggle to keep the fire alight. She dropped the rope of fish atop the jar of groundnuts and sank to her knees with the girls, adding her breath to the fire. At last a strong flame took hold of the winter-damp wood, and a healthy fire began to crackle.

Koleopatchika maneuvered her large stewpot into the fire pit. She produced knives from her supply basket, and soon all three huddled around the pot, slicing groundnuts into the water, chopping the dried fish into bite-size chunks.

"At last," Pocahontas said, "we will learn the secret of Koleopatchika's famous groundnut stew."

Koleopatchika put on a face of stern mystery. "The secret is that *I* make it, child. The spirits have given me a great gift. My groundnut magic can never be replicated by any other hand."

"All the men swear their hearts to you when they get the smallest taste of your stew."

She gave her nieces a sly wink. "Men have been known to call my stewpot the most delicious and satisfying in all of Tsenacomoco."

A deep pink flush crept over Matachanna's face.

"Oh," Koleopatchika said, half-teasing, half-apologetic. "But you are both too young to understand my jests."

"I'm not," Matachanna said stoutly. "I caught the jest. It just . . . startled me, that's all."

Koleopatchika's smile twinkled like a row of stars. "You *are* growing up, aren't you? I suppose it happens to all of us, sooner or later. It's almost time for you to begin thinking about a husband."

"She's already thought about it," Pocahontas said, "endlessly, and in great detail."

Matachanna gave her an ugly grimace. "Say his name, and I will jab you with this knife. I'll stick you so hard, you'll yelp like a kicked dog."

"Who is he?" Koleopatchika hacked at an especially tough groundnut. "Don't be shy. Cooking time is gossip time. You must share."

Matachanna turned her gaze downward, hiding her soft, dark eyes behind thick lashes. But Pocahontas could stand the secrecy no longer. "It's Utta-ma-tomakkin!" she burst out.

"Oh, a fine choice, Matachanna. Handsome *and* touched by the Okeus. And he'll soon be very wealthy, I assume, with the way my brother favors him."

Matachanna glanced up. "Powhatan favors him?"

"Well, I heard that the *mamanatowick* sent Utta-ma-tomakkin all the way to Pamunkey, to conjure the captive white man. Surely that means Powhatan trusts your priest."

"He is not my priest," Matachanna muttered.

Koleopatchika grinned comfortably. "One day."

"Pass the fish to me, Aunt," said Pocahontas. "I imagine we'll see Utta-ma-tomakkin today, when the party arrives from Pamunkey. And then we can watch the spring flowers bloom in Matachanna's eyes as she gazes at her handsome priest."

Matachanna gave her a flat stare, full of sharp and painful promise.

Men's boastful shouts rose from a nearby lane, a sound like a pack of wolves yipping and tussling around a fresh kill. Pocahontas looked up in time to see her half brother Naukaquawis pass by. He grinned as he moved, pleased with his own strength, with his very maleness. A handful of warriors crowed and shoved and laughed in his wake, but Naukaquawis strode ahead of them, apart from them, moving like a thunderhead on a brisk wind, towering with the force of his own spirit. She watched him pass with the sour taste of envy stinging her throat.

Koleopatchika cast an appreciative eye at Naukaquawis's broad back. "Or perhaps instead of a priest, our Matachanna would prefer a *werowance*."

"Naukaquawis? No!"

"Why not? It's not as if your mother and his are related, so there is nothing scandalous in it. And he's handsome. He will make a very fine husband someday. Someday soon."

Pocahontas looked at her aunt sharply, keen as a kestrel staring after a mouse. "What do you mean?"

"My brother has great esteem for Naukaquawis—maybe greater esteem than for Matachanna's priest."

"Don't be coy," Pocahontas insisted. "Cooking is for gossip. Share." A knotted string tightened around her heart.

"Naukaquawis is to come into his chiefdom tonight. Powhatan will announce which territory will be his, but his first great act as *werowance* will be to take the *tassantassa* as his own."

"What?"

The entire town of Werowocomoco knew that tonight Opechancanough would present his captive to the *mamanato-wick*. What purpose such a display would serve was not yet clear. Speculation ran between the yards and cook fires, fast and wild as a river in flood. Rumor of the white man's fate bubbled nearly as hot as the stews that boiled for the evening feast. Most thought the white man would be killed. Some thought he would be set free, made to run back to his fort and chased by men with clubs—a sort of *huskanaw*, the details of which grew stranger and more unlikely as the tale spread.

"Oh, tell us what you know," Matachanna pleaded. Apparently even prim and quiet Matachanna was not immune to the lure of gossip about the captive *tassantassa*.

Koleopatchika gave a tiny, triumphant smile. She seemed to savor her gossip magic nearly as much as her groundnut magic. "Well, I only *heard* that Naukaquawis is to adopt the white man. The captive will be brought before Powhatan, who will sentence the man to death."

"Death? But why?" Pocahontas asked.

"Don't fret. At the last moment, Naukaquawis will save the *tassantassa*. He will claim responsibility for the man's life, and take him as a member of his own family."

"How? Does the Okeus permit such a thing?" Pocahontas had never heard of such a ritual. She gave her aunt a skeptical look as she worked over the stew.

"It's all worked out with the priest. 'I claim this man's life as my own,' Naukaquawis is to say. 'I account for him. Let him be called my brother; let his hearth be joined to my own.' I overheard Naukaquawis practicing the correct words." She glanced about the yard of their longhouse, as if they might be surrounded by spying gossips, though the women and children who passed were intent on their own chores. "Or . . . *somebody* overheard. In any case, the white man, who rules his own kind, will be made *tanx-werowance* to Naukaquawis, since he will owe his life to the one who saves him. Thus Naukaquawis will have reign over the *tassantassas*, as simple as that. It's a very fine opportunity Powhatan presents to Naukaquawis. The *mamanatowick* shows that young man true favor. He'll be an important chief one day, mark my words. Are you still so certain you wish to spurn him, Matachanna?"

Before she could stop herself, before she even knew what she was doing, Pocahontas lurched to her feet. Her knife slipped from her fingers and rang on the edge of the pot. Koleopatchika exclaimed as it fell into the stew with a plunk. She seized a ladle and began fishing for it, hissing curses in Pocahontas's direction, but Pocahontas had already turned away. Her feet carried her blindly down the path, stumbling in the direction from which Naukaquawis had come. She was dimly aware of Matachanna calling "Amonute!" but the sound was far and thin, muted by the roaring in Pocahontas's ears. The slick black limbs of the winter-bare forest had closed over her head by the time Matachanna caught up with her.

Her sister pulled her into a tight embrace. Pocahontas felt sobs welling in her chest, a thick, choking pressure, but she could do nothing more than press her face against Matachanna's cloak. Tears did not even come to her eyes. She merely stood silent, clutching at her own ragged, wracked spirit as Matachanna murmured against her hair.

"Your desire has never left you, has it, Amonute?"

Pocahontas shook her head. She did not need to ask what desire her sister spoke of. It was influence, power, mattering, *being*. The word sifted light and pale as ash through her spirit. *Werowansqua*.

"The *tassantassas* were mine," she said at last. Her voice was small and choked in her throat, and she hated herself for sounding so young and female, so common. "They were my work, my special work, my duty."

"You learned their tongue, and it set you apart from the rest of us." The gentle understanding in Matachanna's eyes was a pain and a relief too strong to bear.

Pocahontas covered her face with trembling hands. "What was all my work for, learning their tongue, their ways, if Naukaquawis is to rule over the white chief? Now it will all be his, all the honor, all the influence with our father . . ."

"Oh, but Amonute . . . my Pocahontas. You didn't truly think you could have ruled, did you?" Matachanna's words were soft as smoke, and like smoke they burned Pocahontas's eyes. Matachanna wrapped the edge of her cloak around the both of them and pulled Pocahontas tight to her warm body. She smelled of familiarity and comfort, the pine resin and fur of their longhouse, the ground-ochre bitterness of pigmented oil. "Sister, what good could you do the Real People as a *werowansqua*?"

Pocahontas bit her lip. She wanted to bar her words, lock them away in her throat, but they fought their way out. "Why must I do the Real People good? Why can't I want it just for myself?"

Matachanna sighed.

"It's easy for you, Matachanna." Pocahontas tore herself away, out from under her sister's cloak. "It's easy for you to scorn me for the things I want."

"I don't scorn you, Amonute."

"You will never want for anything—you, of the high blood!"

Matachanna frowned darkly; a furious bird's-foot track appeared on her pretty brow. "You will never want for anything, either, Sister. You don't want for anything now, except that which will gratify your own spirit."

Pocahontas stamped in wordless fury. The frozen earth was so hard that a painful jolt traveled up her leg.

"The truth is," Matachanna said with careful dignity, "you are selfish and ungrateful."

"Ungrateful? And what have I to be grateful for? Tell me that! Should I bow in gratitude for the privilege of learning how to cook groundnut stew to feed my high-blood kin, while you have the leisure of choosing between a priest and a *werowance* for a husband?"

She whirled and sped through the forest, down the narrow path that would lead her, she knew, to her father's great house. Her cloak billowed as she went; cold air closed around her body like a hunter's snare and she gathered its folds in her shaking hands. The cloak was old, one of Koleopatchika's castoffs. Rows of winter weasel skins alternated with the feathers of snow geese, ragged and frayed.

Matachanna's voice chased after her, high and strained with regret. "I'm sorry, Amonute. Come back. Pocahontas!"

But Pocahontas ignored her sister's cries and pushed through the stiff, grasping underbrush. It had snowed a few days prior, a light dusting that had since turned to a thin, sharp crust of rippled ice. It cracked and broke beneath her moccasins, hindering her speed. She released her grip on the front of her cloak, and it spread behind her, white as an egret's wings. Branches tipped with ice clawed at her arms and left trails of burning cold along her skin.

From the direction of the town, women's voices rose in a warbling cry. Distance and the frozen maze of the forest fractured and distorted the sound. She halted and turned toward the cries. The voices seemed to rise and fall in time with her panting breath. Somewhere near the river, a drum pulsed.

Pocahontas altered her course. She pressed through a bank of dense brush and found herself in a cornfield. The few stalks that had not been pulled up and burned lay half-fallen, weighted by rain and ice, aslant against the earth. A few of their morose brown leaves stirred in a silent breeze. The dark, bare ground of the field itself was patched black and white by its broken crust of snow. The thin long legs of a crow tower were silvered on one side with ice. The platform was empty. The tower's silence stabbed at

Pocahontas's spirit, filling her with a welling poignancy. She was stripped now even of her one useful task. She stood still a moment, and then suddenly ran through the cornfield, the cold air raising tears in her eyes, her feet moving with the furious, helpless, ashamed pounding of her heart.

Beyond the field she found a path that wound its way between houses toward Werowocomoco's broad central lane. Women and children ducked through the doors of longhouses, pouring onto the path, raising their voices in the wavering victory cry. Below the high ululations, the deeper, more sonorous rumble of men's voices stirred, more a physical sensation than a sound, and one fraught with a tight, dangerous coil of excitement. Now she could see the central lane, now the great gray plume of smoke from the communal fire. The Real People thronged the lane, bumping one another like canoes set adrift in a narrow stream. The dark tips of bows rose above the heads of the crowd as it moved in rank down the lane toward the *mamanatowick's* great house.

Pocahontas wedged herself into the crowd, jostled by crying women, pushing children, and old men calling out good-natured curses and laughing taunts. She could not squeeze through to the front. Instead, she slipped sideways, dodging bodies, moving parallel to the parade of bows. Now and then two cloak-wrapped backs parted and she caught fleeting glimpses of the procession: the chest-out strut of a painted warrior; Opechancanough's scowl in rapid, flashing profile; the flicker of a downcast pair of pale-blue eyes and a thick beard, tawny as squirrel skin.

At last she fought her way to the front of the chanting crowd, just as the procession reached Powhatan's residence, breaking from the crush of bodies in time to see the stooped back of the *tassantassa* disappear through the low, rectangular door. He wore the thick, strong-smelling cloth his kind was fond of: *wool*. She'd learned the word from the two runaways, but they had been spirited away, well guarded by her father's men in a tiny village far to the northwest, where their kind would never find them. It had been nearly a month since she had seen them last, and without any means of practicing their language she feared she would lose it. But as she watched the *tassantassa* vanish into the darkness of the great house, the strange, flowing, water-song cadences of their tongue filled her mind. *Wool*, she recited in the isolated quiet of her own thoughts. *Boot, Iing-land, ship, gun.*

Pocahontas watched as Kocoum dropped the flap into place and took up his accustomed station on Powhatan's door. He nodded in a guarded but friendly way when she approached. He had been a fine protector during her work with the runaways, vigilant and with no shortage of hard looks for the white men, but never interfering with her duty. He had shown no interest in learning the tongue himself, and only shrugged when she tried to interest him in practicing the *tassantassa* words. But he had shown patience and respect for the importance of her task. Looking up at his still, observant face, Pocahontas thought perhaps Matachanna was wrong: she might have one friend in the world, this young warrior Kocoum.

"Let me go inside," she whispered.

He tilted his head as though he could not hear her for all the singing and calling. But his eyes sparkled with that quiet, teasing amusement. Of course he knew what she wanted.

"You know I can speak their tongue," she said, louder this time, almost shouting. "My father will need me."

Kocoum smiled at her. It was a small smile, one corner of his mouth tipping up higher than the other. But he did not argue. He stepped aside and swung the door flap open.

Down the great length of the house, the heart fire's glow showed ruddy on the arch of the ceiling. The smell of tense excitement—men's sweat, men's eagerness—eclipsed the usual indoor odors of pine smoke and dried herbs. Somebody had brought a hand drum. The rhythm of it chattered in her bones and blood, shaking her like a priest's turtle-shell rattle. She moved down the dark hall of the *yehakin* with care, trying to order her thoughts but failing to make any more sense of her own emotions than wonder and fear. *Iing-land. Wool. Gun.* The air was hot here; she loosed the tie of her cloak and let it fall away from her throat. Sweat stood out on her bare chest and back, glistening among her strands of white shell beads.

The men took no notice of her, intent as they were on the *tassantassa*. They held him by his elbows in the light of the heart fire. He gazed about him with a strained air, clearly afraid but fighting to banish the fear from his face. He was brave, and intelligent; she could read that much in his sharp, darting eyes, in the dignified acceptance of what he assumed was his fate.

Powhatan was on his feet, trembling slightly as he often did now, but draped in the majesty of his ceremonial robes. They trailed against the black earth, raising a wake of white ash in the close, vibrating air.

"Bring the block," Powhatan said, "and take from this man his life."

The *tassantassa's* eyes widened, though he made no move to escape.

He knows our tongue, Pocahontas thought with dull startlement, with a sudden feeling of fellowship.

A great hewn stump was rolled into the circle of light. The men howled, wolflike, hungry for the climax of the ceremony. At the edge of the shivering light, Naukaquawis stood aloof amid the dancing and shouting, arms crossed casually, as confident and untouchable as the Okeus himself. The stump thudded against the earth. The men holding the *tassantassa* forced him to his knees, bending him double so that his shaggy head rested on the rough, splintered wood. Pocahontas saw the fire of fear kindle in his spirit; those strange blue eyes for one flashing moment betrayed his sorrow and defeat.

The men raised their clubs high above their heads.

There was a drawing in of breath, a sudden, expectant silence. Naukaquawis let his arms fall to his side, shifting his weight as if to dodge forward, but he seemed to move as slowly as a body under water, dragging and thick. Pocahontas moved, too, wondering at her own unexpected stride, emerging from between the men's bodies like a dreamer treading an unreal, unseen path.

The clubs reached the peak of their upward arcs and hung in the smoky air for an instant that lasted an eternity. Naukaquawis leaned, ready to make the saving leap, ready to account for the life of the *tassantassa* and take him for his own. But Pocahontas's body was smaller, quicker, already crossing the ring of firelight. She was a fish dodging the net. She was a flicker of movement, a flash of white beads and sheen. She saw surprise in her brother's eyes, then anger—and then she saw nothing.

Her eyes closed.

She folded atop the *tassantassa* like a dropped cloak, cradling his rough head in her slim brown arms. The clubs fell around her like hail, shuddering the ground where she and the white man crouched, the breeze of their movement stirring the fine hairs of her body.

A stunned silence rocked the great house. The drum, like her heart, stopped beating.

Pocahontas raised her head tentatively. Powhatan stared down at her, his brows high beneath red-and-black paint.

"I claim this one's life as my own." She said the ritual words as easily as though she had practiced them alongside Naukaquawis. Her voice was as high as a bird-leg flute. It piped almost eerily in that place of men, moving between them, twisting into their startled thoughts as lithe as a green snake. "I account for him. Let him be my brother now; let his hearth be joined to mine."

Naukaquawis coughed out a startled grunt.

Powhatan shook his head in wonder. Silver hair rippled, a wind on the river. "Daughter?"

Pocahontas stared steadily up. Her eyes did not blink.

Powhatan drew in a breath, and for a moment she feared he would condemn her, cast her out. Instead, the walls of his great house shook with his laughter.

"By the Okeus," he said, slapping his sagging belly through his ceremonial robe. The rows of shells stitched down the robe's back rattled with his laugh. "If you want this man, Mischief, then you shall have him."

Naukaquawis gasped. "Father . . . !"

"Fear not," Powhatan said, waving his son to acquiescence. "You are *werowance*, with or without a white man at your heel. But after all, it was Pocahontas who saved this man and declared him her brother. Let it be as the Okeus wills it."

Naukaquawis lowered a terrible stare toward his common-born little sister, who still clutched the white man's head in her arms.

Powhatan bent, slowly, ponderously, to look the *tassantassa* in his dirt-smudged, hairy face. "Do you understand, Chawnzmit? You are my daughter's now. You owe her your life."

THE SECOND NAME

Pocahontas

SMITH

January 1608

From the king's long, smoke-dense house, Smith was marched
back through the town, back through the crowing, howling, whirling mass of naturals. Their wild din rang in his ears, and yet it
meant nothing, touched nothing of his thoughts or soul. He was
drifting, lost in a deep mist of confusion and relief. He was aware
of nothing save for the little girl who walked at his side. The hood
of her ragged white cape was thrown back that all might see her
face, round and beaming with triumph beneath a black bristle of
short-cropped hair that framed her features, the long braid swinging from the back of her head. The thin legs, swaddled in doeskin
leggings, stepped in a marching gait as bold as a soldier's. She did
not look up at him, her new prize, but he felt a proprietary assurance radiating from her like heat from a fire. At the fore of their little parade, Naukaquawis stalked in a sulk, and behind him moved
Opechancanough, scowling likewise, his brow as dark and low as
a thunderhead.

They crossed the whole of the large village and moved down
an avenue of oaks and chestnut trees, emerging in a large clearing.
The din of the villagers still filled the forest, though it was a distant
sound; here the men of the party and even the little strutting girl-
child moved with reverence.

A temple stood at the clearing's center. He could identify their temples now on sight, the houses where their dark god dwelt in all his brutal, unseen power. Four tall posts representing the four directions of the winds stood at each corner, stripped of bark, pale as old bone. Each post was topped by a disc of hardwood carved into a unique, twisted face. These were the faces of the spirits that guarded this sacred place, forbidding with their sharp-toothed snarls and glaring borehole eyes. They were fierce as devils, and watched Smith with unblinking stares as he approached.

Outside the temple's door stood a huge quartz crystal, at least two feet broad on each flat, smooth side, lying canted over with its pointed tip angled toward the east. He had never seen a gemstone so large or so flawless. Through its glassy body he could make out the sinuous curves of tattoos on the men's bare legs. The sight of such a large and perfect object was faintly unsettling, filling him with a slow-creeping awe, a sense of being watched by something greater and more cunning and dangerous than the temple's four guardians. Each natural in turn paused to pay respect to the stone, cupping hands against foreheads, making a slow falling gesture as if pouring out some viscous substance upon the altar of the stone. He cupped his hands and poured likewise, and the little girl turned her face up to his with a gleam of approval in her black eyes.

Inside the temple, he was confronted by a conjuring priest, who chanted beneath his hanging shroud of weasel tails and tassels of snakeskin. The rattles crashed like hard rain. Smith's nostrils burned on the pungent smell of the broad-leafed, purple-flowering weed the naturals smoked with great relish. The priest blew a stream of white smoke into his face, and he closed his eyes against the enchantment. He seemed to reel where he sat, though he knew his body held quite still. Sounds bled one into another and ran over his body like oil, slippery and rich, a warm throb of sensation that stirred him, blood and soul, with every bright clash of copper bells or wail of the spinning priests.

"He calls you," said a voice near him, *"tanx-werowance."*

With sluggish surprise, he realized the words were spoken in English. The voice was high, a sparrow's call, the child's voice. He looked at his new mistress with open amazement. Her smooth coppery brow knitted in thought. Her mouth moved silently as she worked out a suitable translation; the dark eyes skated to the side, searching for words in the blackness of the temple's interior.

"Tanx-werowance," she said again, and then, in rough-accented but perfect English, "very small king."

Smith nodded carefully. His head wobbled.

"My brother, Naukaquawis, will be your *werowance.* Naukaquawis is that one." She nodded toward the young man. "Do you understand?"

The ceremony continued. Chanting, the priests brought various strange, musty-smelling objects from the temple's western wall. A rattle shook before Smith's slow-blinking eyes—a blur of turtle shell, a din of thunder. The skin of a great maneless lion passed over his face. It smelled of mildew and animal rage, the claws that still curved from its splayed tawny paws scratching lightly at his cheek. Next a heavy bear's pelt was draped over his shoulders. It weighed him down, pulling him toward the earth with an insistent, dragging gravity.

A mask shimmered and slid through the dark air before him, two small round eyes like bullet holes staring unblinking into his own, the mouth a stern circle through which no light came. The sight of it, its sinister, gliding movement, filled him with rising dread. It pronounced words over him that fell like ringing axe-blows against his ears. He could not make out their meaning. Dark slashes across the cheeks, harrow lines, claw lines.

He was made to smoke the pipe, drawing on the stinging smoke until his head filled with dancing light and unsettling visions, and his throat opened in an animalistic howl. At last they presented a basin of cold water. He dipped his hands with some relief, sensing the end of the ceremony, and a bundle of soft feathers was passed over his knuckles, over fingers that felt much too long and fragile, too sensitive. The feathers lifted droplets of water from his skin.

By the fall of night he was vibrating with exhaustion and the potency of the weed. He found himself, to his confusion and gratitude, standing upon a low shelf of riverbank, blue dark in the twilight, saying his farewells to Naukaquawis and Opechancanough, both of whom stared with eyes as deep and joyless as the eyes of the priest's mask. Three men took up the paddles of a canoe. Smith climbed into it, felt it rock him like a babe in a cradle. He pressed his knees fearfully into the hard sides of the dugout and was glad to note how painfully the wood bit into his flesh. He could trust his senses again. The fresh air seemed to do him good.

The girl Pocahontas leaped into the dugout as well, folding herself on a bark-strip mat with her white cloak for blanket. Long before they reached Jamestown, standing like a harsh black stone against the night, the fur and feathers of her cape moved with the steady rhythm of her breath. In sleep all the pride and challenge drained from her face, and in a world that was sharp and bruising, full of lightless eyes and raking claws, she was soft as a curl of smoke.

It was the girl who bade him farewell on the shore of Jamestown. The night was velvet black, covered in clouds that promised more snow. Somebody shouted a challenge from the fort's wall. A puff of white vapor rose from the girl's mouth. "I will come back, *tanx-werowance*," she promised. "We will speak."

And then she was gone, a smudge of pale gray receding upriver. As he stood watching on the shore, the dim distance closed around the canoe, leaving nothing behind but the gentle chatter of water against its hull and the quiet splash of paddles in the darkness.

A wash of wan, cold light woke him a few hours later. Smith moved carefully on his narrow, hard bed, feeling each muscle of his body complain in turn. The outer edges of his kneecaps throbbed where they had pressed against the inner curve of the canoe. His bladder was painfully full; he eased himself upright, shivering against the dull winter cold, stared around the dim interior of his tiny cabin. It was small enough that he might touch the walls if he flung out his arms. The floor was hard earth, rimmed with frost around the edges where the previous day's dampness had seeped inside. He stared at the white lace along the floor. The holes in its patterns brought to mind the fearful mask that had stared at him in the temple's shuddering firelight. He remembered the feel of the words the priest had spoken over him, the guttural shout, the grating pronouncement. But he could not recall the words themselves.

Smith moved carefully toward his door, shaking the tension and cold from his body as he went. He pushed it open slowly. It came up against some obstacle and stopped.

"Ah," said a man's voice. "He's awake."

"Oh, aye?" Another.

"Go and get Ratcliffe."

Smith pushed harder against the door; the man blocking it stepped aside. It was William Baker, a stout and rather good man, one of the men he had taken along on his ill-fated expedition to the Apocants. Had that been weeks ago? It seemed years. He had spent so long among the naturals as their captive, paraded in fear and failure through village after village, before at last that strange ritual at the feet of their great king, the little girl saving him to keep as her pet. *Weeks only?*

"What's all this, then?" he asked of Baker.

The man shuffled his feet. His breath had frosted in his beard. "Truth is, John Smith, you're to stand trial."

"Trial?" After all he had been through! God in Heaven, was it not enough?

"For the deaths of Thomas Emry, Jehu Robinson, and George Classen."

It was unfortunate, what had become of Thomas and Jehu. They were both good men, worthy and of use to the colony. A shame that they were felled by Indian arrows, but it was a fate that had befallen plenty of men since they had landed in the New World.

"George Classen? What happened to him?"

Baker dropped his head. Beneath his dense shrubbery of dark beard, he looked distinctly green. "After you and the others left with that savage, rowing upstream in the canoe, we stayed aboard like you ordered and waited for your return. But by midmorning the next day, we still hadn't seen or heard from you. Some of the men said you were betrayed by the savage and butchered. They said we ought to take the shallop back home to Jamestown, report to Ratcliffe that the expedition had failed."

Smith scowled.

"But then," Baker went on, "some ladies came out onto the shore. Indian ladies, you see."

"I haven't seen many other types of lady since we landed," said Smith.

"They sort of . . . beckoned to us." Baker lifted his arms, held them out as if beseeching an embrace. "Their skin was all washed of paint, smooth-like. And they stood there without nothing on top, not even paint, so we could see it all, if you take my meaning."

"Aye, go on."

"Well, Classen said to hell with it all, to hell with the expedition and the fort and the rest. He wanted them ladies. We could all see that. I and a couple of others tried to hold him back, but a few of the men japed with him and encouraged him to have at it. He put the landing boat over the side and rowed himself ashore, laughing and carrying on the whole way, making sport of it."

Baker fell silent. An icy fist clutched at Smith's middle. He remembered the scent of the lion's pelt, that clever, slinking musk in the darkness.

"Well," Baker said haltingly, "when he came ashore the ladies surrounded him, started stripping off his clothes, and a few of the men still on the shallop was hooting and hollering at him. And then over the sounds of their voices I heard a different sound, a kind of wild shriek, and . . . and men poured out of the bushes. Savage men, you see. They had bows and axes and them terrible clubs with the hard flat ends. They caught Classen up between them, and the women built up a fire right there on the shore while the men tied him to a kind of . . . a kind of rack." Baker drifted into silence. He swallowed hard.

"Go on," Smith said cautiously.

"They started . . . removing bits of him, John Smith. They'd take off a finger or a toe, and Classen watched—we all watched—as they tossed these pieces into the fire. He screamed and screamed— Christ preserve me, it was worse than a pig at butchering time. Soon they was taking off strips of skin, from his arms and legs and face. After a time he lost consciousness, and then they . . ."

"All right," Smith broke in. "That's enough. And so I am to stand trial for George Classen's death. A man who chose to walk into an obvious trap, a man who chose to get himself killed."

Baker nodded miserably. "And the other two. They followed you; that's what Ratcliffe said. You took them upriver, and that's what got them killed. The savages brought their bodies onto the strand, after . . . after Classen . . . We couldn't do nothing about it, about Classen or the bodies. He'd taken our landing boat ashore, and we weren't anchored within range of our guns."

"The guns," Smith said, clutched by a sudden, desperate fear. He seized Baker by the shoulders. "Tell me you weren't foolish enough to fire on them."

"A time or two," he admitted.

Smith cursed elaborately. Baker blushed at the vileness of his words.

"Don't you see," Smith said, "they know now—they know how far our guns can fire. They know a safe distance, that our weapons have limits."

Baker shook his head like a bear beset by wasps. No, of course this great oaf didn't understand. Of course he did not see how they had revealed their weakness to the naturals. No one saw, no one understood how to navigate this violent, fearful place, save for Smith. And now they would try *him*—and execute him, he had no doubt—for the foolishness of other men.

Smith turned away.

"You're not to go anywhere," Baker said apologetically. "Ratcliffe's orders."

"Fuck Ratcliffe. I need a piss."

He eschewed the usual places and pulled down the front of his trousers against the palisade wall. It was a vindication, if a small one, to watch his piss darkening the very bones of the fort, to watch the steam rise like a banner of defiance into the morning air. By the time he had tucked himself away, Ratcliffe was there, watching Smith with that flat, unfeeling gaze, with all the warmth of a viper watching a mouse in the underbrush.

They wrapped Smith's wrists in a length of rope and stood him before the men of the fort. It was a ragged bunch, less than half the number who had first landed. They ranged in a sickle in the center of Jamestown, staring at him with eyes haunted by cold and hunger. They were thin as stray dogs, and just as quick to snarl and bite.

Ratcliffe read off the charges in a ringing, pompous voice that would have done Edward-Maria Wingfield proud. Negligence, resulting in the deaths of three good men. *At least it's not to be mutiny this time*, thought Smith.

Smith watched Ratcliffe's steady pacing, the hands clasped behind his back, a gesture of thoughtfulness, not of strut.

"I thought you were a better man," Smith said when the president had finished reciting the charges. Ratcliffe turned slowly to regard him, a cold stare in the cold morning, like ice on the river. "You respected me."

"Aye," Ratcliffe said, "I did, well enough. But you reached beyond your place, John Smith. You lost caution. If you ever had a shred of caution to begin with. And now three men are dead. Shall we simply leave that lie?"

"I didn't kill them. Many more than three are dead. Will you stand the naturals on trial, too? Make them answer for all the men they've slain?"

"When we capture some, we certainly shall try them. And make them pay for their crimes."

A few men rumbled their agreement.

"And what crime am I to die for?" Smith shouted. "The crime of being common? The crime of exceeding my place, of doing what you lot cannot or will not do? You've been waiting all this time, Ratcliffe—waiting for a chance to be rid of me." He swept his hard gaze over the crowd, taking them all in, accusing them all of Ratcliffe's madness. "You fools! You're out of your senses. You're desperate. You allow hunger to rule your minds and your hearts. You aren't dealing out justice, you're *starving* . . . and killing me won't fill your bellies."

Ratcliffe moved very close. A sour stink rose from him, of old wool and mud, of fitful sleep and pervasive fear.

"John Smith, I find you guilty of all charges."

"How convenient for you."

"Take him to the top of the watchtower," Ratcliffe barked, "and hang him."

The men surged forward, some of them shouting against Ratcliffe's order, calling for justice, but far more were too glad to seize Smith by the arms and frog-march him toward the nearest tower. Ratcliffe ascended the ladder with an easy grace that was incongruous with his bony, pale form. Smith climbed with greater difficulty, scrabbling with his tied hands, pushed and supported from below by a mob of hungry men. A length of rough rope passed from hand to hand and wound itself like Eden's serpent around the railing of the watchtower. Smith jerked his body out of the grasp of the men who held him. The sad remains of the colony stared up at him from far below, gaunt, pale faces with deep-black pits for eyes. Their mouths moved—in cheers or in cries of defiance—he could not tell the difference. There was a ringing in his ears like axe blows, and he could not make out the words.

A noose dropped over his head. It was heavy as a bearskin on his shoulders. He remembered the slight weight of the little girl falling over him, her oily, herbal smell, the frail body shielding his own from harm.

She was not here to save him now.

A few wet droplets struck his cheeks, so cold they burned: tiny flakes of snow falling into the hair of the men who surrounded him, Ratcliffe's bulldogs. It dusted the matted wool of their shoulders.

From far below, the roll of a drum sounded. *A nice formality*, he thought with giddy wryness. He caught sight of Matthew Scrivener, pale-faced and tight-lipped, watching in wordless anger.

The shouts fell silent.

"John Smith," Ratcliffe boomed, "for the crime of causing the deaths of George Classen, Jehu Robinson, and Thomas Emry, I do sentence you to hang by the neck until dead."

The bark of the last word hung in the air, but in the silence that followed on its clipped heels, Smith heard a rush, a hollow, deep-bellied flapping—the furling of a sail. He turned to stare frantically at the river. Ratcliffe, too, turned, and gaped at the sight. Through the obscuring blur of falling snow, the stark black hull of a ship turned in the current toward land. Men moved in the rigging, small and jerky as puppets, securing the sail as it dropped against the slash of the boom. Through the growing flurry, in a dreamlike trance of disbelief, Smith read the letters emblazoned below the rail. *"Susan Constant."*

"Ahoy!" A familiar voice carried across the frozen spit.

Christ the redeemer, Smith prayed in a hot rush of passion and gratitude, *it's Captain Newport.*

He raised his voice to the men below. It was hoarse, constricted with the force of his sudden relief, but it carried. "Newport! Newport has returned! Food, men! He has food!"

"You are the luckiest man or beast God ever created," Scrivener said, passing a chipped cup of wine to Smith.

Smith noted with amusement that it was the same old porcelain cup Bartholomew Gosnold had used, back when he'd been counted among the living.

"The timing of Newport's arrival was nearly too much to be believed," Scrivener added.

Their work for the day was finished: roofs patched against the intermittent fall of snow, planks laid across patches of icy mud, rents in old clothing mended with new yarn from the stock of supplies Newport had brought from England. A diluted sunset pinked the western horizon, a fitful shimmer through the tops of bare trees. A dense bank of cloud was tinted with rose, stooping toward the muted, slumbering earth with its burden of snow.

The sky promised another icy night with a frigid day to follow, but it was pleasant enough to huddle around the communal fire. Newport had managed to bring a few pigs from the distant home shore; one boar that had grown sickly on the voyage was now roasting on a spit, dropping his fragrant fats into the blaze with a patter and sizzle. A copper kettle was nestled among the orange coals, the bright glow of its belly slowly darkening in the fire. Bits of hearty carrot and turnip rose on the current of the boil, flashing bright as candles in the gathering dusk, and sank again into the depths of a rich-scented stew. The arrival of the supply ship was a miracle so great it seemed nearly beyond the workings of Christ. They would have food now, food and strength and security, stomachs full enough to stave off the demons that drove men to such pointless outrages as vengeful hangings.

Smith sipped gratefully at his hot spiced wine—the first he'd enjoyed in months. It was poor stuff, no doubt, for the Virginia Company had spared every expense it could, and even if they watered the barrels with half the James River, the supply of wine would certainly not last until the arrival of the next ship, due in late spring. But after months of cold water and thin, savorless broth, and following as it did on the heels of his thwarted hanging, the wine tasted as good as any King James himself might enjoy.

"That was the second time in a handful of days I've given death the slip," Smith said. He related the story of his capture to Matthew Scrivener. The man was always a patient listener, always ready to accept an account from a man he trusted, no matter how unlikely the tale. Scrivener rocked with laughter at the description of the daughter of the great king, risking the men's clubs to save Smith as her own pet. "In the days since I've been back," Smith said—*in the days since Ratcliffe tried to kill me*—"I haven't told another soul that tale. What's the use? Nobody would believe it."

"It does somewhat defy imagination," Scrivener said, but he was chuckling over the rim of his cup. "An Indian princess enchanted by John Smith."

The girl was not enchanted by him—Smith had no doubt of that. She was too young for such thoughts. The snub of her nose and the puppy roundness of her face told her age well enough, even if her body was hidden beneath that shabby white cloak. But beyond her age, he'd sensed an air of calculation in her actions. Smith did not quite understand it, but when the girl looked at him, it was with the gleam of a plot in her eyes, not the heat of infatuation. But it hardly mattered that he did not understand her motives. He was alive.

"I wonder if I shall see her again," he mused.

"Hup, men." William Baker arrived with a length of wood balanced on his ox shoulder. They edged aside to give him room to toss the log onto the fire. A great shower of sparks erupted, wreathing the roast pig in tiny gems, crackling as loud as the Indian priests' rattles. Baker threw a quick, shamefaced glance in Smith's direction, and then lumbered away.

"That one wanted me dead," Smith said.

"Baker? Never. He's a good enough sort."

"He's Ratcliffe's man. That much is clear."

"Men don't know whose they are from one day to the next. It was the hunger that did it to them, Smith."

"Ratcliffe still gives me looks full of murder. He slinks about like a shadow, those sly little eyes of his watching me . . . always watching."

"He cannot touch you. Not anymore—not now that we have food. The men will never stand for it. Men are sensible when they're not starving."

There were plenty of men at Jamestown now, too. Newport had brought a full shipload of hopefuls to the colony. Fresh men to shoulder some of the load, to share the burden. They were well fed, or looked to be by comparison with the more established colonists. Stand a lad who had just made an ocean crossing in the dead of winter beside a starving colonist, and it was the only time you might rightfully call a straw-thin sailor well fed.

A wind howled over the edge of the palisade, blowing a scatter of icy crystals down among the trampled grounds.

"Cold night," Scrivener muttered.

The wind picked up, flattening the flames against the ground. The shape of the spitted hog dimmed and receded in the sudden loss of light. Smith set Gosnold's old porcelain cup on the ground and pulled his cloak tight about his body. In that moment, a log on the fire gave an enormous crack; a gout of flame leaped from the log's heart, trailed by a streak of sparks. Smith and Scrivener jumped back from the fire. They watched, holding their breath, as the sparks drifted across the cold blackness of the grounds and settled among the damp thatch of the storehouse's roof.

No, Smith thought, his mouth suddenly dry. *Let it be too wet, merciful Christ.*

Nothing happened for a long moment. The wind died back, and the fire returned to a steady, tame blaze. The pig sizzled. Scrivener drew in a shaky breath as if to speak, and then halted.

Smith saw it, too: a ruddy glow suffusing through the thatch, thick pale smoke rising. He shouted, *"Fire!"*

Men came stumbling from their huts, pulling cloaks about them. The night erupted with cries.

"Buckets! Open the gates! To the river, men! Bring water!"

By the time a chain of buckets passed hand to hand, down to the river and back again, the storehouse was well ablaze. Oily smoke filled eyes and nostrils, tasting of burnt wool and wheat. Men clambered atop the nearest cabins, beating out sparks and tiny licks of flame with wet blankets. They flung water at the storehouse, sending up spurts of steam to mingle with the terrible black smoke, but it was useless. The blaze burned too hot, fueled by the new kegs of oil and the well-tended dry goods inside. The men worked with a fearful energy, the lot of them shivering with a feeling that was near panic. But it was no use. After hours of hopeless battle, the storehouse burned itself out, nothing but a heap of ashes among a few smoldering twigs that had once been stout beams.

Gone. All of it gone. Their hope, their salvation. Even the roasted pig and the stew had burned up, forgotten in the madness of the blaze. As a weak dawn rose trembling over Jamestown, Smith stood, hollowed by exhaustion and despair, staring at white shards lying splintered against the frozen black earth. Even his cup of wine was lost, trampled in the panic of the night.

God almighty, do you want us to starve? He peered up into a dense shelf of cloud filling with morning light. The brightness of it brought a thin water to his eyes. *No food to stop them . . . Ratcliffe will hang me all over again. And nothing to save my hide a third time. It's too much to hope for, that I'll be spared again.*

He staggered to his cabin and fell onto his bed. The interior was choking with the pungent, thick smell of burnt wool. With nothing to hope for and everything to fear, John Smith stumbled into a deep, dragging sleep.

It was a dream that woke him.

He stood on a path in the forest, a luminous cobalt trail that wound among trees the color of twilight, deep blue and smoky violet. Somewhere along the stretch of the trail, in the undergrowth smelling of singed wool and watered wine, he heard a child's voice calling to him.

Very small king.

He gasped as he awoke. Light leaked through the cracks around his door. He had tossed away his blanket in sleep, and now his body was stiff with cold. He lay shivering on his pallet, clinging to the threads of the dream. One by one the blue-violet trees dissipated before the eye of memory. The child's voice faded.

Gradually he became aware of murmuring outside, a busy sound of suspicion and wonder.

"King," Ratcliffe's voice called, clear and demanding, rising above the greater hum of so many men. "What does she mean, *king*?"

She.

Smith lurched from bed and threw his door wide, kicking at the blanket that had tangled around his ankle.

The communal fire pit was black and cold. A sluggish breeze stirred, lifting an eddy of greasy ash from the ruin of the storehouse. Men pressed around the gate, which was flung open, though Smith could not see who stood on the other side. The crowd moved with a tense, bobbing excitement. He scuttled forward, sliding between thin bodies, the worn fabric of their garments full of the smell of fire. The faces in the crowd were alight with hope and hunger.

Ratcliffe again. "What does she mean, *king*?"

Smith shouldered to the front.

The girl stood in the very center of the gateway, the frayed white cape held snug beneath her chin, face framed in a wreath of pale feathers. Ratcliffe was planted in front of the child, challenging her with his height and his flat, serpentine stare. The child ignored him, gazing calmly down at the ground, refusing, politely but firmly, to acknowledge Ratcliffe's authority.

Somebody murmured a greeting: "Ho, Smith," and Pocahontas glanced up at the sound of his name. The dark, almond-slanted eyes hid themselves for a moment behind lowered lids, a slow blink of satisfaction.

"That one," the child said. A small hand emerged from her cape to point in Smith's direction. Her accented English stirred another ripple of excitement among the men of the colony.

"Good God," Ratcliffe scoffed. "She thinks John Smith is the king?"

A few men chuckled. One hissed.

Smith slipped forward to Ratcliffe's side. The president withdrew slightly, not out of deference but from distaste at Smith's nearness.

"Pocahontas."

"*Wingapoh*, Chawnzmit."

"Why are you here?" He said it in her tongue, unwilling to allow Ratcliffe any part of the conversation.

She tilted her face, gave a small, slow grin, foxlike and sly. "I said I would come, and we would speak." She paused a moment, then sniffed the air ostentatiously. "You had a fire."

"Yes. Last night."

"We smelled it."

"All the way to Werowocomoco?"

Ratcliffe threw up his hands. "Speak English, man. Or have the good grace to translate."

Both Smith and Pocahontas ignored him.

"Our scouts smelled it," she said, "and ran to my father's longhouse."

"So there are scouts still in the woods around us, watching."

Pocahontas smiled serenely. "The house where you put your things, the things from the big boat. That is the house that burned."

The skin at the nape of Smith's neck prickled and crawled. Indians watching unseen from the woodland were unsettling enough, but they must have been watching from the treetops or pressed against the palisade wall, to know where the colony had stored the ship's goods. *Ratcliffe, be glad I keep you ignorant, you prancing fool.*

"Yes," he admitted. "We have no food now. All of it is gone."

She nodded. "As my father suspected."

She turned abruptly and whistled, a perfect imitation of the high piping call of some local bird. Soon the men of the fort drew back, gasping and muttering, as a stream of naturals emerged from the wiry undergrowth at the river's edge. Smith had not even seen their canoes; they must have been well hidden, lying low beneath the winter brush. Men and women alike came, a score or more, bearing baskets piled high with dried corn, grass-woven sacks heavy with beans, freshly killed turkeys strung up by their feet. The colonists divided, forming an avenue of amazed stares and welcoming praises. A few dropped to their knees on the frozen earth and prayed aloud.

Pocahontas stood still as the stream of salvation flowed around her. She looked up into John Smith's face, her lips curved in a tiny, triumphant smile. "Here is food," she said offhand, as if she had not just saved them all from a slow and certain death. "Powhatan is good. He cares for his children, and you are his now, *tanx-werowance*. You are *tanx* to his son Naukaquawis, and you are my brother. I claimed you. I took you away from death."

"I know," Smith muttered, bewildered.

She took his hand. Hers was small and warm, and he could not help but smile at her confident and friendly touch. "Then come, Chawnzmit. It is time for us to speak."

They sat together on one of the flat-topped logs surrounding the cold fire pit, conversing as the gifts of corn and birds and dried fish were offered and tabulated. Scrivener took charge of the goods, designating a new cabin as the storehouse, directing the flow of baskets and sacks, and bowing to every natural who passed him. Smith watched in amazement until Pocahontas tapped him briskly on the knee.

She pulled the chain of beads from the neck of her cloak and held it up in her slender fingers. Her face was stern with concentration. "*Roanoke*," she said.

Smith knew the game by now; he had played it often enough with naturals on his trading expeditions. "Beads," he said in English. "Shell beads."

She nodded her approval. Testing him: she already knew these English words.

They worked at their task as the food came in, stringing phrases together from stray, half-understood words, threading sentences like broken necklaces. Pocahontas giggled every time she corrected his speech, shaking her head until the braid hanging down her back swung, full of a child's lighthearted sport. Soon he was laughing, too, showing her the difference between *The beads are yellow* and *The beads are sunshine* with gestures and his poor fragments of Indian words.

"A strange pair we make," he told her, and she smiled, agreeing.

Two days later she returned, again with an escort of men and women bearing more stock for the new supply house. Again they conversed, testing the boundaries of each language, both of them delighting in the joy of new and shared knowledge. Pocahontas visited the fort so regularly the men of Jamestown began to speak of her with reverence, as if she were an angel wrapped in her ragged white wings. At the approach of her canoe, the guards on duty in the watchtower would call out joyously, *"The princess! The princess has come!"*

The snows of winter deepened, piling against the palisade walls, crusting with sharp points of ice that broke the skin of men's legs when they sank into drifts over their boot-tops. The cabins of Jamestown were rounded by snowfall. Within the boundaries of the palisade, the snow stained to gray and less appealing shades, then renewed itself in white as storms rolled up the length of the great river. In time it reverted to its sickly colors again, tramped beneath the weary feet of the colonists.

The men of Jamestown were weary, but they were not hungry. As their stores depleted, Pocahontas came again, bearing her gifts and greetings from her father. The most precious gift of all she gave to John Smith alone: knowledge of her people's language, of their customs and ways.

Many times he would watch her face puzzling over a new phrase, the black brows knitting with her familiar furrow of concentration, and he would wonder guiltily whether she understood all that she gave away. Did her father expect this? Did he send this little ambassador freely, knowing that his new, pale-skinned *tanx-werowance* must be extracting from her the secrets of the Real People, things the king would rather the English did not know? Was it a trade Powhatan was willing to make, for some terrible payment he had yet to demand? Or was he as innocent in the matter as his daughter?

As winter thawed at last into a gray, wet spring, Smith's guilt deepened, for he had come to like the girl immensely. There was a familiar spark in her soul, a flame of arrogant defiance that burned kindred to his own. Her great intelligence was obvious to anyone who glanced her way. It shone from her face, a torch of confident understanding that could not be extinguished. Not so obvious to the casual observer was her ambition. She was possessed of a desire for power so great it might put to shame the Roman emperors of old. Such ambition in a little girl would have been comical, if Pocahontas were not so charming and delightful. Instead, it seemed as natural to her as were feathers to a bird or scales to a fish.

She had confessed her ambition to him once, when she finally understood the meaning of the English word *princess.*

"A princess is the daughter of a king," Smith had explained.

"I am that." Pocahontas nodded in solemn agreement.

"A princess is valuable. A princess marries a great man, gives birth to sons of great standing. Her sons become kings. She is respected, cherished by the people."

The girl's face had fallen. The sorrow that came over her lively, expressive features took Smith aback. "I am *not* that," she said emphatically. "Not a princess."

"No? But you are the great king's daughter."

She had explained then, with obvious chagrin and palpable longing, her place in the world.

"I'm a commoner, too," Smith told her, his chest welling with kinship for the child. He had a sudden urge to fold her in a brotherly embrace, to offer this small creature some shelter against all the terrible unfairness in the world. Instead he sat up straighter, gazing stoically out over the sharp tops of the palisade. "I can never rise above my station, though God knows I have greater worth."

Pocahontas peered up at him. "But you are *tanx-werowance.* That is better than a common man."

"Only to the Real People. The English, the *tassantassas* . . . my people see me as low and uncouth."

She tested the new word. "Uncouth?"

He smiled in spite of his turbulent emotions. "Not a gentleman."

"I am not a gentleman, too."

"No—for a girl, we wouldn't say *gentleman*. We would say *lady*."

"I am not a lady. I am uncouth. But you can be called *tanx-werowance* by Chief Powhatan. You can be given greatness because you are brave and wise."

"Can you not be called a lady? Does your father not have that power?"

She sighed. "Perhaps my father might lift me up. I might rise as high as *werowansqua*—lady-king."

"Queen," Smith said, hiding his chuckle.

She nodded distractedly, as if she already knew the word, though Smith had never heard her speak it. The girl was lost now in her own tangle of thoughts, picking sadly at the bread-crumb trail of her thwarted ambitions. "I would be a leader. I would have my own tribe, if only my father would notice me."

"How could any father fail to take note of a daughter such as you?"

She shook her head. The childish legs swung, kicking the log where they sat.

"What does he notice, then?"

"Warriors," she said, "and hunters. And guns. The guns he wants, so that he can move west, beyond the fall line."

And Smith had quietly tucked the knowledge into a dark corner of his mind, even as he patted the girl's back and strung a few silly words together to cheer her.

In the fullness of spring, when buds swelled on the tips of branches and the mornings rang with the calls of thrushes and blackbirds, Pocahontas came to Jamestown more often. She was often accompanied by a sober young man, a bodyguard of sorts. Sometimes a train of Indian children followed her into the fort, cavorting among the cabins and filling the air with their wild cries.

The Englishmen gave the little boys and girls cheap strings of beads and patted their bristled heads, showed them how to roll the hoops of discarded barrel lids up and down the lanes of the fort. Pocahontas's train in turn would surround Thomas Savage and the handful of other young lads Newport had imported from England. She taught them Indian games, hopping contests and competitions of bragging, in which the children challenged one another to make increasingly outrageous claims. It always amused the men of the fort, to watch the lads attempt to brag in hand signs.

The world was warming, and the Indian children laid off their leggings and cloaks, their loin-wraps and moccasins. They went about in naught but their paint and tattoos, as unconcerned with their own nakedness as beasts of the field. Smith kept as sharp a gaze on the children's play as Pocahontas's unspeaking bodyguard did on her. She was female, after all, and the men of Jamestown had seen no women since leaving England. As she turned feet over hands down the muddy lanes, her bare limbs flashing in the sunshine, shouting for the English boys to try and best her, Smith would often note a man looking on with too avid a stare. He would move into the watcher's line of sight and regard him silently until the man blinked and hurried away.

The girl had called him brother, and like any good brother, he would allow no harm to befall her.

The affection he held for the child was a fierce and precious thing, the first emotion he'd felt since Constantinople that was not desperation or pain, disgust or rage—or bleak disappointment. She was a talisman to him, the sound of her playful laughter a shield against all the bitterness of an uncaring, unjust world. The love he felt for her was quite unlike that he had felt for Antonia, or for any woman before. He did not desire her body. It was her smile and her bubbling laugh that filled him with quiet satisfaction, with certainty in God's goodness, with a peace he had not known for many years. In the light of a bright afternoon he surprised her by telling another child in perfect Real Tongue, "Bid Pocahontas bring me two little baskets, and I will give her white beads to make her a chain." Pocahontas's grin when she skipped to his side warmed him. He pulled a bit of red yarn from his pocket and sat with her, stringing beads as pure as summertime clouds, her stick-thin fingers deft at their work. When the chain was finished, he tied it around her neck. She bowed in the English style, an elaborate gesture of thanks, and the memory of her smile as she bobbed like a foraging bird stayed with John Smith for days afterward.

One bright afternoon the girl arrived with a complement of warriors at her back. They moved up the shoreline in a resolute line, stiff and wary as they trailed Pocahontas's slight, familiar frame. As he watched them approach Jamestown, Smith sensed with a sudden dark tremor that something immeasurably precious was about to be broken and lost forever.

The usual cry of "*The princess!*" drifted from the watchtowers; the gate opened for her as it had so many times before. Smith went out to greet her and the men who stalked along silently in her wake. She looked up at him with a sober, businesslike mien that at once confirmed his fears.

"*Wingapoh,*" he said.

She returned the greeting with no quaver in her voice, but the briefest flash of regret shadowed her eyes. "My father sends me to request a gift from his *tanx-werowance.*"

I am not a gentleman, too. Why did his memory slide backward so, tracking through the happy weeks of spring to that gray day when she had gazed at him with troubled eyes? He thought to lead her to the fire pit, their usual meeting place, but she had mentioned gifts. This was no social visit from the Great Chief's ambassador. It was a mission of trade.

He nodded his understanding. He ushered the party through the gate and sank easily into the traditional squatting posture of trade. Pocahontas did likewise, folding her arms, bracing her thin elbows against her knobby knees. Red excoriations showed through the pale calluses on her joints, a patch of dried scab where she had skinned one knee. *Every bit a child*, he thought, *and yet she is so somber. Does she feel it, too? This thing we have built together, this friendship, about to be shattered?*

Her warriors lowered themselves, too, their dark eyes never leaving his face.

Pocahontas began the negotiation without delay, as if eager to conclude an unpleasant business as quickly as possible. "Now that you are Real People, Chawnzmit, Powhatan expects your aid in his endeavors."

Smith glanced around the yard. Several of the colonists had gathered, eyeing the scene with unmasked curiosity. The younger boys of the fort clustered together and stared at Pocahontas, milling like pups waiting for their master to toss a ball.

Smith spoke in the Indians' language. "Let us use the Real Tongue." The girl was so handy now with English, and spoke so boldly, that anyone might overhear. He did not fancy Ratcliffe learning of Chief Powhatan's endeavors.

"Very well."

"What aid does the *mamanatowick* seek?"

She looked at him for one long moment. There was doubt in her eyes, and a subtle resentment, as if she would have shirked this particular task had she found any way to do so. "Guns," she said at last.

Smith nodded. He had expected this, truly. He had known the day would come, the demand would come. And yet he could feel only sorrow, the dragging certainty that his tie to the sportive little girl, his only happiness in a long year of desolation, was coming unraveled.

"You must know, Pocahontas, that I cannot part with any guns."

"But you must. Your *mamanatowick* requires it."

"My *mamanatowick* is King James—the one across the sea. He has told us most strictly that we are to keep all our guns. Every one."

She frowned at him, not her usual glower of concentration as when she puzzled over a new word. This was a true, sharp scowl, and it stabbed his heart, to see her disapproval directed at him. "Powhatan is your *mamanatowick* now. You entered the temple; you wore the bearskin. You smoked the pipe!"

"All true. Yet what am I to do? Honor requires that I keep my word to my first *mamanatowick*, even though I revere the great Powhatan."

Pocahontas looked away. Her eyes were distant. She turned his words over carefully, examining them from all angles, seeking their weakness. Smith's heart constricted to see the intensity of the child's frown. Constantinople was so long ago. This child was the only company he had looked to with any kind of delight since those languid afternoons with Antonia. *Must we meet now as trading partners, as enemies? My dear child, my little sister, who is a commoner like me* . . . Bitterly, silently, he cursed Powhatan's name.

"We brought food," Pocahontas said. "We kept you and your men from starving. What of that honor? Would you throw that gift into my father's face?"

And there was the weakness. Smith owed his life to the child twice over. He was no gentleman, but honor was real to him. All the English owed much to the naturals who had sustained them through the long and terrible winter. But guns? Put firearms into the naturals' hands, and it would be only a matter of time before one of the stiff, stolid warriors surrounding the little ambassador turned a gun on an Englishman. They were deadly enough with their arrows. Firearms in Indian hands would be a devastation. The colonists had already been fool enough to reveal the range of their shot at Apocant over the sordid business with George Classen. How far had knowledge of English weaponry spread? Did Powhatan himself know the range of a *tassantassa* bullet?

Any mystery that might still surround English firepower was the only advantage Jamestown still held. And the tense, wary faces of Pocahontas's warrior guards spoke plainly of the scant trust on either side of the palisade. No—at all costs, the naturals must not have their guns.

"Very well," Smith said, forming the ploy quickly in his mind, and hating himself even as he spoke the words. "The *mamanato-wick* may have his guns. I shall give him two. Come along with me."

He led the party to the northwest wall. Beyond was the stretch of marsh, bogs that grew wider and deeper by the day as the season advanced. Past the marsh stood the deep tangle of the forest, where Powhatan's spies waited unseen like malevolent birds roosting in the treetops. There two cannons stood, wheels half-sunk in the mud, muzzles pointing out through freshly hewn gaps in the face of the palisade, nosing like two eager dogs through a hedge. They had hauled the things ashore from the *Susan Constant* upon Newport's return.

"Here are your guns," Smith said. "If you can carry them back to Werowocomoco, I will gladly give them to Powhatan, with my thanks and blessings."

The Indian men looked at one another cautiously. Then one seized the great, cold muzzle of the nearest cannon and strained against it. His feet slid in the mud. One or two more men joined him, hauling in concert, rocking it. But of course it was no use.

Pocahontas looked up at him, her mouth flat and thin with shocked disappointment. "You mock us, Chawnzmit. You mock me."

He cringed at the hurt in her voice. "No," he said gently, but she spun on her heel and nearly ran for the fort's gate.

She called a command over her shoulder, and her warriors abandoned their efforts at the cannon. As they passed him, they stared one by one into his face, and their looks were filled with hateful promise.

"Pocahontas, wait," he said, moving swiftly after her. "Don't open the gate," he called to his men.

But they would not contradict the wish of the princess, their savior and angel. They swung the gate wide at her curt request, and her escort of bristling men filed through.

Pocahontas turned one bleak look on him, a wounded stare cast over her thin shoulder as she strode toward the river.

"I'm sorry," he cried out, startled at the pain in his heart. "I have no choice. Don't you see?"

But the gate swung closed behind her. The crossbars dropped into place with a desolate clatter.

She was gone.

POCAHONTAS

Season of Cattapeuk

All the long way home to Werowocomoco, Pocahontas sat rigid and silent in the bow of her canoe while the men paddled behind her. Her shoulders and neck ached from her own stiffness, yet she could not release the anger, the terrible stunned sensation of betrayal that gripped her as tightly as an osprey grips a fish.

The men in her party talked among themselves, low and offended, of the rudeness of Chawnzmit, of his astonishing arrogance. It was so far beyond what any respectable *tanx* was entitled to. All the men talked save for Kocoum, who sat behind Pocahontas as silent as she was. His paddle moved steadily in the current. Now and then a drop of river water was flung from the paddle's tip as he crossed it in the space between them. Her back was soon sprinkled with droplets like tears. They ran in slow, halting streams down her spine, but she made no move to brush them from her skin.

When they reached the shore of Werowocomoco and beached their dugouts, Kocoum offered his hand to help her from the canoe. She rose with a stifled gasp; the pain in her tense muscles was sudden and fierce. Kocoum placed one of his big hands on the back of her neck and squeezed; she sighed as the tension abated.

"What will you tell your father?" he said quietly.

"What can I tell him, other than the truth?"

They made their way to Powhatan's longhouse. She felt the eyes of women and warriors on her as she picked her path through Werowocomoco, past the communal dance circle where a few children squatted in the dust corralling ants with twigs, past the homes of her aunts and cousins who sat weaving new-sprouted silk grass in the sun. She caught sight of Matachanna, smiling as she braided a strand of beads into Nonoma's hair; the smile faded from her sister's face at the sight of Pocahontas marching in obvious disgrace toward the *mamanatowick*'s great house.

She came face-to-face with her father's door flap and stood gazing at it mutely, stupid with loss and humiliation. Kocoum lifted it aside, and she bent automatically to enter.

Down the long length of the hall, she could see that Powhatan was on his feet. He moved about his heart fire with a steadier gait than she had seen him use in many months. Wives chattered in the depths of the longhouse as they worked. Restrained feminine laughter came from the bedsteads along the walls, the thumps of sleeping mats being beaten. A woman hummed as she sorted the contents of a storage bag. Pots of paint and a flea whisk made of pungent dried herbs lay at her bare feet. At the fire, Powhatan fondly patted the heads and bottoms of a pair of young wives, who giggled as they assembled a roasting spit with green saplings and twine made of deer sinew.

Pocahontas's feet dragged as she drew nearer. She had not seen her father so happy in far too long. It was the anticipation of guns, she knew, the growing and flourishing of his grand designs. He relished the thought of falling on the Massawomecks, wiping them from the land like a grease stain, claiming their rich territory for the Real People. He was certain that his time had come at last, his victory inevitable, guaranteed by the Okeus, by this strange and contradictory blessing of *tassantassas* invading Tsenacomoco.

And she must be the one to tell him that his dream could never be. *He will think of only disappointment when he looks on me. I will never be called a* lady; *I will never be* werowansqua.

She hung back, hesitating, gripping the upright post of an arcing, smoke-blackened beam. A low voice said something she could not catch, and Powhatan turned his face toward the unseen speaker, nodded in agreement, his long, silver hair swinging. Pocahontas had not caught the words, but she recognized the timbre of the voice at once, its natural force and intensity.

Opechancanough.

So her uncle had come all the way from Pamunkey-town. No doubt he had come to witness the great triumph, to see the guns with his own eyes, to plot with the *mamanatowick* how the priceless weapons would be deployed against their enemies.

I had best pull this thorn out quickly.

She took a deep breath. The taste of raw meat and the sappy greenness of the roasting spit filled her mouth. Pocahontas moved away from the bedstead, placing herself quietly in her father's path. He stopped his pacing and looked at her with some surprise, and then a grin split his weathered old face.

"There she is now, my little Mischief. What is the news from the white men's fort?"

Pocahontas hung her head. She could feel her uncle Opechancanough waiting, tense and malevolent as a snake poised to strike. "They would not send guns, Father."

"What?"

"The *tassantassas* were deceptive. They mocked your request, and taunted us with the heaviness of their biggest guns. They said you could have them if we could move them, but they were so heavy a hundred men could not have moved them one handspan through the mud." She was dimly aware of the sly concealment in her own words, and wondered at it. *They, not he. They, not Chawnzmit. But it was Chawnzmit who deceived me. It was his own doing—he who I thought was my friend. Why do I protect him from my father's wrath?*

Powhatan's face flushed a livid red. His wives glanced at one another and withdrew, moving quickly down the length of the great hall.

Opechancanough grunted, a sound like a bear waking from interrupted slumber. "I told you, Brother. The *tassantassas* are liars. Perhaps now you see it: they must be finished, removed. They must be crushed like flies on a grindstone."

A bleak vision filled Pocahontas's mind, of Chawnzmit shot through by Opechancanough's bow, his body bristling with arrows, the fletchings dyed scarlet with his blood. She saw his face, that strange wiry pelt of beard and his smile of friendship beneath it, the eyes as blue as the sky in *cattapeuk*, smiling at her with understanding, with kinship. And she saw a blue eye pierced by an arrow, heard a scream of pain and rage. She did not want him crushed—not Chawnzmit. Not the little boys at the fort, either, nor the men on the tower who called out to her, *"Princess! The princess has come!"* Chawnzmit had wounded her with his deception, but he and the *tassantassas* valued her as no one in Werowocomoco did—as her father never would, now that she had failed to secure the guns he so desperately longed for. She could not let them be destroyed. And if she could retain her hold on the *tassantassas*, maintain her value to the fort, she might yet find some way to restore her worth to Powhatan.

But she could not regain her father's favor without the white men. Without them, she had no hope of rising to *werowansqua*.

Her throat was dry with fear and shame, but still she spoke. "Father, though their deception was a grave offense, I know we can still obtain the *tassantassas'* guns."

Powhatan raised his head, a slow gesture of permission; Pocahontas clutched at her racing thoughts, trying to order them, praying to the spirits that she might make some sense to her father. She must speak clearly, with confidence. She must not waver.

Before she could open her mouth, Opechancanough stood. He was tall, broad, sinewy, slow-slinking like a cougar stalking among the trees. His eyes fixed on her a baleful stare, and she shrank in the force of his presence, painfully aware that she was only a girl, and a common one at that.

"It is an outrage," Opechancanough said, his voice tight and quiet with disgust, "that a girl should be allowed to speak to the *mamanatowick* with such impunity. Brother, be your own man again. Stop listening to the counsel of white men and naked children."

Powhatan turned a look of offended dignity on his brother. Opechancanough's arms were folded over the tattoos of his chest, the proud black bows of Pamunkey crossed above his heart. He did not blink under the *mamanatowick*'s stare. He stood his ground, unwavering and unapologetic.

Pocahontas gasped at the sight. It reached deep into her spirit, unsettling her in ways she could not describe, could not fully identify. With a clutch of remembered pain, she recalled the time she had followed Naukaquawis through the forest, years before his *huskanaw*, when he was only a boy with a shaven head, and she just six years old. Far beyond the boundaries of Werowocomoco, they had followed a trail of dung and broken branches to a great clearing where a herd of wood buffalo grazed in the autumn sunshine. Together they had watched two bulls fight for control of the herd. One bull was old, stiff in the shoulders, with small, rheumy eyes ringed by black flies. He had frothed and roared as the young challenger assaulted him, but his aging body could not stave off the onslaught. The younger bull gored him, and the old bull's silence as he limped into the forest had torn at Pocahontas's heart. She had sniffled and cried on the way home, the forest blurring behind her tears. Naukaquawis had teased her for her softness. It filled her with a terrible, cold ache, a trembling wistful sorrow, knowing the old bull would die in the forest, haunted by the memory of his cows and calves, mocked by his own faded strength.

"No," she said quickly. Opechancanough's eyes were as fierce and piercing as a hawk's. She slid her gaze away from him and turned her face toward her father, who was still the *mamanato-wick*. He had not been gored by Opechancanough yet—*not yet*. "Powhatan is wise to maintain good relations with the *tassantas-sas*. I have been to their town. I have seen how they are. I know their ways and their weaknesses."

"What does a girl know of men's weaknesses?" Opechancanough spat the words at her.

She looked up at him. With a tremulous wonder she recognized something of the old, defeated bull in her uncle's demeanor, too, and her eyes narrowed. *What horn might wound one as strong and fearless as he?* In the same moment she asked herself the question, she knew the answer. *Tsena-no-ha.*

"I know more than you realize, *werowance*. I know you still reel from the loss of your wife."

It was a mistake to say it. Opechancanough advanced on her like a storm rolling upriver. She tried to shy away from him, but he seized her by the upper arm. His fingers bit painfully into her flesh as he shook her.

"Do not speak to me of *that*, you pestilent child. You know *nothing*."

"Do not touch my daughter." Powhatan's voice boomed, a ringing drumbeat of authority, a sound of natural power that Pocahontas had not heard in many months.

Opechancanough's hand opened and she jerked her body out of his grasp. The relief of hearing the *mamanatowick's* surge of strength was so great that tears stung her eyes. She dashed them away with the back of her hand.

She spoke quickly, before her uncle could move again. "The *tassantassas* do lie, it is true. But they do it because they are hungry. All their food burned up, as I told you already. We bring them gifts, but it is never enough. They are always fearful, always wondering when their stores will run out. It makes them wary and untrusting. But if they have full bellies, they won't be so desperate anymore. They will be civil.

"Chawnzmit, their chief, is a good man." She took a deep breath, hoping the secret didn't show on her face—her secret knowledge that Chawnzmit was not, in fact, a *werowance*. "Honor is important to him. He will give you all the honor you require, if only he can stop fearing for the survival of his men. Once he knows they will always be fed, he will do his duty to you, *mamanatowick*."

Her words staggered to a halt. She did not know where half the words came from, unless a spirit breathed them into her throat, unless the Okeus himself put them in her mouth. She prayed they were true words, from a good spirit, not from a lurking *manitou* bent on trickery. She kept her eyes servilely on the floor, waiting. The sound of her own ragged heartbeat filled her ears.

At last Powhatan spoke. "What do you propose, daughter?"

"It is the season for planting. Let me take women to the *tassantassas'* fort—and a few men to protect us. Let us show them how to make gardens, how to grow crops. Once they have thriving gardens and know that they can harvest food, they will cease their fearful behavior—and their deceptions." *Okeus, let it be true. Spirits, make it so.*

Powhatan resumed his pacing, walking his circuit around the heart fire. The light of the fire moved fitfully on his skin, dancing on the bold designs of his fine apron. He moved with trembling legs again, the old-bull weakness creeping back into his limbs. Pocahontas turned her unfocused gaze on Powhatan's clustered, whispering wives so that she would not see his trembling.

Her eyes did not want to see her father's growing frailty. She felt Opechancanough breathing hoarsely beside her.

"Perhaps it is as you say," Powhatan said slowly.

Pocahontas heard the desperate hope in his voice—the need for guns, the strength Powhatan could no longer wield with his aging body. He *wanted* it to be as Pocahontas said, and so did she.

Opechancanough sighed, a sound of vast disappointment that edged near pity. Pocahontas cut her eyes quickly toward him, and saw him turn away from the spectacle of the old *mamanatowick* with an abrupt twitch, the knotted lock of his hair clattering its copper and beads as he went. "Weak as a woman," he muttered.

Pocahontas allowed herself a small smile. Women were not so weak, after all, if a woman could unman the great Opechancanough just by leaving his hearth. Even girls were not weak, if their words could influence the *mamanatowick*. Her hands clenched at her sides; her palms tingled as if she held something, something warm and weighty and of great value. She thought of Chawnzmit sitting beside the fire pit, laughing as his tongue tripped over words. She thought of Opossu-no-quonuske, shining in her cape of black birds' feathers.

I will be a werowansqua *after all*, she vowed to no one but herself, her chest swelling with pride and the hot glow of victory. *See if I am not, one day.*

Naukaquawis laid his callused hand on Pocahontas's shoulder, pushing her gently but firmly away from the dugout she was helping to load with gardening tools. He steered her toward the path back to Werowocomoco, where the underbrush would provide them with some measure of privacy. Under the hand of a *werowance*, she could do little to resist. She called instructions to the women over her shoulder as she went. "Don't forget the digging sticks! At least ten—more, if they can be found!"

In the forest shade, she turned a defiant gaze up to her brother's face. He had painted himself with black and red, bold colors to strike awe into an enemy's heart, though Pocahontas still felt sure that the *tassantassas* were no enemies of the Real People. "What do you want, Naukaquawis? I have work to do."

"I intend to remind you," he said slowly, his eyes steady and hard in their red-and-black mask, "who is in control of this mission."

"It was my idea. Powhatan heard the proposal from my lips. You never would have thought of it."

"Chawnzmit is still my *tanx-werowance*, even if I didn't save him from the war clubs. You are a child, low blood, and female. I expect obedience from you. Obedience and respect."

She squinted at him. There was anger in his eyes, carefully controlled but simmering just below the surface. He had not forgotten—no, by the Okeus, how could he forget—that she had taken Chawnzmit from his own grasp, stolen him at the height of an important ceremony before the eyes of many men and priests. Chawnzmit was to be his prize, a reward fit for a chief. Instead the *tassantassa* had ended up the plaything of a low-blood girl. The men must joke about it still, rubbing the humiliation in Naukaquawis's face.

Her brother controlled his spite admirably, and if there was any taunting, he bore it well. She nearly felt sorry for having stolen his prize. He was everything a man of the Real People ought to be: stoic, reliable, loyal, and brave. In the days when they were both children, Naukaquawis had been a kind and patient brother. He would make a very fine chief. He might even rise to be *mamanato-wick* one day, and if that day came before Pocahontas could secure her father's cooperation, it would fall to Naukaquawis to say who would become a *werowance*—or a *werowansqua*.

She bowed her head slightly and pressed a hand to her heart. "Brother, I have not always been fair to you. But I swear that I will defer to you in this work. You are my *werowance*, for as long as we remain with the white men."

He gave a short, sharp grunt of acceptance.

"But," she said quietly, her skin prickling in anticipation of his backlash, "I would ask you humbly to recall that I know their language, and their ways."

"The one called Chawnzmit knows *our* language. Any of us may communicate with him."

"This is true. But only I can speak to the other white men. Chawnzmit is not always near. You will see. And of course, Brother, gardening is women's work. Only we know the lore of plants and seeds. If we are to teach the *tassantassas* to grow their own food, you must allow me—allow all the women—some freedom to act as we see fit."

He paused a moment, regarding her thoughtfully. At last he nodded. "You have your uses. I won't interfere with women's work, nor take away your small honors, Amonute." She bit her lip at the implied criticism of her own actions. "As long as you obey."

When they returned to finish loading the canoes, Pocahontas was startled to find Matachanna and Nonoma working alongside the canoe. Between them, the girls hefted a large basket of seed corn, tied a woven cover in place, and then lashed the basket carefully into the hull of their boat.

Matachanna looked up with her familiar, gently beaming smile. "That's a fifth of the seed corn from our house's cache. Do you think it will be enough?"

Pocahontas nodded. "Are you coming to the fort with me?"

"We both are." Matachanna tucked Nonoma beneath her arm in a quick hug. "We want to see your *tassantassas* up close. And I want to help you, Pocahontas. Sometimes even you need a friend paddling your canoe."

She hooked her finger with Matachanna's. "It's good of you, Sister. And you, Nonoma. I know we haven't always been the best of friends, but I'm glad you'll be with me."

When the canoes were filled, Naukaquawis gave the word; they coasted in twos and threes out into the river. The spirits of all the women and girls were buoyant with anticipation of a great adventure to come. Even the warriors seemed relaxed and happy, those fierce, stoic men who would guard the women as they cleared the *tassantassas*' land and set seeds and sprouts into high black mounds of newly turned earth.

At sunset they reached the fort. Pocahontas lifted a palm in the white men's greeting, called *"Wingapoh!"* and "Halloo!" in her familiar voice. A returned shout of "The princess!" carried across the water, filling her stomach with a warmth as satisfying as well-cooked stew.

The palisade gates opened wide for her, as they had done so many times before. Chawnzmit came jogging out to meet her. His face glowed with happiness and relief at her presence—she knew he was glad to see that their friendship was not irredeemably broken. But she noted that he wore the hard, blue metal helmet, and his shirt of many interlinked metal rings gleamed over his accustomed wrappings of strong-smelling wool.

He took her hands in his own. It was a *tassantassa* gesture of gratitude and welcome, she knew—but she felt Matachanna and the other women stir in surprise. To the Real People, it was an intimate touch. Her face burned hot in the sun, and she dropped her eyes demurely from Chawnzmit's face.

"I'm so glad you've returned," he said hesitantly. "Your father . . ."

"He was very angry at your deception. He will not tolerate such a display of disobedience again."

Chawnzmit was quiet for a moment. Gently, she freed her hands from his grip. At last he said, "I understand."

Pocahontas brightened. "But Powhatan is also very generous. He has allowed me to bring you something better than dried corn and fish. My sisters and I will show you how to plant a garden and how to tend it, so that when *taquitock* comes, you will not be hungry."

The days that followed were sweet. The season of *cohattayough* settled over the land like warm, deep fur, coaxing blossoms from the trees and birds from their nests. The air filled with the perfume of promise, a lush, rich, rounded scent, hinting at the seed beneath the soil, humming softly of growth yet to come. The days lengthened. Sunsets lingered, filling the forest with the long, sideways slant of golden light that heralded a mild night and a warm morning. In the beam and glitter of those fire-orange shafts, newborn tribes of insects danced and shimmered.

Never before had Pocahontas taken such joy in work. She bent her back to the task of clearing a great swath of land beyond the palisade, working alongside the rest of the women with songs and rhymes quick on her lips. They chanted and swung their arms to their own concerted rhythms. "Now we cut and now we clear," left hand gathering the tufts of high grasses; "planting time is almost here," right arm sweeping with the antler knife. The vegetation came loose to the striding cadence, pull and cut, tear and toss: "Beans to plant and corn to grow," the knife cleaving through stout stalks of brush, "secrets only women know!" Stark earth showing bare and startled in the sun.

The men of the fort made shorter work of the nearby trees than the Real People could have done. The women would have built carefully tended fires around the trunks of oaks and chestnuts, corralling and directing the heat with dark-colored mats until the trunks were heavily charred. The char would have been chipped away with bone chisels, and then the process repeated until the trunk was thin enough that the tree finally toppled and was hauled away to become a dugout canoe, a process of more tedious burning and chipping.

But the *tassantassas* merely hacked away with their axes, sending chips of sweet-smelling wood flying, crying out a warning as the trees groaned and cracked and then rushed toward the earth with a jarring shudder and a roar of shivering leaves. The white men cleared the garden space in less than a quarter of the time a proper char-and-chip might take, and the women eyed the blue metal and the sharp beaks of *tassantassa* axes with sly deliberation.

Under the watchful eyes of the warrior guards, the women led the *tassantassas* into the field and showed them how to mound the earth to receive the seeds, how to plant corn and beans side by side so the strong cornstalk might provide a friendly place for the bean to twine and climb in its quest for brighter sun. They taught them how to space squash seeds, so that when the plants sprouted, their broad, glossy leaves would cover the earth and keep the soil damp and soft throughout the whole of the garden.

By day they planted and laughed with the *tassantassa* men. By night, the white men built up their communal fire and shared corn cakes and fish stew. The women danced and sang, spinning in the fresh *cohattayough* air. The white men clapped their hands as the Real Women danced, and now and then one would call out his appreciation to this dancer or that, cupping hands around a wooly beard to shout, "My lady!"

When they had danced their fill, the women retired to the longhouse they had built at the garden's edge. It was a makeshift thing, the saplings that held up its arch rather flimsy and its sides covered with soft woven mats rather than sturdy birch-bark strips. The bedsteads were lumpy and hard, the sleeping mats so old that they would not grow soft no matter how they were beaten. Yet for Pocahontas, it was a place of joy and peace. There she fell asleep each night with a deep current of satisfaction thrumming along her tired muscles, tugging her into happy dreams. Her work with the *tassantassas* was good. They had shown no tendency to deceive since she had arrived to clear the land. The words she had spoken to her father had been true, after all: once they knew they would never again starve, the English would be good allies and honorable subjects. Chawnzmit—who was, like she, no gentleman—would be her true friend once more. She would be free again to talk and laugh with him, the only being in all the world who understood what it was like to dream, to yearn for something more than the dull life of the lowly born.

A week after their arrival, Pocahontas sat in the soft new summer grass on the edge of the *tassantassas'* garden. She, Matachanna, and Nonoma were sorting seed beans into small baskets, which the women would soon tote throughout the garden, driving the seeds into the growing mounds with their sharp hardwood digging sticks. The seeds were dry in her hands, drinking the moisture from her skin. They made a soothing music as they spilled from dusty palms.

"So," Pocahontas said casually, "what do you think of my *tassantassas*?"

"They're our brother Naukaquawis's *tassantassas*, not yours," Nonoma said. But there was no sting of scorn in her voice. Time had worn away the rough edges where Nonoma and Pocahontas clashed and caught. Now they joked and teased one another as if they had grown up in the same *yehakin*. Pocahontas pulled an ugly face, showing Nonoma her tongue, and they giggled together.

"I think they're strange," Matachanna said. "They're pleasant enough, but there is something about them I don't entirely trust."

Pocahontas looked at her over their basket of seeds, brows cocked quizzically.

"I don't know what it is, exactly," Matachanna went on. "But look at them—how oddly helpless they are, and yet how strong. Their axes can fell eight trees in a single day, but they can't puzzle out how to dry fish for the winter."

"It's only because they have no women with them," Pocahontas said practically. "It's always women who do the food work."

"And that is the strangest of all," Matachanna said. "Why would they make a town here without any women? I'd understand them more if they were only passing through, but here they are, a year after their arrival, with a wall and houses built, and those strange, huge boats waiting in the river. But no women at all—not a single one. They are the *oddest* men I've ever seen."

"No wonder they starved in the wintertime," Nonoma said. "Have you ever seen a man bake his own bread or cook his own stew? Okeus! Did they think corn cakes would fall on them from the sky?"

"It's not only the question of food that's strange," Matachanna said. "They have no women to garden or cook, but they also have no women for . . ." She trailed off, her face flushing red, and busied herself with the seeds as if she had not spoken her thoughts aloud.

"Look how she blushes," Pocahontas whispered to Nonoma. "She's thinking of Utta-ma-tomakkin."

Matachanna glared at her. "Laugh all you like, Amonute, but you know it's true. What do the men do for pleasure, if there aren't any women in their town?"

Pocahontas shrugged. "I never thought about it."

"Nor I," Nonoma admitted. "Maybe . . . maybe they lie with each other?"

"Well, they must," Matachanna said, matter-of-fact, tossing a handful of beans into the nearest basket. But her face was still bright with embarrassment. "Have you ever known a man to go long without visiting some woman's bed? Of course not! It's as necessary as breathing for them."

Pocahontas lowered her voice, made it as dark as smoke. "Has Utta-ma-tomakkin told you all about these things? The terrible, driving needs of men?"

Matachanna flung a handful of beans into Pocahontas's face; Nonoma shrieked with laughter.

"I am not the only one who thinks your *tassantassas* are strange," Matachanna said. All trace of blush faded from her face. She was suddenly quite serious. "Our men also talk about their odd ways. I've overheard. The *tassantassas* have curious ideas about gift giving. They won't give up a knife or an axe for anything—not even in trade. Not any longer, that is—they used to trade their tools, or so I've heard. Now they won't part with them, even for the food they so desperately need. Oh, they'll give copper, anything made of copper, and plenty of beads. And sometimes that strange-smelling cloth they wear. But the blue metal . . ."

"They call it *steel*," Pocahontas interjected.

"*Steel.* They will not part with steel even as a gift, as an offering of thanks. Here we are, building a garden for them, teaching them how to plant and grow, and they will not give up a single piece of their precious steel."

"Rude," Nonoma agreed. Then she snickered. "Yet they are too dull to notice when the men take their steel anyway."

Pocahontas tensed. She sat up very straight. "*Take* their steel? What do you mean?"

"The men have made a game of it. They wait until a *tassantassa* is working with one of his tools. Then they walk up and talk to him, engage him in trade. While he is distracted with his tools lying on the ground, the man picks up a tool with his toes. Or sometimes he takes it with his hands, if he can. It is better to take it with the hands, braver. The other men account him better at the game if he can snatch up a piece of steel by hand. But the toes will do. The *tassantassas* don't notice at all."

The white men had unusual customs, peculiar ideas about what was polite and what was rude—that could not be denied. But Pocahontas was quite certain the *tassantassas* did know that their steel was being taken. Faced with the intimidating boldness of a

Real Man, painted in his fearsome colors and puffed by his natural haughtiness, most Englishmen would rather keep silent about such ostentatious "gifting." Yet to the English, the loss of their steel tools was not gifting, but theft. A worm of anxiety burrowed into her gut. How long had the game been played? The *tassantassas* were surely at the limits of the stiff, silent, straight-faced endurance, which they called politeness. While the women danced and sang and took joy in their work, the men—both white and Real—must be hot as stewpots on the verge of boiling over.

The pot did boil over two days later. Pocahontas and her sisters were making their way into the fort, each carrying a bundle of new-made digging sticks for the *tassantassas'* own use. As they passed through the open gate, bare feet sinking into the thick, cool mud of Jamestown, they heard shouting from the direction of the communal fire. Pocahontas tossed her digging sticks in a careless heap against the palisade wall and ran.

A knot of white men surged, pawing at one another like quarreling dogs, their voices clamoring together so that she could make out none of their words. But no—she saw as she sprinted forward that they were not fighting each other. They were shoving and jostling so that each man might gain a better view of whatever held their attention near the fire. Pocahontas squeezed among them, gasping as she was pressed and shoved this way and that. The rank odor of so many white men gagged her. She heard Matachanna call her name fearfully from back among the cabins. *At least she and Nonoma are at a distance*, she thought, and sent up a prayer for their safety even as her spirit chattered in fear for her own life.

She made her way to the front of the crowd, stumbling as she burst forth from the press of wool-covered, steel-clad bodies. She froze and stared in horror at the sight that greeted her.

Two large, burly *tassantassas* held two Real Men, pinioning their arms behind their bodies. It was Naukaquawis and his friend Mackinoe, a sly, grinning trickster who would certainly have taken to the game of liberating steel from the white men with his toes. Mackinoe may have invented the sport himself; he was fond of causing trouble, and was quick with a laugh and a fox-sharp smile whenever he was implicated. He was smiling now, his teeth bared easily in a smugly amused face, even as the big *tassantassa* who held him gave his arms a vicious jerk that straightened his back and arched his shoulders. Naukaquawis's face was only slightly more serious, with a small measure of chagrin beneath his amusement.

Chawnzmit and the dark-haired, snake-eyed man called President Ratcliffe emerged from the crowd a heartbeat after Pocahontas did. She looked desperately to her friend, but Chawnzmit's eyes were still and thoughtful beneath his thick, sand-yellow brows.

President Ratcliffe raised his voice. It was dry as bean dust; it made Pocahontas's limbs shiver. "What's going on here? What is the meaning of this?"

The big man who held Mackinoe replied. "Caught these two trying to lift our knives. And an axe. Right in front of our faces, you know the way the savages do."

"Aye, we've lost enough steel to them already," said Naukaquawis's captor. "Time we ceased to turn a blind eye to their thieving."

A whoop split the air. Two Real Men had scrambled onto one of Jamestown's watchtowers; they nocked arrows to their bowstrings, aimed among the *tassantassa* crowd. Chawnzmit's hand fell to the butt of his weapon. Giddy, her spirit lost in a mist of fear, Pocahontas repeated the word for that terrible piece of steel over and over in her mind. *Snaphaunce . . . gun . . . gun.*

Naukaquawis's sharp, commanding voice leaped above the angry commotion of the crowd. "Hold your arrows! Do not shoot a single *tassantassa*. Leave us be. We'll get out of this ourselves. Do you think we can't?"

The bowmen lowered their weapons. Chawnzmit eyed Naukaquawis, his stare hard with suspicion, but his hand left his gun. In the momentary silence that followed Naukaquawis's words, Pocahontas heard her sisters' distant sobbing.

Pocahontas staggered forward. She made a bow to Chawnzmit and Ratcliffe—she knew the English appreciated such things, knew it was a gesture of great respect. "Chawnzmit, may I speak with you?"

He took a step toward her, but Ratcliffe held out a hand. "No, Smith. The men are right; we've had enough of the savages' thievery. It's not right that they should come to our fort and mock us to our very faces."

"They don't see it as thievery," Chawnzmit said. His voice was laden with derision. "And if you had listened to me and allowed me to give them gifts, it never would have come to this."

"I will not be chided, Smith. Watch yourself."

Chawnzmit's face reddened. "You sent me out to learn of the naturals' ways. You said yourself we needed their knowledge, their skills, to survive. Yet when I tell you they expect gifts, you disregard me. Why waste my efforts? Why waste the lives of good men—George Classen, Jehu Robinson, Thomas Emry?"

"Do not speak those names to me. Were it not for you, all three of those good men would still be alive."

"You're every bit as bad as Wingfield. Arrogant, ignorant, too impressed by half with your own high birth." Chawnzmit spat into the mud. The crowd of *tassantassas* gasped and murmured like a distant storm.

Pocahontas felt rage buffeting her from all directions, falling on her like physical blows from Chawnzmit and Ratcliffe, from the crowd of white men, from Naukaquawis and his warriors. *I must stop this somehow—now, before they kill one another, and me, too. Oh, Okeus! Defend me!*

She bowed again, low, and clasped her hands in a show of desperate entreaty, a gesture she hoped the white men understood. "Please, allow me to . . ."

A rough hand took her by the chin and lifted her upright. For one wild heartbeat she thought it was Chawnzmit who handled her so unkindly, and her stomach curdled with fear and sorrow. But it was Ratcliffe who stared down into her face, Ratcliffe's pale cheeks marked by angry blooms of red. The crowd of *tassantassas* gasped. They did not approve of their princess being used so coarsely. She heard Naukaquawis issue a warning hiss.

"I will allow you to do only one thing," he said, his voice low and dark, calm with the weight of his fury. "Go back to your father, little princess, and tell him what we have done. Let mighty Powhatan see that England will not be so crudely treated."

Her eyes slid away from his face, sought out her friend Chawnzmit. She pleaded silently for him to intervene. He glanced toward Naukaquawis, then back to her. Something shadowed his blue eyes, regret or sadness, or perhaps hard determination—she could not be sure. But when he turned away from her, the pain was greater than the pain of Ratcliffe's steely grip. The president released her with a jerk; she stumbled and clutched a hand to her bruised face. Tears blurred her vision. "Chawnzmit," she called, but he did not look back at her as he walked away.

She paced all night on the bank of the river, eyes blinded by hot tears. Her spirit cried out like a wounded beast, inarticulate and wracked with pain. Again and again she saw Chawnzmit, watching her struggle in Ratcliffe's grip, and then turning deliberately away. She had defended him to her father, had fought to help him and his people—and he had shown himself to be no true friend. She wore a track in the underbrush, her restless feet beating at vegetation silvered by moonlight, her unfeeling fingers breaking off twigs and shredding leaves as she moved in her unceasing distress. The only person who had truly understood her—the one who was like she was, low blood, common, but dreaming of more, knowing she deserved more . . .

With a pain that cramped like hunger, she felt Matachanna's old words fall heavy into the pit of her spirit. They dropped like chestnuts into a deep basket, round and cold and hard. *As far as I'm concerned, you don't have so many friends to spare.* Matachanna was right. If Chawnzmit was not her friend, then no one was. Oh, how it burned to admit it, how sour was the knowledge in her mouth!

She walked up to her calves in the river. The cold lanced into her flesh; she stood still and welcomed it. The harsh bite of cold water chased away the dull ache in her chest, suffusing her body with a shivering, sharp awareness. Night insects buzzed in the grasses. A hunting owl called once and was silent.

Into the momentary peace, Matachanna spoke again. *The truth is, you are selfish and ungrateful.*

Pocahontas bent her knees and dashed her hands against the surface of the river. A glittering arc of spray curved into the night, pattering back into the water. The words gripped her spirit as hard as Ratcliffe's fingers had held her jaw, yet she still resisted the truth. Her dream was too grand, too important. Her desire for influence, to be the focus of all eyes, could not be abated by something as simple as truth. She cherished her dream every bit as much as Powhatan clung to his dream of guns and conquest.

Powhatan. If I tell him exactly what happened today, it will all be over. He won't risk Naukaquawis's safety. Chawnzmit might be no friend to her, but she was still the master of the English tongue, still the best resource the Real People had for dealing with the fort. Her skill with the *tassantassas'* language was the one lever she could still use to move her father. Water lapped around her legs, raising the tiny hairs of her body. *I have a very small and frail arm to draw such a mighty bow.* She wrapped her arms around herself.

She was nothing but a little fawn, thin and fragile as a baby clam's shell. *Am I equal to this task? Can I bend Powhatan—the whole of Tsenacomoco—to my will? I will not give up so easily. I will not walk away, as Chawnzmit walked away.*

Her teeth chattered.

Dawn stole through the forest, leaching the deep blues and violets from the spaces between trees, replacing them with a pale gray, the gentle sheen of new-strung pearls. Birds began to wake in the branches. Their tentative morning songs stirred the air as a paddle stirs weeds in shallow water with a languid, dancing slowness. Pocahontas splashed back onto dry land. Her legs were numb from the cold; she stamped and shook them, rubbing her hands vigorously over her body to warm her skin.

As the sun crept above the horizon, she formed her plan, turning it over and over in her mind like a woman working red clay into a pot. It was a good plan. Like a good pot, it would hold and withstand the heat of her father's hottest fire. She made her way back through the wakening wood. The women's temporary shelter loomed into view, the arch of its roof painted with a bright-yellow slash of morning light. The door flap lifted, and a woman ducked out, straightened, and flicked her apron to remove some speck of dirt.

The spirits are good to me. It was just the woman she needed.

"Anawanuske," she called.

The woman paused midstretch and glanced, startled, toward Pocahontas. Anawanuske was a new bride of Powhatan, having arrived in the capital of Werowocomoco only a few months before. She had seen perhaps sixteen winters, but in spite of her youth she was not an especially pretty woman. One of her eyes drifted away from whatever she looked at, and her chin was too small. But she was very kind, and had a wicked humor with a wit nearly as sharp as Pocahontas's own.

But of far greater value than her face, Anawanuske was the eldest daughter of Wowinchopunck, *werowance* of the Paspaheghs. Wowinchopunck remained embittered over Powhatan's too-soft treatment of the white men, and some whispered that the Paspahegh were prepared to split from the union of tribes and stand on their own against the *tassantassas*—and to stand against the entirety of Powhatan's confederacy.

Powhatan had wasted no time in marrying Wowinchopunck's daughter as soon as she was ripe for a husband. Any child Anawanuske produced might have weak eyes, but her offspring, sired by the *mamanatowick*, would do much to bind the Paspahegh more tightly to Powhatan. She was a woman of value—a woman to whom her father would listen.

When Pocahontas waved urgently for the woman to join her on the edge of the clearing, Anawanuske glanced around the garden and peered into the forest, searching for the cause of Pocahontas's urgency. Seeing nothing, she shrugged and left the yard of the women's house.

Pocahontas greeted her with hand to heart. *"Wingapoh."*

"What is it, Amonute?"

"I have a task for you. I need you to carry a very important message to your father."

"Wowinchopunck? Why?"

"Paspahegh is the closest town. We need their aid. You have heard, haven't you, that the *tassantassas* captured some of our men?"

"Yes, of course. As far as I care, they may keep Mackinoe. I never liked him—always grinning and licking his lips like a dog. But Naukaquawis . . ."

"Exactly."

"Powhatan will be furious."

"This is an opportunity for Paspahegh to regain Powhatan's esteem."

Paspahegh, of course, cared very little for Powhatan's esteem just now. Did Anawanuske know of her own father's anger? Pocahontas pressed her lips together and hoped, but a moment later, Anawanuske tilted her head. "How do you mean?" she said slowly.

"The white leader—the one they call President Ratcliffe . . ."

"Is he their leader?" Anawanuske asked, startled. "I thought it was Chawnzmit."

"Chawnzmit is a *tanx*. Ratcliffe is his *werowance*, and he told me to return to Werowocomoco and tell my father that they have captured his favorite son. He means to provoke Powhatan, to start a war. But wouldn't it be better if we returned to Werowocomoco with Naukaquawis? What if we returned bearing the message that Wowinchopunck has liberated Naukaquawis from the fort, and that the peace Powhatan has worked for is still intact? Imagine how my father—your husband—will celebrate. Paspahegh will be lauded as the bravest and best of all the tribes."

"And how exactly is Wowinchopunck to liberate Naukaquawis?"

Pocahontas had considered this already. "He mustn't kill anybody. He must do it without violence. But you have seen how eager the *tassantassas* are for food. It will be many weeks before the garden produces any corn or beans. If he offers a share of corn . . ."

"You know how terrible the summers have been, Amonute. For years our corn yields have been far short of what they should be. Wowinchopunck will say that Paspahegh has no corn to spare. And he will be right to say it! All the tribes send tribute to Powhatan, so you are used to seeing full stores at Werowocomoco. But it is not that way in the smaller towns, where we must pay our regular tributes to the *mamanatowick*. We have suffered through these dry, hot years."

"Fish, then—there are still plenty of fish running. Bring them many, many fish, and whatever bits of corn can be spared, and I know they will let Naukaquawis go. And that repulsive Mackinoe."

Anawanuske sighed. "I suppose it might work. I do want to see my mother and little sisters again. It's an excuse to visit them, even if only for a day."

Pocahontas hooked her finger with Anawanuske's, in friendship and gratitude. "Thank you. And remember: no violence. Your father must free Naukaquawis through peaceful means only."

"I'll remember."

Once she had seen Anawanuske off in the smallest and lightest canoe, Pocahontas stole into the women's longhouse and slept for a few fitful hours. Her dreams were shadowed by a strange, half-seen vision, a world of gray stone crowded with people, a sour smell that made her feel at once hopeless and thrilled. Her body jerked her out of the dreamworld. She lay beneath her wolfskin, mouth dry, staring up at the smoke hole in the roof. A ring of blue sky stared back at her, unblinking and thoughtful, like Chawnzmit's stare as Ratcliffe held her in his hard, angry fist.

Pocahontas slid from beneath the wolfskin. The air here was warm. Outside the longhouse it would be like a festival fireside, a *cohattayough* midday shimmering with heat visions and the movement of insects. A sheen of sweat dried and cooled her. She took deep breaths to steady her spirit, and smelled the familiar, homey scents of the longhouse: the forceful, warm odor of pine smoke; a whiff of bear grease and earthy mineral pigments; the green brightness of drying herbs; and the faint salty undercurrent of preserved fish. Comforting scents. And yet she felt no comfort. She drew deeper and deeper breaths, drinking the longhouse, savoring it like cool water on a scorching day. The more she breathed it in, the further from it her spirit receded. The sensation unsettled her, filling her with a desolate yearning, a tremor of unbearable loss.

She made her way to the door flap and stepped out into the full force of the midday sun.

She worked in silence in the hot field, stabbing her digging stick automatically into the mounds of earth so that Matachanna could follow behind and drop her seeds into the soil. No one spoke. The women were subdued and frightened, yet still they clung to the hope of the garden, praying that their gift would soften the *tassantassas'* hearts and set their men free.

Sweat ran down Pocahontas's skin, streaking the greasepaint she had applied to ward off the mosquitoes and biting flies. She longed for the evening chants, the call to leave off work for another day. She imagined that when the women finally made their way to the shoreline to bathe, she would wade deep into the river and sluice the day's worries from her skin. Her fears would fall from her body as leaves fall from autumn trees. They would drift in the current, clouds of yellow and red and mud black, and the river would carry them far, far away.

At last the evening chant was called, just as the rich odor of corn-and-fish stew began to waft from the longhouse. Pocahontas wedged her digging stick deep into a garden mound. Her hands were sore from the work. Blisters would form by tomorrow; she must ask Matachanna for her good salve.

As she joined the stream of women making their way toward the bathing spot, she noted movement on the river: the swift cut and pull of a lone paddle and the low glide of a dugout canoe. *Anawanuske!* Pocahontas broke from the line and ran to the low shelf of riverbank where the canoe would come to ground. But something was not right. The figure in the canoe was too broad through the shoulders, too square of jaw. It was a man. A Paspahegh shield hung over the near side of his vessel.

A terrible weight of failure, heavy and cold as a snowdrift, fell upon her as she watched the canoe beach. She felt footsteps on the path behind her and knew without turning that Kocoum was there. His silent presence was as familiar to her as her own thwarted dreams.

The Paspahegh man sprang from his canoe. A furrow marred the space between his brows; his face was dark with blood-angry *puccoon*. Pocahontas stared at him, unable to speak.

"You have a message from Paspahegh?" Kocoum said quietly.

The messenger jerked his chin upward in a curt, wordless acknowledgment.

Kocoum laid one hand on Pocahontas's shoulder. "You must give it to me, I suppose," he said. "Our *werowance* Naukaquawis is . . . inside the white men's fort."

"The message is for the white men. I am to tell it to the girl who speaks their tongue."

"This is the girl." Gently, Kocoum pushed her forward.

Pocahontas's chin trembled as she looked up at the warrior. Her spirit writhed, savaged by fearsome beasts: guilt, terror, and loss. Each one had terrible teeth, and talons as sharp as steel.

"You are to tell the *tassantassas* that we have taken two of them as our prisoners," the messenger said. "We caught them out hunting. They are ours now. We will keep them until they release the Real Men they hold. If Naukaquawis and the other are unharmed, then their friends will remain unharmed . . . more or less. But they shall not have them back until we have ours."

His duty discharged, the Paspahegh man turned abruptly and shoved his canoe back into the river.

Pocahontas stood on the riverbank, still as a deer bemused by torchlight. All her thoughts clamored at once, and over the strange ringing in her ears, mournful words repeated. She heard them in Matachanna's voice. *What have you done, Pocahontas? What have you done?*

Kocoum took her by the arm, but he did not handle her roughly. When he spoke his voice was as soothing as a man's ever could be. "Come, Amonute. We had best deliver the message to the fort. One foot in front of the other—that's the way. And after you have told the *tassantassas* what you must tell them, I will take you home. All of us are going home. The Okeus alone knows what will happen now, but we will all be safer at Werowocomoco."

Two days later, as Powhatan raged from his bedstead, his wives cowering around him, word reached Werowocomoco that the *tassantassas* had moved in retaliation. The white men had fallen on a Paspahegh village, setting fire to the houses and burning the precious dugout canoes that took so much labor and care to build.

The spirits could be thanked for one small mercy: no women or children had been harmed or captured. Only three men were lost, cut down by English guns, their bodies broken and burned and stinking of sulfur and blood. Thirteen men were taken as captives, joining Naukaquawis and Mackinoe in whatever nightmare prison the *tassantassas* had made for them.

The spirits were kind to spare so many lives, but the burning of the town left every heart in the *mamanatowick*'s capital despondent. It would take the Paspahegh women weeks to rebuild their homes, recover their food stores, and resurrect the crow towers and stockades of their gardens. And the dugouts—their destruction was a senseless waste, breathtaking in its vicious spite. Up and down the lanes of Werowocomoco, women keened in sympathetic sorrow and men kicked stones, slashing at the air with their war clubs and promising vengeance on the white men.

Pocahontas hid her face in the furs of her bed, listening in horror to the cries of anger and loss that echoed through the town. A ravenous creature seemed to gnaw at her heart, and its teeth were made of hard, cold guilt.

That evening she felt Matachanna's slight, warm weight sink onto the sleeping mat beside her. A tentative hand rested on her shoulder.

"Pocahontas, my sister."

She did not respond. It took all the effort her spirit could muster to breathe around the suffocating force of her shame. How could she hope to sit up and look into Matachanna's face?

"Please, Amonute." She pulled a corner of the wolfskin blanket away from Pocahontas's eyes. Matachanna's pretty face was long with concern. "There is something going on at Father's longhouse. Something I think you need to see for yourself."

"I can't. I don't want to."

Matachanna found her hand, buried in the wolf pelt. Warm fingers laced together; she squeezed. "I know you are fond of Chawnzmit. I think it's important that you witness all that is happening now. Please, come and see. Do this for me, Sister."

With dragging steps, Pocahontas allowed herself to be led through the lanes of Werowocomoco to her father's house. Even before Kocoum allowed them inside, with a sympathetic glance at Pocahontas's bed-creased face and guilt-ravaged eyes, they could hear men shouting inside. Pocahontas balked at the door flap. She knew, some whisper on the wind had told her, that the final thin sinew holding her dreams to her heart was about to be severed.

Many *werowances* from nearby tribes clustered around the heart fire, though more still were absent. It was a hasty meeting Powhatan had called. A peace pipe, still smoldering a thin wisp of tobacco smoke, lay forgotten beside the fire. The chiefs surged and boiled like a pot left too long in the coals.

Propped up on his accustomed high bedstead, Powhatan watched with a stiff air of offended honor while his chiefs argued below him. Behind the *mamanatowick*, in the deep shadow of his sleeping place, two or three young women crouched, ready to attend to any of his needs. One of them leaned forward to whisper something in the *mamanatowick*'s ear, and Pocahontas started, recognizing the wandering eye and small chin of Anawanuske. Her eyes were downcast, contrite. Anawanuske's own sense of guilt at the part she had played was palpable, and Pocahontas's misery redoubled, knowing that she had led another down the path of shame.

Seated just below Powhatan's tattooed knee, Opechancanough watched the discussion with keen black eyes. He turned his hard-carved face from one man to another, trying to discern their words among the fretful din of the longhouse, as if he considered each man's righteous anger in turn, and found this storm of bitterness to be as sweet as a *cohattayough* breeze. The discs of copper in his hair gleamed like night fires.

Powhatan raised a shaking hand for silence. "They have sixteen Real Men now. Three more have been taken by the *tassantassas*, men of Paspahegh. And it was a Paspahegh village that was put to the torch. I will hear Wowinchopunck speak first, as he has been the most wronged."

"All of you know the story in full already," said Wowinchopunck. His voice was harsh and low, tense with a fury he could barely control. "There is nothing to add, save that one man in particular led these outrageous attacks. All the *tassantassas* acted under his command, and all that was done to Paspahegh was done at his orders."

"Which man?" Chopoke demanded.

It was Opechancanough who answered, the words uncoiling like a snake at the thaw of spring. "Chawnzmit."

Pocahontas tightened her grip on Matachanna's hand.

"There is more proof of Chawnzmit's treachery," Opechancanough said. "This morning he released a prisoner from the fort. That man is here. He will tell you all how he was treated at the hands of our *brother*, the good *tanx-werowance* Chawnzmit."

From among the crowd of men, Mackinoe rose on trembling legs. For once he did not grin like a fox; his face was grave and pale. He blinked repeatedly at the firelight.

"Last night," Mackinoe said, "I was taken before Chawnzmit to be questioned."

There was nothing unusual in this; enemy tribes often captured and questioned one another. It was a point of pride to resist the flaying knives and the pain of lost fingers or toes in order to protect the secrets of one's tribe. If a man died in the questioning, then it was a brave and honorable death, especially if he did not cry out. This was a hazard all warriors accepted, part of the risk of being male.

But Chawnzmit did not go about his questioning in the usual way.

"The *tassantassas* laid me on the ground, tied my hands and feet to stakes in the mud," Mackinoe said. "Rather than using knives, rather than presenting the opportunity to resist my death, as any proper men would do, six of them simply pointed their guns, the long ones they call *musket*, at my exposed body."

He shuddered, recalling the terror of the moment, and in spite of her personal misery, Pocahontas welled with sympathy for Mackinoe. The experience must have been horrific if its memory caused him to tremble before the eyes of the chiefs. *Chawnzmit could not have done this. No—my friend was always kind to me.* Until he turned away, and left her bruised in the clutch of President Ratcliffe.

"And then what happened?" Opechancanough prompted.

Mackinoe hung his head. "I told them what I knew."

The men raised their voices. Opechancanough let the sound swell for a moment, and then drew it in again with a smooth wave of one hand.

"I told them," Mackinoe stumbled on, "that three tribes have been plotting an attack. That Paspahegh planned to ally with Chickahominy . . . and with my own tribe, Pamunkey."

Powhatan grunted once, a hoarse, startled sound, the sound a buck makes when the arrow punches home. The *mamanatowick* turned wounded eyes on his brother. "You, Opechancanough? You plotted against the fort, knowing my designs?"

Opechancanough made no answer, but stared steadily back into the old chief's eyes.

"When they had that confession from me," Mackinoe said, shame-faced, "Chawnzmit took the rest of our men by groups off to various parts of the fort. And we heard gunfire, were led to believe that each group we could not see was being put to a dishonorable death, and the same would befall us unless we also told what we knew. In this way, through this deception, Chawnzmit confirmed the truth of the plot. And when all our warriors had confessed, we were reunited, unharmed."

Powhatan's mouth worked soundlessly for a moment, chewing on his fury and his feebleness. His eyes roved the shadows of the longhouse. They were eyes nearly blanked by confusion and despair, but when they fell upon Pocahontas's face, their dark stare sharpened, and a blaze kindled in their depths.

"Amonute," Powhatan boomed. "Come here."

She gasped and clung to Matachanna's hand. She wanted to flee, run from the great house and never return, leave Werowocomoco altogether—but the *mamanatowick*'s command could not be disobeyed. She forced her fingers to uncurl from Matachanna's. Her feet dragged as she made her slow, halting way into the firelight and stood with her head dropped in fear and shame.

"The alliance with the *tassantassas* is well and truly broken," Powhatan declared. The gathered *werowances* murmured their approval. "Chawnzmit is no brother to any Real Person—not even to you, Amonute, who saved him from death. But you will return to the fort one final time. You will go and beg for your brother's freedom. For I will have Naukaquawis back at all costs. Am I understood?"

Her eyes crept up the platform to her father's face. It was weathered as an old moccasin, creased by uncountable lines, sagging at the jowls. She saw again the ancient wood buffalo retreating into the forest, dropping blood on the trail where his own hooves trampled it among memories of his former glory. A wave of sadness struck her, cresting over her head and pulling her beneath a dark and tumbling current. She thought she might be swept from her feet, might fall among the painted bodies of the *werowances*, taut with their hunger for war. Yet some miraculous intervention of the spirits kept her standing.

She looked away from her father's face and found the stern, red-painted brow and burning black eyes of her uncle.

"I understand," she said to Opechancanough.

Pocahontas stared intently at the great wooden palisade of Jamestown, at its gate on hinges that screamed like birds, the strange peak-roofed houses, even the thick, sucking mud of the common area. She would impress every detail, every puddle and knothole, into her memory and heart. This was the final moment of her ambition; all her hopes, all her most cherished wishes would culminate this day in disappointment and stinging shame.

With Kocoum at her side, she moved through the crowd of Englishmen. She clutched haughty dignity about her like a worn and thin-patched cloak. The *tassantassas* still parted for her, still called her princess. They still bowed as she passed, mindful of all the good she had done them, all the kindness she had shown. And yet these men had tormented her people, threatened honest warriors with an undignified death, used their fear to shame and manipulate them. These men had burned a village, made a ruin of precious canoes. *Chawnzmit did it—all done at his command.* She could not deny the truth any longer, not even within her own heart. But where sorrow had once dwelt, there remained only resolve.

At the communal fire she found Chawnzmit waiting. He removed his stiff wool hat at her approach—another strange sign of English respect—and in the hesitant rigidity of his body, in the downcast blue eyes that never quite met her own, she read his regret and self-loathing as plainly as if he had shouted a confession into her ear. He shuffled his feet, but did not speak.

She, too, lost all words to an unseen thief. While the *tassantassas* murmured around them, she watched Chawnzmit's thick, rough hands twist the brim of his hat. At last she said, "You will ruin your hat if you keep worrying at it."

More footsteps—the shuffle of many men walking. She glanced up just long enough to see the line of captives; the Real Men tied in a line by their hands, with Naukaquawis at its head. She quickly dropped her eyes again, refusing to see them in their weakness and shame. She could at least spare them the dishonor of being seen by a low-blood girl-child in their deplorable captivity. She owed them at least that, after having led them all into this terrible affair.

"Powhatan has sent his favorite daughter," she said, choking on the words, "to seek the freedom of these warriors. The *mamanatowick* would have peace with you again, Chawnzmit." It was not true—the old bull was in no state to enforce a peace even if he wanted one—but she could say no other words, not if she wanted to see Naukaquawis freed.

"Aye, I suspected that was why you'd come."

She dared to steal a glance at Chawnzmit's face. He looked stunned beneath his thick yellow hair, as if he, too, sensed the end of their friendship but could see no way to halt what he had begun.

"May I speak to you alone?" she said.

Kocoum was reluctant to allow them privacy, but at last agreed to remain out of earshot but within bowshot, provided Chawnzmit turned his snaphaunce over to one of his fellow Englishmen. Pocahontas led the white man who was once her brother outside the walls of Jamestown. They walked together in silence, deep into the garden. The first spindly stalks of corn had just begun to sprout. She trailed her fingers along the edges of leaves, the new greenery whispering beneath her hands. Squash vines had begun to reach tendrils along the bare ground, their dark leaves still folded in tight buds. Weeds had already begun to sprout, and there was no sign that the white men had attempted to pull them.

Pocahontas looked back toward the fort. A few *tassantassas* gazed curiously from the watchtower, where the sun glimmered on their steel helmets. Kocoum stalked along the edge of the field, vigilant, bow half-raised with an arrow in his free hand. Pocahontas smiled lightly at the sight of him; she was incongruously cheered by his presence.

Chawnzmit took the smile for himself. "It is good to see you again, Pocahontas."

She tossed her head. Matachanna had laced white feathers into her braid for good luck and strength, and they made a slicing sound in the air. The sound filled her with a curious kind of magic, a tiny wellspring of eagle fierceness. "How did our friendship go so wrong, Chawnzmit? You were my brother, and now you have done"—she waved her hand toward the fort, unable to find adequate words in her language or in his—"this."

Chawnzmit lowered his gaze. He stared at the weeds for a long moment, as if he might find some acceptable answer there. At last he said, his voice halting and low, "I respect you, Pocahontas. God knows I do. I respect you and your people alike. But I mean for my people to survive. Our survival must be my highest concern. Surely you can see that."

Survival—wasn't that why they had given the *tassantassas* this very garden? And even this gift they could not tend properly, nor did they show any gratitude for it. "I am wounded, Chawnzmit, that you cannot treat me or the Real People with greater kindness. I have shown you such goodness, been such a useful sister to you. And yet . . ."

"You are more than useful to me, Pocahontas." He spoke with such feeling that she stepped back a pace, startled by his sudden passion. He reached out a hand, but it closed on empty air. "In truth, you have been my only happiness here, in this miserable land. I have delighted in you, my little sister."

"Then why? You have been terribly cruel to us, Chawnzmit. You must return to loving me again, loving *us* again as a good friend, as a brother. We must have no more of these insults, burning houses, destroying canoes, tormenting men, terrorizing women . . . what good does it do?"

A shroud of pain fell over his face, distorting his mouth with a pure and unfettered sorrow. "Oh, child," he said, "would that my people could love yours. Don't you see? The alternative to . . . to what I do . . . terrorizing women and children . . . is not love, but war."

She shook her head, a wordless denial.

"It's true, Pocahontas." His hand cupped her chin. She flinched, remembering Ratcliffe's grip, but Chawnzmit's touch was gentle, warm with compassion. "Child—beloved sister. Your uncle Opechancanough, and more men—Wowinchopunck, others— they plot against us, even if your father does not. Opechancanough does not love us. Don't you think I know it? Don't you think I see? He will find ways to destroy us, sooner or later, and he will not stop until all my kind are dead."

She could say nothing. It was true; she had seen it in her father's longhouse. And there was more that Chawnzmit might not yet know: Powhatan would not be Powhatan for much longer. He had at most a handful of years before death claimed him, or his weakness could no longer be concealed. When that day came, Opechancanough would take up the mantle of *mamanatowick*, and any small protection the *tassantassas* had enjoyed under the old Chief of Chiefs would vanish. She could all but see the blood glistening on Opechancanough's horns.

"I do not like it, any more than you do," he said. "But if I cannot strike fear into Opechancanough's heart now, my people will never be safe."

"Opechancanough is not an easy man to frighten."

"I know," Chawnzmit whispered. "That is why I must do as I do."

"Is there no other way? Our people traded once peacefully. Perhaps we can again."

"Perhaps. I will not give up hope of it. I swear that to you. But you must understand, Pocahontas: I will do anything I must to ensure that my people survive. If your father were standing where I now stand, the leader of strangers in a foreign land, he would do the same. Because he is a good man, and wise."

She turned away. Tears tracked hot down her cheeks and fell like warm rain on her lip. She licked them away, salty as ash stick.

"Because I will do as I must," Chawnzmit said, "it is not safe for you here. Not anymore." He caught up her hand, holding it tightly as Matachanna so often did. "Believe me when I say that you have been the truest and most welcome friend I have had in many a year. You are a good girl, bright and honest. You do credit to your father—to all your people."

"And you, Chawnzmit. You taught me many things. I also do credit to you."

He smiled ruefully. "I cannot agree with you there." He released her hand, all but the first finger, which he hooked with his own. "But I promise you, once my people are secure, I shall strive to win your friendship once again. I shall strive to be worthy of you, Princess."

In spite of the pain swelling in her heart, she laughed. "I am not a princess. Remember?"

"You are, and a lady, in every sense of the word. One day you will see it. One day all the world will see it."

They made their way back to the fort. Kocoum fell dutifully in step beside her, wary as a lone wolf. She turned to him with a reassuring smile. "It will be well," she whispered, but Kocoum squinted past her shoulder at Chawnzmit, who restored his well-crushed hat to his head.

Back in the presence of Naukaquawis and his fellow prisoners, Pocahontas kept her eyes on the ground, but she felt them shift expectantly as she and Chawnzmit approached.

"Ratcliffe," Chawnzmit called into the crowd. "Bring the naturals' bows and knives. The princess has moved my heart with her pleas for mercy. I am returning the prisoners to her tender and worthy care."

As the bonds were cut from the warriors' hands one by one, Chawnzmit bent his head close to Pocahontas's ear. "You must not return, Princess. I cannot guarantee your safety—cannot say with honesty that you would not be taken a prisoner, too, and used to sway your father to English whims. Promise me you will stay well away from Jamestown."

Kocoum paced a vigilant circle around them while she considered his words for a long moment. At last she turned to him with a hand pressed to her heart, and said only, "*Wingapoh*, Chawnzmit."

SMITH

September 1608

When the *Susan Constant* landed for the third time at Jamestown, nosing against the slow, deep currents of the James River, the men stood aside and allowed John Smith the honor of being the first to greet Captain Newport. Of course, they were not without their muttered curses or hateful looks. There were still many among the colony who had little love for Smith. They had not forgotten his coarse tongue, his arguments, or the overconfident mien, so unexpected in a common man. It was that natural swagger which had caused Edward-Maria Wingfield to declare Smith mutinous, and none of the luster had scuffed away from Smith's boldness. If anything, the events of that fearfully hot and dry summer had polished his arrogance to a slick, high sheen.

Throughout the long months of the season, Smith had maintained his assertive stand against the naturals, unwilling to yield a foot of ground lest Opechancanough perceive a chink in English armor, the weakness for which the cunning warrior was ever vigilant. It soon became clear that no naturals—not even armed men— would approach the fort to trade. The garden built by Pocahontas and her women scarcely produced three bushels of corn and beans at the season's first harvest, and whatever they did put by was quickly half-eaten by the rats that had accompanied them from

England. Jamestown felt the specter of winter privation loom once more, an oppressive, all-penetrating fear that seemed to tower over the palisade walls like a gallows. Smith had taken to the shallop and visited every Indian village within a few days' trek, extracting trade goods by any means necessary.

Most of the time, the tribes were willing enough to part with some of their stores; copper and beads—and, when they were especially tight-fisted, the occasional steel blade—were of even greater value now that Chief Powhatan had forbidden his subjects to visit Jamestown. Smith, however, did not fail to note the tight-eyed, wary glances of those men who agreed to sink into the customary trading crouch. Powhatan had most certainly declared harsh penalties for those caught giving food to the English. *He thinks to starve us out*, Smith had confided to Matthew Scrivener one day, *but by God, I will not be starved again.*

When villages flatly refused him, or fired arrows at his shallop to drive him away, Smith retaliated with arrows of his own: arrows dipped in fire. Their canoes, he had learned, were especially vulnerable. A single dugout took many weeks to create, and represented the concerted labors of several women and men. Assaults on canoes yielded the fastest results, although the threat of capturing and enslaving women or children was useful with especially adamant tribes. When the naturals perceived that they had no strength to refuse, with guns and fire arrows trained on their people and their shelters, their women would lift the covers to their secret stores—and weeping, speaking in fear of the dry summer, the poor harvest to come, the children who would go hungry through the bitter winter, they would yield baskets of preserved food to the English.

Smith could have hated himself for those moments, for the weeping women and the hungry little ones, but for Opechancanough, who was always there, stalking his thoughts, silent and malevolent as a cougar in the woods.

In spite of his success at securing food, a large faction of the colonists still despised him. For most, it was the same oft-sung melody: John Smith was no gentleman, and had no business as a leader of men. For others, it was the memory of George Classen's grisly death. For still others, it was simply Smith himself: his brashness, his haughtiness, his pervasive certainty that he was *right*, always so blasted right.

But I am *right*, he thought sourly, watching the men give way before him, some of them spitting into the mud as he passed. *I am right to do as I do.*

The sailors secured the *Susan Constant* against the flimsy dock, but Smith saw nothing of the ship, nothing of the men. He saw only his memories of Indian women—the poor women, faces tear-stained, crying for their lost stores, weeping for the extra labor of digging *tuckahoe* roots from hard winter ground; their babes with empty bellies in the long, cold nights. Smith had done this to them. He had taken their final winter stores and left them destitute, because he must—because he would not see the English starve.

For all those colonists who despised him, there were some who loved him. Not only had Smith found a way to feed the hungry mouths of Jamestown, but he had rid the fort of a curse that was nearly as bad as starvation.

Early in the summer, on returning from a trading expedition with the shallop brimming with corn and oysters, Smith had found the fort practically empty. The sounds of hammers and saws echoed through the wood, and the scruffy ship's boys, small and bony as the corpses of birds, informed him in an excited clamor that President Ratcliffe had gone mad.

"Mad?"

"Aye, he's taken to the woods, sir, told all the men to build him a palace, sir!"

"They've been at it for days. Ratcliffe's orders!"

"No one's been hunting, no fishing . . . not that they're any good at fishing, sir."

"Only there's no food, John Smith! Did you bring food from the savages?"

"You mustn't call them savages, lad." *Savage* implied an animallike simplicity, a childish innocence, an ignorance of sophisticated ways. Opechancanough lacked nothing of sophistication, and although the girl, Pocahontas, might be innocent, she was brighter than a dozen Wingfields and half a brace of Ratcliffes.

Smith handed out strings of dried oysters among the boys and they wore them looped around their necks like beads, each boy chewing and sucking on the end of his fine prize. They led him through the forest to Ratcliffe's palace.

A gentleman to the end, Ratcliffe sat in quiet dignity upon a rough-hewn stool, watching as the men of the fort labored over boards and beams, erecting the frame of a very large and very fine house in the middle of nowhere. Smith had stood silent among the milling boys, watching the men scuttle about their useless task, hunched, eyes shifting and downcast like whipped dogs. When one of them caught sight of Smith, he had thrown down his plane. *John Smith, thank God. Do something.*

He had done something indeed. Ratcliffe blustered and roared, and those flat, unfeeling eyes had filled finally with something— seething hate at the sight of Smith, come to put an end to the gentleman's lofty palace. A fist to the jaw had silenced him, and Smith had marched the stuttering, raving president back to Jamestown in time to bundle him onto the *Susan Constant* before it cast off for England.

The ship had borne a load of ordinary dirt, useless ballast that some of the men, Ratcliffe especially, insisted contained flecks of gold, and would make all the shareholders of the Virginia Company wealthy beyond imagining. Smith was only grateful that the *Susan*

Constant would return again, with its too-small hold packed with oats and barley. He had prayed it would arrive before winter set in.

"What would we do without you?" Scrivener had said when the door of the ship's cabin closed on Ratcliffe's indignant shouts.

"You might have thought of hitting him yourself."

"But that was mutiny, you know."

"Hang me, then," Smith chuckled. "It wouldn't be the first time."

Now, in the pale sun of late September, the *Susan Constant* had returned, and Smith shook Captain Newport's one remaining hand at the foot of the dock. No one had declared Smith president—not formally. But a general sense of inevitability had fallen over the colony. It was clear to all that John Smith's first concern was for Jamestown, not for himself, and that alone set him apart from the presidents who had come before. It was good enough for now. *Good enough, until a fresh gentleman comes along.*

A line of new men filed up the dock, wide-eyed at the sight of the palisade and its watchtowers, at the pervasive dark mass of the forest pressing in on Jamestown. Amused, Smith watched them stagger and stare. *Did I ever look so fresh and fearful?*

Newport tugged at the sleeve pinned over the stump of his missing arm. "I've brought plenty of food, Smith: grain, oil, flour, some salt pork."

"I am glad to hear it."

"Let us watch our fires this time, eh?" He laughed, a rhythmic rasp like a saw pulled slow through timber.

"And the bushels of earth—what came of those?"

Newport grunted sourly. "Nothing. Not a blasted thing. The king put all the men he had to analyzing the samples: scholars, chemists, even alchemists. The bits that shone were . . . something else. I cannot recall the name now."

"Not gold."

"Aye, not gold, nor silver. There is naught in the earth here to make a man rich."

"As I told you—as I told Ratcliffe and Wingfield long ago. If there were gold here, the naturals would be wearing it in their hair instead of shells and copper. Even the copper they get in trade; they don't dig it from the ground."

"The naturals will be wearing gold soon. Or one of them will, at any rate."

Newport called for a particular case from the hold of the ship. When it arrived, he lifted the lid with a flourish. Inside, a crown lay on a cushion of red velvet. Each pointed ray that lifted from the circlet bore a faceted jewel.

Smith glanced warily at Newport. The captain gave a hearty laugh.

He lifted the crown, testing its weight in his hands. The feel was all wrong for solid gold. Leafed copper, Smith guessed. The gems set into the metal were cloudy just below their glittering surface sheen. Glass.

"As the Virginia Company plans to stay for a spell," Newport said, "King James will make this Powhatan a tributary. Let the savage keep his kingdom and his throne made of sticks and bones."

Smith dropped the crown back into its crate. "A tributary? In Christ's name, what does King James hope to gain from this?"

"Loyalty. Cooperation."

"The Virginia Company has gone as mad as Ratcliffe."

"Many great men have made a substantial investment in this colony, John Smith. It's clear the samples we sent contained no gold. You claim there is no passage to the Indies—no passage on this river, at any rate. What, then, is our purpose?"

"I wish I knew."

"The king wishes he knew, as well. If you want to keep a name for yourself in London, you will find some use for this land."

"I had no name in London to start," Smith interjected, but Newport sailed on.

"A gold mine, a passage, silver . . . something of value, Smith, something worth investing in. The shareholders are growing impatient."

"Not half as impatient as I, I promise you."

"Finding the worth of this worthless mud pit will take time. If we make Powhatan a tributary, he will owe King James his loyalty."

"And you think he will see it that way? You don't know the man. I do. This business with the crown—it's folly, Newport. It will gain us nothing, and could lose us all."

"Powhatan will be grateful for the guidance of King James."

"Guidance!"

"They are savages, Smith. They need us to . . ."

"Need us? That garden, there, beyond the palisade . . . that was built by a handful of little girls. These people live off such gardens, feed whole cities from plots of land smaller than that one, and yet we could not make it yield enough to feed us for a fortnight! Tell me again how they need us."

Newport glanced at the garden, at its tattered cornstalks trembling in the breeze and spent leaves hanging in yellow folds. He turned back to Smith with a frown. "Powhatan will be crowned. This is the order of the Virginia Company—it is the order of your sovereign. Find a way to do it, Smith. The investors will hear no excuses, and neither will King James."

It was a brave group of men who agreed to accompany Smith upriver to Werowocomoco; all the English knew that Smith's trading expeditions had soured the naturals considerably. Hands tightened on the handles of guns, and helmets slid firmly into place as the shallop rounded the final bend before Werowocomoco.

But the town was remarkably quiet. No figures stirred in the wide lanes, fringed with brush shot golden and red with the coming autumn. The furrowed, muddy shore where the naturals landed their canoes was deserted. A few pale puffs of smoke rose from an arched roof here and there, and in the distance, from the direction of the cornfields, Smith heard a child laughing.

"Gone?" Scrivener asked, pawing anxiously at his gun.

"No. Not all of them," said Smith.

"Do they see us?"

"Of a certainty."

They dropped anchor. The shallop drifted in the current to the end of its chain, and then hung quivering in the water.

"I'll go ashore myself," Smith said.

"No—you ought to take at least a few men with you."

Smith looked around. The party shuffled and coughed. He thought he heard someone whisper, "Classen."

"Listen," he said. "I suspect most of their men are gone—hunting or on some mission of war. If there were any quantity of men here, they'd be firing their bows at us already. Now I'll go ashore, and any man who wishes may accompany me. I shan't force any of you. Stay here if you like."

In the end more than half the men crowded into the landing boat. It was a tight enough fit that rowing was difficult, and whenever a nervous man twitched, the boat rocked and the shallow draft welcomed a spill of water over the side. Their boots were sodden by the time they landed at Werowocomoco.

Evening was fast advancing, the sky tinted with shades of rose-gold. A final steadfast flight of gnats whirled in defiance of the coming chill, shimmering in a sideways shaft of light that cut brightly through the forest, blinding the eyes. Smith raised an arm to shade his vision. The brush nearby crackled.

The men gasped and Smith heard the softly metallic clatter of guns pulled from belts, smelled the sulfur trace of burning matchcords in the sudden disturbance of the air. In one moment of frenzied despair, he feared that he had been wrong, had read the signs all wrong, Opechancanough had lured and deceived him at last; the forest was alive with Indians, rising from the black shadows like vengeful gods.

"*Wingapoh*, Chawnzmit."

"Pocahontas."

Scrivener turned in a cautious circle, his firearm extended, and then, satisfied that the forest was empty, he shoved it hard back into his belt. "Almighty preserving Christ. It's only the princess."

She stood in the shaft of sunset light, her slender brown body wreathed in a halo of fire. The brilliance of it bent and distorted around her, and all Smith could make out was the outline of her form, breaking and rippling as she moved like a heat mirage on a far horizon. He squinted, blinking back tears at the brightness of her.

She stepped from the light and onto the forest trail. A leather cap was tied with a knotted lace beneath her chin, and from her crown rose a rack of deer antlers, stained red as blood by precious *puccoon*. Face and shoulders, arms and legs, were red, too, save for the places where a violent ochre, lemon bright, streaked through. A line of black paint crossed her flat chest, and another divided her face from hairline to chin, so that each wide, slanted eye seemed to peer at him from around a dark corner. In the division of her face, he saw two princesses, each watching his party, poised and silent, perfect in symmetry. Over her paints she had dusted that native glimmering mineral, the one Ratcliffe and his supporters had mistaken for gold dust. She shifted. It was a tiny gesture, a casual turn of the head, a half shrug, and she sparkled as she moved, the metallic flecks dancing on her skin like stars reflected in water. Quietly, the men exclaimed. Smith had never seen her like this—none of them had. Their princess, the angel sent by an orderly God, stood before them a wild and beautiful heathen.

She blinked up at Smith through her red-and-black mask. "Why have you come? To take our food, as you took the food of other towns?" English words. She wanted all the men to understand.

"No. We come bringing gifts to your father."

"He is away."

"Where has he gone?"

She lowered her antlers, slashed them like a buck in an autumn thicket. "Uttamussak."

He recalled the name. The most sacred temple in all the Great Chief's territory. "And when will he return?"

She shrugged, a childish gesture. Her painted skin shimmered and shone. "When he is done praying. When the Okeus speaks."

Smith asked in her own tongue, "Where are all the men?"

"Hunting."

"Who guards the women?"

"Men."

"You are being evasive."

She smiled at him. The dimple in her chin showed clear and deep in the line of black paint.

"Are we in danger, Pocahontas?"

Again she lowered the antlers. "Perhaps you are in danger," she said in English. Behind Smith on the trail, the men crowded together uneasily. But she looked up laughing, shaking her head as if at the folly of a small child. When she said his name, her voice was fond and happy.

She explained as they walked toward the town. Most of the men who had not accompanied Powhatan to the great temple had left to hunt. So many of the surrounding towns had traded away all their surplus goods, even though her father had instructed them not to—and here she paused to cut a stare at Smith—that Werowocomoco received little in tribute, and expected a lean winter. The men thought to bring in meat early, so that it might be dried and laid away even before the traditional hunt began. Some men remained, and knew of Chawnzmit's coming. "But as your men looked frightened and weak, and hesitant to leave the ship, they decided you were not worth shooting full of arrows."

"I am grateful."

She turned to him with a serious glower. "My uncle Opechancanough would sooner see you dead, no matter how many arrows were wasted."

"I know."

"You are lucky that Powhatan still rules here. We were ordered not to go to Jamestown, but my father did not say you couldn't come to his capital and give him gifts."

They reached the center of the town. A few young men positioned drums around the huge fire pit. They looked in the direction of the English with sharp, defiant stares.

Smith caught Pocahontas by her thin elbow. "Tell me, little sister. Are we safe?"

"Yes," she said. "I swear it. Opechancanough does not hold all of Tsenacomoco in his sway. Not yet. My father still hopes for your guns, Chawnzmit, even if it is a secret hope. Tonight, at least, you are safe. Until Powhatan says otherwise." She pressed a hand to her heart.

The sky burst into color and flame, painting wisps of cloud with the blood of the dying sun. The drums spoke, a sudden roar of tight hide and thunder, and the fire in the pit leaped high. A piercing racket—the high, ululating wail of women—erupted from among the houses. They came to the fire in one great rush. They were painted as men going to war: red and black, sharp lines to ward off the deadliest spirits, those who brought ill luck and sudden cowardice. Slender bodies twisted, bending at the curve of hip; breasts swayed in paint of ochre and *puccoon*, ash-white and fawn-spotted, bouncing under chains of copper and bead as they stamped. High-stepping knees kicked decorated aprons high, exposing in the flash of fringe and firelight the dark joining of their thighs. The women of Werowocomoco screamed and turned, chanted and whirled. Antlers grew from heads, bears' teeth weighted braids of black hair that lifted from painted skin as bodies spun. They mimed the swing of a war club, the firing of a bow. They mimed prey falling, men falling.

The Englishmen pressed close to Smith, fearful and fascinated. The light, pliant bodies spiraled from the ring of light into the growing dusk. In the half darkness their hands brushed pale skin, clutched for a moment and released, whirled away. A smear of *puccoon* traced across the back of Smith's hand, dark as a spill of wine. He licked it away. It tasted of earth and sage, bestial musk and the bright waters of a mineral spring.

A small hand slipped into his own, tugging and insistent. Pocahontas stared up at him from her pagan mask. A careless hand had smeared the perfect line of black; the dark paint tracked across her cheek like smoke from a distant fire. "Dance," she commanded, and caught in the net of drumbeat and fire, he followed her into the ring.

The bodies flowed around him, moved with him, passed him skin to skin. He heated with a lust he had not felt since Constantinople; through the smoke of the fire and the pounding of the drum he caught the secretive note of rosemary on the wind. The other men joined in, hooting, jigging gracelessly, and he watched with bemused wonder as the painted women wreathed them in caresses. He felt those same hands on his own skin. His soul seemed to pull free of his body, hanging in the air in a haze of blue-white smoke.

But always, as he danced, as he sang wordlessly, as he caught a woman's wrist and held it, feeling the graceful bird-leg bones turn slowly in his palm before he released her, he was aware of a small but stately presence. Pocahontas. She bore her antlers proudly, crowned in a rack of blood and firelight. She stepped endlessly around the perimeter of the fire ring. She paced, surveying the dance and his part in it, watching with approval. Her eyes were always on John Smith, and they glittered with amused satisfaction. As the night wore on, as one by one the men were towed, staggering, from the circle by laughing women, as they faded into the animal cries of the forest, her face darted from light to shadow. The tips of the antlers glowed.

See, her smile said, receding into the velvet of the night. *See how love is better than war.*

Smith woke fearful and dazed, eyes stinging from a night of precious little sleep. The hard, damp wood of the landing boat pressed into his shoulder and back. He sat up carefully. His cramped body prickled and burned. One boot pressed into a groaning man's leg; his hand came down on the chest of another. He was laid out with the rest of the landing party in the bed of the rowboat. Those men who could not fit inside slumped on the ground, leaning against the boat's sides and each other. They snored softly.

Smith made a quick count. They were all there, each man accounted for and all, so far as he could tell, alive and unharmed. Pocahontas had kept her word.

A watery yellow dawn was rising, the sun climbing steadily into a shroud of thin, vaporous cloud. When the men aboard the shallop noted him stirring, they called out to him. Smith waved. He was well—mystified, taken aback, and considerably exercised in his person, but well.

The landing party soon stirred to life, too. Groggy men wandered into the brush to relieve themselves. Their cheeks and the backs of necks still bore traces of paint or the scratch marks of nails. Smith sent a man to the shallop for food, and they broke a cold fast in silence, eyeing one another with wonder and doubt.

By the time the final crumb of hardtack was gone, Smith grew aware of a rising sound from the depths of Werowocomoco. It was a great, deep swell of voices, masculine and low, punctuated by staccato bursts of chanting—or perhaps it was laughter. The landing party glanced uneasily from one man to another. Finally all eyes landed on Smith.

He stood, brushing his palms together. "The Great Chief has returned."

The *mamanatowick* was gracious in receiving Smith—more gracious, in truth, than he had any cause to be. When Smith was admitted into his presence, Powhatan accepted his bow in dignified silence, the lined face betraying nothing of the loathing he must surely feel for the English and their devil of a spokesman, Chawnzmit. He ordered his women to bring food to refresh his guest, and Smith, knowing the conventions, engaged in polite, inconsequential talk until it arrived. He avoided touching upon the true nature of his call until the chief at last stared down at him from his high bed with wry, expectant eyes.

"Great Chief," Smith began, "I would ask you to come to Jamestown, for we—that is, my own *mamanatowick* and I—have a valuable gift for you."

Powhatan received this in silence, and for one moment of soaring relief, Smith believed the man would accept, that his work would be done and he could return to his tiny cabin at Jamestown and never set foot in Werowocomoco again. Then he saw the tremor of fury that shook the chief's frame. The old face was still as a grave, but the eyes crackled with sparks of disgust.

Smith perceived the problem at once. He hurried to explain. "We invite you to Jamestown so that we might do you the respect you deserve. Allow us to feast you, *mamanatowick*. Let us show you that we know how to honor a chief of your standing."

But it was no use. In one smooth movement, Powhatan stood. The old chief drew himself to his full height; the shoulders lost the stoop of age, and the back gave up its bend of weariness. He towered over Smith where he sat cross-legged beside the heart fire. The curtain of silver hair slid over one shoulder, releasing into the longhouse the smell of herbs and animal skins, the tang of the sacred smoke that brought visions. The odor disquieted Smith. He remembered with a shiver the mask confronting him from the shadows and the rake of the cougar's claws against his cheek. *The smell of the temple*. Powhatan was still imbued with the power of the sacred space. It buoyed him up, filling the sails of his hatred for the English with a hot and mighty wind.

"I am the *mamanatowick*, Chawnzmit. I do not come to your call like a tame dog. If your little chief would give me gifts, you shall bring them here, to me."

Smith bowed his head in acquiescence.

"There is only one thing I want from your people," Powhatan said.

Smith did not wait for the chief to say it. "Guns."

Powhatan made no reply, and Smith dared to glance up at him. He caught him in the act of lowering himself back to his perch. Smith noted how the old man's arms shook as he eased his weight onto the bed.

"I will not bring you guns," Smith said, choosing his words with care, "but I will bring you a great honor from my *mamanato-wick*, who recognizes your might even across the great sea."

Powhatan's eyes narrowed. His curiosity was piqued equal to his ire. *His curiosity may be all I need to get this mad business over with.*

"Go, then, Chawnzmit. I would see how your kind honors Great Chiefs, though I doubt you know the meaning of *honor*."

Captain Newport himself came to Werowocomoco three days later to bestow the crown and declare Chief Powhatan a tributary of King James and England. He traveled in as much ceremonial pomp as Jamestown could muster, sailing the *Discovery* upriver until Smith feared its keel would catch and hold in the deep, silty mud when the tide inevitably receded. Word traveled fast through the forest, faster than the *Discovery*. Long before they reached Werowocomoco the riverbanks filled with naturals, who milled and waved, chanted and sang. Smith stood at the rail beneath the tight canopy of the foresail, watching the crowded banks slide past. Now and then over the barks of the crew and the groan of wind in the lines, he caught the words of the Indians' chants. More often than not the songs mocked the English, volleying acerbic rhymes against the *Discovery*'s unfeeling wooden hull. Oblivious, the Englishmen grinned and waved and shouted their innocent greetings. Alone among them, Smith stood still, watching and listening, ever alert for the shade of Opechancanough sliding through the whispering trees.

Smith was, of course, among the handful chosen to come ashore, bearing Powhatan's crown. He remained surly and quiet in the landing boat, staring at the box that held the crown as if it contained a knot of vipers. He could feel Newport's eyes upon him, smugly cheered by Smith's own silence, no doubt glad that Jamestown's harshest critic had been cowed at last. He refused to meet the captain's eye, slipping unthinkingly into the custom of the naturals, paying Newport all the attention and respect he was due.

Warriors helped pull the boat ashore, pressing hands to heart and vowing friendship and safe passage. They eyed the box Smith carried with open curiosity. Some of them touched it or tapped upon it, but none dared remove it from Smith's hands. All knew these gifts were for the *mamanatowick*—the mysterious box and more. King James had heard that the Great Chief enjoyed hunting and made use of dogs—though certainly no mangy Indian creature could equal a good English hound. He had sent a pure-white greyhound, tall and sleek, to improve the *mamanatowick*'s stock; this both men and women exclaimed over with open admiration as Newport coaxed the dog from the rowboat. A wooden bedstead followed in pieces, finely carved in English oak and oiled to a rich glow. Finally, the men produced a few bottles of good white wine.

Powhatan deigned to meet them out of doors, at the communal fire pit where the women had danced on that strange, starshot night. The reason for the meeting place was clear: so that all his people, not just his favorite wives and his select *werowances*, might witness the spectacle of the English bringing tribute to the Great Chief.

His wives piled mats until they were hip high, and then draped the stack with several plush wolf pelts. Powhatan made his slow and methodical way from the direction of his smoky hall, wide shoulders draped with a long leather cloak painted black as cold ash. It dragged in the dirt behind him; the people he passed gave the train of his trappings a wide and respectful berth and fell into step behind him, singing and shaking dried gourds over their heads. Their rattles made a din like a hailstorm, a sound that shut out all other senses save for sight, and Smith's eyes were full of the majesty of Powhatan. His long gray hair spilled down his back. Here and there one of his wives had braided a lock, and these few thin braids hung heavy with ornaments: bird claws and weasel tails, clusters of animal teeth and flat discs of copper, which winked and dazzled in the midday sun. On his brow, the crown of red-dyed deer hair bristled tall and proud, a more royal sight by far than any gold leaf and glass gems King James might contrive.

Powhatan lowered himself onto his makeshift throne of wolf-skins. His wives sank to the ground around him. The people of Werowocomoco thronged about the fire pit, children and women pressing side by side with hunters and warriors. The murmur of their voices was like a wind in an autumn wood.

"Great Powhatan," Newport said, gesturing grandly with his hand. "I am charged by King James, sovereign of England and of this land, with presenting these tokens of the king's esteem to you, his loyal subject." Newport glanced sharply at Smith, waiting for the translation.

Smith drew a deep breath. He caught sight of Pocahontas in the crowd, peering out from her place between a young woman and the big-eared warrior guard who had ever been her shadow when she had visited the fort. Her smooth brow was furrowed with confusion. When she caught his eye, her look was dark with wounded disbelief.

"*Mamanatowick*," Smith said in the naturals' tongue, "the *mamanatowick* across the sea sends gifts in acknowledgment of your greatness."

The men of the crowd muttered their approval; a few women raised an ululating cheer. Pocahontas's face pinched in bewilderment.

One by one, Newport presented the offerings, and Smith translated at his side. Powhatan accepted the wine and the bedstead in polite if unimpressed silence. The dog he gestured for, leaning from his throne to examine it with his hands, watching it trot around the fire pit at the end of its lead. He nodded, well satisfied with this gift, if with no other. A dog was a thing of real value, of obvious utility. The greyhound was large and clearly swift, and its unspotted white fur was a novelty not seen among the hunting dogs of Tsenacomoco. "Suitable," he said to Smith.

"There is one gift more," Newport said.

Smith ducked his head close to the captain's ear. "I implore you, give him the crown in the box; do not make a spectacle of placing it upon his head."

"Nonsense. He cannot swear fealty to King James if he does not kneel to accept his tributary crown."

"He cannot swear fealty in any case. He does not understand what you do today, and wouldn't swear if he did."

Newport's glare was sharp. "We have discussed this already, Smith. Open the box."

"We will lose all," Smith said. One last warning, one last attempt. It was all he would make, this final effort to spare the colony from further disaster—and then let Newport hold the responsibility for Jamestown's fate in the one hand that remained to him.

Smith opened the box.

The ripple of awe ran through the crowd. The crown blazed in the sun, bright as lightning in a nighttime storm. Powhatan leaned toward it with interest.

It fell to Smith to cajole the old chief into standing. Powhatan could not be made to understand why he ought to rise, but his curiosity in English custom was enough to coax him to his feet. Kneeling, however, was unthinkable. When Smith halfheartedly suggested the *mamanatowick* take to his knees, his detached, stoic resolve broke and he stared openly at Smith and Newport in shock. Several of the English demonstrated, and Powhatan watched them sink into their subservient crouches in open disgust.

At Newport's word, two or three men pressed on the old chief's shoulders, hoping to force him to his knees. A few of the chief's warriors started forward with protests on their lips, but Powhatan waved them back. He preferred, it seemed, to face English customs on his own. Despite his great age and encroaching weakness, Powhatan bore up with noble grace, resisting the hands of the English as if their leaning weight were no more than the bite of a flea, unworthy of his notice.

His neck did bend slightly with the effort, though, and Newport accounted it enough a gesture of submission to satisfy King James. He placed the crown on Powhatan's head among his red bristles of deerhide. The cheap metal and glass glittered atop the *puccoon*-dyed tufts. Smith turned away from the sight.

The twisted masque of a coronation concluded with the requisite feast. Smith sank to the earth in relief as baskets of corn cake were passed, as the women shared out jugs of sweet nut milk and fillets of fish roasted in wrappings of leaves. He picked at the food while the dances commenced, and watched with a grimace of distaste as Powhatan's most favored chiefs inspected the crown. Presently a small, warm weight settled beside him. He peered from the corner of his eye at Pocahontas, her coltish legs folded beneath her, facing partly away with a basket of bread between them. The string of white beads hung from her neck, his red yarn peeking between the baubles.

"You cannot speak to me openly?"

"Not with my father so near. He has forbidden it."

"Then you took a risk, when you danced in your antlers."

"I had to show you."

That love was better than war. Smith nodded, though she did not see his tacit agreement.

The girl bit into a corn cake. Flecks of golden meal clung to her lip. She wiped them away with the back of her hand. "You do not eat, Chawnzmit."

"I find I have little appetite."

"Is your spirit troubled?"

"Very much."

"I understand why."

"Do you?"

For one brief moment she turned, looked full into his eyes. Her face was long and wise, and pale with sorrow. "Powhatan may not understand what you have done today, Chawnzmit, but I do."

He dropped his eyes. He could not bear to look at her, that accusing, knowing stare, that innocent and loving face. "Do you, Pocahontas?"

"One day he will come to understand what you meant by this ceremony. And he will not be pleased."

"I hope that day is a long way off, for all our sakes."

"That is my hope, too. But I fear the day will come sooner than any of us would like. You are still my brother, Chawnzmit, no matter what my father commands. Our spirits are the same. I would not see you hurt in this war, if war cannot be avoided."

"I would not see anyone hurt, if I could make it so."

She gathered herself to rise and reached to pick up the basket. Her hand brushed his arm, a brief, warm gesture, full of more sympathy than he deserved.

"I know," she said gently, and walked away.

POCAHONTAS

Season of Taquitock

The harvest was thin. Cornstalks dried weeks before they should have, and their leaves were pale and limp, shot at the edges with golden yellow long before the cooler days of autumn set in. The ears were small and sparse and hugged tight to the brittle stalks. When they were cracked away from their secretive pocket between leaf and stem, the scent given off by the broken plants was dusty and weak, not the robust sweetness of harvests past. Beneath their sheaths of thin, crackling husk, the kernels were small and gray and fell short of the ends of the cobs, leaving empty white spaces like the unfilled cells of a honeycomb. On the bean plants, pods hung like the thin, bony fingers of old men. Squashes were undersized and had to be hunted out on hands and knees. The women rooted beneath spreads of leaves grayed by dust and came up with small gourds barely larger than a fist. At least, they said with forced smiles, the flesh of the squash would be especially sweet this year.

The weak harvest was an ill omen. Pocahontas noted the changes in her body, the tenderness as small breasts began to jut from her chest, the down-soft fuzz just beginning to darken between her thighs. She pinched herself in anger, as if she might reproach her body into delaying its progress into womanhood. Such flagrant ripening was unseemly at a time like this, with the crops slowly failing. Did the spirits mean some cruel joke, ushering her into her years of fertility and magic while the very earth failed? Or did she have some uncontrollable magic already, draining the land of its fecundity so that she might fuel her own strange and compelling fire?

And compelling that blaze was. Pocahontas found herself watching with rapt fascination while the boys practiced their archery. In the mornings their mothers would throw clods of earth or pieces of wood high into the air, and the boys would line up to shoot, eyes intent, brows furrowed with concentration. No boy could have his breakfast until he'd shot down his target, so this was the only time of the day when their attention was fixed, when Pocahontas might stare with impunity, and without fear that she might be noticed and become the target of boys' rude songs when everyone gathered that evening to dance and pray. Peering around the edge of a longhouse, she would watch the shapes in their arms change as they drew their bowstrings, the muscles standing out sudden and wiry, their bodies lively and strong as fish thrashing in a net. It was the eldest boys she watched most avidly, those who were only months away from their *huskanaw*. Most of them, like Pocahontas herself, had already obtained the first of their tattoos. The way the black-and-red ink slid over the tense, lean muscle of an arm or back brought a rush of heat to her face and filled her nights with restless kicking and turning.

As she ripened, she grew ever closer to Matachanna. Not only did she now understand her half sister's blushes and sidelong glances at Utta-ma-tomakkin, but her friendship with Matachanna was more important than ever. With womanhood approaching, its rites of magic and times of blood, Pocahontas felt keenly her lack of friends. Who would join her in the sweat lodge to celebrate her first woman's courses? Who would help her dedicate her moon's blood to the spirits, who would giggle with her as her thighs were painted red with *puccoon* and covered with a fringed apron? Her drive to learn the *tassantassa* language had frightened away most of the girls of Werowocomoco—those who had not already abandoned Pocahontas for her sharp tongue and mocking nature. No, the truth of Matachanna's long-ago words was plain to see. Pocahontas was not well loved. Her mocking war dance that summer night when she had worn antlers and led the women of Werowocomoco to weave a wild spell around the *tassantassas* was still spoken of with fond humor among the lanes and longhouses of the capital. But that was not the same thing as being well loved.

She felt her loneliness most sharply when she allowed her thoughts to roam back to Chawnzmit, to the days she had spent at the fort, learning the *tassantassa* tongue by his side. She had not seen Chawnzmit since the day he and his one-armed fellow had crowned Powhatan. Even had he still been her adopted brother, he could not have ushered her into the sacred lore of womanhood. Men were forbidden from that realm. But she missed him all the same. Matachanna was a good sister, and could be counted on to make a beautiful apron for Pocahontas's blood ceremony. But Matachanna could not understand the stark yearning in her half sister's heart, the unquenchable thirst. Matachanna did not know what it was like, to be *not a gentleman* in a gentleman's world. Chawnzmit was the only one who understood, the only one who felt the cold stab of that particular pain.

Gentleman. Pocahontas smiled rather sadly as she broke another ear of corn from a dry, rustling stalk and dropped it in the basket at her feet. *It is strange how readily* tassantassa *words still come to my mind, though I have not spoken to a white man for nearly a whole moon.*

Matachanna stumbled upright from where she knelt, rustling beneath a low spread of squash leaves. She clutched a few gourds against her stomach. They were small, but their yellow flesh was streaked and speckled with green as bright and glowing as sunlight on summer leaves. "Let's put these aside for our own supper tonight," Matachanna said. She piled the squashes carefully beside Pocahontas's basket. "I love the first roast squash of *taquitock*. It's always delicious, but look how pretty these gourds are. Won't they look lovely with the glowing coals all around them? I will braid your hair while we watch them cook." Matachanna straightened, dusting her hands together. She peered sharply at Pocahontas's face. "What are you smiling about?"

"Roast squash."

"You are not. You hardly heard a word I said, and just for that, I'll eat all the squash myself and you'll get mix-pot stew." She tugged fondly on Pocahontas's braid. "I know that wistful look. You were thinking about boys."

Pocahontas flushed; her sister's arrow had struck too close to the target. It would never do for anyone to know how often she thought about Chawnzmit.

"Who is it?" Matachanna reached to snap ears of corn off a nearby stalk. The dry leaves rustled against her arms.

"No one."

"You can tell me."

"No," Pocahontas said desperately, "I *can't*."

A poor choice of words: a misstep. Matachanna's corn ears thudded into the basket, and she gaped at Pocahontas, wide-eyed and half-grinning. "Chawnzmit? You're in love with him!"

"Quiet! Father will be furious if he finds out you ever spoke that name. You know how he feels. And besides, I am *not* in love with Chaw—with that man. He was only a good friend, and I miss his company."

"Imagine loving a white man, anyway. I am glad you haven't given your heart to . . . to that man, Amonute. You could never marry a *tassantassa*. Such a thing would only bring sorrow. They are too different from us."

"Are they so different?"

"You know they are."

"But the women who danced that night . . . who lay with the white men . . ."

"Oh, they all say the *tassantassas* are made like Real Men, only hairier. Otherwise they are the same in matters beneath the apron. But I'm not speaking of *that*. I'm speaking of marriage."

"Well, I don't want to marry a white man."

"Then who *do* you wish to marry?"

Pocahontas tore a corn leaf from her stalk. She twirled it between her fingers, brushed its crackling dryness over her lips. "I don't know. I haven't thought of it. Your heart is still set on Utta-ma-tomakkin, I suppose."

Matachanna's dark lashes veiled her eyes. "Yes. And I know he wants me, too."

"You know? Have you spoken to him of marriage?"

Matachanna giggled. She hid her face among the corn leaves. A breeze moved through the field, coaxing a last song from the spent plants, a dry whisper. Dapples of light and shade moved across Matachanna's shy, beaming face. A deep stab of jealousy pierced Pocahontas, a fierce envy for the life of beautiful ease her half sister would lead. A powerful priest to marry, willing women to serve at her fire, happy children, ropes of pearls for her neck and her hair. Matachanna, stepping in time to the ordered dance of a contented life. Wanting for nothing. A place in the world.

"What did he say?" Pocahontas asked, struggling to keep her voice light, to be glad in her spirit for her sister's happiness.

"He said he will speak to Father as soon as my first blood comes." Matachanna's face grew suddenly long. "Oh, Pocahontas, will it *never* come? I'm nearly the oldest girl who hasn't entered the sweat lodge! I've asked the priests how to make my blood come faster, and they gave me herbs to eat and told me the dances I must do alone in the forest to entreat the Okeus and the moon spirit. But still, nothing."

"Perhaps you should ask Utta-ma-tomakkin to pray for your womanhood to arrive."

Matachanna sighed. "I have. He has been smoking and chanting for it, and he has sweated himself twice to speak directly to the Okeus. But still, I have no apron."

"I have heard the old women say that when harvests are poor, fewer girls enter the sweat lodge. But you are only fourteen. Sometimes it takes sixteen or seventeen winters before the courses come." Matachanna's face fell all the more. Pocahontas cast about for some way to cheer her. "Take comfort. Now is a terrible time to speak to Father, anyhow. The spirits are only protecting your heart, so that when Utta-ma-tomakkin finally goes to him, Father will be happy and will agree to send you off to your handsome priest's longhouse. Then he will put together the biggest and best bride gift Tsenacomoco has ever seen!"

Matachanna smiled at that, but she shook her head. "Father *is* terrible to speak to these days. He stares off into shadows with a haunted look in his eye. Half the time he doesn't seem to hear anyone at all, even when they speak directly to him. Winganuske cannot even hold his attention for more than a moment, and she is his favorite wife. I'm beginning to fear a *manitou* may have hold of him."

"No," Pocahontas said slowly, reluctantly. "It's not a demon. He has been in this state ever since the *tassantassas* placed that metal hat on his head."

"You're right. I never realized it." Matachanna worked at the corn in thoughtful silence. At last she said, "The hat must have a spell on it. What else could steal away Father's spirit? The *tassantassas* must have done it on purpose, to weaken him and humiliate him before the eyes of all his people! How could they, after we have been so kind to them?" She paused. A crow called in the momentary quiet—an omen of ill luck—and Matachanna glanced around sharply. Pocahontas saw the tiny hairs on her sister's arms raise. Matachanna muttered, "I didn't even know *tassantassas* had priests, but who else could work a spell into a metal hat?"

Pocahontas knew the crown was not enchanted, though it certainly held a peculiar power. She did not fully understand the words Captain Newport had spoken on that fateful day, when the men leaned their weight against her father to bend his proud neck. But she had grasped the magic of those words. *Sovereign. King. Loyal subject.*

Over the next several days, she often stole away from her duties, not to dance in privacy to incite the moon's blood, as Matachanna did, or even to spy on the boys shooting for their morning meals. Instead, she wandered deep into the forest, trailing her hands absently over the boles of trees, feeling the turn of the season stirring beneath the rough bark, the subtle, fragrant vibration of rising sap and dying leaves.

As she wandered, Pocahontas rolled the English words about like a pebble in her palm, watching them shift and flicker with her spirit's inward eye. *Sovereign. Subject.* Here was *tassantassa* magic, and she alone understood how the spell had bound her father. Sooner or later, Powhatan would remember his useless, common daughter, the one whose meddling had shamed his bloodline and landed his favorite son in dangerous captivity. He would remember Pocahontas and call on her, and she would have no choice but to speak the truth.

Taquitock drew to a close. The gardens were stripped of their last small, precious yields. The harvest celebration went on for days, longer than any other festival in Pocahontas's memory, a loud clamor of rattles and cries, of dancing and drums, ringing defiance against the thin stores packed away in the storage pits, the baskets half-full of half-naked corn ears. *Popanow* gathered in towers of high, gray cloud. The coming winter milled like a flock of crows on the eastern horizon.

When the harvest celebration was over, and the men left Werowocomoco for the annual deer hunt, those women who were not engaged with gathering nuts or digging *tuckahoe* turned their hands to a new longhouse. It was to be a fine, large one—a *yehakin* fit for a powerful chief, even though the *mamanatowick*'s great house already stood at the center of the village.

Pocahontas and Nonoma hauled a brace of freshly killed turkeys to the town's central fire pit. They were weighty birds, fattened on the forest's ample crop of acorns. The girls' arms were weak with exhaustion by the time they settled beside the crackling embers of the great fire. Pocahontas pulled a turkey onto her lap and tore the gray down and shining brown coverts from tender, pale skin.

"Why must we do this here, Amonute?" Nonoma spat as a stray clump of down drifted into her face, and she swiped at her tickling nose. "Our own longhouse's fire is as good as this fire. And anyway, I hate plucking birds."

"I want to watch them build." Her hands moved of their own accord, sorting the feathers by touch, casting the small, soft pieces into the fire pit, tucking the strong flight and tail feathers into a silk-grass pouch for later use.

Now and then the breeze would shift, blowing the pungent, choking smoke of burning feathers into her face. She fanned the smoke away along with Nonoma's complaints.

Winganuske oversaw the effort of building. She snapped out commands to her team of women, who bent the cured and soaked saplings into high arcs and lashed them together with new sinews. By the time the girls had plucked six turkeys between them— Pocahontas doing most of the work—the frame of the longhouse had grown to nearly twice the length of an average home.

"It's going to be awfully large," Nonoma said.

"Another great house."

"Is Father moving, then?"

Pocahontas shook her head. A blunt fear had begun to pound inside her head, a small and queasy worry. "I haven't heard any word that the *mamanatowick* intends to move to a new *yehakin*." She and Nonoma shared a long look. "I suppose," Pocahontas said slowly, "another important chief may be moving here, to Werowocomoco."

"But that makes no sense. Why should any other *werowance* live here? They have their own territories to look after."

Pocahontas made no reply. There was only one *werowance* who might stake a claim in Powhatan's capital. Winganuske's gestures were avid and sharp, her body and voice brusque with the expectation of perfection. *She wishes especially to impress my uncle when he arrives.* So the finest and most beloved of the old bull's herd was already planning to leave him, to cast off her old loyalties and bid for the favor of the new *mamanatowick*.

"I never did like Winganuske," Pocahontas said.

Nonoma tossed a handful of feathers into the fire. White smoke lifted in a thick cloud. "Why?"

"Never mind."

The women lashed long, straight saplings across the upright frames. Birch-bark strips would be threaded through these in the springtime, when the new sap running through the trees would leave the bark soft and flexible. One of the women finished tying her length of sinew and stood back, rolling her shoulders to loosen a cramp. She turned and caught sight of Pocahontas with her heap of turkeys. The woman waved, a tentative, almost shy gesture, and made her way across the grounds to the fire pit.

"Anawanuske."

"Hello, Amonute."

"It's a fine new longhouse you're building."

"I cannot talk long. Winganuske will want me working. But Powhatan asked me to send you to his side if I caught sight of you."

Pocahontas held her breath. The day she had long feared had come. The air seemed full of spirits, crowding around her, pressing her with urgent, forceful hands. She closed her eyes; she could not tell in which direction she was being pushed.

"Nonoma, take the turkeys back to our house."

"By myself?"

"Run home and fetch Matachanna. She'll help you. I don't know when I will return from Father's great house."

It was not Kocoum who held aside her father's door flap, but a young warrior unfamiliar to her. Kocoum had joined the hunts this year. She imagined him moving through the violet twilight of woodland shadow, draped in a deerskin, crowned with the face and ears of a doe. She pictured the furtive dance of deception, the gentle step and bent neck of fellowship, the doe's placid face offered to the prey while inside the skin, the slick and hairless body of a predator was waiting, deadly and eager.

Powhatan sat on the edge of his high bedstead. His hands lay folded on his apron. Beside him, gleaming dully in the light of the heart fire, the English crown crouched with its sharp spines erect. Pocahontas halted, wordless, waiting, her eyes caught by the crown's bright jewels like a fish in a weir.

"Amonute. Pocahontas." His voice was soft, resigned. From outside, at the center of Werowocomoco, a rhythmic pounding rose like drums in a distant wood: the sound of the women building Opechancanough's longhouse. "Long have I looked at this strange hat, this gift from the white invaders. It has some meaning that I cannot discern. Some power."

She shuffled her feet in the dust of his fire ring.

He lifted a hand to point toward the crown. The hand shook with his old man's tremor. "Tell me what this means, child."

A hard and painful lump formed in her throat. She swallowed with difficulty. "I don't know, Father."

"You do. Tell me."

She heaved a deep, hollow sigh. A heaviness pulled at her heart, dragging her down, as if a *manitou* had sunk its black claws into her spirit. "It . . . the crown . . . makes you subservient to the white *mamanatowick*. It makes you no more than a *tanx*—at least in the eyes of the *tassantassas*."

Powhatan stiffened. His eyes seemed to stare far beyond her, beyond the walls of his longhouse. "They think to have all for themselves. They think to cow me, to make me small."

There was a day when Pocahontas would have protested, a time when she would have argued for the goodness of Chawnzmit, if for no other white man. But she could no longer deny the truth of her father's words, and so she held her tongue as he summoned the few men who remained in Werowocomoco. She sat at his feet, holding a gourd full of water to serve the men as they approached to receive their instructions. She listened as the men repeated the message they would carry to every territory in Tsenacomoco, to even the smallest of villages, the most insignificant *tanx*. She gazed down into her gourd, watching her dim reflection tremble with the ragged beat of her heart. Again and again she heard the men recite Powhatan's command: *No one is to trade with the* tassantassas, *even if they come to you. Even if they use force. Anyone who provides the white traitors with food or other succor shall be killed—man, woman, or child—and any tribe that aids them will be destroyed as the Chessiopiak were destroyed, wholly and completely, down to the merest babe.*

When the last messenger had departed, Powhatan stood. Pocahontas followed him down the length of his dark and empty hall, giving him her shoulder to lean upon as he ducked through the flap of his own door. They stood together, blinking in the brightness of day. A cold wind gusted through Werowocomoco. It stripped a great flurry of red leaves from the trees and scattered them down the lanes of the capital, tossing and playing them among the figures of the women whose backs were bent to raise Opechancanough's longhouse.

Powhatan watched the leaves swirl around the dark dot of the communal fire pit. His eyes avoided the new construction, slid away from the sight of Winganuske hard at work on another man's dwelling. The *mamanatowick* grunted in knowing approval at the wind and leaves. "It will be an especially harsh winter, little Mischief. The white men will starve without our aid. It is certain. They will drop like flies in the frost."

She dashed the tears from her eyes with the back of her wrist, before Powhatan could see them fall.

Popanow closed over the land, choking light from the days with a cold, hard fist. The season was as bitter as Powhatan had predicted it would be. The covers on the women's storage pits froze in place beneath thick ice; the steel axes and knives that had been traded or stolen from the white men passed from hand to hand as the people of Werowocomoco labored to reopen their caches. Women took to the marshlands, wrapping hands and feet in strips of fur-lined leather. They hacked at the hard, frozen ground with digging sticks and axes, prying long, pale *tuckahoe* roots from the mud. The tubers were wrinkled and tasted dry and bland, but they would stretch the meager stores of food until springtime.

During these dark and terrible days, Pocahontas spent more time with Powhatan than she ever had before. Since that autumn afternoon when she had seen him in his trembling wonder, helpless before the spell of the *tassantassa* crown, Pocahontas had taken on a significance to her father that she scarcely understood. He clung to her presence, keeping her as close as a priest kept his best talisman. But Pocahontas was under no illusions. This was not the role she had long desired, a place as her father's trusted advisor, hard won through excellence and useful service. Her proximity to him was almost punitive, as if he feared that if his daughter went free, all of Werowocomoco would learn of his shame, the strange thrall the white men's *tanx* hat had inflicted upon him.

And so it was that Pocahontas was at her father's side when news arrived of Chawnzmit's aggressions. She had joined with his wives in refreshing the mix-pot stew. They clustered about the large pot—copper, a prize won from the *tassantassas* in exchange for some corn, no doubt, or a basket of beans, goods Powhatan's women would likely prefer this winter to the ostentatious gleam of trade copper. The stew retained the fishy scent of a season's worth of oyster and sturgeon. The sweet, herbaceous tang of autumn's deer fat still laced richly through the thick broth, and juicy kernels of corn bobbed to the surface as Pocahontas stirred. But the pot was more than half-empty, and they had nothing to renew it but thick slices of starchy *tuckahoe*, a handful of dried oysters, and a small measure of withered beans. By the end of the winter, the copper stewpot would be the most dismal place in all of Werowocomoco.

The *tuckahoe* slices plopped drearily into the broth. Over the sound of her stirring, Pocahontas caught men's voices raised in tense conversation. The sound came from just outside the door flap. She craned toward the sound, but Winganuske dealt a quick blow to Pocahontas's ear.

"Mind your task, Amonute."

Pale winter light flooded briefly into the hall as the door flap opened and then quickly closed. Pocahontas blinked into the returned darkness, unable to see the men striding down the length of Powhatan's great house. She could hear their footsteps well enough: hard, direct, heavy with purpose.

Winganuske made a fluttering sign with her hands; the women seized their food and tools and retreated to the bedsteads lining the room, where they sank silently into the shadows. Pocahontas hugged herself close to an upright beam and watched with shallow, careful breaths, cheek pressed against the smoke-blackened wood. Opechancanough strode past; the white feathers in his hair trailed behind him, bright in the dimness of the longhouse, like the tails of falling stars. A handful of men followed. One moved among the others, surrounded by them, with the dragging steps of a subdued prisoner.

"What is this?" Powhatan's voice rose above the sounds of the men, the rattle and click of bead and copper, of animals' claws and arrows in quivers.

"Word from the Appamattuck," said Opechancanough. "Word of treason." He pushed the subdued man forward.

The Appamattuck was young, no older than Kocoum. Many of the tattoos that ran jagged along his arms and back were still unfinished. He bowed his head in the presence of the *mamanatowick*.

"Speak," said Powhatan.

"Great Chief, I come to offer myself in place of my people."

"Offer yourself?"

"Appamattuck knows the law. We know of the edict you issued in *taquitock*. We agreed to it in good faith."

The edict. The command not to feed the *tassantassas*, on pain of death. More than death: destruction of one's whole tribe.

"Opossu-no-quonuske knows her misstep was grave," the young warrior went on, "but she had no choice but to give the *tassantassas* what they demanded. She begs humbly that you will spare the tribe, and take only her life and my own."

"She fed *tassantassas*?"

"They came calling. We resisted, as you instructed us. We tried to drive them away with arrows. But they came in their large ship, the one with those guns they call *cannon*. They fired their great gun into our midst. Two men were killed, and a huge oak tree fell, scattering our warriors. In the confusion, while we regrouped, some of the *tassantassas* came ashore. They fell upon us while our ears still rang with the *cannon's* thunder, and we could not hear their approach. I was taken, and two other men. And with us, three boys not old enough for the *huskanaw*." The man paused. His head drooped for a moment, in shame or in careful thought, Pocahontas was not sure. At last he continued his story. "Their leader, the one called Chawnzmit, threatened us with guns. He demanded that we give up our winter stores. I looked into his eyes, and there was a desperate hunger there, something that went beyond winter privation. He was like a *manitou* prowling for the spirits of men, possessed by a need to devour. Nothing else mattered to him. He made torches with pine branches." The young Appamattuck's voice did not waver. "And he burned our skin. Mine, and the skins of the other grown men."

He turned slightly in the firelight. Pocahontas gasped aloud when she saw the livid wounds on the man's chest, the raised blisters amid the charred and bleeding skin. The pain must have been all but unbearable, and yet this man delivered his story with dignity and control, as if the burns hurt no worse than his first tattoos.

"Still we did not give in, *mamanatowick*, for what is pain, or even death, beside the Great Chief's command? But when he threatened the boys with fire, Opossu-no-quonuske put a stop to it. She yielded half of Appamattuck's stores to Chawnzmit, and made it clear to him that there was nothing more she could give, hoping the *tassantassas* would never trouble Appamattuck again. She is prepared, as am I, to die for Appamattuck's crimes against you. But she asks that you spare the rest of the tribe."

A stifling, expectant silence fell down the length of the great house. Pocahontas could feel the women in the shadows trembling, sensed the burning in their chests as they held their breath.

Powhatan's dry, hollow voice cracked the silence. "Why do you offer yourself?"

The young man stared down at his feet. He had to force the admission from his mouth. "I cried out when Chawnzmit burned me. Only once. Even the little boys did not cry when he turned on them with his burning torch. Take my life and spare my tribe, and I swear before the Okeus, I will die bravely."

Powhatan turned to his brother. Their eyes locked in a long stare. Powhatan's face sagged with weariness while Opechancanough's was tense with hatred.

"Our own sister," said the *mamanatowick* sadly.

Opechancanough turned to his men. "Take this young warrior to my longhouse. Find some women to treat his burns. Feed him, too. I would speak to my brother alone."

When none remained in the longhouse but the *mamanato-wick's* hidden women, Opechancanough sighed and pressed his fists against red-rimmed eyes. "You cannot kill Opossu-no-quonuske."

"Of course not."

Pocahontas, arms wrapped tight around the beam, released her pent-up breath.

"By rights, you should. You vowed you would destroy traitors completely. A *mamanatowick* who breaks his vows impresses no one, Wahunse-na-cawh."

The name struck Pocahontas like one of Winganuske's blows. She flinched. All her life she had thought of her father as Powhatan; rarely had she heard his true name used, and never in such a brusque, scolding tone. She glanced away, so as not to witness her father's shame.

"I was hasty," said the *mamanatowick*. "My anger had the better of me."

"The only thing to do now is to cleanse you of the vow. It is the only way you might save face with the *werowances*."

Powhatan's bedstead creaked as he shifted in thought. "Yes. It would be just the thing to spare Opossu-no-quonuske. She only did what she thought she must to save her people from the *tassan-tassas'* cruelty. I cannot fault her in that. But how will we keep the rest of the tribes from trading with Chawnzmit? I know he burned a longhouse at Nansemond not three days ago."

"But they drove him off. Nansemond did not give him so much as an ear of corn."

"And now this threatening of little boys. He grows ever more persistent."

"It's a sign that he is desperate—his men must be close to starvation. We have almost won. We need only wait."

"And in the meantime, he will fire his *cannon* and torture children to obtain our food. By the Okeus, is there any way to defeat this demon?"

"There must be. We will find a way. Let us think on it and pray about it. I will set the priests to work, conjuring the spirits day and night until we have our answer. But in the meantime, we must cleanse you of that vow. Let us do it now, before Opossu-no-quonuske takes her own life in shame."

Powhatan nodded. His dark eyes wandered into an unseen distance, sorting through the frayed ends of memory. "I saw it done once, this cleansing. We need a few things: the sacred weed, of course . . . the temple will have a supply. A pure-white gourd for dipping water. And we need two girls who have not yet entered into a woman's magic. They must make bread with their own hands, and carry it themselves to the temple." He turned his head. The firelight deepened the lines of his face as he gazed into the shadowy place where Pocahontas clung to her post. "Amonute. I know you are there."

She stepped forward cautiously, limbs trembling.

"Run to your longhouse and fetch one of your unblooded sisters. Make new bread, as quickly as you can. You are coming with me to the temple of Uttamussak."

The bread was still warm from the fire. She had packed it into a silk-grass pouch, which she hung from one shoulder. Beneath her white cloak, the pouch's woven strap itched against her bare chest, but Pocahontas did not dare scratch her skin. She and Matachanna sat silent and stiff in the center of Powhatan's largest canoe. They clutched one another's hands. Pocahontas knew her palm must be as clammy as Matachanna's, but she did not pull her fingers from her sister's grasp to dry and warm them. Behind them, in the rear of the dugout, four strong warriors paddled in time. The boat surged downriver with every stroke, speeding toward the sacred grounds of Uttamussak. In the bow of the canoe, Powhatan huddled beneath a great wolfskin cape, the hood pulled up to cover his long silver hair. He sat with his back to the girls, facing out upon the world, quiet and immovable as an ancient mountain. The pointed, smoke-brown ears of his wolfskin cloak twitched now and then as he jerked his head to peer at the river's banks.

As they traveled, now and then Opechancanough's canoe would leap ahead, his warriors straining at their paddles in silent intensity, backs and arms taut with power and rage. Then Opechancanough would glance toward Powhatan perched like an ancient eagle on a broken roost, and his paddles would slow, and his dugout would fall back once more.

Pocahontas noted the spirit posts well before the canoes angled toward the riverbank. Here and there amid the trees, a trunk stood pale and cracked, stripped of its bark and lopped off at the height of a man's head. The spirit masks held aloft on the posts leered through *popanow*'s dark tangle of branches. The sharp teeth of a wolf flashed as they passed, the furrowed flesh of a cougar's snarl, the forbidding visage of a bear. More faces watched her, faces she could not identify: the precise black holes of *manitou*'s eyes, the lolling tongues of demons. She gripped Matachanna's hand more tightly, watching wide-eyed and helpless as the terrible faces emerged and receded from the brush like storm fronts rising and falling, inevitable, a force beyond any man's control.

Most terrifying of all, though, were the faces of men. The man posts were more numerous as they pulled close to the low shelf of riverbank where they would land the canoes, and the closer they

came to Uttamussak, the fiercer the faces grew. The hard wood
of the masks seemed to writhe, roiling with emotion as the water
above a fish weir ripples with the thrashing of the creatures trapped
below. Anger twisted the mouths of the masks; hatred burned like
black fires in their empty eyes. They were shouting, calling for
blood, straining at their white posts to leap into the forest on their
strange, long-limbed spirit bodies and dance destruction throughout the land of Tsenacomoco.

Powhatan's canoe turned for the shore. They beached with a
hollow scrape of dugout on mud and stone, a vibration that echoed
in Pocahontas's bones. She was stiff and reluctant as she climbed
from the canoe and made her way onto the shore. Matachanna
regained her hand, and they stood together, staring at the trail that
reached back into the damp winter forest with suspicion. The man
posts lined each side of the trail, seething out at the river—toward
them—in silent rage.

"Uttamussak is where your handsome priest lives," Pocahontas
whispered, no hint of teasing in her voice now. "Are you sure you
wish to marry him, and join him at such a hearth?"

Matachanna said nothing. Pocahontas heard her sister swal-
low a hard lump in her throat.

When all the men came ashore and the canoes had been pulled
well out of the reach of the river's high tide, they formed a silent
procession to the temple. Pocahontas clutched her bag of fresh
bread close to her chest. Beside her, Matachanna held the pure-
white dipping gourd in trembling hands. It was they who would
have to lead the party to the temple, so all the *manitou* would know
that the men came in the spirit of purity, untainted by any magic
and as free of guile as innocent girls.

"We must be brave," Matachanna said softly, "as brave as boys
at their *huskanaw*."

Pocahontas nodded, but as they stepped onto the trail she felt
the masks turn on their posts to stare at her, look through her flesh

and bones to her weak, quaking spirit. She summoned the courage to glance back, and saw only the backs of the posts, not the black pits of their eyes, not their faces snarling down at her. A small relief. She sighed and cradled the bread against her body.

After what seemed an endless walk through the forest of masks, they emerged into a clearing. An undisturbed skin of snow lay over the ground, sparkling in the sun, icy hard after many days and nights of thawing and refreezing. A lone, dark trail cut across the snow like a knife slash through buckskin. It led in a perfect line to the door of the temple.

The temple itself waited like a ghost crouched on a precipice, pale, softly breathing, watching the life that moved below with a knowing, cruelly distant smile.

Pocahontas hesitated. The men milled anxiously on the trail behind her. The door flap of the temple opened and a figure emerged, familiar even across the brightness of the snow-white clearing, even through the paint on his face.

Matachanna gave a small squeak of surprise and relief. "Utta-ma-tomakkin!" She led the way across the narrow path through the snowfield.

With regal stillness, Utta-ma-tomakkin watched the party's approach. His ceremonial robe, a long, trailing cloak of buckskin painted black as old coals, gathered in soft folds about his feet, as stark against the snow as a bird traversing a clear sky. A row of white-shell beaded spirals crossed his back from shoulder to shoulder. In the center of his cloak, the sacred cross of the four winds blazed in pearls dyed with *puccoon*, while beneath the cross the cougar and the deer reared in their delicate balance, life and death confronting one another across an expanse of ashy blackness.

A flat black stone stood outside the temple, not as fine as the great quartz crystal of Werowocomoco's temple, but still emanating an air of majesty. The girls bowed at the altar stone, hands to foreheads. Utta-ma-tomakkin produced a rattle from beneath his

cloak, two halves of turtle shell so aged by the smoke of the temple that they were nearly as black as the cloak itself. Pocahontas
held herself tense and still as the rattle shook its bright thunder before her face. It passed over her shoulders, her heart, her
belly, and her back, hissing and chanting, unhooking the claws of
unseen, malevolent spirits from her skin. Matachanna, too, was
cleansed by the sound. Then Utta-ma-tomakkin reached once
more beneath his cloak. His fist emerged, closed, and approached
Pocahontas's face. Just in time she saw the white powder trickling from his hand, and she squeezed her eyes shut and held her
breath. The priest's breath puffed against her skin. A cold sensation
prickled along her forehead and cheeks. She blinked the powder
from her eyes and watched as Utta-ma-tomakkin blew the white
clay onto Matachanna. Matachanna gasped; her face was entirely
coated in white, the powder building tiny ridges along her eyelids
as she squinted in startlement.

"You are cleansed," Utta-ma-tomakkin pronounced in his
smooth, resonant voice, "and the spirits approve. You do not come
to this place wreathed in woman's magic. You do not come cloaked
in guile. You come in purity, seeking purity. Enter."

A high, desperate voice cracked across the snowfield. It took
Pocahontas a heartbeat, a terrible, slow stretch of time, to realize
that the words were English.

"Naturals! They must have food!"

She spun in the doorway of the temple, the ends of her ragged
white cloak lifting and flying. Opechancanough barked a command, and the warriors' bows rose, arrows whipped from quivers like blackbirds rising startled from a garden. Five *tassantassas*
staggered from the woods. They were thin, gaunt with hunger.
Their legs moved slowly as they stumbled on the crust of snow.
One held a torch aloft, which burned with a sickly yellow flame.
For a moment she wondered why he carried a torch during the
day. Then, as she watched wide-eyed, one of the *tassantassas* lifted

his long gun and held a trailing bit of pale sinew to the torch. *Matchlock.* She remembered the word. The burning sinew would light the powder within the gun's black, cold body, and soon the lead balls would fly, deadly and fast.

She seized Matachanna's hand.

"Into the temple," Utta-ma-tomakkin said. He pushed Matachanna through the door and Pocahontas, clinging to her arm, staggered after. As the *tassantassas* advanced in a wary crouch, guns at the ready, Pocahontas saw Powhatan fling aside his wolfskin robe. He drew a war club from the belt of his winter tunic, and for one moment, her father was not a staggering old bull, but faced his enemies as tall and strong as a buck in the first vigorous blush of autumn.

Then the temple's door flap swung closed, smothering the girls in thick, smoky darkness.

"What is it?" Matachanna said. Her words came fast and panicky. "What do they want? Why are they here?"

"Runaways. They left the fort seeking food. They have none. I'm sure of it." Pocahontas squeezed the strap of her bread bag in one trembling fist.

The men shouted at one another across the field, Real Tongue and English words mingling in one roar of anger and fear.

Pocahontas glanced around. At the far end of the temple, light dropped in a bright-white shaft through the smoke hole in the roof. The heart fire burned below it. There was nothing else but shadow, pressing in from all sides, and outside, men with guns and clubs and arrows.

"Come." She took Matachanna by the arm, pulled her quickly toward the shaft of light.

Matachanna balked. "No! It's forbidden. We can't be here without a priest."

"He cleansed us. He told us to enter." Pocahontas felt her sister shivering. *Is she more afraid of angry spirits, or angry men? Okeus, help us!* "We must get away from the door, Matachanna. We have no weapons, no way to defend ourselves! We must hide!"

Matachanna sobbed, but she took a few steps toward the heart fire.

The shouts rose in a sudden pique, and the crack of a gunshot split the air. A small circle of fiery white suddenly appeared, hanging in the darkness. A moment later, Pocahontas realized the *tassantassas'* bullet had pierced the temple wall. The odor of sulfur and heat, of fragmented bark, filled the long, dark hall.

Matachanna screamed and lurched about in the darkness, casting herself into the arrow-thin beam of light that shone through the bullet hole. It flickered over her face, which was white from clay dust and terror. Pocahontas froze, and the whole world became Matachanna's wide, terrified eyes, the clay cracking on her face and falling like snow, her mouth open wide in a howl of fear. Pocahontas clapped her hand over her sister's mouth. As if her spirit watched from far away, Pocahontas saw her hand pressed beneath Matachanna's nose, pulling at her sister as they flashed in and out of the beam of light.

"Come! We must hide!" Pocahontas tugged harder, but Matachanna broke away. She staggered back into the darkness, away from the heart fire, fleeing Pocahontas's hands.

Outside, a man screamed in pain. Pocahontas could not tell whether it was a *tassantassa* or a Real Man. Another shot exploded, a sound like a tree limb snapping beneath the weight of winter ice. Sending up a prayer for her sister's safety—for the safety of all the men—Pocahontas fled deep into the temple.

She halted at the edge of the smoke hole's ring of light. Motes moved in a lazy swirl, sparkling in the bright column. Their placid dance made an otherworldly counterpoint to the sounds of violence outside. The largest log in the heart fire's stone ring split with a pop. Pocahontas leaped back as sparks streaked upward like a thin red arm reaching for the hole in the roof, grasping at the clay-white winter sky. She inched away from the pool of light, suddenly afraid, against all reason, that the *tassantassas* would see her through the walls of the temple unless she veiled herself in shadow.

Beyond the heart fire, in the deepest blackness against the temple's rear wall, her hands found a row of chest-high platforms. She moved along the wall of niches, groping blindly, searching for a place to hide. She collided with a post and gasped at the sound of many bead chains clattering together. Her fingers found dry bundles of herbs; in her haste she crushed one, and the scent of sacred tobacco blossomed beneath the smell of years' worth of dust. *What is this place? Where can I hide?* With a great effort, Pocahontas slowed her feet and hands, and her racing thoughts. She felt around her with more deliberate care, exploring the darkness with cold fingers.

She reached into one of the niches on the high platform. Her hands rested on something smooth and soft: buckskin. Beneath it was something hard as stone but light, rocking easily beneath her touch. She squeezed through the buckskin shroud. It fit easily into her palm and her fingers wrapped around it like the handle of a ladle or a digging stick.

All at once she knew what she held. Her scalp prickled, and a roaring in her ears blotted out the sounds of fighting outside. *Bone.*

It was the ossuary, the final resting place of *werowances* dead for generations. Once his bones were laid in a temple, the spirit of a chief would not return to the cycle of life, to be reborn endlessly in a new body, to live a new life as someone else. Instead, they joined with the Okeus in the world of the eternal, and never suffered the disintegration of self. It was the privilege of the *werowance*, to *be* for all time, intact and whole, never forgotten.

Pocahontas pulled her hands away from the bones quickly, as if burned. Then she touched them again, fearful and wondering. This was what she wanted. This was her ambition, her life's dream: to be a *werowansqua*, powerful and strong, and in the end, to be *herself* forever. She ran her fingers down the length of a thighbone, feeling the knot at its end like the head of a war club. She trailed her touch over the curved sticks of ribs, the symmetrical stones of a spine. The old desire for influence sprang up in her spirit again.

"Speak," she whispered to the bones, to the chiefs of old. She clutched at their dry remains through their burial bags, but the *werowances* had no words for her. The bones only shifted, moving together with a soft sound like rain on the river, like the clatter of a pigeon's wings, a brief tumble of movement—then stillness—then the ancestors' spirits were gone.

She thought of Matachanna, of the feather-thin ridges of clay around her eyes. She thought of Kocoum, rowing at her back, the drops of water from his paddle falling soft against her skin. She thought of her aunt Koleopatchika dropping groundnuts into a pot. None of them were chiefs. None would ever be. They were, had been, would be, other spirits, dug up out of brief, nameless bodies, turned back into the soil of life to sprout and grow anew. They were temporary. Their names were short and fragile things, to be chipped away by time and forgotten. But they were warm, present, flashing through her world in bright colors, *puccoon* and ochre, pearl and ash. They were drums at sunset, calling, real.

Here in the ossuary there was only darkness, and the bones were dry and cold.

Something sank deep into Pocahontas's heart. It was a barb, an invisible arrow with a head sharper than flint. Its magic spread through her blood and pulsed along her trembling limbs. Her bones lit with a strange and poignant fire, and with her spirit's eye she saw into her own body, and the marrow inside her glowed red and golden, ochre and *puccoon*. The well of her ambition gave one last heave as she clutched at the dead *werowance*'s bones. It bubbled, sighed, and bled itself dry. Where that dark, compelling water had once flowed, this new magic coursed like a gentle stream. It tasted of obligation and guilt, but also of love—love and joy, and the beautiful brevity of a life well lived. The savor of it was bitter and sweet.

A noise above her head ripped Pocahontas from her trance. Something clattered and rolled down the temple's rounded roof. She jerked her hands away from the bones and listened in stunned fear as the object slid down the roof and then caught in the cracks of the bark instead of falling from the temple into the snow. Over the men's war whoops and shouted commands, a crackling rush grew until the sound of it filled the entire world. Thick smoke pressed into her nose and mouth. This was not the smoke of the heart fire; it was dense and oily, rushing and hot.

The tassantassa's *torch! He threw it onto the roof!*

The wall of the temple bloomed in the darkness like a red flower.

From far away, near the temple's door, Matachanna called out to her. "Amonute! Pocahontas!"

She is safe, Pocahontas thought, watching the fire race along the wall of the temple, detached and accepting. *Thank the Okeus.*

The blaze lit up the interior of the temple, beating back the sacred mystery of shrouding darkness. Animal skins hanging along crossbeams smoldered; their claws and teeth cast leaping, jagged shadows into the hot red light. Rows of masks, hung on their pegs, stared downward as if in defeat. The wreaths of dried herbs that encircled each mask caught and blazed, ringing the spirits in haloes of fire.

"Pocahontas! Where are you?"

She moved toward her sister's voice, toward the temple door, choking and gasping. She passed a niche in the wall, its beams licked by yellow flames. Inside, the dark figure of the Okeus himself stood defiant. She paused, staring up at the god in wonder. His body was as haggard as a starving man's, the ribs and bones carved into the blackened wood in sharp, harsh relief. The face was hard as an eagle's talons, all fierce angles and angry leer, the mouth open and ringed with teeth like a wolf's fangs. White shell eyes stared back at her, knowing and sad. Then the hair caught fire, blazing in a knot of writhing red around the god's stunned and helpless face.

Pocahontas ran.

She raced the fire down the length of the hall, her arms extended, pushing her way through the smoke. Hands caught at her. In the sickly light Matachanna held her and shrieked words that Pocahontas could not hear above the roar of the fire. She was still white from the sacred clay. Clinging together like beetles on a stem when the wind blows hard and fierce, the girls fought through the smoke and out the temple door.

The bitter cold of *popanow* was never so welcome. They ran from the burning temple and collapsed together in the field, weeping, heedless of the ongoing battle between the *tassantassas* and the Real Men. Pocahontas coughed again and again, hunched in the snow, a tearing paroxysm that left her weak and nauseous. Her throat was raw and painful, but finally she could breathe again. Matachanna pulled her upright, and Pocahontas stared at her sister, needing to satisfy herself that Matachanna was truly alive. The girl's white clay mask was streaked with sweat and tears and darkened by soot—but she was well.

Pocahontas threw her arms around her. Tears of gratitude stung her eyes more fiercely than the smoke. *Thank you, Okeus.* The god's last magic before he burned: he had spared Matachanna.

Still holding Matachanna, Pocahontas dared to glance around the clearing. The snowfield was trampled and, where the *tassantassas* had fallen, painted bright with blood. Wisps of steam rose from their bodies, from the places where their life's blood drained away into the snow. A harsh wind blew through the forest. It fanned the flames of the temple and shivered the arrows protruding from the *tassantassas'* chests.

But not one of the Real Men was harmed.

Powhatan lifted his wolfskin cloak from the earth and wrapped it carefully around his body, again stooped with age. His war club lay discarded in the snow at his feet.

Utta-ma-tomakkin knelt in the snow, rocking before the sight of Uttamussak in flames, his face cradled in his hands.

A hoarse, wordless scream ripped through the air. Opechancanough stormed to the body of the nearest *tassantassa* and kicked it. The dead man's arm lifted under the blow, and then fell with a limp thud, like a stone dropped into a mudhole. Opechancanough seized the man's arm and hauled the body onto his shoulder. His warriors scrambled to heft the bodies of the other *tassantassas*, following Opechancanough down the trail toward the canoes.

Pocahontas and Matachanna stared at each other, silent and shivering in the snow. Then Pocahontas rose stiffly. She pulled her sister to her feet. Together with Powhatan, they followed Opechancanough down the trail.

The *werowance* of Pamunkey dropped the dead body in one of the dugout canoes. The rest of the *tassantassas* slid from the warriors' shoulders like deer carcasses after the hunt.

"Food," Opechancanough raged. Paint had rubbed from his chest in wide smears; the crossed bows of Pamunkey burned like proud scars through the remains of his ceremonial trappings. "Do they want food? Do they want bread?"

His eyes fell on Pocahontas. He was upon her in three swift strides. She cowered, but he did not want her. Instead, he seized the soot-blackened bag of fresh bread that still hung from her shoulder. He tore it from her body with a violent wrench; she staggered and her singed cloak ripped away, leaving her exposed in the wind.

"Bread for the *tassantassas*! Bread for our brother Chawnzmit!"

Opechancanough reached a fist into the bag. He pulled out a great lump of bread; the golden cornmeal crumbled between his tight-clenched fingers. He pried open the mouth of one of the dead *tassantassas,* stuffed the fistful of bread inside. Pocahontas did not dare to breathe, let alone speak or weep, as her uncle forced the remaining ceremonial bread into the mouths of the dead men. Opechancanough hurled the empty bag into the river.

"If the white men want our bread," he snarled, raising one foot to the bow of the canoe, "let them have it." And he shoved hard, sending the dugout into the rising tide. It glided, hanging for a moment, motionless in the center of the river, and then drifted slowly downstream, toward Jamestown.

Shaking, Pocahontas retrieved her cloak from the riverbank. She bundled herself in its warmth, but the chill had sunk deep into her spirit and bones. She recalled Chawnzmit's words as they stood together in the garden of Jamestown. *Because I will do as I must, it is not safe for you here. Not anymore.*

Opechancanough stalked up the muddy bank. His face was calm, his rage, for the moment, spent.

Pocahontas raised her voice, never knowing where her courage came from. "Chawnzmit will be even more desperate now." She sounded so small, so weak and impermanent, standing among these men who still thrummed with the heat of war. "He will be desperate enough to attack the capital—he will fall on Werowocomoco."

Powhatan turned to stare after the drifting canoe.

"I agree," said Opechancanough. She looked up at him in surprise. His voice was deceptively gentle, his eyes far too calm. "We must be prepared, Brother."

Powhatan nodded. "The time has come. It is certain. We must do away with Chawnzmit, for the good of all."

SMITH

January 1609

John Smith eased himself to the ground, edging as near Powhatan's fire as he dared. The Great Chief's longhouse was warm and dry; even the earthen floor was dry. It was a luxury no structure in Jamestown could boast. Try as they might, the cabins and tents of the fort remained cold and wet. The freezing damp of the New World winter had become a part of Smith's being, as much a fact of his life as beard and bones and flesh—what little flesh remained to him. The warm days of autumn seemed a lifetime ago, a time so long past it had acquired the trappings of legend. But here, at Powhatan's fire, he could recall that the ancient myth had been born out of fact. A thousand years gone, John Smith had been warm and dry. In spite of the obvious danger, knowing full well he had walked willingly into a trap, Smith gave himself over to the sheer pleasure of physical comfort. Christ alone knew when such a blessing might come again.

Seated to his left, John Russell also huddled close to the flames. The man had once been large—exceedingly heavy, in fact. But months of privation had stripped him down, peeling away his fleshy exterior as easily as an Indian maiden peels husks from corn, until only a frame of broad bone remained. Russell, though a gentleman born and bred, had never raised a word of complaint about the conditions at Jamestown. The man had always been quick to lend his considerable strength to the work of maintaining the fort. He was a rare breed, intelligent and capable in spite of his heritage of lofty privilege, and so John Smith had brought him along on this mission, a task he knew would be both dangerous and delicate.

Smith held his palms out to the fire. He glanced up at Powhatan. The Great Chief sat aloof on his pile of furs. For once no wives lounged about him and no maiden daughters worked in the shadowy corners of the longhouse. Two stocky warriors stood like well-made statues to either side of Powhatan's bed.

Smith was no fool. He knew what the absence of women meant. Every snap of a twig that carried through the longhouse walls, every scrape of moccasin on snow, set his heart racing and his mind on edge, even while he affected a posture of casual unconcern. Hunger had made him animalistic, had sharpened something inside him. He was alert for the signs of ambush, all his overtaxed senses straining for information. Had he been a horse or a hound, his nose would have lifted to taste the cautious air, and his ears would have twitched unceasingly.

"So," Smith said, speaking the Indian tongue. Now that his hands were thawed, he kept one hand upon his buckler shield, and the other never strayed far from the butt of his snaphaunce. "You invited us here to trade our guns for food. Here we sit."

Powhatan made no reply, not even a grunt. He looked pointedly away from Smith's face. It was a gesture of dismissal, a great rudeness from a natural. *These Indians with their particular and prickly sense of propriety, their very strange concepts of etiquette and decorum!*

Smith tried another approach: "We have only come at your summons, *mamanatowick*. Had you not called us, we would not be here."

"And when will you be leaving again?"

A response, of sorts. It was better than silence. "We came for the food you offered."

Powhatan lifted a hand and flicked it: a curt dismissal of a lie, though Smith had spoken the truth. The Great Chief had offered them food.

"I never said I would feed you, Chawnzmit."

Smith nodded to each of the silent warriors. "Ah, but Chief Powhatan, the two men who carried your message to Jamestown stand here before me. Do not think I don't recognize their faces. They know the truth of it. Your own people know you offered food for guns."

The old chief's face cracked suddenly, a wide grin. His eyes twinkled with real mirth.

A jape, Smith thought with some relief, still straining for the sounds of men creeping up outside. *If he japes with me, perhaps the situation is not as dire as I feared.*

"You have me there, Chawnzmit. If you want the food, then, you had best give me your guns and swords first."

Swords? Not a part of the original offer. Not that Smith had intended to hand over firearms to the naturals. The runaways who had been sent back to Jamestown in a dugout canoe, arrows in their chests and corn bread in their gaping mouths, had been stripped of their guns. Somewhere in the Tidewater, five warriors were already slinking through the forest with matchlocks lit and murder in their hearts. They were five too many for Smith's liking.

"I cannot give you guns, as you well know," Smith said. Powhatan scowled deeply, all the humor gone from his face in an instant. Smith said quickly, "But I heard that your temple was destroyed. It was ill done, and you were right to take the lives of those runaways who burned it. I will not give you guns, but I will send strong workers to rebuild Uttamussak."

Powhatan's shoulders jerked, a silent bark of laughter. "You have no strong men, Chawnzmit. It is winter, and you have nothing to eat but ice and sticks." He leaned back comfortably on his furs. "If I do not get my guns, you do not get your food."

"Do you think you can while away the days until my people die of starvation?"

Powhatan watched him levelly, unblinking, the smallest and coldest smile on the Great Chief's mouth.

Of course it was precisely what the *mamanatowick* intended: allow the weather, the vile, harsh Tidewater itself, to do the chore of eradicating the English pestilence. Christ knew the land had done a fine enough job already. Brackish water, meager game, gardens that could not produce more than a handful of thin beans and dry corn. Illness spread through the very mud of Jamestown like a wine stain through linen, and when illness was not dropping men like shot drops a flock of birds, the haunting vastness of the woodland turned the English mad. Ratcliffe and his palace; Wingfield and his secret stores.

The Indians needed do naught but wait. And now they knew it; Smith saw the truth of it in Powhatan's conceited stare.

"I cannot spare any of my weapons," Smith said. "We need them to defend ourselves against your people. However, I will make a sacred oath that I will not turn a single one of my weapons on any Real Person. Nor shall any of my men harm your people in any way, if you will freely give us enough food to see us through *popanow*. None of us shall violate this sacred oath, unless you force us to do so with ill treatment."

A dark intensity came over the *mamanatowick*'s face. He sat forward, leaning his elbows upon his knees. Smith thought for one wild, victorious moment that the old man would agree to the oath. Instead, the Great Chief asked a question for which Smith was not prepared: "Why are you here, Chawnzmit? Why did you come to Tsenacomoco? This question has plagued me since you first arrived. It has haunted me like a crying ghost in my dreams. Do you intend to make this land yours? To take it from me, to drive my people out, or kill us entirely? Tell me. Tell me why you came."

Smith could not form a suitable answer. A shower of words tumbled through his head, English and Real Tongue falling together in a confusion, pouring through his mind like the gush of a waterfall. He grasped at them, but the words were slippery as fishes. They darted away again, silver and flashing. How could he make Powhatan understand any of it? The Virginia Company, the search for gold, shareholders and kings, a passage to the Indies . . . How could he explain the greatness of the explorer, immortality on the page of a book, a place in history? The fishes dodged and fled, and Smith could only stare at the chief flatly.

"Listen to my words, Chawnzmit. This"—Powhatan gestured in the space between them, as if delineating an invisible chasm that separated them, or perhaps a tie that bound them—"is not what I want. I am old. I am only growing older. Because you are a young man still, you do not yet feel it, but the same will be true of you. Listen to an old man's wisdom. All I want is a life of quiet ease. I cannot continue to fight, nor can I run. I would rather enjoy what few years I have left, lying with my women, laughing with my children. Making a friendship with all who come to my land— even you, even after all you have done." The Great Chief's voice rose slightly, carrying just a bit farther than it had before. The men guarding his person drew themselves up. It was almost imperceptible, but Smith, sharpened as he was, found it signal enough.

"I will strike a bargain with you," Powhatan said, "a trade, if you swear to me that you will deal from now on only with me. You and all your kind must let all my people alone, in Werowocomoco and in all my other towns, all my other territories."

Smith ducked his head, a grudging acknowledgment. "If I had intended to harm any of your people, Chief Powhatan, I should have harmed them long before now." He turned abruptly to Russell, said rapidly in English, "Get back to the shallop. Tell more men to come ashore, armed and ready for a fight. Be quick."

He said smoothly to Powhatan, smiling, "I have sent my man to bring some steel goods, gifts for you—tokens of our good faith."

As they waited for Russell to return, they spoke lightly of the treaty, suggesting terms, waving acceptance. Smith could see in Powhatan's sly, steady eyes that the old man's promises were as false as his own. Russell was admitted once more into the longhouse. Several women followed, carrying baskets of hot food.

"You must excuse me," Powhatan said, rising on unsteady legs. "I find I have more need of the privy pit with each year that passes. My women will entertain you until I return."

The women laid out a small feast, corn dumplings swimming in oyster stew accompanied by baskets of dried mulberries and the soft, sweet meat of chestnuts. Smith's mouth watered; his stomach clenched painfully, so sudden and fierce that he nearly cried aloud. He stuffed a dumpling into his mouth and muttered to Russell, "Brace. They will attack any moment."

Russell, too, packed his cheeks with food, frantic as a starving squirrel. When they had both gulped down all they could in a few moments' time, Smith nodded abruptly. They lifted their bucklers, drew their guns, and barged down the length of the longhouse while the women screamed the alarm behind them.

Smith threw himself past the door flap. He hoisted his snaphaunce and fired a shot into the air. White smoke, reeking of sulfur, spread in a ring above their heads and dissipated rapidly on the breeze. Russell pointed his gun at the nearest Indian, who was already drawing back, already holding his bow out to the side, as were they all, retreating a step or two from the perilous firearms but still tense and ready to spring.

"Hold your shot," Smith barked to Russell. "We may need it. I can't reload as we are now."

They raced for the shallop, glancing over their shoulders as they dodged through the trees. An arrow punched into a tree as Smith fled past it; Russell lifted his buckler in time to deflect another shaft. Before they reached the riverbank, a charge of Englishmen came through the woods to meet them, yelling like devils, matches alight and glowing in the locks of their muskets. The pursuing Indians drew up short, shouting among the trees.

"Back to the boat," Smith said. The riverbank was not far off, where Scrivener waited on the shallop with a crew of men.

They retreated in a body, bucklers raised in cautious defense. Smith watched the forest warily. The men milled at the landing boat, trying to organize themselves in the best way for a successful flight to the safety of the shallop.

A gray shape moved among the trees. Powhatan emerged from the wood, dressed in his robe of wolfskin. He raised a hand to the Englishmen.

"Chawnzmit, my friend. What is this misunderstanding? Why do you flee? Come, let us return to our talk of a treaty."

"Talk of a treaty, while I am surrounded by men armed with bows? I think not."

"I sent bowmen only to guard the corn I will give you."

"Guard it? From whom?"

"From your own men, in case they tried to take it from you and overthrow your leadership. Look at them. They are ready to shoot at the least provocation. Starving men can never be trusted. Why should they not turn their guns on you?"

Smith cut his eyes toward the Englishmen who stood with their muskets trained on Powhatan.

"Look," Powhatan said. "See the corn we bring you."

Scores of men emerged from the wood, each one straining with a basket heaped with food. Some carried corn, some beans, others small colorful gourds, but all brought a wealth of goods.

Smith's mouth watered. He swallowed convulsively as the line of baskets stretched down the length of the shoreline.

Powhatan approached, his hand stretched forth in friendship. "Set down your guns, Chawnzmit. Allow us to prove to you that we are your friends, on this day and for all days to come. We shall watch over your guns while you load the food onto your boat."

For answer, Smith moved close to Powhatan's side. He lifted his snaphaunce, pulled the wheel lock back into a cock. The click of steel was as loud as the pounding of his heart. Immediately he heard the metallic clamor of more firearms cocking as the men of Jamestown steadied their weapons.

"Tell your men to load my boat," Smith grated, his voice dangerous and low. "And to show we are friends, I will not kill you."

The English made a brave show, standing armed over the bushels of beans and corn while the naturals loaded the shallop with extreme care. They did the job so methodically that by the time the goods and the English were aboard, the tide had run low. The shallop, sluggish with the weight of food and men, sank its keel into the mud and could not be persuaded to move.

Smith spat a few choice curses at the naturals, in this tongue and their own. A few of them grinned as they slunk back and forth along the shoreline like wolves around a sheep pen.

"It will be hours before the tide lifts us high enough to sail," Russell murmured. "And by then, we'll be in pitch blackness and cannot navigate."

"Aye. They have us, and no mistake," Smith said.

Powhatan raised his voice. It carried across the water, hoarse and gruff, thick with amusement. "It seems you are rather stuck, Chawnzmit."

"True enough," he called back. He felt as mad as Ratcliffe in his palace; a wild laugh pressed at his throat, threatening to rattle loose and wing across the river.

"It seems you had best come back ashore, you and all your men. We have plenty of food left in our stores. Let us feed you well, and we shall bed you down in a good longhouse. I give you a promise of safety. We are all friends here. Let us pass a night together as brothers."

The old man pressed a hand to his heart, grinning and chuckling.

Smith had no choice but to return the gesture. Beneath the thin, ragged wool of his tunic, through the cold skin of his mail, John Smith felt his heart hammer like a blacksmith at his forge.

The longhouse was dry and warm. In that, at least, Powhatan's promise had been truthful. Smith set his own men guarding the door flap and the inside perimeter of the building, while outside Indian guards paced a black ring through the skiff of snow.

"Now what?" Scrivener muttered, cradling his gun close against his chest.

"You may as well try to rest," Smith said. "We are stuck here until morning."

"Meanwhile, they will send their canoes out to rob us of every last kernel of corn. I have no doubt that the shallop is floating free this very moment."

"Wish we was aboard," somebody agreed from the depths of the longhouse.

"Sailing at night?" Smith mocked. "Have you a cat's eyes, then?"

"What if they cut the shallop free? How will we return to Jamestown?"

If the naturals decided to cut the shallop free, they would not leave the English in any fit state to return to Jamestown. Corpses did not make the finest of sailors. Smith thought it far more likely that a few of them would be singled out to die bravely, subjected to the same trial they had given George Classen at Apocant, while the rest of the English watched. The survivors would be bundled back aboard their empty shallop and sent home to spread the news that Powhatan had finally struck in all his terrible power. And then, Jamestown would be left alone, the final handful of men allowed to starve or die of exposure.

Smith felt little fear. Powhatan still held some small measure of respect for him, he knew—a grudging admission that Smith was a survivor, a leader, a man with the natural gifts of the *werowance*. He would not be left to starve. He would be offered the honor of a brave death. It would not be quick, and Smith would not be brave. But it was preferable to slow starvation and encroaching madness.

Secure in this certainty, a blanketing peace fell over John Smith's soul. He leaned back against the sapling frame of the longhouse and sighed, accepting his bone-deep weariness and the simple comfort of the warm, dry shelter. He was tired. He would sleep, and when he woke, he would die.

From across the longhouse, a faint scratching sounded. The men near it looked around in startlement.

"Chawnzmit," a voice called in a half whisper, urgent and high. A child's voice.

Smith forced himself upright. He staggered on aching legs toward the sound. Small fingers poked into a crack between bark strips, pried, slipped.

"Pocahontas?"

"Hurry," she said. "The guards will come back to this side of the longhouse soon."

He leaned against the patch of bark. It gave against its lashings; the frame of the longhouse creaked. Pocahontas worked her hands into the gap and tugged. The strips gave way, opened just enough for her to wriggle through onto the hard-packed floor.

"Princess," a few of the men said. They helped her to her feet, squeezing her shoulders with reverent hands, touching her arms and her hair, as if her presence might bestow on them enough luck to save their lives.

She tipped her face up and stared into John Smith's eyes. The dimple in her chin quivered.

"Why are you here, Pocahontas? You're in danger; you know that."

"I shouldn't be here. I should leave you all to your fates."

He stepped back, struck by her bitterness. It seemed an emotion too real for this sportive, sweet child, too adult.

"I saw the temple burn, Chawnzmit. I saw what your men did to our sacred place."

"I am sorry for it. I never ordered it. I would have stopped it, if I could."

She dropped her piercing, fierce, unchildlike black eyes and he exhaled in relief.

"I know," she said. "I am here only because I believe what you said, those many months ago. Do you remember, Chawnzmit? You told me . . ."

"That the alternative to what we do is not love, but war."

"Yes. I believe it. After what I have seen, I understand that there can be no love between us. *Tassantassas* and Real People can never live as one. We can never love. But neither do I wish war. My father is old. War would break him—kill him. He is too old now to die bravely in battle. He would die weeping and ashamed, and I would consign his bones to darkness."

He took her hand. He could think of nothing else to do, no word or gesture that could bring comfort to her wracked soul. Her fingers were limp and cold in his hand.

"I do not wish for war," she went on in her stilted English, "therefore I come to warn you. Soon my father will send food for your men, and the warriors who bring it will wait until your starving men are eating. While they are distracted by the food . . ." Her voice stopped abruptly. The crunch of moccasins in snow moved along the outer wall and then faded into the night. She exhaled, squeezing her eyes shut as she drove away the momentary fear. "While they are distracted by the food, my father's warriors will draw the swords from your men's belts, and cut them down with their own blades.

"Your people are cruel, and broken deep in their spirits. But this ambush will only lead to more attacks, more temples burned, more lives lost. So I am here to put a stop to it. Take your men and leave, Chawnzmit. Leave and never trouble my people again. You must stay far from us, and we from you. It is the only way any of us will survive—it is the only way we might have peace again in Tsenacomoco."

Smith nodded, and kept nodding, stunned to speechlessness by her bravery, and wounded by the curious pain he felt on her behalf. She was so naïve, so full of hope where there was no hope to be found. And Smith knew it was he who had instilled it in her, he who had led her to trust.

God will damn me for breaking your heart, he told her silently. *And I will deserve it.*

He caught her chin in his hand and held her gently while he gazed one final time into her face. In all the New World, and in the Old World, too, she alone was a kindred soul. She alone could he trust and esteem. And even she was changing—already changed— touched by a deep, harrowing sadness, her eyes brimming with the power of a revelation he could not understand.

He would give her some token of what had been, some small thing to remember him by. He sensed they would part forever now. He could feel the truth of it crackling around them like sparks from a bonfire. He reached into the pouch he wore for trading and pulled out a string of blue beads. Wordlessly, he offered the string to her.

Pocahontas looked down at his hand but she made no move to reach for the beads. When she looked up again, her face was twisted with tragedy. A hot flood of tears washed her cheeks.

"Chawnzmit," she said, "you think to buy this information from me?" She shook her head, disbelieving and sad. "I give it freely."

She ducked into shadow, pressing herself against the panel of bark, and with a twist of her body she was gone, silent as smoke dissipating on a night breeze.

OPECHANCANOUGH

Season of Popanow

The messenger from Werowocomoco was near collapse. He had run through the forest from the capital to Pamunkey-town. With Chawnzmit on the loose, manning his strange white-winged boat with its thunderous weapons, the river was no longer safe. It took a long time for the messenger to catch his breath. He sat well back from the heat of the heart fire, wheezing, eyes shut, one hand pressed to his racing heart, until at last he was able to gasp out a few words: "They are coming."

Opechancanough, pacing up and down the length of his long-house, eyeing the empty bedstead where Tsena-no-ha had slept, allowed himself the smallest of smiles. "Good."

When the messenger had recovered enough to gulp down a gourdful of water, Opechancanough crouched beside him. The young man's body still trembled violently from his heroic exertion. His face was pale and slightly green around the mouth.

"Chawnzmit received my invitation, then?"

"It seems so, *werowance*. Either he received it, or he decided to come of his own accord. He was angry as a beestung bear when he left Werowocomoco. He is coming here full of violence and hate."

I will meet him with the same.

Opechancanough had offered Chawnzmit food, and sent a man to tell him that he must come to Pamunkey-town, too, for Opechancanough had not yet moved to his new longhouse at Werowocomoco, and he wanted the honor of feasting him, as Powhatan did. He implied that he would not demand guns, but would be satisfied with swords in exchange for many baskets of corn.

The messenger had nearly caught his breath now. "As he was leaving, Chawnzmit made some mention of Pamunkey being more honest than Werowocomoco."

"I must assume he received my invitation, then."

Opechancanough was not shocked to learn that Chawnzmit had slipped through Powhatan's grasp. Of late, Wahunse-na-cawh's thoughts were turned only to ease and lightness, to resting in his bed and chuckling over the antics of his many young children. The great mind that had united all the tribes of Tsenacomoco, the unifying force of the Real People, had dwindled to an old man's doddering. No wonder the *tassantassas* had eluded him.

It happens to us all. If we are not killed honorably in war or lost to the dangers of the hunt, we decline until we are but husks of our former selves. Wahunse-na-cawh, my strong, good brother. One day I will be like you, too.

But that day had not yet come. Opechancanough was still powerful, if not exactly young. And he was a Real Man. A gang of mere *tassantassas* was no match for the *werowance* of Pamunkey in all his cleverness and righteous rage.

"Tell me how Chawnzmit escaped my brother."

The messenger described the Great Chief's plot—a good enough one, perhaps even exceedingly clever for an old and weakened man. By delaying the loading of the *tassantassas'* boat until the tide was well out, and stocking it overfull of heavy dried goods, they had managed to stick the vessel deep in the mud of the river's bed. The white men were put up for the night in a single longhouse.

"But when our warriors came bearing the feast, Chawnzmit would not admit them into the longhouse. He made them stand outside and taste every dish with their own mouths, to ensure the food was not poisoned. When he was satisfied that it was safe, he made the men leave the baskets on the ground. His men carried the food inside and ate it there."

"Alone, without any Real People?"

"Rude," the messenger agreed, with a shrug that said, *But what can one expect from tassantassas?* "In any case, the plan was not to poison the *tassantassas*. We were to wait until they were eating, then pull their swords from their belts and cut their throats, like deer rounded up in the hunt."

"Ah." Half-grudgingly, Opechancanough adjusted his opinion of his brother's capabilities. It *was* a clever plan, one Chawnzmit should not have seen coming.

"But the strangest part is this: listen to what I heard from the men of Werowocomoco. As they were setting their baskets on the ground, some of them saw through the longhouse door. The *tassantassas* had pulled the swords from their own belts, and were sitting upon the flat edges of their blades as if they were woven mats at the fireside."

Opechancanough squinted at the messenger.

A woman entered with another large gourd of water, which the messenger took with a grunt of thanks. He drank deeply. When the woman departed, Opechancanough said, "How did the white men see through the plot? How did they know you intended to cut their throats with their own blades?"

The messenger shook his head slowly, his face drawn with exhaustion and dismay. "I don't know. I asked myself the same question, all the while I was running through the forest to you. I cannot think how, unless they have some great magic that is beyond our reckoning."

Great magic. The slightest, smallest pinch of doubt twisted in Opechancanough's gut. He pushed the sensation away in disgust. Chawnzmit was coming to Pamunkey-town, and he would be dealt with today, in this place, with Opechancanough's own hands. The menace of Tsenacomoco would be eradicated, crushed like a flea against a fingernail. Vengeance for Uttamussak. Vengeance for the Okeus, who burned in his temple. There was no room for doubt, no room for fears of unknown magic.

"You must rest now," he said gruffly to the messenger. "I would let you lie here in my longhouse, but when our guest arrives this will not be a restful place."

The man staggered to his feet. His shoulders sagged with weariness and his steps dragged as a village woman showed him to a quiet bed. Opechancanough followed them out into the common grounds of Pamunkey-town. Word of Chawnzmit's imminent arrival had spread. Women called for their children in the snow-crusted lanes, rushing the little ones indoors. Men checked the strings on their bows, gesturing to one another with the silent signs of hunt and war. They melted into the surrounding trees, pale winter buckskin fading among the frosted vegetation, and took up posts where homes as well as food caches could be defended with ease. A blunt-faced woman crouching in the door of her longhouse slid an antler knife from its sheath. Her eyes were hard and fierce.

Someone gave a call of alarm, a double-noted rising whoop, repeated three times. Opechancanough answered with a long, falling whistle. The signal. He felt rather than saw the men of Pamunkey move into position. The forest surrounding the town seemed to hold one long, shivering breath. The treetops vibrated with eagerness.

Opechancanough gazed toward the river. A high, bare staff glided smoothly upstream, peeking over the tops of the winter-black trees. Chawnzmit's boat. The staff was the great post to which his boat's white wing fastened. Opechancanough walked to the town's central fire pit and stood waiting, arms crossed, back straight, the picture of casual welcome, while inside his spirit writhed with eagerness, clamored for blood like a wolf harrying a wounded deer.

The *tassantassas* landed their small, squat canoe with its two long paddles like a spider's legs. Chawnzmit led four other white men across the commons. His face was gaunt beneath his thick, wiry beard, and his body moved in nervous twitches. They carried with them the now-familiar white-man smell. Opechancanough would never grow used to that odor: sour and bitter as unripe fruit, musky and thick, like the fear stink of a dog. He inhaled a deep lungful of the smell as Chawnzmit approached, looking wary and keen. Today would be the last day the *tassantassa* miasma would drift across the land of Tsenacomoco. Though his nostrils pinched against the white men's nearness, Opechancanough savored the smell like the perfume of a springtime rain.

He pressed a hand to his heart and made himself smile. "*Wingapoh*, Chawnzmit. It is good to see you again."

Without a word, Chawnzmit returned the gesture. His hand came to his breast slowly, carefully, and his small blue eyes shifted this way and that, darting like the eyes of a crow.

"You bring swords, I see."

"We have guns, too," Chawnzmit said. His tongue flickered out to lick at the long hairs of his face. Through the thick beard, Opechancanough could see cracks in the man's pale lips. The cracks were deep, angry red, rimmed with cold white skin. The winter had not been kind to these men—no, not at all. "But you shall not have our guns, Opechancanough. Your brother tried to trick us, to take our weapons. We made him look a fool."

"The *mamanatowick* is an old man. Old men are often foolish. Come. I have hot food. It is warm inside my longhouse. Keep your guns. We shall talk of trade that is more favorable to you."

At his heart fire, Opechancanough tasted each basket of bread and dried fish, each bag of smoked venison, smiling ironically at Chawnzmit as he chewed. When the white men were satisfied that the food was not tainted, they fell on it like vultures at a carcass, tearing and gulping, heads bobbing to peer with suspicious eyes into the innocent shadows of the longhouse.

"Your men seem to have a great liking for Tsenacomoco, Chawnzmit."

Chawnzmit swallowed his mouthful of bread. "We have no love for this land. It is wild and hard. Brutal."

"Your homeland is much more kind, is that it?"

"It is." Chawnzmit sat back, watching Opechancanough with open mistrust.

Opechancanough gave a friendly chuckle. "The place you come from must be safe as a cradleboard, safe as a mother's breast. And yet you do not return to that gentle place. Why do you stay here if you find our land so disagreeable?"

"My *mamanatowick* has commanded us to . . . explore."

"Loyalty to your *mamanatowick* has ever been your greatest concern."

Chawnzmit frowned. The subtlety of the comment was not lost in that shaggy yellow head. "Powhatan was never my *mamanatowick*."

Opechancanough waved a hand, brushing away the simmering argument before it could boil over the edge of its pot. "As you have decided to stay in Tsenacomoco—as your *mamanatowick* has decided that you must stay—we must try harder to be friends."

"Yes."

The man was so small, so weak. He could nearly see the edges of bones pressing through the layers of Chawnzmit's thick clothing. Opechancanough shifted, bending lightly to the side as if working a minor cramp from his back. As he twisted he felt the reassuring pressure of the knife's handle press against his skin. He had wedged the blade sideways into the wide belt of his tunic. The leather of the belt was thick enough to conceal the blade perfectly. When the time was right, he would slide the knife free with one smooth, practiced motion, and open Chawnzmit's throat. Simple. It would be an unthinking, easy motion, like a child dancing stones across the surface of a pond. He would do it here, in his own longhouse, if need be, though better by far to do it outside where his men could witness the act. Let all the men see it, and the women, too. Let them watch, just as they had watched Tsena-no-ha walk away.

Opechancanough made the proper noises about trade, offering and counteroffering, eyeing the *tassantassa* swords, although they refused to place one in his hands for inspection. He made outrageous promises of corn and beans, swearing to provide quantities that far exceeded what the women had laid away in their cellar pits. All the while he watched Chawnzmit's face, watched the white man watching him. He saw the desperation in the *tassantassa's* eyes. It tangled with determination and that flame-hot vein of reckless bravery, which Opechancanough still, despite his hatred for Chawnzmit, admired. The skin around Chawnzmit's sunken eyes tightened, even as his mouth curved in an easy, placid smile. *He knows this is a farce. He knows I know it, too. We are playing one another, openly and boldly. But only one of us can be the fish tricked into the weir. And it is not I, Chawnzmit. It is not I.*

The light streaming through the smoke hole slanted and dimmed by the barest degree. The sun had moved half a hand's breadth across the sky. Opechancanough allowed his hand to drift to his belt and he traced the shape of the knife with one furtive finger. The knife was *tassantassa* steel. He allowed himself to feel the humor of that fact, the sweet weight of justice. He grinned broadly just as the rustle of many feet sounded outside.

One of the *tassantassas* leaped up and dodged for the door flap. Opechancanough rested his chin on his fist, watching the man peer outside. Words flew about the longhouse, the long, slurring sounds of the *tassantassa* tongue mingling in one discordant song of panic as all the men spoke at once. Their faces were urgent, snarling, like circling dogs preparing to leap and bite. Opechancanough's eyes slid half-closed with satisfaction. He did not need to understand their tongue to know what they said. *There are hundreds of warriors outside. The longhouse is surrounded. Opechancanough must have raised every man in Tsenacomoco for this fight.*

A rich, prickling sensation flooded his limbs, a wash of deep satisfaction and gloating triumph. It was like winning a contest of boasts, like felling your first deer, like spilling your seed inside a woman. *Try to escape this time, Chawnzmit. Try to trick your way free.*

Chawnzmit still had many armed men aboard his winged boat, but even if they had had their landing vessel, they would never reach the longhouse in time to free their leader—not through Opechancanough's forest of bowmen. True, the five trapped here beside the heart fire were only a handful compared to the infestation of *tassantassas* at the fort. But Opechancanough had long ago discerned that Chawnzmit was the spirit that kept the fort alive. Once he was killed, the rest would drop dead quickly enough.

Chawnzmit was on his feet, making emphatic gestures to calm his men. He turned on Opechancanough. Beneath the beard, Chawnzmit's jaw clenched and unclenched in a furious rhythm.

"All right, Opechancanough. You've snared me." He did not sound particularly surprised; but then, having only recently slipped Powhatan's snare, Chawnzmit was surely on guard for more trickery. "You have many men outside."

Opechancanough stood slowly, hands out, smiling easily. "Many men. Scores. Hundreds. You will not leave Pamunkey alive."

"I had to try. If there was any chance you might have given us food . . ."

"There is no chance. Before the ice thaws, you will all be dead, one way or another. You will blight my land no more."

"Your land? It is Powhatan's realm."

"Go on thinking that, if you must. It makes no difference now, at the end of your life."

"You seem very sure of that—sure it's the end of my life. Perhaps it is the end of yours."

Opechancanough laughed. "Is it? You're thin as a featherless chick in the nest."

Chawnzmit glanced around at his men. He hesitated, and Opechancanough could see desperate thoughts dart and dash behind those blue eyes. He could all but taste the fear that curdled on Chawnzmit's tongue. Opechancanough's mouth filled with water.

"You can have me, take my life, torture me—anything you like. But let these men go free. In fact, I will make you a trade. My life for corn."

Another bark of laughter cracked from Opechancanough's chest. "So we have come back to trading."

"Unless you're afraid to try me. You and I will fight hand to hand. I will give my gun to my men. None of them shall harm you. You may choose any kind of weapon you like."

I choose tassantassa *steel.*

"You amuse me, Chawnzmit. Very well. We shall fight hand to hand, but not with weapons. We shall wrestle, just like boys at the *huskanaw*. If you can throw me, I will give you all the corn you desire. If I throw you, well . . ."

Of course, it would never come to throwing. His hand itched to pull the blade from his belt, but Opechancanough schooled himself to patience. *Now is not the time. But the time is soon, Okeus, soon.*

Chawnzmit nodded his acceptance. They moved toward the door flap together. Opechancanough bent to lift the flap aside, biting hard at his lip to keep from erupting in laughter. He felt giddy, hot with victory.

Before he could so much as cry out or fling up a hand to defend himself, the hard, grasping talon of Chawnzmit's hand seized the loop of braid on the left side of his head. Chawnzmit twisted the braid about his wrist until his hand was caught in a black tangle, a turkey's foot in a snare. Opechancanough gritted his teeth against the tearing of his scalp. His hand flew to his belt. The knife emerged, flashing in the patch of light that was the half-open door flap. Chawnzmit's other hand descended like an osprey diving. He bent back Opechancanough's finger until the knife fell into the dust. Opechancanough stifled a cry of pain.

Chawnzmit hauled viciously at Opechancanough's braid, maneuvering the *werowance* through the longhouse door ahead of him. A hundred bows were raised on the instant; a hundred flint arrows glimmered in the pale winter sun.

Chawnzmit shielded himself with Opechancanough's body. With his free hand, the *tassantassa* pulled the gun from his belt. The weapon made a single, cold click, a sound like steel against stone. The gun's hard muzzle pressed against Opechancanough's face. The stench of the white man's body choked in Opechancanough's throat.

"Put down your bows," Chawnzmit said. His voice carried far. There was not a hint of a tremor in it. He was as unfeeling and deliberate as a snake in a nest of mice. The white men tumbled out of the longhouse, the smoke from the burning wicks of their weapons hanging like an acrid fog in the air.

Shame burned in Opechancanough's chest. Bad enough that all these men had witnessed his wife leave his hearth for the *tanx* Pepiscunimah. Now they saw him helpless as a deer on a roasting spit, trussed by his own hair. He threw his arms wide, made a broad and easy target of his chest. "Kill him, you cowards! Shoot through me! Chawnzmit cannot be allowed to leave this place!"

He heard the creak of bows tensing, the hiss of arrow shafts along steadying fingers.

"If you kill me," Chawnzmit shouted, "my *mamanatowick* will never cease to hunt your people. He will send hundreds upon hundreds of men just like me, to seek vengeance for my slaying, and no one who calls himself Pamunkey shall ever know a moment of peace again."

A few bows lowered.

Chawnzmit bellowed on as he wrenched Opechancanough's hair. "If you shed so much as one drop of my brothers' blood, or steal the least bead from any of my men, I will not cease in my revenge until I have hunted down every last person who admits to being a Pamunkey: man, woman, or child. Pamunkey will be finished—no more—wiped from Tsenacomoco as if your tribe never existed!"

The rest of the bows dropped.

"Kill them," Opechancanough cried. His voice was hoarse and raw. "Kill these dog-fucking *tassantassas* now, or none of you are men!"

Chawnzmit pressed his gun harder beside Opechancanough's ear. "I am leaving with food, one way or another. Give me food and your *werowance* lives, as do your wives and children. Give me food and we will never cross your path again. We will be content, and leave you alone."

From somewhere in a nearby longhouse came the sounds of hysterical weeping. The women and children were hidden from sight, but they heard Chawnzmit's words as clearly as Opechancanough did.

"Or I will shoot him," Chawnzmit said, "and my men will despoil your women and kill your sons and daughters."

The weeping intensified; the men glanced at one another with fear in their eyes. Opechancanough knew what they were thinking: these *tassantassas* still had their great guns that could shatter trees. Only the Okeus knew what weapons they might deploy against their families.

Chawnzmit sensed his advantage and pressed on: "And when my men have destroyed every last one of you, I will open your stores and take your food for myself." The sound of children sobbing was too much for Opechancanough's warriors. Bowstrings relaxed; arrows returned to quivers.

No. Opechancanough's hand closed helplessly on a knife hilt that was not there. When Chawnzmit released him, he dropped to his knees in the snow, felled by the double blow of shame and defeat.

SMITH

January 1609

Smith took half of what he could find in Pamunkey's frozen cellar pits. It was not much—clearly the village had suffered through a meager harvest and a disappointing hunt. Women uncovered their stores and stood with faces downcast, tears dropping to form pock-marks in the snow. Threads of steam rose from the tiny holes like wan, lost ghosts. Again he felt the dreadful twist of self-loathing writhe like a clubbed serpent in his chest as he set his men to work, rifling through baskets and bags and clay jars that were not nearly full enough. Children wept, burying their faces in the hems of their mothers' winter cloaks. The men scowled, their mouths thin, and their bitter eyes swearing hatred and promising revenge.

Smith did not breathe a sigh of relief until he was back aboard the shallop and the vessel was clear of Pamunkey's shores, leaving Opechancanough and his warriors far behind. Opechancanough was a large and powerful man, and no coward. Smith had made a desperate gamble. It was only by Christ's mercy that the gamble had paid out.

John Russell, convinced at last that the Indians were not going to retaliate from the riverbank, slung his musket over his shoulder. He cast an appraising eye at the Pamunkey spoils. "It isn't much, is it?"

"No," Smith said. "Not much. It will last us a few months, perhaps, if we take care to keep the rats away. There was still half a barrel of oats at Jamestown and three-quarters of a crate of hardtack. There should still be a bit of salt pork left, too. We will eat precious little, but we'll eat."

"And when this food runs out?"

Smith shook his head. "I will think of something."

Russell clenched one broad, hard fist. "Fills me with ire to think of all the food their Great King gave us, only to rob our boat again while we cowered in their longhouse."

"Aye," another man put in, "there's much more food at their big city—whatever they call it, Werey-way . . ."

"Werowocomoco."

The man's lips moved, trying to form the word. He gave up with a shrug. "We all saw that they have more food there."

It was true. During Smith's many months of trade, he had come to know the naturals' customs well. At every harvest and every hunt, they sent a portion of their goods to Powhatan, a tribute for his protection, to placate the old man into continued benevolence. Werowocomoco was a far richer prize than Pamunkey or any other village Smith might raid. And yet it was full of angry men whose peculiar Indian sense of pride had been badly bruised when Smith declined to offer up his throat for the cutting. The rush of quivering energy that always followed a confrontation had drained from Smith's limbs and the very thought of returning to Werowocomoco, of facing a pack of enraged Indians who thirsted for his blood, made him heavy with exhaustion and despair.

And yet, if they took even just a quarter of Werowocomoco's stores, they would need fear hunger no more. It would be more than enough to see them through the winter and beyond. They would survive in comfort until the next harvest, when, God willing, their garden would mature and produce enough food to carry them securely through winter's black months. With a fraction of

Powhatan's stores, they could fend off starvation—even if no more supply ships came from England.

Werowocomoco would be on guard. Or would they? The shallop moved downstream faster than any natural could run; Smith was sure of it.

"Right," he said, bracing his trembling body, girding his weary soul. "When you see the banks of Werowocomoco, drop anchor. I will go ashore."

A few hours later, with the shallop anchored once more off Werowocomoco's shore, Smith boarded the landing boat alone. He ducked his head low as he rowed. A scattered shower of icy snowflakes blew across the river, tinkling like tiny crystalline chimes against the steel of his helmet. The shallop rested quiet and dark on the silver glass of the river. The men watched him in strained silence, hands gripping the shallop's rail like the claws of birds, pale, bony, twitching.

He expected a shout of alarm, the whip of arrows through the air, their hiss and quiet splash as they buried themselves in the water around his boat. But the woods were dead and still; there was no hint of voices or movement on the riverbank, or beyond in the lanes and commons of Werowocomoco.

He landed the rowboat and paused, turning slowly, expecting the specter of an Indian warrior to loom over him, war club raised and face twisted in a rictus of hatred. But the shore was empty. Specks of icy snow gathered in the indentations of many footprints, dimples and pits in the black river mud.

Smith made his way up the trail toward the capital, snaphaunce drawn and at the ready. A few birds chirped listlessly in the cold, bare branches of oaks and mulberries, but no human voice so much as whispered. He gained the great clearing, the communal flat of trampled earth. The huge stone ring of the central fire stood black and round as the eye of a mask. Its coals were raked flat.

Not so much as a heat shiver stirred above the ashes; the fire was thoroughly extinguished. Under leafless shade trees, the lashed and bent sapling poles of houses arched naked in the wind. The bark-paneled walls were stripped away, leaving thin, lonesome skeletons of longhouses. Paler earth showed between the saplings, clean and flat, demarcating the remains of warm, dry floors, already gathering a dust-thin layer of ice.

Smith moved cautiously toward the cellar pit of the nearest home. He lifted the cache's lid, a light but sturdy contrivance made of woven branches and tight-lashed sinews. The pit was empty, the entire stock spirited away, down to the smallest bean and pumpkin seed.

He moved from house to house, inspecting each cellar in turn, though after peering into the first few, he was certain he would find them all empty. Werowocomoco was deserted. Powhatan had taken everything. Not one crumb would be left to the pillaging monster the old chief had once called a member of his own family.

Smith made his way to site of one longhouse in particular. The mulberry spread above it, the familiar crooked limb reaching like the hopeless arm of a drowning man.

Pocahontas had not only visited him in their days of friendship. Smith had also paid her several calls at Werowocomoco, bearing gifts for her and for Powhatan. He remembered her house, recognized it even with its bark stripped away, though without its covering the place looked decidedly less welcoming. The black saplings of its framework bent like threatening bows above the earth. Smith walked below the framework. He touched one arch with a tentative hand and then gripped the post hard. The cold dampness of the wood seeped into his skin. He remembered the previous winter, when this house had been warm and full of laughter. He remembered Pocahontas staring up at him with a furrowed brow, testing an English word, working at it with the determined confidence and natural alacrity he so admired.

Boot, her voice said across a great distance, *wool.* Simple words, ordinary. They raised a terrible pang in his chest, a white, burning stab of loss and regret.

Smith found the cellar outside the house Pocahontas had shared with her sisters and unmarried aunts. He pushed away the large flat stone that covered it. He thought he would find it as empty as the rest of Werowocomoco's caches, but something lay inside—a long chain of white beads, looped and twisted back upon itself, cast aside like the pale shed skin of a snake.

He lowered himself into the cellar. The beads were frozen against the earth. They came away one by one as he tugged gently on the string. Smith held the beads up to the light. Through the stain of old mud he could see the red yarn peeking between the bright-white globes. He remembered stringing it for the girl, remembered speaking the words she taught him as he worked, her sly, testing smile, her clever fingers toying with the chain. *Bid Pocahontas bring me two little baskets, and I will give her white beads to make her a chain.*

Smith slipped the chain of beads into his pouch. He climbed from the cellar pit and looked once more around the abandoned town. Hunched under the weight of memory, with a pain worse than hunger gnawing at his very center, he made his way back to the rowboat. With every step he clutched and kneaded the leather of his pouch. He felt the roundness and sameness of the beads, repeating in his hand the echo of a girl's voice fading on a distant shore.

Smith led his ragged troop through the palisade gate of Jamestown. The peaks of thatched roofs and canvas tents had gathered a crust of snow. In the trampled center of the fort, where the communal fire pit had once stood, a sturdy plane of dark-gray ice had formed over the mire of puddles and sucking mud. Jamestown was not a pretty sight—it never had been. But after the desolation of the abandoned Werowocomoco, the fort's utilitarian ugliness seemed as delightful as a Turkish palace.

Men rushed from the small, dismal cabins and hobbled from their tents, stiff with cold, their joints ablaze with the pain of malnutrition. A relieved cheer went up when the men spotted the baskets and jars of Pamunkey goods making their way through the gate.

Smith pushed open the rickety door of the supply shed, eager to take stock. Combined with the dwindling stores Jamestown still possessed, Smith could stretch the Pamunkey spoils for several months. And during those months, he could finally rest. No more expeditions, no more raids, no women wailing in dismay, no mighty chiefs stripped of their dignity, brought low before the eyes of their people. Sleep, sleep and reflection, and the walls of Jamestown hiding John Smith's gaunt, hot-eyed face from the New World.

In the slant of light falling through the open door, Smith considered the storeroom. Empty crates and kegs were heaped in one corner, tipped on their sides, yawning. From among the pile of refuse, he heard a constant scuttling sound. The thick stench of rat piss permeated the dark room.

Smith pried up the lid of the remaining barrel of oats. In the sudden burst of light, a nest of rats squealed and thrashed, leaping up the side of the barrel, and scampered into the shelter of the piled crates. Smith stared down into the barrel, his empty stomach roiling with disgust. There were as many pellets of rat droppings as there were oats. An uneven hole ringed by pale, gnawed wood showed where the pests had worked their way inside.

"Christ," Smith cursed. He pounded the lid back on the barrel, tipped it, and rolled it through the door and into the frozen commons.

By now the dandies had gathered, expecting their dole of food. Their tailored woolens hung on their emaciated frames; they were

thin as poppets in a wheat field and yet they had done nothing—
nothing—to protect their last bit of food.

Smith kicked the lid from the barrel. Oats and rat shit spilled
across the ground.

"Good God," one of the gentlemen cried, "what do you think
you're about, Smith?"

"Put down the food from the naturals," Smith commanded
his men. "Right here, in the commons. Not a kernel of corn shall
go into that storehouse until the rats are all dead and the refuse
cleared away."

A few of the dandies moved toward the baskets of beans,
the hard winter squashes painted in bright, tempting splashes of
orange and green. Smith drew his gun and trained it on them.

"Not another step. You get nothing until the work is done. And
properly, too, as it should have been done the whole time I was
away. Look at you! The lot of you couldn't kill a few rats? You might
have eaten them even; only gentlemen do not eat rats. Is that the
way of it?"

Thomas Savage's mouth twisted in a wry grin. The ship's boy
was stunted and small after his hungry years in Jamestown; Smith
saw the truth of his assumption reflected in the boy's face.

"Savage, have you ever eaten a rat?"

"Aye, Captain Smith. I eat 'em when I can catch 'em. They roast
just like a bird. It's the best use any of us has made of the storehouse since you've been away."

"We will all eat rat tonight," Smith declared, "and what a feast
we will have. There are dozens of them in that storehouse, feed-
ing on your oats, making new generations of their kind to beggar
Jamestown, while you *gentlemen* do nothing but lie in your tents
pining for England."

"Watch yourself, Smith," one of the gentlemen growled.

"I do. I have. I've watched myself risk life and limb to secure
food for you shiftless jackanapes. I've watched myself destroy all

the good relations with the naturals, those bonds I worked so hard to create, all in the name of keeping you lot fed through the winter."

"You are not the president. Nobody has declared you president. By what right . . ."

"By right of my wits," Smith roared. "By right of my back, which I have bent in labor in the name of England and the Virginia Company, while you lot have slumbered like babes on your cots." He clutched at the beads in his pouch, his fist locking around them convulsively; he could not drop the pouch, could not let go. "By right of the bonds I have forged and then shattered that *you*, undeserving curs that you are, might live."

Matthew Scrivener stepped forward. "If you must hear Smith declared president in order to respect his command, then I shall be the first to declare him."

"Aye," said Russell, hulking above the Pamunkey baskets with his hand upon the strap of his musket. "And I declare him, too. I saw this man fight the king of the Pamunkeys, a great strong ox of a savage, hand to hand. I saw him work us free of two Indian traps, using naught but his wits and his words. Here is a president worthy of Jamestown if ever the place had one."

The men of his expedition raised their voices. "Aye! Aye, President Smith!"

Smith was too incensed to feel any rush of triumph or pride. *That they would prefer to lie in their cots, stoically awaiting death, rather than turn their fine, soft hands to labor . . . ! Christ help us all, for it's clear we shan't be bothered to help ourselves.*

Smith paced before the spilled oats, the baskets of fine Pamunkey wares. "There you have it, then. I am declared. By order of your president, not a man shall touch this food until the work is done, starting with salvaging these oats. Every rat dropping shall be picked from them, and the good grains will be packed away properly and stored. Half of you on the task. The other half will set to ordering the storehouse. Haul out the refuse. Stack it well away from the building. And kill any rat you find."

Most of the men set to their tasks quickly enough, though their faces darkened with resentment. Smith did not care.

A few walked away and turned their backs on Smith, no doubt thinking to wait out the labor and help themselves to the food when it was done.

"I tell you now," Smith shouted, "and I shall tell you only once: he who shall not work shall not eat."

The gentlemen hesitated, looked around. Something in Smith's voice caught and held them—a new note of command, the deadly assurance that he would follow through on his promise. Or perhaps it was his countenance, his wide-legged stance, the square of his shoulders, the way his hand clutched at his leather belt pouch like a soldier's fist upon the hilt of a sword.

One by one, the dandies of Jamestown gave in. They lent their hands to the labor, working in offended silence side by side with more honest men. Overseeing the work with a terse word and an imperative stride, John Smith stalked through their ranks like a stone monument come to life. The mantle of president was new and sudden, but it hung with rightful ease around his neck.

THE THIRD NAME

Matoaka

POCAHONTAS

Season of Cattepeuk

The season of running fish came again. Throughout the forests of Tsenacomoco, the tips of branches swelled with new growth, the promise of budding leaves hanging like green pearls in the tree-tops. Birds squabbled and tussled in thickets, warring for their minute territories, building soft new nests to woo their tiny wives. The woodlands thawed. Streams clamored in the deep cuts of their beds; the river swelled, and its current ran deep, fast, and cold, tasting of earth and tree roots. The falls, invigorated by the gush of thawing snow, filled the lanes and fields of Orapax with their distant but constant voice.

For the first few weeks in Powhatan's new capital, many days' journey from Werowocomoco, the sound of the falls disturbed Pocahontas. It filled her days with an unsettled tension and her nights with strange dreams of talking spirits. The falls were a dangerous place, for they delineated the border between Tsenacomoco and Massawomeck territory. The Massawomecks were a frightening specter, armed with plenty of trade iron and steel, darting like lightning in their birch-bark canoes. They had no love for the Real People, and their nearness placed a constant strain on Powhatan's subjects, women and warriors alike. And yet they were a preferable enemy to the *tassantassas*—to Chawnzmit, who had proven

himself more reckless and cunning than any of them had suspected. Chawnzmit, the unpredictable leader of a band of starving
beasts.

At least the Massawomecks thought—and made war—like
people. Theirs was a preferable sort of evil, a danger less sinister
than living in proximity to white men.

Several weeks after they settled in Orapax, Koleopatchika rose
early on a bright morning and began stripping the old bark strips
from the longhouse. The intrusion of sunlight into the peaceful
dark of the house's interior chased Pocahontas from her sleeping
mats. She helped her aunt thread the strips upward and backward,
freeing them from the lashed-sapling frame, while Matachanna
and Nonoma trampled flat the new sprouting grass, creating a
wide bed on which to lay the bark.

The bark was stretched out to dry in the sunlight. The trek
from Werowocomoco to Orapax had been hasty, and bark strips
were not the only household necessity damaged by Powhatan's
flight through the wintry forest. Pots and baskets had to be set
beside roaring fires before they dried enough to store food, and the
sleeping furs were chilly for several nights until they, too, finally
gave up their dampness.

The warped bark from their old longhouse had let too many
drafts into the new *yehakin*; Pocahontas looked forward to tight,
smooth walls once more, and a house that held in the warmth of
the heart fire and its thick, homey smoke.

By the afternoon, the springtime sun had flattened the curled
and kinked ends of all but a few of the strips. Nonoma and
Koleopatchika smiled and gossiped as they wove the dried bark
back into place. Matachanna took up a good flint knife and a carrying bag, and made her way into the forest to pare new bark slices
from the wide boles of ancient trees.

Though she had not been invited, Pocahontas tied her own knife to her waist with a strip of leather and ran to catch up with her sister.

They did not go far. It was unwise to wander beyond the boundary posts of Orapax. One never knew when the Massawomecks might come sneaking through the outer fringes of Tsenacomoco. Fortunately, Orapax had been so long unused that plentiful bark was ready for the taking within shouting distance of the town. Matachanna set to work on a vast birch, scoring the trunk with her knife, the lines even and neat. The sap of springtime was high and sweet in the trees, and gave off a pleasant scent like the nectar of flowering herbs.

Pocahontas chose the tree beside Matachanna's. Now and then as she worked she licked the birch sap from her knuckles or the handle of her knife. It prickled and danced on her tongue.

"The sap is sweet this year," Pocahontas said. "That is some consolation, if we must live at Orapax."

Matachanna made no reply. She did not look up or smile, either—she only sliced methodically at her birch tree, face turned carelessly away, as if she worked alone.

It had been this way since Chawnzmit's attempt to raid Werowocomoco. The final weeks of winter had passed in agony for Pocahontas as she strove to make peace with her sister but met only icy disregard.

She threw down her knife. "Enough, Matachanna. Please. Won't you tell me why you are so angry?"

Matachanna worked her fingertips beneath the edge of her bark and pulled. The bark came away in one long, perfect strip with a sound like a blade cutting through buckskin. The bark's pale underside filled the forest with its sweet perfume. Pocahontas waited while her sister rolled the strip carefully and tucked it inside her bag. Then Matachanna turned to Pocahontas with a frown so direct and accusing that she stumbled back as if shoved.

"I know it was you who freed Chawnzmit."

"I . . . I didn't free him." That was true; she had only warned him of the coming attack. Chawnzmit had freed himself. Matachanna's scowl bore down upon her, and under the ferocity of her sister's gaze, Pocahontas hung her head. "I told him what Father had planned, that the warriors were to kill the *tassantassas* with their own blades."

"Pocahontas, how could you?" Matachanna's dismayed wail set a flock of pigeons clattering up out of her birch tree, winging in a panic through the wood.

"I did it to stop the . . ."

"After he burned Uttamussak!"

"It was not Chawnzmit who burned the temple."

"What does it matter? One *tassantassa* is exactly like another. And everybody knows Chawnzmit commands the white men. Whatever any of them does, he does by Chawnzmit's orders."

"If only you had heard the things Chawnzmit said, Matachanna! We spoke, he and I, that day when I got Naukaquawis out of their fort."

"No doubt you did speak to him. No doubt you told him all our people's secrets."

"I would never . . . !"

"You should have left him alone in that longhouse—Chawnzmit and all his vile men. You should have let Father do what had to be done. We would all be better off if the *tassantassas* were dead—every last one of them, starting with that crow Chawnzmit."

"Don't you see, Matachanna? If we initiated open war with the *tassantassas*, it would never end. Their weapons are greater than ours. Before we could destroy them, they would take as many Real People with them into death as they possibly could! What I did, I did for the Real People."

Matachanna laughed bitterly. She seized another strip of bark and ripped it viciously from the tree. "Oh, indeed. You thought only of the Real People. You may be able to lie to Father, Pocahontas, but you cannot lie to me. I see you for who you truly are. What you did, you did for yourself. Because you want to be a *werowansqua*. Well, look around you. See where your selfishness has landed you, and all the rest of us, too. *Orapax*." She kicked a stone; it flew into a nearby thicket, crackling among the branches. In the momentary silence that followed, the sound of the rushing falls seemed to grow in volume. It was as if the place itself closed slowly in upon them, hiding its subtle menaces behind a soft cloak of springtime green.

Pocahontas shook her head in wordless sorrow. She remembered the feel of the unknown *werowance*'s bones beneath her hands, the dark, compelling smell of shadow and tobacco and herb. She remembered the Okeus's face wreathed in flame. "No, Matachanna," she said. She choked on her own voice, and it came from her chest in a hoarse whisper. "I don't want to be a *werowansqua*. Not anymore."

"Well, I don't want to be your friend. Not anymore. I told you a day like today would come when I'd finally had enough of your selfishness." Matachanna sheathed her knife, slung her bag onto her back, and settled the wide strap across her forehead. "Goodbye, Amonute."

Pocahontas watched Matachanna stomp down the overgrown trail. The bag of bark strips flopped from side to side as she hurried toward Orapax. Pocahontas picked up her knife from the loamy soil and returned to her work, recalling Matachanna in the temple, her clay-white face full of love and relief when she had seen Pocahontas stumble through the dense smoke and flames. She scored the bark, pried and pulled, scored again. Now and then she paused to wipe tears from her cheeks. The taste of salt mingled with the sweetness of birch sap on her lips.

She returned to Orapax at sunset. She approached the longhouse from the rear, hesitant as a tree vole in the evening hours, when the forest filled with the white ghosts of owls on the wing. Koleopatchika was busy with the walls, deftly weaving the new bark strips over-under through the sapling framework. Pocahontas dropped her bag of coiled bark at Koleopatchika's feet. Her aunt looked up with a smile of tender sympathy. Then her sparkling black eyes slid to the house's half-formed yard; a sly, encouraging spark flickered in her gaze.

Pocahontas looked up. Kocoum sat upon a large stone, patiently wrapping an arrowhead to the shaft of a new arrow.

She approached him and stood in shy, tentative silence several paces away. She had not seen Kocoum since Werowocomoco. His duties to the *mamanatowick* had carried him on lengthy missions through the latter part of winter, patrolling the borders of Orapax for white men and Massawomecks. Kocoum had been her protector and shadow while she had worked with the *tassantassas*, and yet, through the long and distressing weeks of settling into this new life at Orapax, she had nearly forgotten what he looked like. Pocahontas watched in quiet contentment as he worked, reacquainting herself with his features and his habits. His fingers moved in a careful, precise rhythm, twining the sinew neatly, folding and securing it, testing the knot. One leg was crossed upon the other, his tattooed ankle resting on his knee. Even with his face turned down, she could see that his mouth was serious with concentration, as it so often was. It was good to see once more the arch of his bold nose and the straight line running down his scalp from forehead to nape where his unshaven hair was pulled neatly to the side, caught up in a heavy loop of braid. Red-painted turkey feathers dangled from his hair, moving gently in a rising evening breeze that smelled of river fish, of fertile earth and growing things.

He looked up and slid his arrow into the quiver propped against his knee. "Pocahontas."

"*Wingapoh.* Why are you here?"

He stood and stretched the cramp of long, patient work from his back and shoulders. "Walk with me."

They strolled to the river in companionable silence, each content with the sound of the other's footsteps. They halted on a shelf of stone high above the bank. The river was far narrower here than at Werowocomoco. It moved rapidly, a strong, compelling rush so unlike the smooth, contented flow, the lazy tidal rise and fall, of the river she had known for most of her life. Purple twilight gathered at the edges of the forest. Early stars shone in the dusky sky like the pale eyes of spirits. From the riverbank a canoe pushed out onto the water. The men aboard paddled smoothly for the river's deep, blue-dark center. At the bow, one man held a pine torch close to the water's surface; just behind him, another waited with a knotted silk-grass net on a long pole, ready to scoop up curious fish that came to bathe in the flickering star of torchlight. The torch was reflected in the current, the mirrored golden light breaking and rippling downstream as the bow gently parted the river.

Kocoum spoke. "I am old enough now to have my own longhouse. To set up a household."

She glanced at him from the corner of her eye. The dusk cast a shade upon his skin, painting his body the color of tobacco flowers. "You will need a wife for that, won't you?"

"Yes. I have one in mind."

She laughed. "Kocoum, I'm not a woman yet."

He glanced down at her chest, which ripened month by month like fruit on a vine. "You will be soon. Your aunt Koleopatchika is right. Something has changed in you since we left Werowocomoco."

Since the burning of Uttamussak. She turned her face downward and tracked the night fishers with brimming eyes. "You have been discussing me with my aunt?"

He shrugged. "You are a daughter of the *mamanatowick*. I cannot find your mother to discuss the matter with her."

"Why me?"

He brushed her shoulder with his fingers. His touch was gentle and warm. "Because I like Mischief." Before she could swat his hand away, he tugged on her braid. "Think about what I've said tonight, Amonute. I know I am young, but I have much to offer a wife. I'm a good hunter—one of the best, in truth, though you'll never hear me speak of it in the boasting contests. I don't need to boast. Boasting doesn't kill game."

She smiled. "Certainly you are not boasting now."

"It's only the truth. I am a good warrior, too. I'm brave, reliable, and loyal to your father."

"What of my uncle?" she asked suddenly.

"Opechancanough?" Kocoum's brow furrowed, but he seemed to grasp her meaning and continued. "Opechancanough is a good man, strong, an excellent *werowance*. I know some men mock him for being captured by Chawnzmit, but I respect his bravery. I would never hesitate to fight at his side. If the time comes when the men of Tsenacomoco must swear loyalty to Opechancanough, I will do it without reservation."

She turned back to the torch on the water. The canoe rocked, and the men below shouted as they hauled the net aboard. It was full of movement and sound, the muscular twist of long silver bodies, the copper-bell splash of water.

"I would make you happy, Amonute."

"I believe you would."

"Then if you like, I will go to your father and ask him to pledge you to my hearth when your time comes to enter the sweat lodge."

A strange, dense cloud engulfed her spirit, thick and white as a wolf's fur. She would never be a *werowansqua*—but quite apart from being an impossibility, it was no longer her dream. Thank the Okeus that she was no high-blood girl. She could marry whom she pleased. Kocoum was all the things he said he was—a good provider, a sturdy and respectable man. And like Pocahontas, he was lowborn. At his hearth, she could retreat into a life of quiet obscurity, finding contentment in a woman's work until the day when she, like Kocoum, like Matachanna, was turned back into the soil of life, her name lost to time, her spirit free to start anew.

She wanted to accept. She wanted to beg him to go to her father that very night. But once Kocoum's plans were set in motion, and her blood finally arrived, she would be a wife first and the daughter of the *mamanatowick* second. She needed to speak to Chawnzmit one final time while she was still free to do so. She needed to know that she had done the right thing in saving him from death.

"Before I can answer you," she said slowly, "there is something I must do. I do not know when I will do it, nor do I know how—yet. It may be many months before I have the opportunity."

"What must you do?"

She shook her head curtly. "I cannot speak of it to anyone."

Kocoum took a wary step back. "Women's magic?" All men were suspicious by nature of women's magic, of the blood that gave life and the other mysterious rhythms of female flesh.

"Yes," she said quickly. "A man cannot know."

"I understand."

"I will give you my answer, Kocoum, as soon as I am able. I ask you to be patient until then."

"Very well."

He lowered himself onto the shelf of stone. His legs hung over the edge, swinging boyishly in the soft night. He leaned back on his hands and watched the pine torch slip downstream like a spirit walking. In the spring night, soft as a rabbit skin, comforting as a well-loved sleeping mat, Kocoum was the very image of contented patience.

She joined him on the edge of the overhang. The stone was cool and faintly damp with the promise of a heavy morning dew, the kind that set the world shimmering like the inside of an oyster's shell. She kicked her feet in the crisp air. She was happy at Kocoum's side. The rent in her heart caused by Matachanna's hatred did not ache as fiercely as it had. She rested her head on his shoulder.

"When I've done what I must do," she said quietly, her voice barely carrying above the splashing of the night fishers' net, "my answer will be yes."

Cattapeuk burgeoned, green and soft. Warm days raised moss-scented mists in the forest of Orapax. Shoots rose bright and eager from the loam, unfurling leaves that gathered morning dew in their cups like gourds beside the river. Mulberry trees shook their green tassels of flowers in soft breezes, and the plum trees donned cloaks of sweetly scented, snow-white blossoms. Along the edges of trails, strawberries tumbled like pearls rolled in *puccoon*, shining in the shade of their dark, glossy leaves. Smoking racks sprouted like mushrooms in the yard of every longhouse. Each afternoon was colored by the smell of smoked fish, a salty-sweet, woodsy tang that settled into clothing and hair and hung about the branches of trees.

All through the season, Pocahontas waited for her chance to slip away from her father's new capital. Jamestown lay far down-river from Orapax, a journey of many days. Often she would find herself pausing in her work, setting a half-full gourd of strawberries aside or dropping her bags of smoked fish to wander to the riverbank and stare downstream.

In truth, nothing prevented her from leaving Orapax. The memory of Chawnzmit, of the kinship of their spirits, pulled at her like a bone fishhook set deep in her heart. She knew before she could accept a new life, a new identity as woman and wife, she must see him one last time and learn for herself whether she had been wise or foolish in sparing him from a violent death at his own blade.

She also knew with a placid certainty that once she saw Chawnzmit again, once she spoke to him, her childhood would be forever behind her. She would drop Amonute the girl as a tree drops its final dry leaf in winter. The last thin shred of her old ambitions would fall, too, never to be retrieved. She would content herself with the life of a Real Woman—that and nothing more.

Perhaps it was that certainty that held her fast in Orapax as *cattapeuk* blossomed and flourished. Perhaps there was some secret corner of her spirit that was reluctant to release its hold on its former dream, a territory of her own, the rich prize of immortality, of being ever herself.

Or perhaps it was Matachanna. Pocahontas had thought no pain could be more severe than Matachanna's ostentatious scorn, which she heaped upon Pocahontas whenever they were near to one another. Matachanna would fall into icy silence as Pocahontas approached, and then turn deliberately away from her. Soon, though, her rejection became not a show but a simple habit. And that was a torment beyond her calculated disdain. It was at least as compelling as the hook Chawnzmit had set into her spirit. Day by day Pocahontas looked for some sign that she was forgiven—a glance or a softening of her sister's mouth. But day by day, Matachanna drifted further away, a loosed canoe on a rising tide.

Too soon, *cattapeuk* yielded to *cohattayough*. The spiked and filamented flowers of the passion-fruit vine withered, and in their place the soft-skinned fruits hung, round and full like silk-grass bags on women's backs. The fish runs slackened. Young turkeys strutted in the dappled light of the forest, picking for acorns and insects beneath patches of last autumn's leaves.

Pocahontas gave herself over to the rhythm of work. Her digging stick was a welcome distraction. On days when Matachanna's scorn or Chawnzmit's distance were too much to bear, she would jab and lever it into the black earth of her garden, working the soil with a grim focus that brought soreness to her muscles and blisters to her hands, but a semblance of peace to her spirit. She often stayed in the garden until after sunset, plucking caterpillars from the young squash leaves, tearing weeds from the feet of corn plants, even while the rest of the Real People gathered at the communal fire to boast and dance.

The blisters healed. The corn grew tall and strong, the stalks shrouded with bean vines. Ears grew in the joints of the corn leaves, seeming to appear overnight, swelling to the length of a hand almost as soon as they had emerged. And then *cohattayough* was nearly over. Soon the days would grow shorter, the nights colder. The harvest would commence in two more turns of the moon.

Where has the year fled to? Pocahontas dropped her digging stick and lay back in her garden. The sun had already departed in a blaze of pink and gold. Night as dark as the flesh of a plum stole around the edges of the sky. Above her, the corn swayed and whispered in a soft breeze. Drums carried, a heartbeat pulsing vital and loud at the night's fire. Women's voices rose in song. It was a joyous sound, the simple gladness of being together, of being alive. Pocahontas felt far removed from that gladness. It drifted around the edges of her spirit, fading away like the trace of an echo.

She watched the stars emerge. They were like white bead shells in the sky, scattered by a careless hand and forgotten. Beneath the soil she felt the earth itself stretching, unfurling like a coil of bark drying in the sun. What was that sense of opening, of slow, inevitable blooming? Images crowded her mind: a crack in a butterfly's chrysalis, a turtle's limbs emerging from its shell with deliberate care. She thought of deer leading fawns through the dusky forest, of the moon riding high and round against a purple sky.

She understood that the time had come to go. She could wait no longer, for soon—very soon—she would have a new name.

Pocahontas rose to her feet. She held still for a long moment, listening to the last birds of the evening calling out to the dancers at the fire. She waited for her legs to tremble under the weight of her vision, but they never did. She found her digging stick beneath the squash leaves, brushed it clean, and lifted her hand to her face. The smell of rich damp, earth dark and moist, clung to her palm. It smelled new and forgiving. Good.

While the village of Orapax danced, Pocahontas gathered what she would need. Sleeping mats, bundles of dry tinder, baskets of food, a sturdy gourd for her water. She packed a bag with grease-paint to keep the flies from her skin, two antler knives, and a pot of salve for blisters and wounds. The bag felt heavy in her hands, but when she hoisted it to her back and fixed the strap against her forehead, it weighed less than a feather on the wind.

Pocahontas crept through the lanes of Orapax, stealing between the shadows of the longhouses. No one saw her go. At the trail to the riverbank, she paused to look back at her home. The fire was bright in the center of town, ringed by song and laughter. Through the leaping, shimmying light she saw legs move and stamp; she saw bodies and arms bend, whirling, clapping. A shadow raised its arms in the ecstasy of dance—a young woman's form—Matachanna? Another moved through the firelight, chest out, proud as a turkey beneath an oak tree. Kocoum?

"Good-bye," she whispered.

As she picked her way through the darkness toward the beached canoes, she thought she heard Matachanna's voice call after her— *"Sister!"*—in answer.

Paddling was nearly as good as gardening for soothing the mind and quieting the spirit, though the old calluses from her digging stick were no protection against the harshness of her oar. Blisters appeared in new and tender places: in the center of her palms, on the fleshy pads and the lined joints of her fingers. When the river was broad and calm enough to permit it, she would tuck her paddle into the hull and allow the small dugout to coast. She trailed her hands in the water to take away the heat and pain. When the cool river water was no longer sufficient, she dabbed her hands with ointment and wrapped them in strips of soft buckskin, tying the knots with her teeth and stiff, aching fingers.

Pocahontas paddled for a few hours the first night, and then secured her boat against a snag in a quiet eddy. She slept until dawn, made a hasty breakfast of dried fish and water dipped over the side of her canoe, and continued downriver in the pink morning mist. Well before the sun was high, the sound of the falls faded, taking with it the spectral threat of a Massawomeck ambush. Freed from that particular worry, she allowed herself to slip into the easy rhythm of the canoe: dip and pull, lift and cross. The current and her own wiry strength carried her downstream as fast as a rabbit bolting.

Two days passed, filled with nothing but the river and the simple, mindless, soothing act of paddling. Fish darted away from her bow, and deer startled and watched her pass, trembling in the shallows, water still dripping from their black muzzles. Birds cried, and Pocahontas called back to them. She smelled the outflowing of brooks and streams that carried the rich loamy scent of woodlands down from the hills to mingle with the faint salt of the river.

By night she beached, exhausted, on the edges of the various territories through which she passed. It was not precisely dangerous for a girl to travel alone through Tsenacomoco, yet Pocahontas had no desire to be sent back to her father at Orapax by an overly cautious *werowance*. Her arms were nearly too tired to work the fire stick, but each night she made a tiny fire and slept huddled close beneath her mats. Even in sleep she kept her shoulders visible so that any warrior who might chance upon her would see by her tattoos that she was Pamunkey, and a girl: no threat to anyone.

On the third morning she rose up fresh and ready like a sapling sprouting from the forest floor. Her body had adapted to the hard work of rowing—even her blisters had hardened, and her hands flexed with a strength and eagerness that surprised her. Her spirit, too, felt changed. The knowledge that Matachanna would never love her again did not bring the fierce, desperate sorrow she had felt in Orapax, nor the anger that kept her isolated in the gardens while the world went on dancing and living without her. Rather, her sadness was a small thing—still real, still bitter, but something she could contain like corn kernels inside a priest's rattle. The sadness would still shake, and she knew its noise would sometimes be great, but it was her own hand on the rattle. She could master it and tuck it away at will. It would never again blot out her spirit completely.

All day she paddled, rejoicing silently in the new strength in her body. She smiled at herons wading in the tidal mud of the shallows. She laughed when they took indignant wing, calling hoarsely, scolding her for her unseemly speed. By sunset her lower back began to ache, as did her stomach. She had eaten little that day, too caught up in the pleasures of solitude and the rhythm of the river to stop.

She cast about for a suitable spot to land her canoe, and realized with a dull, creeping surprise that she recognized this place. Why had she not known it sooner? The shelf of riverbank was low and muddy, still scored deeply with the tracks of many dugouts. The trails leading back into the woods opened before her eyes like friendly hands.

Pocahontas beached carefully, dragged her canoe above the tideline, and made her way inland to Werowocomoco.

In the fading red light, she walked the remembered lanes of her childhood home. Frames of longhouses still stood, but an encroaching growth of passion-fruit vines draped over them, dangling copper-bright fruits into spaces where once the smoke of heart fires had hung. The ground surrounding the communal fire pit was still flat and dusty, and here and there she could make out the pale ghost of a human footprint. But the grounds had been danced over by many other feet in the months since Powhatan had left Werowocomoco. The round-padded feet of coyotes or wolves stalked the edges of the ring. The pronged prints of birds showed here and there, stark in the dust like fresh tattoos. The sharp, cloven tracks of a deer indicated where a brave buck had walked across the ashes of the fire pit. Along the eastern edge of the ring, the sinuous trail of a snake moved like the path of a stream, fluid and mysterious in the fading light.

A cold breeze moved through Werowocomoco. It shivered the passion-fruit vines, which danced darkly in the gathering twilight. Pocahontas crouched still beside the fire pit, watching, all senses alert like a rabbit emerging from its scrape. But not even ghosts moved in the old capital.

After a time she built her fire there in the communal fire pit where so often she had clapped and sung, side by side with Matachanna and the other girls. Her fire was small, but she held her hands up to it, and it lit her skin with a vibrant, hot glow.

She stood, turning to rummage in her food basket for an evening meal—and paused, one hand on her cramping belly. At first she was afraid an illness had seized her insides. But she held her breath, and felt the pinch of pain ebb like the outflowing tide. Then it gathered itself to surge again. She remembered lying in her garden and saw once more the delicate moth's cocoon splitting, the creature inside struggling to break free.

She touched between her thighs. There it was: the dark smear of blood on her fingertips. She knew it would be there even before she inspected her hand in the firelight. She had not reached Jamestown in time.

Pocahontas laid out her sleeping mat. She unwrapped an old, hardened dumpling from its silk-grass wrapping and set it beside a strip of fish and a strip of venison. She sat gazing at her supper. She knew certain rites should be observed, knew that proper dedications must be made to the spirits for luck and fertility, for magic and long life. But it was other women who knew the lore. Only women could dedicate her—women who had entered the sweat lodge and received the rites from those who had crossed that magic threshold before. She gnawed on the tough fish, mulling over her predicament with a calmness that surprised her. Was it more dangerous to go about in the world as a woman undedicated? Or was it worse to perform the rites incorrectly? Which would offend the spirits more, causing them to cover their eyes when she passed? Which would leave her more vulnerable to attack by ill-tempered *manitou*?

She did not know. There was no one to tell her. She gazed earnestly into the fire until the brightness of the light stung her eyes and left echoes of the flames flitting across her vision as bright as chokecherries on an autumn tree. *Okeus, I saw you burn. You know me. Guide me correctly; bring me safely through this passage.*

Pocahontas rose. Beyond the vine-covered bones of the longhouses she found an ancient oak, found the soft moss at its base by feel in the darkness. She recovered from her traveling bag the buckskin strips that had wrapped her hands. These she fashioned into a belt, but did not tie it yet between her legs.

She sat again beside her tiny fire. She drew into her mind the image of the Okeus, his hard black body circled by flames, the leering, white-eyed face emerging and vanishing again through a drifting veil of oily smoke.

Speak, Okeus. Guide my hand. Make me strong against manitou. *Make the spirits pour out their favors on me, like water from a gourd. Make their blessings sweet as nut milk. Let me not offend.*

A voice filled her ears. It was loud as a hundred rattles; it was low and dark, forcible as thunder. *"Woman's blood is magic. Woman's blood makes life. Woman's blood is fire."*

Pocahontas trembled.

"Blood is the fire that drives copper from the orestone. Blood is the fire that simmers the pot, that bakes the bread, that makes one cake out of water and meal.

"*Blood is the fire that consumes the forest, tree and root, spirit and flesh. Blood is the fire that fells the tree and hollows its heart, that it may carry men upon the river.*

"*A fire may cleave or a fire may bind. A fire may destroy. A fire may create.*"

Breathless, eyes closed, she waited.

"*Your blood is your power. Anoint yourself with the blood. Direct your power. Make of yourself a mighty fire, girl-who-was-Amonute.*"

She opened her eyes. *Don't think*, she told herself as her spirit shuddered and gasped. *Don't ruin this vision. Move like the river moves, flowing between the high banks that guide it.*

She dipped her hand once more between her thighs. She touched the dark, earthy wetness to her forehead.

Make me wise, she commanded the blood.

Her hand went to her heart, streaking a track of magic across her breast. Its coolness burned against her skin. *Make me loving. Make me give, and not take.*

The voice chuckled. It was an ominous rush, a prickling whisper like the sound of the falls at Orapax. "*Wisdom, love, generosity? That is all you seek?*"

It is all.

"*And power? Influence? A territory of your own, werowansqua? What of immortality? Do you not wish to be remembered for all time, to be your own self for all time?*"

She could not speak, even in the confines of her awestruck spirit. She shook her head and lowered her eyes to the earth. She recalled the shapes moving around the fire on the night she left Orapax. The movement of those silhouettes, both familiar and mysterious. The way their dance called to her, the thrum of their song repeating along her bones. The simple goodness of a brief, honest, common life. Oneness with the whole was not immortality. But it was wholeness.

"*Then sweat,*" the voice commanded.

A brisk wind moaned down the length of Werowocomoco. The fire blazed yellow and hot, like summer sun on the cornfields. She pulled a sleeping mat over her head and opened it like a heron's broad wings. The heat of the fire pressed against her body, cupped in the shadowy lodge of her bark-woven wingspan. She rocked, singing under her breath, and felt the blood dry on her forehead and heart. The sweat emerged like dew along her limbs, gathered in the crease of her neck.

I am alone, she chanted, mournful, resigned. *Aloneness is my fate. I enter womanhood apart from all women, and apart I will always stand.*

My wings are isolation. My cape is a wall. My lodge is small and empty. I am drained of the things Amonute lived for. Her desires are dust in the wind.

The sweat broke. It ran in streams down her back, her chest, her face. It left a prickling on her skin, a trace of heat and magic. The sweat carried Amonute away.

Okeus, you know me. Okeus, I saw you burn. Fill me with wisdom and generosity. Make me a basket that is useful; fill my being with love. For even though I must be a woman alone, I would be a woman who is wise. I would be a woman who gives.

When she could take the heat no longer, Pocahontas let the mat fall to the ground. She gasped when the cold night air touched her skin; a great, forceful burning suffused her limbs, the fire that was blood. She drank deeply from her gourd and then tied her new moss belt between her thighs. The deep, booming voice spoke no more. She was alone with the silence of Werowocomoco, alone but for the light of her small but vigorous fire.

Pocahontas tucked herself between the mats. Stars painted the sky in a white, glittering swath, and across the band of light she saw silhouettes move: women bending and stooping, twisting in the joy of dance; men strutting and leaping; all of them rising together like a flock of birds lifting from the earth. She was apart, but she watched them glide across the brilliant night sky, and the perfect oneness of their movement was as beautiful as pearls on a chain.

She did not know, as she fell toward the sleep of total exhaustion, who she would be when she awoke. She had no true name now; Amonute was gone in a streak of sweat and blood.

In the deep night, in the night that turned and shuffled, leaped and swayed like dancers in a ring, Pocahontas dreamed.

Wings stretched from her body—long, pale wings with ragged white feathers. She sprang into the air, beating at the sky with broad, feathered arms, digging like a canoe paddle churning the river. She called out as she flew, but no one answered; she was a bird without a flock.

She glided. Wind moved over her body, through it, teasing tears from her eyes. Words brushed her skin; the wind was made of words.

Wool.

Boot.

Gun.

Bid Pocahontas bring me two little baskets, and I will give her white beads to make her a chain.

Her bird feet tangled in a length of red string. She bent a long, strong neck and sliced the string away with a heron's bill.

Far below her, against the blackness of the earth, a tiny fire danced in a wide circle of ash. She dived toward it. As she came closer, she saw that the fire reached out red hands and pulled dry sticks into its own heart. And it grew warmer. Never larger—never great. But warmer and brighter, pushing the darkness away. People drew near. They held their hands up, smiling at the warmth and nodding their heads.

Her feathers fell from her wings. When they landed in the flames, the blaze was hot and cheery. *Ah*, the people said, speaking in one voice. *This fire is good.*

She woke to the croaking of a heron, calling from somewhere at the river's edge. Though she ached from a restless sleep on the hard, cold earth, she held her body very still, clinging to the images of her dream. They were fading quickly, slipping from her grasp like fronds of riverweed, slick and wispy in the hand.

I have a name, she realized. The knowledge of it filled her with quiet pride, with a hot, trembling wonder.

She sat up abruptly. There was a pot of greasepaint in her bag; she worked the tight lid free and was glad to see that the paint was red. Not *puccoon*—she was a common woman, and such luxuries were not for her. But it was bloodroot, and the color was right.

She painted her inner thighs with the bloodroot. She was aware that the painting was a blessing a female relative should have bestowed: Koleopatchika, perhaps, or Matachanna. But she was a woman alone now, a woman apart. Her fingers could paint as well as any other's.

The silk-grass cloth that had wrapped her bread would have to do for an apron, at least until she returned to Orapax. She spread the cloth beside the ashes of her fire, and, smiling, she traced her chosen symbols with one bloodroot-covered finger: a heron in flight above the ring of a small fire.

She stood and fixed the apron of womanhood in place with her last long strip of buckskin. Then she declared her new name to the bones of Werowocomoco.

"Matoaka." *A kindled fire.*

She reached Jamestown late the same day, just as the afternoon light began to slant lazily from the west. She had forgotten the harsh smell of the place, the sharp acridity of white men's sweat and damp wool, of waste and rot and gunpowder.

Their great ships rested in their accustomed place, tied by heavy lines to the largest and sturdiest trees near the water's edge. The flags on the ships' central posts lifted and flapped on a stray breeze, exposing for a moment the red cross on its white field. A group of crows squabbled along the taut line of one ship, and they glared down at her with sharp, malevolent eyes as she paddled beneath the tight-strung ropes.

She smiled to hear the watcher cry "Halloo!" from his high lookout tower. It brought to mind happier days, when she had come bearing gifts from her father, when there had been hope in Powhatan's longhouse that the *tassantassas* might become allies and the old *mamanatowick* had brimmed with youthful energy.

She beached her canoe and moved carefully up the strand, slipping in the thick, stagnant mud.

"Who goes there?" came the *tassantassa* challenge.

She pressed a hand to her heart. "I am the princess."

The palisade gates flung wide for her. Men gathered in their accustomed throng, staring and murmuring. Many faces she recalled, but several were new: in the months since Powhatan had vacated Werowocomoco, the *tassantassas* had brought more men from their far-off land. They still looked thin and underfed. The dark-blue circles beneath their eyes showed plainly in their pale faces. Their bushy beards did little to disguise the sharpness of their features. Privation had hacked at them like a stone axe against soft wood, leaving rough edges in its wake.

She smiled at them as she entered the fort, reassuring them with gestures and words that she came in friendship, even though she brought no gifts of food.

The fort itself had grown. More of the peak-roofed buildings had sprouted, and some had merged together like longhouses; the fresh new planks that joined them stood out bright and golden against the older, weathered wood. The trampled mire in the center of the fort was crisscrossed with flat wooden walkways, damp bridges that barely kept the men's feet out of the water as they rushed forward to greet her.

"Princess, what news do you bring?"

"Have you any food for us?"

She held out her empty hands. "I have come to speak to Chawnzmit."

A silence fell over the crowd. The men twisted and crushed their hats in their hand. She remembered how Chawnzmit had done the same as he stood in the garden she had built for him. She recalled the sunlight limning the edges of his beard with copper brightness.

"Where is Chawnzmit?"

A big man stepped forward, ducking his head in apology. His eyes were sad, and shifted this way and that as if he could not bring himself to meet her gaze. She searched through her memory for the man's name. Chawn-russ-l.

"I am sorry, Princess," Chawn-russ-l said. His voice was as mournful as a brown dove's. "Chawnzmit is dead."

OPECHANCANOUGH

Season of Cohattayough

Opechancanough worked his knife carefully into the new mulberry bow. He had chosen the best and most flexible sapling he could find, and planed the staff carefully while it was still wet from soaking. He sheared away strips of fresh white wood with a broad flint cutter until the staff was perfectly flat on both of its long faces. The handle he had left round and thick, and he had teased the wood with a knife and handfuls of sand, rubbed beneath a scrap of leather, until it fit exactly in his palm. The notches at each end were the final touch. They had to align in perfect symmetry, small enough to hold the sinew-braid bowstring securely, but wide enough to allow the correct degree of give and snap as the bow was bent and fired.

He had not intended to soothe his spirit with bowmaking. It was only a chore that needed doing; his old bow was beginning to show the first signs of failure—minute cracks near the handle and an alarming catch in the song of taut bent wood when he drew upon the string. It would not do to dwell so near Massawomeck territory with a faulty bow, and so he had set about making a new one. As he worked, however, the process of creation seemed to settle something deep in his chest.

As the mulberry sapling bent beneath his hands, the image of Tsena-no-ha faded from his mind. When Opechancanough brushed away the sand from the staff, leaving a smooth luster, he also brushed away his fears for his aging brother. He concentrated on the knife in his hand, the responsive spring of the mulberry wood, and the whippy lightness of his fine new weapon. As he did, he flung aside the dark cloud of anger that had stalked him for years like a *manitou* in the forest.

He sat cross-legged, engrossed in his work, occasionally glancing up to smile at the women who bustled about his yard. They were painted and adorned finer than women ought to be for the mundane work of storing groundnuts and sun-dried berries in his cellar. Each woman hoped she might become the mistress of his hearth, his new wife—or one wife of many, should he assume the mantle of the Chief of Chiefs.

Winganuske moved through the women like a canoe down-river, direct and smooth, gliding with a confidence none of the others possessed. Opechancanough's smile faded when he saw her. She was as beautiful as ever with her round, wide face and enchanting eyes—the favorite of Powhatan, the great love that warmed the old man's heart. Opechancanough knew what she wanted, but when the time came for him to choose a wife, he would not choose her, even if she left Powhatan's hearth willingly. He would not take *everything* from his brother. Not everything.

The flock of women whispered and laughed as they beat softness back into his sleeping mats, shook out his furs in the sunlight, and picked moth casings from the edges of the plush skins. The sound was good—the laughter, the feminine joy. It renewed the grin on his face and brought a slow, appreciative chuckle to his chest. Months after the move to Orapax, when the straggling Massawomeck scouts had finally been warded away with constant patrols through the woods, he was finally settling in. This new longhouse was beautiful—well built with a good, tight weave of bark on its walls and roof. The bedsteads inside were springy and comfortable, and the heart fire tended with affectionate care by his youngest sister, Koleopatchika. He wanted for nothing but a special woman to manage such a fine house.

Koleopatchika ducked through the door of the *yehakin* with another bundle of furs. She cast some bawdy joke at the women as she handed the furs around, and they began shaking out the dust and accumulated ash in the yard. Opechancanough raised a hand in greeting, thinking to call out his thanks to his sister. But she stared beyond him, her mouth forming a shocked dark circle. "*Oh!*" she cried, the wolfskin hanging limp in her hands.

Opechancanough sprang from his rock, whirled about to face the forest. He expected some danger, an enemy, a Massawomeck warrior raiding for blood or—Okeus protect him, the hated *tassantassas* come to shatter his fragile, newfound peace.

What he saw only redoubled his surprise.

A strange specter emerged from the wood. It had the body of a very young woman, barely out of girlhood, with a curiously thin and flimsy apron draped over its loins. The hair had been sliced off bluntly at chin length, and ruffled in the slight wind of her movement. Above her ears and brow, bristly dark hair grew out from the shaven pate of childhood. It would not be shaven again. He realized with a sudden twist of anxiety that he looked upon an initiate, a new wielder of the life-giving blood.

Superstitiously, he stepped away, averting his eyes. Women were full of unpredictable magic at this turn of their lives, the bend in the trail that a man could never comprehend. Spirits might hang close about her—or *manitou*.

But as his gaze slid from her body, he caught a brief flash of the dimple in her chin, and recognized the new-made woman.

"Amonute."

"Uncle."

She came to stand at his side. Cautiously, he glanced at her face. The dark, slanted eyes were still familiar, still the same eyes she'd had as a girl. *What else did you expect, you fool?* The simple sameness of her face calmed his fear of magic, and yet he detected something in her countenance that was not the same—something lost, something brushed away like the sand from his new bow. Something that was gone forever.

"I have a new name now," she said quietly. "Matoaka."

He nodded. Of course she had a new name. All Real People took new names at the great moments of their lives, when they *became* again, when the world changed them, or they changed the world. Boys emerged from the *huskanaw* with new names. Chiefs took new identities when they claimed their territories.

"I would speak with you, if I may, Uncle."

Opechancanough sent the women away. They went muttering, casting wondering glances back at Amonute as they left. He held the flap of the door aside for her to pass, and then followed her into the cool shadows of his longhouse.

She sank to the floor at the heart fire, waiting patiently while he shifted his weight from one foot to the other, caught in indecision. Should he sit beside her, as a brother would do? Or should he seat himself upon his bedstead, high and strong like a chief? He was unused to this indecision, this softness and muddle.

I am a werowance, *after all—and her* werowance, *no less, for she is Pamunkey-born.*

Opechancanough settled onto the bed. Without furs or mats to cushion him, the frame creaked loudly beneath his weight.

"What would you speak of, Amo . . ." He caught himself and laughed in embarrassed apology. "Matoaka?"

"I have come to tell you that I wish to marry the warrior Kocoum."

Opechancanough heard this in silence, allowed that silence to stretch. An orphaned girl might approach her *werowance* about her marriage wishes, but Matoaka's father still lived. Powhatan lay in his longhouse not far from here, dreaming in the dark of his own faded strength. At last he said, "Does your father know of this?"

"I have not told him yet. I have not seen him. I've only just returned."

"Returned from where?" He recalled hearing the concerned whispers among his train of hopeful women, rumors that little Amonute had vanished in the night. That was more than ten days ago. He looked at her more closely, peering through the red mist of his own superstition, his mistrust of newly realized blood. Her body was strong and lean. The girlish arms were hard with taut new muscle. "You have been paddling."

"For many days."

"And where did you go?"

Her eyes flicked up to meet his; she held his gaze with an impertinent stare, and then dropped her face once more.

It's her old boldness that's gone—or mostly gone. She is softer now. Changed.

And yet she did not answer immediately, which was a boldness in itself.

"I have not yet told my father of my preference for Kocoum, because I know who truly holds the power in Tsenacomoco. I saw you kill the *tassantassas* at Uttamussak. I saw you fill their mouths with bread. I saw in that moment that Powhatan is not the man he once was. After all, here we are in Orapax, and not in Werowocomoco where we belong."

"Powhatan's reasons for leaving Werowocomoco were sound."

She tilted her head as if considering his assertion. The ends of her short, tufted hair turned ruddy in the firelight. "We will soon call another man Powhatan, I think."

"Not I. There are some things I will not take from my brother. His name is one of them."

She shrugged. "*Mamanatowick*, then."

At the sound of the title, a swell rose in his middle like a great sea wave, pressing from below against his heart. He felt twin blades cut at him, gratification and fear, cleaving into his spirit with a sudden, sharp force. No one had yet called him *mamanatowick* save for this child—this woman. But the title felt right. Right, and inevitable, and weighted with sorrow.

"Matoaka, you once relished your work with the *tassantassas*."

She flinched, an almost imperceptible twitch of her mouth, but she waited in silence for him to continue, her hands folded patiently in her aproned lap.

"When I am *mamanatowick* in truth—when all the world knows it—the *tassantassas* must be driven away or killed. Do you understand why?"

"Yes," she said at once. He had expected a thoughtful silence, perhaps even a childish protest. But she did not hesitate. "I will not interfere with your plans. My ambitions cost our people much. I know that, and I am sorry for it. But those ambitions belonged to Amonute, not to Matoaka. Matoaka wants only what is best for the Real People."

He sighed, gave a weary exhalation. "I don't think it is your fault, woman. I doubt you are as much to blame as you might feel. Chawnzmit is crafty. He would have found a way to take our food, to make his weak people prosperous no matter what any of us did. He is more *manitou* than man. You are not to blame—not entirely."

She hung her head. Opechancanough could not be sure whether tears shone in her eyes or whether some reciprocal spark glittered back at the firelight.

"Tell me," he said, "why Kocoum?"

"He is a good hunter, a good warrior . . ."

"Oh, yes. All women say that of the men they wish to marry. What else draws you to him?"

"He is common. Like me. As his wife, I can fade from the sight of the Real People. I can hide from my shame, my involvement with the *tassantassas*. I will sit beside no *werowance*, displaying myself before the eyes of my tribe, reminding them of the part I played in"—she gestured helplessly, limply, indicating Orapax beyond the longhouse walls—"this."

"That is wise," he said, approving and rather startled to hear such serious thoughts from the mouth of the same little Mischief who had thrown herself across Chawnzmit's body, fearlessly stealing the boast from her brother.

Wise. The word caused her to glance up and quickly away again, a shy smile of satisfaction on her lips.

"But allow me to offer you some advice, Matoaka. It is not wise to wall yourself up, to keep yourself away from your tribe. I understand the impulse to fade away, to hide from your shame. Okeus knows I understand shame better than most men. But seclusion will only wound your spirit in the end."

She leaned away slightly, as if pushed by an invisible hand. Her face turned away. In its soft lines, still round with the traces of childhood, he saw a cloud of sorrow rise and eddy like a plume of smoke in a windless sky. It was all she wanted now: seclusion, and a respite from pain. After what she had been through—what they all had been through—he could not fault her. He wished for one heartbeat that he might have the same. A quiet life, laughter with a good woman beside him, the pounding of children's running feet in his yard. Easy hunts, ample harvests, a fine mulberry bow that he never had cause to string, let alone to shoot at another man.

But he was the *mamanatowick*. Or he would be, one inescapable day.

Matoaka fixed a cheery smile to her face. She did have a lovely smile, open and bright. It flashed above her dimpled chin. "Have you any advice for me, Uncle? How shall I be a good wife to Kocoum?"

Opechancanough huffed a laugh—abrupt and hoarse but not bitter. He recalled Tsena-no-ha waking away, how it inflamed his rage to know that she had found happiness at Pepiscunimah's hearth rather than his own. He recalled with a clutch of shame how that rage had burned hot and wild in the ensuing years. Had Tsena-no-ha's love ever been worth that twisting, sharp-toothed fury? Now that he had lost so much more—Werowocomoco, his brother's strength, his dignity when Chawnzmit had caught him up by the hair and held him like a day-old pup before the bows of his own men—now he knew the hollow ache of true loss. Now he knew the banked, glowing smolder of true and righteous anger.

"Yes, woman, I would give you advice," Opechancanough said. His voice grated with stifled emotion. He wished with sudden, dizzying surprise to find Pepiscunimah, not to harry the man with insults or violence, but to clasp his finger with his own. He wished to place a kiss on Tsena-no-ha's lovely, imperious brow and wish her years of happiness. "Love your people as much as you love your husband. Serve your tribe, for the bond you have with your people is as important as the bond you will have with your mate. Perhaps it is more important."

Matoaka bowed her head in acceptance. Her newly short hair swung forward to hide her face. He did not need to see her face to know that his advice had been a disappointment to her, heartfelt as it was. The young woman was not the child; Matoaka was not Amonute. Matoaka had no desire for a public life, no appetite for power, no need to caper for the *mamanatowick* and charm him to her whims. She would retreat into the privacy of her longhouse as soon as she was able. Tsenacomoco would forget her, and she would be content.

"Go to your father's longhouse," he said quietly. "Tell him."

She made her way down the hall. Already she moved more like a woman—not with a woman's round-hipped sway, not with the fluid, appealing grace of Winganuske, but with a straight-backed confidence that even the child Amonute had not possessed.

She lifted the door flap; white light flooded in around her. She paused, and turned back to face him. She was a silhouette: dark-featured and backlit by a bright and dancing sun. "You should know, Uncle. Chawnzmit is dead."

She ducked out. The door flap closed behind her with a soft, hollow thump.

Opechancanough drew in a deep, ragged breath. For the first time in nearly a year, he felt hope stir. Perhaps the *tassantassas* could be destroyed after all, and sooner than later.

POCAHONTAS

Season of Cohattayough

Downriver, far from Orapax, Pocahontas's braid was adrift in the deep currents. She pictured it, tumbling end over end, slow as a snowflake drifting. Its ends unraveling, a black wavering net through which the tiny silver fishes darted and played. It might be out to sea now, surging and pooling with the movement of the waves, dancing like the long ropes of weed that greened the deepest tide pools.

When the *tassantassas* had made her understand at last that Chawnzmit was dead—that he had been killed by a great, terrible, roaring burst when a spark had fallen on a keg of gunpowder, and she was too late—she had pushed her way back through the men's hands to her canoe. The crows gathered along the great ship's line had burst into flight as she rowed past, screaming their mockery through a cloud of black feathers and a clatter of wings.

She had paddled hard upriver, arms burning against the current, eyes burning with tears. When her vision finally cleared, she let her paddle rest and fell back downstream, the dugout spinning broadside into the current as she fished her knife from her traveling bag.

She had seized the braid of her girlhood and sawed at it with her bone blade. The hair made a tearing rasp, and swung in sudden freedom around her face. She dropped it over the side, not bothering to salvage its few poor ornaments: the handful of shell beads, the shining copper disc, the white feather she had worn for luck.

Her childhood drifted down into the secret places of the river, into the cold and the unknowable darkness. It was finally over—Chawnzmit, Amonute, the *tassantassas*—done.

The trek home had taken many more days than her trip downriver. She paddled in silence; her small body strained against the hard thrust of the current, neck tense, shoulders aching. She made landfall every afternoon, unable to row any farther, panting from the exertion and the ill luck of it all. How the spirits mocked her, that she should travel so far only to learn that Chawnzmit was dead! At night she changed her paddings of moss and threw her blood magic into the fire—burning her spirit, turning all her power to smoke, wafting away the last vestiges of who she had been.

It was a wise voice that had directed her to Opechancanough's hearth. And once she had told him the news of Chawnzmit's death, she presented herself at Powhatan's fire, too.

The old man lay bundled on his bed. The white dog the *tassantassas* had given him sat nearby, one slender paw on Powhatan's furs, taking morsels of food from his fingers while a woman crooned a gentle song from somewhere close by.

Pocahontas stood in front of him and allowed him to take in the sight of her with braid shorn and forelock growing, with the apron of womanhood—such as it was, that poor scrap of silk grass—hanging from her narrow hips. The old *mamanatowick's* eyes had filled with a mix of pride and loss, but he gave his blessing to her union, pronouncing Kocoum a fine and fitting husband.

She kissed his wrinkled cheek, avoiding the dog as it tried to lick her hand, and walked quickly from the stifling confines of his great house.

She found the trail that led to her own small longhouse. The strawberries had ceased to fruit, and the few berries that had been left unharvested lay soft and cloying in the dust of the trail. Persimmons slowly ripened on the boughs of their shrubby trees. A rabbit startled and bolted across her path, the flash of its white tail winking like a star in the undergrowth.

She rounded a bend. From the direction of her longhouse came the rise and fall of many women's voices, passing the rounds of a chant through their ranks.

A woman comes, a woman comes
She comes with digging stick and bowl
She comes with basket, gourd, and bread
She comes to warm her husband's bed!

The wedding song.

Pocahontas broke into a run, loping like the rabbit in long, bounding strides. She burst into the yard of her longhouse. A ring of girls and women moved in a circle, stepping sideways, turn and clap, and the song started again, first from this side of the ring, then the other.

A woman comes, a woman comes
She comes with mill and stores of corn
She comes with blood that brings new life
She comes with sheath for husband's knife!

Within the dancing ring, a handful of unblooded girls clamored, holding pots of paint high, shaking between them a long cape of fine, pale buckskin. Koleopatchika directed them with quick words and sharp gestures—Koleopatchika, sister of the *mamanatowick*, standing in the rightful place of a mother. It could only be a daughter of Powhatan, motherless here in Orapax but never alone, who went to her marriage bed.

Pocahontas pushed through the circle of dancers. "Matachanna!"

The unblooded girls looked up from their work. They held between them the marriage cape; it stretched across the yard like a cloud come to earth.

Pocahontas's eyes traveled up the length of the cape. It was embellished in *roanoke*, the purple-black beads worked into row upon row of tight spirals. At its center, the blocky form of a male body stood out against the snowy leather, and from the figure's head rose a pair of spreading, jagged antlers. A fitting symbol for the bride of a priest.

Above the cloak, a face finely painted in ash and *puccoon* stared back at her. A black line divided Matachanna's face at the cheekbones, tracking over the bridge of her nose; she was red to the hairline, and her astonished eyes looked all the rounder in their mask. Her chin was still swollen and pink between the vertical bars of her new tattoo: the mark of a high-status wife.

For one cold-clutching moment, Pocahontas feared Matachanna would scorn her again, as she had so many times. But Matachanna yelped, a high bark like a wolf calling to its pack, and rushed through the crowd of girls to Pocahontas's side.

"Pocahontas! I thought you were dead!" She pulled her sister into a tight embrace. "Oh, won't you please forgive me? I was terrible to you, and I'm sorry."

"It's I who should beg forgiveness," Pocahontas said quietly, close to Matachanna's ear, to be heard over the renewed round of the wedding song. Her sister smelled of smoke and sweet herbs, of tobacco and salt tears. She smelled of home.

"I won't hear it. My Mischief. I would kiss you, but I'd smear my *puccoon*."

Pocahontas smiled shyly, glanced down at her makeshift apron. "I have a new name."

"Okeus! You're a woman now, too. Think of it, both of us in the same month. It is powerful magic. We are bonded together."

"More than sisters," Pocahontas agreed.

They whispered their new names, smiling, laughing, clinging to one another tight as burrs.

"Matoaka is a good name," Matachanna said. "but I will never call you anything but Pocahontas."

"And you will always be Matachanna to me, even if everyone else calls you Coanuske."

Snow woman. Pocahontas burned to know the vision that had inspired her sister's new name, but of course such a thing could never be told. And she ached in turn to share the mystery of her own name vision: the rush of flight, the words on the wind, the fire that kindled itself for the good of all the people who gathered around its small but brilliant light. She pulled Matachanna into another embrace and felt her spirit throb against her sister's skin. She felt the magic of their two visions mingle, Pocahontas's fire and Matachanna's secret snow.

Matachanna pulled away, grinning. "I want you to carry the white beads today, Pocahontas."

A singular honor. Pocahontas blushed as she accepted the long strand of pearls. She twined them through her fingers while the girls pinned the white cape about Matachanna's shoulders. The dancers sang the final chorus, and together they led Matachanna to the dancing grounds of Orapax, where Utta-ma-tomakkin stood beautiful and proud at the fireside, waiting to receive his bride.

They swore their hearts to one another and clasped hands above a gourd full of water. Pocahontas stretched the cord of pearls tight and brought it down upon their hands. The chain broke with a loud snap. Pearls showered over the dancing ground, bouncing and rolling, and the girls who had led Matachanna scrambled in the dust to collect them.

Pocahontas looked out through the laughing crowd as the drums began to pulse. The broken ends of the bead chain still swung from her fingers. She caught sight of a welcome face passing through the gathering, the solemn brow and strong nose emerging between smiling faces, and then vanishing again as he made his way out of the ring.

She pushed through the crowd to catch him.

"Kocoum," she called, taking hold of his elbow.

"Amonute." He took in the shortness of her hair and glanced down at the apron with its heron and its ring of fire. "Oh."

She slipped her hand into his. A breathless thrill filled her chest, quaking her body with every step. But she did not pull away. She tugged him away from the crowd, and they made their way once more to the shelf of stone that stood high above the river, where they had watched the night fishers in the purple twilight. There were no night fishers now. The sun was full and soft on the river as all the world celebrated the union of Matachanna and Utta-ma-tomakkin.

"You are a woman now," Kocoum said sensibly.

She smiled at the undisguised expectation in his voice. "My answer is still yes. I have told my father and my uncle of my choice. I have told them I choose you."

He bent and kissed her—not on the forehead or the cheek, as a friend would do, but full on the mouth. She gasped; the quivering in her body rose in pitch like a paddle drum when its skin is tightened. A very unwomanly giggle threatened to burst from her chest. She quelled it with a bear-strong effort.

When the season of *nepinough* arrived, calling grapes from the vine and ears from the corn plants, it was Pocahontas who donned the white cape of marriage. Her cloak's design was simple: a heron in white shell beads, barely visible against the pale drape of doeskin. Her chin was not tattooed, for she was only a common wife, and her red paint was bloodroot. But as she stood in the center of the dancing ring with Kocoum, she had never felt so grateful, nor had she felt so blessed.

Matachanna stretched the white chain in the air between Pocahontas and her husband. The shell beads snapped across their clasped hands, filling the autumn-blue sky with a shower of stars.

OPECHANCANOUGH

Season of Popanow
One year later

The troop of warriors sank to their bellies in the cornfield. The late-season husks did not give so much as a whisper to betray the ambush. The spent leaves of the plants drooped, yellow and dry, like the white-and-red flags atop the *tassantassas'* ships. Opechancanough surveyed the field, satisfied by its silence, and moved to the garden's edge to await the arrival of his trading partners.

Chawnzmit was dead. The ravening white wolf was truly gone. Only a shiver of loathing remaining in Opechancanough's bones to remind him that the ill dream called Chawnzmit had ever truly walked Tsenacomoco. When the new-made woman Matoaka had brought him the tidings, he had not dared to believe them, though his spirit vibrated with hope and renewed resolve.

But more than a year had passed, and no one had seen a hint of Chawnzmit's presence. The previous winter, when the *tassantassas* ventured out to raid the southern territories, their efforts were easily rebuffed—something unheard of under Chawnzmit's rule. Throughout the cold, wet seasons when nothing would grow, Opechancanough had taken advantage of the *tassantassas'* new meekness and obvious desperation to lure them into snares. His other chiefs had done likewise, and hardly a month went by without some warrior boasting of taking a *tassantassa*'s life. Soon enough the white men no longer left their fort at all, withdrawing behind their high palisade to lick their bleeding wounds.

But *popanow* had come once more with lowering skies, with mornings whitened by frost. The *tassantassas* knew, as Opechancanough knew, that they would soon be like wounded bears backed against a cliff wall: roaring in fear, wielding their deadly claws . . . but desperate and frightened enough to blunder.

He watched as the large, white-winged boat they called *shallop* appeared around the river's bend, lumbering like a wood buffalo in a muddy wallow. There were many men aboard that boat. They watched from the rail with strained, pale faces, and even at a distance Opechancanough could feel the hope gasp in the white men's thin breasts. He made the sign of welcome as they anchored and filled a smaller boat with men. He gestured as they came onto the shore, wary, crouched, like kicked dogs slinking away from a cook fire.

Here, Opechancanough said, motioning with both hands to row upon row of baskets heaped high with corn. *Here is what I give you.*

The men eyed the corn as they eyed him, their stilt-thin legs stepping nervously and heads bobbing like wading birds probing in the mud. Opechancanough smiled and spoke soothing words, though they did not understand. He gestured eagerly, encouraging the men to take the bait.

One of them shouldered his musket and stooped to lift a basket. It came up quickly, far lighter than it looked. The *tassantassa* exclaimed in dismay; he upended the basket to reveal how its bottom had been pushed up to create a high mound. The corn was piled atop that mound—far less grain than a basket ought to hold—so that what had seemed a heaping pile of corn was nothing but a thin skin of trickery.

Their leader barked harsh words and pushed close to Opechancanough's face. His breath smelled of rot.

Opechancanough smiled.

The *tassantassas* leveled their guns toward him while their leader went on barking, no doubt demanding the full allotment of corn, as Opechancanough's messengers had agreed.

Let them clamor like crows in a naked tree. They will not shoot me; they need my corn, or they will starve. His grin widened.

Opechancanough turned his head away from the white man's foul breath. He gave a great whoop, high and sharp, then dropped to his belly in the dust.

The cornfield released a loud hiss as warriors rose from among the clattering leaves with bows drawn. The *tassantassas* wailed in dismay. A few shots cracked the air; the stink of their weapons singed Opechancanough's throat. But none of the Real People grunted in pain. The *tassantassas* were poor shots these days, their eyes weakened by hunger and their arms always shaking.

Most of the white men fell in the first volley of arrows. Four threw down their guns in a panic and made for the shore. Their guns were useless now—Opechancanough had learned that guns took time to reload. They could not be armed as quickly as one nocks an arrow to a bowstring. Still, even emptied of their bullets, the guns might be useful. He would collect them when his business here was finished.

Opechancanough watched from the ground as the next flight of arrows dropped two in their tracks, as easily as deer are picked off in an open meadow.

The men still aboard the shallop shouted and scuttled over the deck of their ship. The anchor came up, and the boat lifted on the current, moving swiftly downstream while the abandoned pair of *tassantassas* cowered and cursed on the strand.

Opechancanough raised his fist, and the warriors subsided.

He strolled casually down to the riverbank. The *tassantassas* wrestled the landing boat out into the water, eyes wide, panting and frothing like deer run into the ground. They shoved off in their small boat, the oars tapping weakly at the water. The white men cried out for mercy as he unslung his bow from his shoulder.

Pushed-up baskets, he mused, chuckling as he took aim. *Too simple.*

Opechancanough fired. One white man gurgled and slumped; the boat spun in a rapid circle as the remaining *tassantassa* rowed frantically. His keen of terror was like a bird's thin cry.

Chawnzmit would never have fallen for pushed-up baskets.

Opechancanough fired again and the last oar dropped into the water.

But Chawnzmit is dead.

An especially harsh winter fell over Tsenacomoco that year. Snowdrifts grew to knee deep, ponds and marshes froze solid, and the roar of the falls was almost silenced. Now and then great chunks of ice would drift past the deadened shores of Orapax, evidence of a mighty freeze beyond the fall line, unlike any seen in Opechancanough's memory.

Word traveled slowly in such conditions, but still rumors crept upriver against the icy currents and tumbling ice. The ferocity of *popanow* dealt a heavy blow to the *tassantassas*. With Chawnzmit gone, there was no sharp mind to control their trade, and the white men quickly bartered away all their valuable goods for meager quantities of food. Now no Real People would visit the fort with sacks of cornmeal or baskets of *tuckahoe*, for the *tassantassas* were known to possess only trash—and guns, which they still could not be made to part with. They starved now in earnest. Those scouts who made their delayed reports to Powhatan told of white men dying so rapidly that those still living could not dig graves in the frozen earth fast enough to bury them. And as the weeks of bitter cold and darkness ground onward, reports arrived that the *tassantassas* had resorted to eating their dead.

Opechancanough spat in disgust when he heard it, though in truth he had expected the white men to gnaw each other's bones long before this. Had not Chawnzmit admitted that his people ate the flesh of men those years ago, when Opechancanough had led his captive in triumph from village to village?

Yet, even as his hatred for the *tassantassas* grew, an assured peace burrowed into Opechancanough's spirit, nestling like a pup at its dam's belly, warm and contented. This was truly the last season of the *tassantassas*. He had only to persevere a few weeks more, and the last of them would be gone.

Opechancanough's contentment was rudely strangled at the first hint of a thaw. The falls swelled and began to roar with a redoubled voice. Blue blocks of ice drifted in greater quantities, flashing by Orapax on a rapid current. The snow rotted beneath a crust toughened by warming mornings and freezing nights. Now when Opechancanough made his way through the forest clearings to meet the southern messengers, wrapped in a wolfskin cloak, he broke through the crust with every other step, and his shins were soon cut and bruised from the icy edges of his own deep footprints.

A messenger waited for him in a patch of yellow sunlight. The man was bundled in a cougar's pelt, and a hood of weasel skins was tied close about his ears, but the dark vertical tattoos of Paspahegh showed in the gaps of his fur-lined leggings.

"What news from Paspahegh?" Opechancanough said.

"Wowinchopunck, my *werowance*, sends his greetings and respect to his old friend Opechancanough."

Opechancanough's chest tightened with a queer sensation that was somewhere between elation and sinking. He was not the *mamanatowick*—not yet. But Powhatan had retreated so far into himself, into the world of his wives and his private thoughts, that

Opechancanough may as well have been declared the Chief of Chiefs already. None of the territories would send either greetings or respect to Powhatan—not unless the old man was close by. It was Opechancanough whose favor they all sought now. This had been the way of things all winter long.

Opechancanough nodded.

"New ships have entered the capes near Paspahegh. They carry more white men for the fort."

"Ships." More white men. There seemed to be an unlimited supply of them, like ants marching from a sand hill.

Opechancanough took the message to Powhatan himself. But the *mamanatowick* only shook his head and pulled his fur robe tighter around his wasting body.

As the year unfolded, Opechancanough began to doubt his god, for it seemed the Okeus had turned his face away from the Real People. The planting season of *cohattayough* came late. The gardens would be small and sparse. *Nepinough*, the season of growing and early harvest, was thin and poor. Drought plagued the land for the fifth year running. Or was it the sixth? The seventh? Opechancanough found he could no longer recall the seasons, could not summon up the chronicle of years as he once had. The twin plagues of the tenacious white men and the failing harvest beat at him, and his spirit was mired like a moccasin in a bog.

The *tassantassas* ate through the food their ships delivered, like grasshoppers loosed among tender leaves, and soon the white men ventured out of their strange wooden village for the first time in many months, seeking trade with the nearby villages. The Real People rebuffed them, of course, for there was no surplus to spare—not for any price—not even, with such a pathetic harvest to come, for guns.

Violence flamed, fanned by hatred and desperation, and crises erupted and spread through the forest of Tsenacomoco like brush fires. *Tassantassas* fell upon a village, sacking the caches of food.

The men of the village apprehended scouting white men, and took their scalps to diminish their spirits when they returned in a new body. The friends of the scalped men threw torches into canoes, and laughed and hooted as the priceless dugouts burned. It went ever on, each act connected to the last, rolling ever faster like the Great Netted Hoop, the Universe itself, spinning in the dark sky.

Nepinough drew to an early close. A hasty harvest ensued, rushed by the untimely departure of the season as much as by the specter of the *tassantassas*, who were assumed to lurk about the edges of every field like *manitou* prowling for human flesh.

Before the last of the corn was in, another visitor arrived at Orapax: Japazaws, *werowance* of the Pattawomecks. He was a stout, squint-eyed man given to licking spittle of greater men, ingratiating himself with any man whom he thought could further his own standing. Opechancanough had never liked Japazaws, and he liked him even less as the man settled at the edge of Powhatan's fire.

"Why have you come yourself?" Opechancanough demanded. "Does Pattawomeck not need the guidance of its chief at a time such as this?"

Japazaws made a noise that was dangerously close to a woman's giggle. He nodded. "It is true, Opechancanough; the days are terrible. Even more terrible at my village, close as we are to the white men. I assure you, none of my tribe enjoy the luxury of distance as our great *mamanatowick* and his fearless brother do, here in Orapax."

"Stop," Powhatan said. His voice was barely more than a whisper. "I will not stand for this foolish baiting. Why have you come, Japazaws?"

The little man puffed himself like a grouse strutting in a springtime lek. "I bear a very important message. Too important to trust to any man who is not a *werowance*."

Opechancanough gestured impatiently. "Let us hear it, then."

"The *tassantassas* have a new *werowance* at their fort. He arrived several days ago from their homeland, the place they call *Iing-land*, and he called me to his presence with a message for you, O Powhatan.

"He demands that you order all hostilities against his people to cease. He also demands that any Real Men who have recently killed *tassantassas* be sent to Jamestown to receive his *mamanato-wick's* justice."

Opechancanough leaned toward Japazaws, looming close in the firelight. "You seem to speak the white men's tongue well, to understand their chief's message so precisely."

"I am a skilled man," Japazaws bristled.

"You must trade often with the *tassantassas*, to speak their tongue so easily. Or have you already moved into their fort, Japazaws?"

Japazaws allowed the accusation to slide over him. "There is more to the message," he said, and turned to face Powhatan as if Opechancanough were not there. "He demands the return of any *tassantassa* runaways who might have taken refuge over the winter with any tribes of the Real People, or else he swears to recover such cowards by force.

"Finally, he reminds you, Powhatan, that you swore your friendship and homage to his *mamanatowick*, King James, when you were crowned."

At mention of the crowning, Powhatan's face darkened. "Enough," he growled.

Opechancanough's scalp prickled. A surge of rage and strength seemed to rise in Powhatan's spirit, so that he filled his fur robe, bellying outward like one of the white men's ships sailing in a high wind.

"What is this white chief's name?" Powhatan said.

"He calls himself Lord-del-a-wair."

Powhatan eyed Opechancanough sharply. "Brother, find your best runner. Send a message to my daughter Matoaka. She lives on the outer edge of Orapax in her husband's longhouse, not far from the falls."

"I know the place. It is not far—a quarter of a day's walk, there and back."

"And when your runner has gone, take this man who calls himself a *werowance* and put him under guard in one of my smallest houses. As he is fond of carrying messages like a boy shy of his *huskanaw*, I shall give him one to carry at first light."

Matoaka arrived as night was falling, ever obedient to her father's summons—or perhaps to her uncle's. She had wrapped herself in a white feather cape against the early autumn chill. Opechancanough smiled when he saw her, despite his disgust at Japazaws and his *tassantassa* friends. Marriage—womanhood—agreed with Matoaka. In spite of the difficult year, her face was smooth, free of any mark of worry, and she looked up at him with a radiant, intelligent openness, a willingness to serve that kindled a sudden optimism in Opechancanough's spirit.

He took her cloak and hung it on a peg. His hand trailed over the soft feathers, and beneath the swell of hope he felt a poignant pain as he recalled the brash child she had once been. A recollection of her flashed into his mind, sparking in brilliant colors: the girl Amonute standing with hands on hips, demanding of her father that she be allowed to serve at his fire.

"You used to have a white cloak like this one," he said quietly, almost wistfully. "Though I recall it was ragged and patched."

She laughed. "That old rag! It was handed down to me from Koleopatchika." She shook her head. "I must have looked like a pigeon carcass in it, but I loved it. I thought it was so very fine."

"Your new cloak is beautiful."

She blushed, gazed down at the floor. "Kocoum gave it to me."

"He is good to you? You are content?"

"More than content." The flush on her cheeks deepened. Then she tossed her head, sending the blunt-cut, chin-length hair flying and the short fringe above her brows swinging. "But you did not call me here to talk of cloaks or of husbands."

"No. Come, we have much to discuss."

She shared a long, sober look with Opechancanough as they settled together on mats at Powhatan's feet. Her expression darkened all the more when Opechancanough relayed the message from the fort.

"Lord-del-a-wair," she said, quietly musing. The firelight leaped and shivered in her dark eyes.

"And so," Powhatan said, "we must compose a . . . suitable reply. A challenge like this cannot be left unanswered."

"You know the *tassantassas'* ways better than anyone else," said Opechancanough. "Suggest how we might respond to this . . ."

"Outrageous offense," Powhatan grated.

Matoaka's brows rose. "You wish to send them an insult?"

Opechancanough shared a look with his brother. At last Powhatan said, "Yes."

Matoaka clasped her hands atop her apron, studied her fingers as if she might read some trace of an answer in the crisscrossed lines of her own skin. Now and then her lips worked silently as she tasted the white men's words with meticulous care, testing them gingerly like unripe berries on the tongue. There was something bitter and dark in her eyes, and Opechancanough sensed that even she, who had once been so proud of her mastery of the *tassantassa* tongue, had had enough of the white men's presence.

At last she looked up and met Opechancanough's eye, and then, with an apologetic shrug, she addressed herself to Powhatan. "Chawnzmit once told me that *kings*—white *mamanatowicks*—are always approached with great ceremony, and addressed with a display of honor and respect. And so I suggest you tell this Lord-del-a-wair the following . . ."

At first light Opechancanough hauled Japazaws from his well-guarded house, a drafty hut barely larger than a cellar where the man surely had passed an unpleasant night. At Powhatan's fire, Matoaka made the little man rehearse the message until he had memorized it to her satisfaction.

I am given to understand that in your land, kings are always addressed with great respect. Therefore, do not send another message unless it is accompanied by a coach and three horses.

Opechancanough could not understand what a *coach* or *horses* were, but it did not matter. Matoaka assured him, with a hint of her old mischievous sparkle, that the message would work its way under Lord-del-a-wair's skin like a splinter of wood, stinging and impossible to ignore.

The thought of this pompous white *werowance* twitching and moaning under the goad of taunting words buoyed Opechancanough's spirit as he marched Japazaws back to his canoe. He saw the messenger off with an admonishment to leave nothing out of Powhatan's reply, and stood waving his farewell until Japazaws was no more than a dark speck lost in the tangled horizon of forest and river.

Lord-del-a-wair's sharp reply came two weeks later, as Orapax hummed with tense focus. The village was making ready for the hunt, and a treacherous season it was expected to be. With *tassantassas* roving, falling upon villages with torches and threats, many hunters were required to stay home to protect the women, children, the small caches of precious food and the prized canoes, so costly and difficult to replace once they were crudely hacked and burned. More men at home meant fewer hunting, and less meat to see them through a winter that already promised great difficulty. But the hunt must be undertaken, this year of all years. Summer after summer of drought had finally taken its toll on Tsenacomoco.

Opechancanough checked his supply of fresh bowstrings and tucked them into his carrying pouch. He issued a few orders to the women who flocked about his longhouse. Despite the threat of *tassantassas* rising like a black tide across the land, the women were still hopeful. He inspected the bag of food one of the women had prepared for him to carry on the hunt and nodded in approval. He was about to speak to her, for she was an exceptionally pretty and hard-working woman, and might make a good wife if she survived the coming winter. But before any words of praise could leave his throat, a hoarse, ragged wail cut through the trees.

The women dropped their work and fled for the safety of the longhouses.

Another wail shivered among the dying leaves of the canopy. It struck the chill of *popanow* deep into Opechancanough's bones.

Manitou, he said silently. His thoughts were slow and blundering.

And as he thought the word, a woman cried it from inside the longhouse. *"Manitou!"*

Opechancanough snapped from his reverie. He tore the bow from his shoulder, nocked an arrow in one swift, sure movement. He would face the *manitou* single-handed if he must. No demon could be worse than the *tassantassas*, and he had already faced them bravely more times than he could count.

The longhouse fell silent, the women inside cowering in mute terror. Or perhaps the roaring in his ears deafened him to their cries. It did not matter. The mulberry bow creaked as he drew it, and his arm did not shake.

A figure emerged from the forest, stumbling and staggering, shoulders drooping in weariness, or with a sorrow too great to be borne. Its feet dragged as it moved; the clawed hands rose to tear at the flesh of its own chest, its bloody and distorted face, its hair.

The hair.

Opechancanough watched as the thing gathered its loose black hair in a blood-smeared fist and pulled. As it did, he could see that the hair grew from the left side of the scalp, with the right side clean-shaven.

He lowered his bow. *Not a* manitou, *but a man. A man of the Real People.*

The bedraggled man threw back his head and cried again. The wail rent the air, tearing into Opechancanough's heart with cold claws as the man collapsed to his knees in the dust, still keening.

And in that moment, Opechancanough knew him.

"Wowinchopunck."

The *werowance* of Paspahegh sat shivering beneath a wolfskin robe, staring into the heart fire with eyes as dull as a chip of old stone. Opechancanough and Powhatan reclined in their shadowy corners, suspended in awkward silence, assailed by the man's palpable misery, unable to do more for him than remain close at hand with their eyes cast politely away from his display of grief. When Wowinchopunck's cries had finally ceased, Opechancanough brought him food and water, but the gourd and the small basket of venison and dried berries sat untouched.

An hour passed, and then another. Now and then Wowinchopunck twitched or gasped as his memories came to vivid life again, but still he would neither speak nor eat. Finally Opechancanough uncoiled himself from the bedstead and sank to the ground beside his friend. He placed a hand on Wowinchopunck's shoulder. "Tell me."

Wowinchopunck inhaled, a ragged, desolate sound, a wind over a frozen marsh. His eyes focused on Opechancanough. A light of pain kindled there, burning away the merciful dullness. Then he glanced up at Powhatan on his high bed. The *mamanato-wick* sat forward; the frame of his bedstead moaned.

"Several days ago—I do not know how many, for I have rowed and walked long, almost without stopping—a ship came to the shore of Paspahegh. It went under the command of a man who called himself Lord-del-a-wair. We thought they came to trade, and we warded them away, telling them with signs and words that we had nothing to spare and did not wish to trade with them in any case. But many of them came ashore—more than I have seen in one place, all of them armed with guns.

"This Lord-del-a-wair made it known that he wished to speak to the *werowance*. So I faced him, of course. I tried to find some reason in his shouting and waving, but his face was as dark as a half-ripe mulberry, and the veins stood out upon his forehead. He could not be reasoned with, and I turned my back on him.

"He hit me on the back of the head with something. His gun, I suppose, for he had no club that I could see. I fell, and my wife . . ." Wowinchopunck stammered into silence. Opechancanough feared that he would return to his silent trance of misery, and glanced up at Powhatan anxiously. But Wowinchopunck summoned his spirit and went on. "My wife rushed to my side even though the *tassantassas* were all about, and raging.

"Some of the white men seized her, started dragging her toward the small boat they use to go to and from their large ships. Of course my men began firing, but the *tassantassas* were wearing their metal clothes. The arrows broke, or stuck in places that only wounded, and we did not fell a single man.

"My wife began screaming—she is brave, but no one expects women to remain silent when they are captured. My two . . ." Again he choked, again the veil of pain fell across his face. Opechancanough squeezed his shoulder again, hoping to impart some strength to Wowinchopunck's wavering heart.

"My two sons heard her cries, and rushed out to save her. The *tassantassas* captured them, too, for you know they are only little boys, years short of the *huskanaw*." He drew another deep, rattling breath. "*Were.* They were little boys."

Opechancanough swallowed the hard knot that rose into his throat. "Go on."

"The *tassantassas* pointed their guns at my family, and so I commanded all my men to cease firing. I called out to this Lord-del-a-wair, hoping to entice him into some trade so that I might buy their freedom. But he ignored my shouts, and bundled all three of them onto the small boat with his men.

"I rushed to the edge of the water, and even waded in, as if I might swim out to save them. But I knew it was no use. I pleaded with the white men to return them. I pleaded with the Okeus to intervene. My men took to their canoes, but the men aboard the little boat fired upon them, and they could not draw close enough to harm the *tassantassas*.

"They took all three aboard the ship: my wife and my two little sons. Lord-del-a-wair kept shouting down at me, words in his own tongue, words I did not understand. But I remember two, because he repeated them so many times. *Coach* and *horses*."

Opechancanough, mouth dry, stared at Powhatan. The *mamanatowick* blinked several times; his nostrils flared, but he gestured for Wowinchopunck to continue.

"Then, when I did not respond—what response could I make?—he threw my boys off the ship and into the water, one after the other. They swam toward shore, crying out for me, and I thought they would make it, thought they would reach one of the canoes that went out to retrieve them.

"But the *tassantassas* aimed their muskets down from the top of their ship, and fired."

Wowinchopunck's hands lifted to cover his twisted face. He wept in near silence, with only his breath hissing between his fingers, a faint sound beneath the crackle of the heart fire.

No need to ask whether the boys had survived the horrifying ordeal. Opechancanough shared another long look with Powhatan. To his surprise, tears shone in the *mamanatowick*'s eyes. The old man blinked them away and leaned back into shadow, gazing over Opechancanough's head into the long dark hall of the great house.

"And then, while my wife screamed piteously for her sons, some of the white men tore off her apron and passed her about, using her before my eyes, and the eyes of the entire tribe. After a while they stood her up, and called down to me, to my men circling the ship and shouting for vengeance, for white blood. She was bloody and bruised, and her face was terrible, blank, like a dead thing.

"I thought they might let her go, after all they had done to her. But Lord-del-a-wair shouted once more about *horses* and *coach*. Then he drew his sword and . . ." Wowinchopunck made a stabbing motion toward his own middle. He seemed to crumple around the self-inflicted blow, drooping beside the fire like a stem wilting in summer heat. He stayed on the ground, his body shaken by silent sobs.

Opechancanough tucked the corners of the robe around his friend's face, covering his shame from sight.

Powhatan's hands worked at his own hair, tearing the silver strands with jagged, fierce, helpless talons. He rocked in grief, and a hoarse cry reverberated through the longhouse. Opechancanough did not know whether it came from the *mamanatowick*, from Wowinchopunck, or from his own burning throat.

Silence settled again.

Wowinchopunck stirred and straightened beneath the wolf-skin. He rose on shaking legs to stand before Powhatan. When he spoke, his words were strong and calm: not the voice of a grieving father and husband, but the voice of a *werowance* who faces his enemies with club and bow in hand. "The time has long since come to destroy these *tassantassas*. If you do not agree to it, Powhatan, then I say, *there* sits the true *mamanatowick* of Tsenacomoco." He pointed at Opechancanough.

Opechancanough held himself as still as a rabbit when the hawk's shadow speeds across the grass. He did not dare glance toward Powhatan, for fear that he would see defeat in the eyes of the brother he loved so dearly. For fear that he, Opechancanough, would be the cause of grief in the old man's heart.

But Powhatan grunted in assent. Opechancanough's eyes flew to the *mamanatowick's* face. The old man nodded, face stark and haggard in the firelight. "We can no longer run, no longer hide. Now we return the *tassantassas'* violence, blow for blow. And then a blow more."

POCAHONTAS

Season of Cattapeuk
Three years later

Kocoum took the bag of venison and berries from Pocahontas's hands. It was her best bag, woven tightly with the softest strands of grass, and dyed with bloodroot and ochre and bright-white clay. Two fine, even red lines crossed over one another, woven along the flat loop of the carrying strap. Each tiny knot of dyed silk grass lay flat and precise in its field of white. It had taken her days to make it, and her fingers had been cramped and stiff for many more days afterward. But whatever she did for Kocoum, she did with her whole heart.

He laid the bag carefully in the belly of his canoe. When he stopped for the midday meal, he would find the sweet dumplings she had hidden inside, wrapped in mulberry leaves. They would bring a smile to his face, even on a day like this, when he went to make war with the *tassantassas*.

It seemed Kocoum was always off making war. For three years Powhatan and Opechancanough had sent their men against the *tassantassas*, to harry the white men fiercely like a pack of wolves at the heels of a herd of sickly deer. And each time the *mamana-towick* called, Kocoum answered. He was as loyal to the Chief of

Chiefs as he had sworn to be, those years ago when he had told Pocahontas he wanted her for his wife. She could not fault his honesty, nor his bravery.

But her seventeenth winter had just passed, and still she had no child. They tried, when Kocoum was not off making war—the spirits knew how they tried! But as aggressions against the white men increased, she saw her husband less and less, and each month the moon's cycle mocked her fragile hopes.

Kocoum lifted her chin with a gentle hand. His kiss was soft and lingering. "I will think of you every day and every night, Pocahontas."

She was Matoaka now, of course, but Kocoum had never ceased calling her by her old name. She was glad of it. She never wanted him to stop.

The canoe rocked and chattered against the gravelly shore as he settled himself inside and took up the carved handle of his paddle. "When I've killed a few more *tassantassas*," he said, grinning, "we'll make a son or two!"

And then he was pushing off, turning the dugout away and gliding out into the fast current as confident as a buck in *nepinough*. Pocahontas remained on the riverbank, watching his strong arms flash in the sun as he paddled. She sent up a prayer for the spirits to protect him, the *manitou* to shun him, the Okeus to shield him. It was the same prayer she said every time he went to war. It was a part of the routine of their lives, a thing woven into the fabric of their marriage like one of the neat, red knots on his bag. Long after he'd vanished around the bend, Pocahontas remained, staring after him.

She longed for Kocoum's company even more than she longed for a child. Their *yehakin* was secluded, well hidden on the fringes of Orapax. No one had ever troubled them here, not enemy tribes or white men or even Real Women. Usually Kocoum was her only company, if he was there at all. With gardens and children to tend, fish to smoke, meat and fruits to preserve, the women of Orapax were not at leisure to stroll through the forest to Pocahontas's heart fire and share their idle gossip.

Matachanna made the trek a few times a month, and she and Pocahontas would spend blissful hours weaving or stretching and scraping hides in the sun while they talked of old times and new hopes. But Matachanna saw her husband far more often than Pocahontas saw Kocoum, and someday soon Matachanna's belly would swell, children would gather about her feet, and the visits would come to an end.

It is no matter, Pocahontas told herself firmly, turning her back on the river. *I knew womanhood would mean isolation.* She had seen it clearly the night she sweated alone among the bones of Werowocomoco.

She made her way up the shaded trail toward her small longhouse. The rich mineral scent of spring bloomed all around her, damp and soft and cool. She remembered Werowocomoco in the firelight, the passion-fruit vines hanging from the longhouse frames like the weasel-tail fringe of a priestly headdress. It had been so long since she had seen the place. Was it still abandoned? Had the vines overtaken it completely, choking the gardens and yards, blanketing the dancing grounds like a glossy green snow?

I would like to see it again. Werowocomoco, and all the southern villages. So many years have passed, and so much has changed in Tsenacomoco.

Lost in her thoughts, she did not see the man standing patiently beside her longhouse until she had almost reached her door. She stifled a shriek and stood staring at him, tingling.

"*Wingapoh,*" he said. "You are Matoaka, daughter of Powhatan?"

"Yes . . ."

The man nodded briskly. "Good. Your father has sent me to escort you to Orapax."

She shook her head. "I don't understand. Escort me?" Did Powhatan wish to keep her close while Kocoum was off at war? Anxiety curled tight and hard beneath her heart. Was this battle expected to be worse than the others? Did her father believe Kocoum would not return?

"The *mamanatowick* wishes to speak with you. He has a task for you. That is all I know of it."

Pocahontas stiffened. She had hoped her days of aiding her father were at an end. Kocoum had told her—reluctantly, of course—the terrible fate that had befallen Wowinchopunck's family. For three years she could not sleep without dreaming of it, the children thrashing in bloodred water, the woman standing blank-faced at the ship's rail. And always the English words echoing through her spirit, mocking and sly. *A coach and three horses. A coach and three horses.*

She wanted no part of her father's schemes. Or her uncle's. She had paid many times over for her arrogant childhood dream of influence and power. Her solitude, the danger Kocoum faced, her empty womb, Uttamussak burned, Wowinchopunck's family destroyed . . . all of it came from the *tassantassa* plague, and the *tassantassa* plague persisted because of her.

But she thought of Kocoum paddling bravely away, his back strong and beautiful as it bent to the task of rowing, the hint of his black tattoos showing through his ochre paint. *Kocoum always answers the call faithfully, and the Okeus has always brought him home. Perhaps the god will be kind to me if I answer the call, too. One final time, to honor the bravery of my husband.*

The Pattawomeck shoreline came into view, a black shelf of mud sloping into the broad, still eddy of the landing place. Several dugouts rested on the bank, in plain view of the river. The canoes gave Pocahontas pause. All down the great length of the river, as she traveled from Orapax to Pattawomeck territory, the canoes of the

Real People had been scarcely visible, hauled far above the water-line, dark masses half-concealed by the new growth of riverside vegetation. No village risked the burning of their dugouts; the *tassantassas* were too quick to set them alight when they were left unattended. The white men sometimes roamed far upriver, and so all the territories had taken to hiding their canoes.

Canoes well hidden, in every village but this one. Perhaps my father is right after all.

Powhatan's frail appearance had startled her when she'd answered his summons. She had not seen him in three years—not even at the harvest festivals when she made the long walk to the center of Orapax. He had remained in the seclusion of his *yehakin*, and she had been too ashamed of her role in the tassantassas' survival to face him. Had Powhatan truly grown so much thinner and weaker in those years, or had he looked this way for many seasons, the silver hair fading to the white of dirty snow, the skin hanging loose from his once strong and blocky jaw? Perhaps it was her memory that was at fault, not the strength of Powhatan.

The old man's eyes had been sharp enough, though, shining at her keenly from his wasted face.

"You must go to Pattawomeck territory," he had told her in a voice that both whispered and grated. "The *werowance* of that tribe, Japazaws, has grown too friendly with the *tassantassas*."

Opechancanough had brooded in the corner as Powhatan spoke and Pocahontas listened with bowed head and blinking eyes. His body was tight-strung with watchful tension, his suspicion of Japazaws plain to see on his face.

Powhatan feared a defection; feared Japazaws would ally his tribe with the white men and spill the secrets of the Real People like blood on snow. He believed Pocahontas could stop Japazaws. Pocahontas was not at all sure she could, but she had answered her father's call. She had gone to honor Kocoum, who gave so much and never stopped striving for the well-being of the Real People.

Throughout the long trek from Orapax to the village of Passapatanzy, as the green water of spring slid by and the rowers' paddles lifted and fell in a quiet, regular rhythm, Pocahontas pondered the task the *mamanatowick* had set before her. If Japazaws was truly ready to sell his tribe to the *tassantassas*, then Pocahontas could do nothing to stop it—whatever Powhatan or Opechancanough might think. She was only a lowborn young woman. She was not even a mother—even that shred of status eluded her.

She had expressed her reservations as forcefully as she dared. But Powhatan had been adamant.

"You will be useful in this, Matoaka. I know it. You recall a particular young daughter of mine, the girl you once served as handmaid."

"Nonoma." No—what name had she taken when she reached womanhood? Pocahontas struggled to recall it. "Musqua-chehip."

"You recall," Powhatan said, "that I gave her in marriage to Japazaws, thinking to bind him more closely to me, as I suspected his heart might waver toward the white men."

"The plan seems to have failed," Opechancanough interjected smoothly. "Our scouts report that Japazaws trades with the *tassantassas* ever more frequently, and that he has even made some small noises about an alliance."

"Why not simply remove him from power?" Pocahontas asked.

Powhatan frowned. His eyes were distant with his troubled thoughts. "If it comes to that—if he can't be brought back under control—I shall. But our power is scattered, our warriors and chiefs blown like leaves in the wind. It will take time to swear in a new chief properly. We must try to salvage Japazaws first, if it can be done."

"Why me, Father?"

"You were friends with Musqua-chehip when you were girls. Is that not so?"

Pocahontas could not keep an ironic smile from her face. "I don't think Nonoma—or, Musqua-chehip, I should say—and I could ever have been called friends. Not truly." True, she had reached a sort of truce with Nonoma, but years later, Pocahontas couldn't think of the high-born girl without a certain cautious reserve. She glanced uneasily at Opechancanough. "Are you certain this is a wise plan?"

Powhatan caught the direction of her question and he lurched forward on his bedstead. "I am *mamanatowick* here, not my brother. A woman like you would do well to remember it."

She dropped her eyes meekly. "I only meant . . . I am not certain that Musqua-chehip can be influenced. Or made to influence her husband. As a girl she was always flighty and selfish."

Powhatan grunted. "As were you, Pocahontas."

This time when he used the pet name of her childhood, there was no affection in it. It was an accusation. She glanced up at his face and met his cold, commanding stare, harsh even in the gauntness of his features. *Perhaps it is not only years that have aged him. Perhaps it is the strife we have been through—all the suffering we might have been spared but for my childish ambitions, my disastrous need for influence.*

In the end, it was her guilt—even more than her sense of duty to her father or her desire to make Kocoum proud—that sent her downriver. If only she could influence Musqua-chehip for good, Pocahontas hoped she might turn the current of the war, and undo a small part of the damage she had caused as a child.

The *mamanatowick*'s warrior guards landed her craft and helped her step ashore. But standing in the thick, well-trodden mud of Passapatanzy's shore while her father's warriors retrieved her two small travel bags, she stared at the ostentatious canoes in dismay. It seemed Japazaws truly had no fear of *tassantassa* violence. Against such bold confidence, what could one lowborn woman do?

A high, piping voice called from the trailhead. "*Wingapoh!
Wingapoh*, dear Pocahontas!"

Even with the chin-length hair of a woman, the thick black
fringe falling to her brows, Pocahontas recognized Musqua-chehip
at once. As with Matachanna, she could not help but think of her
by the childhood name—*Nonoma*. She would always be the same
haughty, *puccoon*-covered child to Pocahontas. Nonoma danced
on her toes among the thick springtime foliage, one hand waving
gaily in the air. Several pearl and copper bracelets ringed her wrists,
and around her neck strings of beads clattered as she bounced. The
beads were not the type usually sported by *werowances'* wives—
pearl and dark-violet *roanoke*, or carved shell rubbed with *puccoon*
so the incised patterns shone bright against sun-darkened skin.
Nonoma's necklaces were made of glass trade beads. Pocahontas
could tell the difference even from several paces. The beads sparkled in rich, exotic colors: yellow fiery as autumn flowers, orange
clear like a butterfly's wing, and several shades of blue and green
that called to mind the river dancing below a summer sky.

There was a time when Pocahontas would have envied the fine,
rare beads. But now, knowing they only could have come from the
tassantassas, the sight of them roiled the midday meal in her gut.

She slung her bags across her back, secured both straps to her
forehead, and gave her thanks to the guards. Then she made herself rush into Nonoma's embrace, fixing a smile in place and praying that her feet did not drag.

Nonoma kissed her cheek and squealed. Then she stepped
back abruptly, smoothing an apron liberally decorated with more
bright glass beads and wide swaths of *puccoon*. "Oh, spirits save
me from myself. I am acting just like a little girl. But it's so good to
see you again!"

"It's good to see you, too, Nono . . ." Pocahontas caught herself
with a quick shake of the head. Nonoma was ever prickly about

receiving proper respect. She would not appreciate being called by her girl's name. "Musqua-chehip."

"And I must call you Matoaka, I suppose."

Pocahontas hung her head, hoping her cheeks colored. It would be an appropriate response to a high-blood woman who humors one of low status. "You may go on calling me Pocahontas, if it suits you."

"Mischief." Nonoma gave a sharp laugh. It rang with a note of the girl's old arrogance. "Well, let me show you around Passapatanzy, and you must tell me all the news from Orapax."

Pocahontas did her best to concentrate on Nonoma's chatter as they wandered the lanes of her village. She answered Nonoma's queries about Orapax as honestly as she dared, sharing tales from the dancing grounds, telling of new children born and new men returned from the *huskanaw*—and pleading ignorance when Nonoma pried for details about Orapax's food stores, number of warriors, and the health of Powhatan. Nonoma led her from one longhouse to the next, introducing Pocahontas to women who wore too many glass beads and used too many steel tools to work their stretched skins or repair their husbands' fishing nets. Passapatanzy seemed to glitter with copper and steel and the sinister brightness of glass beads. Light reflected from these hard tokens of *tassantassa* friendship as the sun glints off each scale of a snake's skin.

At last Nonoma hooked her arm through Pocahontas's and declared, "And now you must meet my husband!"

They found Japazaws in the dusty yard of his longhouse, gingerly tipping an old clay cook pot with one flat, dirty toe. He seemed displeased with the thing, though Pocahontas could not imagine why a man might interest himself in pots. Japazaws was not a tall man; his body was square and shambling, and his eyes were pinched in a perpetual squint. Pocahontas peered through her forelock at the *werowance*; he brought to mind the image of a mole scrabbling aboveground, groping for the entrance to its burrow. A laugh threatened to form on her tongue, and she pressed her lips together to chase it away.

When Nonoma called brightly to him, Japazaws glanced up with an expression of mistrust—though perhaps it was only his natural squint that made him appear suspicious.

"So you are Matoaka," he said, eyeing her with the same grudging interest he had directed at the cook pot.

She stared down at her feet, smiling meekly. She felt the weight of his narrow gaze press upon her spirit. *Does he know why I have come? What does he suspect?*

"My Musqua-chehip has told me much about you."

Pocahontas flushed with mortification. She couldn't imagine Nonoma saying anything kind or flattering about their shared childhood. Despite Nonoma's display of hand waving and happy gossip, Pocahontas was certain Nonoma had never forgiven her for spitting into her face the first day they met.

"Well," Japazaws said gruffly, eyeing the pot once more, dismissing Pocahontas, "we are glad to host you here. You shall stay in Musqua-chehip's longhouse. No doubt she will feed you well and show you off at the dancing ring tonight."

In Nonoma's longhouse, Pocahontas was treated to another tour: this time of Nonoma's many exotic possessions. Each of the bedsteads, every rack and peg was draped and piled and hung with rich, soft furs, many of which seemed to have come from creatures Pocahontas did not recognize. *More trade with the white men.* The brightly dyed lengths of wool had certainly come from the fort. Nonoma stroked a piece of the green cloth against her cheek and closed her eyes dreamily.

"Oh, isn't it strange and wonderful? It's too scratchy to wear, of course, and it smells unpleasant when it's wet. But I love to touch it and look at it."

"You certainly have a good deal of it." Pocahontas lifted the edge of a length of blue wool. It was long enough to make two cloaks. *The* tassantassas *never had so much cloth to spare in the days when Chawnzmit lived. They must be thriving at Jamestown.*

"Japazaws is a wonderful husband," Nonoma said. "He allows me anything I desire. He never denies me. What is your husband like, Pocahontas?"

"Kocoum? Well, he's very brave. He is often . . . away." She nearly said *at war*, but she did not think Nonoma, cooing among her draperies of exotic furs and colorful wool, would welcome talk of killing *tassantassas*.

Nonoma giggled. "I remember Kocoum." She pulled on her ears until they stuck out through the locks of her hair. "Such a somber man, too. Does he ever laugh with you? Japazaws is so merry! I know he's many years older than I, but life is so easy with him. I hardly have to work at all. What a lovely thing, to be the wife of a great man." She cut a swift, mocking glance toward Pocahontas.

"Matachanna is married to Utta-ma-tomakkin," Pocahontas said hotly, "as you well know. He is the highest priest in the land—and she takes great pleasure in working hard."

Nonoma tipped her head to one side, as if Pocahontas were no more than a witless child. "*Matachanna?* Oh, I could have sworn she'd received a new name. Did she not, after all? How tragic."

Pocahontas blushed. "Coanuske is her name."

"At any rate," Nonoma said, as if Pocahontas had not spoken, "a priest is not the same thing as a *werowance.*"

Anger surged, but Pocahontas shoved it into a distant part of her spirit. "I am very tired from the journey, Musqua-chehip. May I sleep now?"

Nonoma left her alone with an admonishment to be fresh for the dancing at nightfall. When the door flap closed, Pocahontas rummaged through Nonoma's belongings until she found a plain sleeping mat and a simple deerskin, untainted by the touch of Jamestown. She curled beneath it and lay scowling into the darkness.

This is hopeless, her spirit cried again and again, *hopeless.* Nonoma would not be made to influence her husband for the good of the Real People. She was too in love with fine and rare things, caught by the *tassantassas'* lure like a rabbit in a slipknot. She and her husband were best left to strangle in their pretty snare.

In the morning I will tell my father's warriors to take me home. I must face him in failure, but at least I will bring him the truth: Japazaws is already too far gone to return him to Powhatan's control.

When Nonoma came to wake her for the dancing, Pocahontas rose feeling every bit as cramped and foggy. She had not slept at all. Her spirit hung like a dried leaf on a cornstalk, limp and spent. The evening's dance only depressed her more. The women of Passapatanzy had dressed in their finery to honor the visitor from Orapax—and as she stood swaying and clapping halfheartedly, everywhere Pocahontas turned she saw the shimmer and flash of bright-colored beads. As soon as a few women began to drift toward their longhouses, Pocahontas excused herself from the circle, too. This time she did not need to feign exhaustion. But when she crept beneath the deerskin, wiping silent tears away with the coarse, earthy hide, sleep still evaded her.

"But I *want* to!"

A squealing voice woke Pocahontas, sharp and high against the sweetness of morning birdsong. She rubbed her gritty eyes, wincing at the ray of pale light that descended from the smoke hole. The interior of Nonoma's longhouse smelled of wool. The scent raised memories of Chawnzmit, rippling and indistinct like a distant cloud. He smiled at her through a mist; tried the Real word for *dawn* on his clumsy tongue. A dull pain, a slow throb of regret, pulsed in Pocahontas's head. It raised a prickling flush to her cheeks. Motes spilled down the beam of morning light like ice flowing on the river. She recalled in wonder the English words for sunrise and sadness. They were the same. *Morning, mourning.*

The voice whined again, like a pup caught up by the scruff of its neck, as Pocahontas rose from her bed. This time the sound was just an inarticulate, halfhearted yelping. Pocahontas ducked through the door flap and stretched. Nonoma stood there with fists on her narrow hips, facing the *werowance* and stamping her foot in the dust. When she saw Japazaws glance suddenly toward Pocahontas, Nonoma spun toward her with wide-eyed surprise.

"You're awake!"

"I suppose the birds chased me from bed," said Pocahontas wryly.

Nonoma rushed to her and seized her by the hand. "There's a ship on the river—an absolutely huge one, not the little *shallop* the white men usually take about for trading. I want to go see it. Oh, don't you wish to see it, too, Pocahontas? Don't you?"

The only vessel Pocahontas wished to see was the canoe that would carry her back to Orapax. She would be glad to leave Passapatanzy behind, with its shining skin of treachery and its uncomfortable echoes of the luxuries she'd once longed for. But Nonoma peered at her so eagerly, pleading with her eyes and her quivering lip, that Pocahontas felt it would be cruel to flee Passapatanzy that very morning. What could it hurt, after all, to eye an English ship from the safety of the shore? The *tassantassas* were clearly on good terms with Japazaws, and even they would not dare to harm the wife of their pet chief. She realized the white men probably knew Nonoma by sight. It would be safe enough.

"Maybe," she said, squeezing Nonoma's hand. "But it's only first light. Let's bathe, and if the ship is still there, perhaps we can look from the shore. If you approve, *werowance*," she added hastily.

Japazaws shrugged. "It is time to bathe, indeed. When I am clean and proper, then perhaps I will feel like indulging you, wife. Perhaps I will even accompany you myself."

They made their way to the women's bathing place, Nonoma skipping along the trail. She chattered like a blackbird in a marsh as they left their aprons on the grassy shore and waded waist deep. Pocahontas nodded and murmured in response without hearing any of Nonoma's words. She immersed herself chin deep, and then ducked beneath the surface completely. But when she rose up again, a strange veil seemed to hang over the world, obscuring her senses, wreathing her in a smoke of dull confusion. The veil numbed her skin, so that the bracing chill of the river hardly raised its usual prickles on her arms. An English word floated through her thoughts. *Morning.* Or perhaps it was the other word: the one that meant sorrow.

A breeze parted the long reeds that shielded the cove. She peered through the swaying cloak of grasses, staring downstream as if she might see the ship from here—see it, and be free to turn her back on Passapatanzy and its strange, treacherous *werowance.* Return to Orapax, to Kocoum, to her home.

But the ship was not so close; the river was empty. It stretched away between the green walls of the forest, until the wind died away and the curtain grasses closed together, and Pocahontas could see nothing more.

"Come," Pocahontas said with sudden resolve. "Let's find this ship." *So I can leave this place and never return.*

The ship, when at last they found it, was indeed grand, even if it belonged to the *tassantassas.* Secured by a heavy chain, it rested midstream where the river was wide and deep. Near the water's edge, a little landing boat lay just above the tide line.

Anchor. She remembered the word, remembered Chawnzmit repeating it so she could hear the subtle nuances of sound. Other words came back to her in a hot rush, tumbling through her head like stones in a streambed. *Sail. Mast. Sailor.*

Nonoma scuttled from their hidden trail onto the shore. The woman was completely without fear of the *tassantassas*, oblivious to the danger like an infant reaching for a hot coal. Pocahontas hung back, crouching instinctively behind the cover of a low thicket. But Japazaws followed his wife out onto the bank with a confident, swaggering step, and Pocahontas, left unprotected in the forest, swallowed hard. Her throat was dry as a fireside stone. She slunk from cover like a shy deer.

"Oh," Nonoma sighed. "Isn't it lovely, with the sun shining on that folded white wing? What is it called, husband? You know the words, do you not?"

Japazaws made a great show of forgetfulness, tapping at his shaven scalp as if he might dislodge the answer by force.

"*Sail*," Pocahontas croaked. "It's called a *sail*."

"It's very bright."

"The things are quite large when they are unfolded," Japazaws said, "those *sails*. A sight to behold. They fill with wind and grow tight as a drumhead, and then the boat speeds upriver—even against the current—as quick as a wolf running."

A sudden rustle sounded in the woods; Pocahontas jumped and spun. A white man appeared on the trail they had just vacated. The man paused in apparent surprise, and then held his hands out slowly, as if to reassure them that he held no gun.

Pocahontas stepped back quickly and collided with Nonoma's chest; the girl hooked her arm through Pocahontas's and grinned. "Don't run, you dim little fish! It's only Argall. He won't hurt you."

The *tassantassa* bobbed his head and muttered a few words as he made his way slowly down to the shoreline. His pale hands were still outstretched. They contrasted brightly against his dark wool sleeves and tunic. His face was round and shiny, with a high forehead and ashy, backswept hair. His thick beard was cut blunt, straight across, with two pointed corners. It had the look of a half-filled carrying bag lying on his chest. Below a long, straight nose, his mouth twisted as he mumbled. Pocahontas could not tell whether he spoke to her or to Japazaws—or to himself. His words were quiet and low, like a hunter soothing a flighty dog. Argall's eyes watched Pocahontas with piercing avidity. Those eyes unsettled her most of all, with their unblinking wideness and pale hunger.

Japazaws greeted the man in accented English. "Good day, Captain Argall."

"Japazaws, my friend."

Pocahontas clutched at her fluttering stomach. She was astounded by how quickly the words came back to her. She had not spoken English, or even thought of it, since the disaster of the coach and three horses. Yet the words had not left her.

"It is good to see you here," the white captain said. "You and your lovely wife."

He took Nonoma's hand and raised it to his lips. Pocahontas's eyes narrowed. Was this man one who had raped the wife of Wowinchopunck? Had he shot the little boys as they swam in panic and terror for the shore?

He turned to Pocahontas with a half bow. "And who is this dark beauty?"

"Pocahontas," Japazaws said. His voice rose in pitch, ringing with a queer emphasis. "The favorite daughter of Powhatan. She has come to visit my wife, who is her sister."

"How lovely, how lovely," Argall said, glancing between Pocahontas and the little landing boat that waited on the strand. "Japazaws, because you have been a good friend to me, won't you please join me on my ship for a feast? I would celebrate our friendship with good food and rich drink, and perhaps we will trade."

Japazaws translated the invitation to Nonoma, and the young woman's eyes lit up. She clutched harder at Pocahontas's arm and shivered, stifling a girlish squeal. "Oh, we must go aboard, husband—when will I ever have the chance again?"

The *werowance* thumbed his chin, considering. "It is a rare opportunity; that is true. Yet I have heard sad tales of women who were ill-used on these *tassantassa* ships. I would not risk your safety, Musqua-chehip."

"Pocahontas knows the *tassantassa* ways. And they used to revere her. All the white men adored her!" Nonoma said. "I am sure they remember her still, and will treat her with great honor. No harm can befall me if Pocahontas goes with us."

"I won't go," Pocahontas said quickly. She shook off Nonoma's arm and staggered away. Argall tensed, and she turned her face abruptly away from him in scorn. "No," she said in English.

Nonoma wailed. "Pocahontas, why not? It's as safe as can be! And, oh, think of all the wonderful, exotic things we might see! I'll never have a chance again to board a *tassantassa* ship . . . never!" Tears spilled down her cheeks. "I thought you'd learned to be more kind and generous, but I see you're still the haughty girl who spat on my face when I was frightened and alone!"

Pocahontas flushed with mortification. She felt so hot that she pressed her cool palms against her cheeks. *Perhaps Nonoma is right, after all. Surely the English still remember me, and with Japazaws aboard they would never dare to harm us. I'm being foolish. The sooner Nonoma's whims are satisfied, the sooner I can return to Orapax.*

She took Nonoma's hand. "Very well. I'm sorry—please stop crying. I will go aboard with you, so long as we stay close to your husband."

Like the sun parting a bank of thunderheads, Nonoma's face lit with a triumphant smile. "Oh! Pocahontas, I promise you, this will be a day neither of us will ever forget."

Argall rowed them slowly from the shore toward the dark hulk anchored midstream. Pocahontas watched with growing apprehension as the ship loomed larger. As the oars splashed and

Nonoma vibrated with excitement, as Japazaws conversed with the captain in low tones, speaking of trade, Pocahontas strained to catch the English words. But Nonoma chittered like a squirrel in her ear, and Real Tongue and *tassantassa* speech rolled into one hopeless tangle.

The rowboat turned, drifting toward the great wooden carapace of the ship, sucked against its mass like a twig pulled into the swirling wake of a fast canoe. Pale faces peered down from the rail above; their ruddy cheeks and sharp noses, and their hair of strange, earthy colors stood out boldly against the morning sky. One lowered a climbing device made of thin, even planks of wood, tied at regular intervals along two parallel lengths of cord. *Rope.* Pocahontas recalled the proper word for the thick, rough cord as she climbed unsteadily from the rowboat. *Ladder.*

In spite of her queasy fear, she could not help a gasp of admiration when she stood on the ship's deck, clutching the smooth, polished rail in white-knuckled hands. It seemed she could see nearly all of Tsenacomoco from this height. A short distance upstream, the haze of Passapatanzy's cook fires hung above the treetops. Here and there she could make out the arch of a longhouse or the tall, thin posts of the crow towers in the fields. The river wended north and east, a long stripe of silver green edged by the rich deep cliffs of forest. Behind, toward the sea, she could see from her lofty vantage how the river widened, opening into the languid, salty regions of the Tidewater.

A few of the white men bowed to her, and among their murmured greetings she thought she heard her name, and a whisper of "princess." So Nonoma was right. They did recall her—some of them—and would treat her kindly. She smiled at them, cursing her lips for their trembling.

Japazaws reached the deck and turned to help Nonoma aboard. She squealed and clapped when she stood to her full height, and twined her arm through Pocahontas's.

"It *is* lovely. I knew it would be. Aren't you glad you came? Look, see all the strange things the *tassantassas* have!" Nonoma set to inspecting the riggings of the ship, fingering the heavy ropes and the round wooden devices around which they were coiled.

Argall called for a table, the raised eating platform Pocahontas remembered from Jamestown. One was set on the *aft deck*, as the square-bearded captain called the rear portion of the ship, so that they might enjoy the sweeping view as they ate. Pocahontas found the chairs uncomfortable. If she could not sit properly on a mat on the ground, she would rather have stood to eat from the table. But she did her best to remain still throughout the meal, although her bottom ached and her legs felt strange, stuck out in front of her and bent like a hard-drawn bow.

She'd expected a pot would be set in the middle of the table, from which they each would dip their midday meal a scoop at a time. Instead, Argall's men presented each of them with a container of a steaming jumble that was not unlike mix-pot stew. The containers were curved like large turtle shells, flat on their undersides so that they stood securely on the table's surface. Little wooden paddles followed, each with a scooped end. Pocahontas stared at the paddle lying beside her container of stew. She tried to imagine some use for such a strange object. Was it waved like a priest's rattle to bless the meal?

Then Argall dipped the scooped end of his paddle into his stew, lifted the dripping thing to his mouth.

Ah! The paddle is like a dipping shell, with a digging stick's handle. She had seen the men of Jamestown eating often enough, it was true—but always with their hands, or by spearing bits of meat on the ends of their short knives.

She tried the *tassantassa* way, plunging the paddle into her stew. It wobbled when she lifted it, and the chunks of meat splashed back into the container.

Nonoma giggled. "Not like that. Here—hold it this way."

Pocahontas stared at Nonoma in shock. "You have feasted with *tassantassas* before?"

A thump sounded under the table and Nonoma jumped as if a wasp had stung her backside. Japazaws shot his wife a swift warning glance, a flash of squinting eyes that did not escape Pocahontas's notice.

He kicked her foot; that's what made the thumping sound.

"Oh, Japazaws got some of these things for me in trade. The white men call them *spoons*. My friends and I had great fun learning how to use them." Nonoma's smile was strained; her eyes overeager.

A sudden wave of suspicion swelled in Pocahontas's spirit. She dropped her spoon on the table and lifted the container of stew to her lips. It was heavy, and she nearly spilled it down her bare chest, but she managed a mouthful of broth before she returned it to the table with a loud thud. Argall looked at her steadily as she licked the stuff from her lips. She glared back at the captain. The broth was as salty as the river at Jamestown, and tasted of scorch and fire.

Japazaws chuckled uneasily. "Pocahontas was ever a wild thing. My wife could tell you tales about this one."

"I could tell tales," Pocahontas retorted. The English words formed easily on her tongue. "I could tell tales to my father, Japazaws. And to my uncle, Opechancanough. I wonder what tale I ought to tell him about *you*?"

Argall's chair scraped against the deck as he stood. "Perhaps it is time to bring these pleasantries to a close."

Pocahontas jerked to her feet. Her chair fell with a crash. "Yes. It is past time. Return me to the shore."

Japazaws ignored her. He slid close to Argall, and his voice wheedled. "We discussed the terms. It is agreed. You must give me what I am due."

Argall called to one of his men. "Bring the copper kettle from my berth."

Trembling, Pocahontas moved close to Nonoma, but the girl stepped away. There was no longer any warmth in her eyes—not even feigned warmth. She slid behind her husband and peered around his shoulder at Pocahontas with a hard, vengeful glare.

Heart pounding in her constricted throat, Pocahontas spun away from the table. She ran across the deck like a rabbit bolting from the underbrush, searching for the place where she had climbed aboard, pushing through the mass of sailors who moved to block her way.

"Stop her," Argall called.

Hands seized her, closing around her wrists, and a strong male arm fell across her chest. The hands were reluctant and gentle, but they held her fast; she could not break free, no matter how she twisted or thrashed. She was a fish in a weir, helpless in the trap.

"Be kind to her," Argall's voice snapped. "I won't have her harmed."

"Aye, Captain."

Pocahontas pulled against the sailors, kicked, gnashed her teeth near faces and ears that flinched away before she could bite. "Let me go!"

"We won't hurt you, Princess," a man's voice said behind her. His words were soft and soothing, but all Pocahontas could think of was Wowinchopunck's wife, raped on the deck of a ship just like this one, and then speared like a sturgeon.

With a terrible, trembling effort, Pocahontas stopped struggling. She hoped her stillness might lure the men into complacency. Then she would break free. She would dive from the ship's rail and swim to shore, hold her breath beneath the water until her lungs screamed and the bubbles rushed from her nose. She would pray to the Okeus that she might surface out of range of the *tassantassas'* muskets.

When she was still and silent, the men turned her about to face Captain Argall. The man spoke a few words to Japazaws, leaning close to his ear, smiling genially. Beside them, Nonoma cradled a copper cook pot in her arms, cooing as if she held a newborn babe. The sun flashing from the kettle's surface struck tears into Pocahontas's eyes.

They've sold me for a tassantassa *kettle.* No telling what else Japazaws had already traded with the fort in exchange for Nonoma's finery, for the steel and beads that littered Pattawomeck territory like fragments of shiny shell around a crow's nest. *I must be calm and quiet. I must await my chance to break free and warn Opechancanough of this boil festering in the flesh of Tsenacomoco.*

Nonoma and Japazaws made their way through the ranks of sailors toward the rope ladder. The girl clutched her prize against her body, absorbed in its smooth, polished gleam. But she looked up as she passed Pocahontas, who was still circled by the sailors like a deer ringed by torches in a twilight hunt.

"Don't worry," Nonoma said. "Japazaws has told the *tassantassas* to send for your father, to trade you back. You're to be exchanged for all the goods the Real People have stolen from the fort. They will treat you well. Argall gave his word."

"The word of a *tassantassa* is as good as the word of Japazaws. Or his wife."

Nonoma grimaced. "Don't be so wild, Pocahontas. It won't do you any good. You'll be back home before you know it."

She turned her back on Pocahontas, but Nonoma's grim, cold-eyed smile was reflected in the surface of her copper kettle. The glossy curve of the pot distorted her reflection. Her face wavered and danced like a spirit mask in a darkened temple.

POCAHONTAS

Season of Cattapeuk

Were it not for the three-corner palisade, Pocahontas would never have recognized Jamestown. Wooden houses clustered within the walls, crouched close together like sparrows in *popanow*. Gone were the cloth tents, the wallows of mud. Even the fire pit where she had often practiced words with Chawnzmit had vanished, replaced by a group of small cabins. A pathway of planks, fitted as tightly together as the bark strips of a longhouse wall and raised a hand's breadth above the ground, wended through the center of the fort. What had once been a great sloppy puddle churned by the *tassantassas'* boots was now a sward of short green marsh grasses and half-solidified ground ringed by wooden houses.

What surprised her most, though, were the women. Had Chawnzmit not told her of ladies and princesses, Pocahontas would have doubted the *tassantassas* had any women at all. Now, however, they moved about the cramped, narrow lanes of Jamestown with small, stiff strides, enveloped in wool garments that covered their bodies like too-long winter capes, falling in colorful folds to the ground. Their faces were smooth and hairless, their skin even paler and more translucent than the men's. Wide necklaces of some unusual fabric, pale as well-worked buckskin and decorated with intricate cutouts, clung high and tight about their necks, reaching almost to their small, pointed chins. *Tassantassa* women grew their hair long, at least as long as a Real Man's, but no part of their scalps were shaved, nor did they loop their hair in ornamented braids. Instead, they gathered it at the backs of their heads in thick, round knots, or piled it beneath tall hats that looked like clay pots upended on their brows. The women lifted the hems of their long, swaying robes as they moved. Now and then she saw the dark blur of little pointed boots on their feet.

So they have brought their women at last.

If anyone had ever questioned whether the white men intended to stay, there could be no doubt now. With women would come gardens and harvests to see the men through the winter. With women would come children, and the *tassantassa* villages would only grow.

Jamestown itself was growing, even outside its palisade walls. Pocahontas had noted the outbuildings as Argall and his men rowed her ashore, shacks and storehouses rising from the marshland like mushrooms in the autumn wood. A new stockade was taking shape near the neck where one could cross from the boggy spit into the forest. A pen of low, long-bodied, grunting animals, watched over by a pair of boys, smelled even stronger than the *tassantassas* did.

Okeus save me, they have doubled in number since we have been hiding at Orapax—tripled! Opechancanough cannot hope to eradicate them now.

Argall led Pocahontas onto the plank pathway. They crossed the grown-over mud pit, Pocahontas moving with her head erect and her shoulders proud, hoping she did not look as vulnerable as she felt. The brush of their gazes left a sharp prickle on her skin, like the kiss of a nettle. Argall's steps were heavy; the thump of his boots against the wooden path sounded as hollow as her heart and sent a disorienting shiver through her bare feet and legs as she walked softly beside him.

Argall rapped at a cabin's door with one hairy knuckle. Metal hinges squealed as the door swung wide. A white woman peered out, mouth agape in surprise. Her round face was just beginning to show the lines and sag of age. Hair the color of an old copper bell, shot here and there with strands of silver, was swept back severely from her brow. Watery, pale-blue eyes gazed at Pocahontas beneath eyebrows so fine and colorless the hairs were nearly invisible.

"Mary," Argall said. "This woman is my guest, and will be staying at Jamestown for . . . a time. I thought you might enjoy her company. She speaks English passably well. You might outfit her properly with civilized garments and teach her how to get along in the colony."

"Oh," the woman said, touching her lips with small, slender fingers.

"Her name is Pocahontas," Argall supplied.

"By the saints' mercies," Mary said. "It's the princess."

"Treat her as such. She must be used kindly if she's to be any good to us at all." He pushed Pocahontas forward. "God knows I have gone through enough tiresome wrangling to get her. Japazaws, indeed!"

With that, Argall was gone, stomping back across the planks and melting into the bustle of Jamestown.

"Well," Mary said with a resigned sigh, "we had best get you settled in, child."

Mary moved placidly about the tiny house, fussing with the table and chairs, spreading extra blankets of heavy wool on her bed with its thick, crackly sleeping mat. She spoke in low, soothing tones as she worked. Her soft voice reminded Pocahontas of Matachanna, and tears misted her eyes.

The cabin was small, its walls dizzying in their straightness. Pocahontas could not stop herself from glancing up at the ceiling whenever she thought Mary's eyes were turned away. The ceiling was low and nearly flat, peaked slightly in the middle but much too near the crown of one's head. It made Pocahontas feel as if she stood inside a clay jar with the lid tamped down tight, packed away like a groundnut in a cellar.

"What are you looking at, child?"

Pocahontas glanced uneasily at Mary. She knew her fretful staring must seem queer, but she could not ignore the low, oppressive roof. She pointed up and Mary followed her gaze, shaking her copper head, uncomprehending. Then understanding broke over Mary's face.

"Ah. The ceiling. This is not like your home. Is that the way of it?"

"No . . . that is to say, *yes.*"

"What is your own house shaped like, then?"

Pocahontas could not think of the English word; she cupped her hands above her head, miming the high, comfortable roof of a longhouse.

"This must seem a very strange place to you." Mary crossed the small room in three strides. She took Pocahontas's limp hand, squeezing gently. "Tell me more about your house, love. If it doesn't make you too miserable to talk of it."

Pocahontas spoke while Mary bent over her table, cutting a skinned rabbit into pieces with a large knife. Now and then the woman asked questions and seemed genuinely curious about Pocahontas's life: the way she cooked, the tasks she performed as a wife, how she tanned deer hide and kept biting insects from her skin. But as with Nonoma, Pocahontas stepped deftly around any question that touched on Powhatan, or the strength and capabilities of Orapax.

Mary carried the rabbit to a stewpot suspended over a small fire. Bitterly, Pocahontas looked away from the sight of the copper kettle.

As the days passed, Mary was persistent in her kindness, as good a companion as Pocahontas could have wished for. Had she not been a captive, she might have enjoyed the time she spent at the older woman's side. Mary told her of her own life, of the husband who died on the voyage from England and the kindness she had found among the other women of Jamestown. She told Pocahontas, too, something of Argall's plans for her.

"Do you know, Argall wants me to put you in a dress."

"Dress?"

"Aye, like this." She tugged at the long wool robe she wore, exposing the tips of her pointed boots. "You know, Pocahontas, we English think it is terribly bold for a woman to go about with her skin uncovered."

Pocahontas crossed her arms over her breasts. "Why?"

Mary tipped her chin to one side and gave a small, tinkling laugh. "I don't know why, and that is the truth. Oh, the priests will go on about Adam and Eve and the Garden of Eden, and I suppose I don't know as much as a priest knows. But I do know this: God brings us into the world without a stitch, so nakedness can't be all wrong in the sight of the Lord."

Pocahontas clutched herself tighter. Mary's rush of strange words left her spirit spinning.

"But I like your . . . your garment," Mary went on. "It's pretty, with those red-and-black shapes. It looks very soft indeed."

Pocahontas touched her doeskin apron with a trembling hand. She traced the lines of the flying heron, the ring of kindled fire. Lost in her memories of home, she did not see Mary cross the room. She jumped when the woman laid a cool hand on her shoulder.

"There is no rush to put it aside, child. All the time in the world to learn to wear a proper dress. You need not fear going about as you are—not with me."

"But I won't be here for long," Pocahontas insisted. "Argall is to take me to my father, to trade me for stolen tools." *I am valuable to Powhatan—to Opechancanough*, she told herself firmly, struggling to beat back the fear and certainty that gnawed at her. *They will trade for me. They will send for me soon.*

Mary's smile was tight. "Of course, child. Of course."

"He'll do it soon."

"I am sure he will." Her voice was soft and wrapped with sympathy as tightly as sinew wraps an arrowhead.

Days passed. Mary took Pocahontas about the fort, introducing her to the women, who looked rudely away from Pocahontas's bare skin. Some of them gasped and flushed red at the sight of her, as if she had smeared herself with filth and gone about unbathed.

She learned how to draw water from a tiny house at the edge of the settlement—a well, Mary called it—so that she might wash at each sunrise. She hauled the sloshing, gurgling bucket up from the earth-scented depths hand over hand, and soon her arms grew strong from the daily work. The *tassantassas* had no rituals of cleanliness as the Real People did, which Pocahontas now understood accounted for their pungent smell. But Mary was accommodating, and dedicated her largest cook pot to Pocahontas's use. Each morning as the rising sun fought its way past the roofs and chimneys of Jamestown to spill weakly through the cabin's window, Pocahontas stood over the pot to rinse her skin with tepid water. It was not the same as wading into the brilliant cold of the river and sinking up to her chin, greeting the new day with the private chant of her spirit. But it was better than leaving her skin dusty and dry. Each morning as the water trickled from her cupped hands to run down her shoulders, as it renewed the dark of her tattoos with its wet gloss, the same phrase repeated in her heart. *Let me go home. Let me go home.*

When half a moon had passed, Pocahontas began asking Mary when she would be returned to her home. Mary looked miserable and said she did not know, but answered the pitiful query each time she was asked, whether Pocahontas asked her once a day or a hundred times.

Soon her thoughts were consumed by Kocoum, and a hard, sharp grief sank into her heart. She had been gone from their hearth for too long. He would assume she had walked away from their marriage, and he would find another wife. Or would he come seeking her? She feared for him, if he did. Kocoum did not have the wealth to buy her freedom. As likely as not, the *tassantassas* would kill him rather than suffer him to plead for Pocahontas.

When a full moon had turned, when the days began to lengthen and the warmth of approaching summer hung like a haze over Jamestown, Pocahontas tore away the cloak of her dignity. When her morning bath was finished, Pocahontas stood panting over the pot of water, staring down at the ripple and sway of her shadowy reflection. Drops of water fell from her nose into the pot, and the reflection shattered and rolled.

"Pocahontas?" Mary said tentatively, sitting up in the bed they shared. The sleeves of her nightdress were puffed and rumpled.

But Pocahontas did not answer. She flew for the cabin's door, not even stopping to tie her apron about her waist. She raged through the fort, screaming for Argall, beating on doors and walls, on posts, on anything that came before her. The plank pathway rattled like thunder beneath her feet. Early rising women fled from her, averting their eyes from her nakedness, hoisting their skirts to hasten out of her way. The men tried to calm her with outstretched hands, their mouths round with shock inside their heavy beards, but she charged at them, making her fingers into talons, shouting Argall's name.

He came from the deck of his ship. The palisade gate opened with a hoarse creak, and Argall moved through the crowd of gaping, silent English at a near jog, his stern, intense eyes locked with Pocahontas's own.

She cried out when she saw him, a high keen of rage as lonely as a wolf's howl.

Argall took her by the shoulders, held her tightly in his strong hands.

"Let me go! Take me home!"

"Calm yourself, girl."

"I won't! Take me home, you crow, you *manitou*!" She did not know whether the words came out in Real Tongue or in English. Or both, perhaps. She breathed deeply several times, gasping, a fish pulled abruptly into a night hunter's canoe. She wrestled with the words on her tongue, sorting them into English so he would understand. "You told Japazaws you would trade me to my father."

Argall grimaced. His words sounded almost regretful. "In truth, Princess, I told Japazaws no such thing."

"What?"

"He suggested the trade to me, but I gave no word indicating what I would do with you."

She tried to pull away from him, but his grip was as cold and unbreakable as steel.

"Listen to me, Princess. I *will* trade you, and no mistake, for you are no good to me here, running about Jamestown like Bathsheba on the roof. But we must *wait*."

"For what? For how long?"

"Until the time is right. Until you can be leveraged for maximum effect."

She did not know these last words. They meant nothing to her, except for the raw, piercing certainty that whenever Argall might deign to return her to Orapax, it would not be anytime soon.

"Oh!" She dropped to her knees in the damp soil. The talons she had aimed at Argall flew like arrows to her face. She raked herself until her cheeks were scratched and torn.

"God's wounds," Argall cursed. "Where is Mary? Somebody fetch the widow Mary!"

Pocahontas threw back her red-streaked face and wailed at the uncaring sky. "Kocoum!"

Soft arms wrapped around Pocahontas's shoulders and a familiar scent surrounded her like a soft-furred pelt: the well-worn linen of Mary's nightdress, the oily, warm smell of her copper-colored hair.

"Come now, child, stand up," Mary said. "Stand up. Don't carry on this way. It's not proper."

"Kocoum! Kocoum!"

"What in the name of Christ is a kocoum?" Argall muttered.

Somehow she was raised to her feet, and was led, stumbling, back toward the cabin. Mary's wool blanket was wrapped about her shoulders and the woman's gentle touch guided her blind progress. Pocahontas gasped and choked on breath hot with the surety of loss. Inside the cabin with its terrible straight walls and its roof like a confining lid, in its dark, cramped prison, Mary eased Pocahontas onto the bed. She crawled with her beneath the blanket and lay holding her, rocking her gently, cooing and singing as a mother does to a restless child.

In time her gasping sobs eased and the well of tears ran dry—if not the ocean of sorrow. Pocahontas slept in Mary's arms.

Her spirit walked the dreamworld, traveling a blue path through a forest shaded in violet. She found the trail that led to a familiar clearing. At its heart stood her longhouse, far on the fringes of Orapax, the sound of the falls whispering on the air.

She ducked through the door flap and found Kocoum sitting alone beside the heart fire. On the ground beside him lay the fine bag she had woven. Along its strap, the red strands of dyed grass linked and twined like the hands of lovers.

"Kocoum," her spirit called.

He looked up, looked through her, saw nothing. The light of the heart fire edged his braided knot with the golden flicker of torches on the river, of night fishers moving on a silent current. The light colored his ears with a red glow and she smiled as her misty blue fingers caressed one ear, tugging it affectionately, then traced the shape of his sharp cheek and his strong, stoic jaw.

"Mischief?" he said into the darkness. But his voice sounded uncertain. It was already fading.

When she woke in the afternoon, groggy and sick, cramped on the hard straw mattress, Pocahontas knew the dream was true. It was a vision sent by the cruel, unfathomable god. This was her punishment, her penance for the horrors her selfish ambition had unleashed upon Tsenacomoco.

She blinked at the posts of Mary's bedstead, which were as upright and stern as the spirit posts at the four corners of a temple. Mary had hung Pocahontas's apron from one of the posts. She reached for it, pulled it onto her lap, and smoothed it atop the woolen blankets. The doeskin was as soft as the velvet of an antler. When she pressed it to her face, the smell of home flooded her senses: pine smoke and moss, the hard earth floor, bundles of herbs that hung drying by the door. She smelled wolfskin and deer hide, the sweetness of woven mats, the salt of dried fish, and the unchanging, wholesome richness of mix-pot stew.

And Kocoum. Him most of all.

Pocahontas rocked as she cried, holding the apron close.

In her heart, she knew she would never see Kocoum again.

Reverend Whitaker smiled softly as he caressed the worn black leather of his Bible. He was always smiling. He seemed to gaze upon the world with the soft, half-focused stare and benign innocence of a babe in a cradleboard. Pocahontas eyed him warily from across the chapel, where she sat on a rough-hewn bench, as rigid as an oak stump. The small table in front of her was stained and pocked with the markings of ships' boys who, having grown bored in their lessons, had taken knives to the planks while the reverend was distracted.

The reverend, she quickly learned, was often distracted. After lecturing her on the nature and preferences of the *tassantassa* gods, especially the one called Christ, he would instruct Pocahontas to pray. *Pray* did not mean wading into the river to feel the spirits of current and air against her naked skin. *Pray* did not mean chanting, nor dancing at the fireside, nor entering the sweat lodge to hear the voice of the Okeus. *Pray* was not tobacco smoke, circles of cornmeal, tassels of weasel- and snakeskins. Instead, for the *tassantassa* priest, to pray was to sit with hands folded and head bent, staring at the tabletop, hearing nothing but the creaking silence of the Jamestown chapel, thinking nothing, doing nothing, and feeling nothing, save for the ache in her neck. *Pray* made her wish she had a knife of her own, to stab at the little table that held her like a rabbit in a snare.

Often while praying, she would peer through the hanging fringe of her hair, and find Reverend Whitaker standing and gazing up into the rafters, hands clasped behind his back, his neat, ash-colored beard trembling as he muttered to himself. When he was lost in his own thoughts, the reverend noticed nothing of the world about him. He was as lost among the world of the spirits as a priest of the Real People smoking in his temple. Then Pocahontas would lift her head, work the cramp from her shoulders, and unclasp her hands and stretch them, letting the air of the chapel cool the sweat of her palms. Sometimes the reverend would see one of her small movements and glance her way as if surprised by her presence. But he never scolded her for ending prayer early. He only smiled at her.

Pocahontas blinked and focused on the words as Reverend Whitaker read from the Bible.

". . . delivering thee from the people, and from the Gentiles, unto whom I now send thee, to open their eyes and turn them from darkness to light, from the power of Satan unto God, that they may receive forgiveness of sins, and inheritance among them which are sanctified by faith which is in me."

Oh, yes. It was this tale once more. It was the reverend's favorite theme: the duty of all *tassantassas* to tell other peoples of Christ. Pocahontas sighed. She gazed out the narrow window of the chapel as the reverend's soft, easy voice slid through the warm air. Summer was at its full height, the sky pale with heat in midday. Jamestown lay subdued by the sun's rays; the dingy smoke from its chimneys seemed to ripple and dance in the heat mirage that hung like a curse over the growing town.

Sweat gathered in her armpits and clung beneath her high collar, stiffening the fabric of her dress. Only after many weeks had Mary been able to coax Pocahontas into a semblance of a white woman's garb, though in truth it was not Mary who convinced her. Pocahontas had begun to notice how men leered at her, staring at her bare chest and legs with an intensity she had only seen before in Kocoum's face. She eyed the men carefully, watching them move through the lanes of Jamestown from a crack of the shutter on the cabin's lone window. It was true that Englishmen looked at most of the women they passed, sometimes even turning their heads to stare after the women if they thought their impertinence would not be noted. But few of them stared at the other women with the unsettling, avid eyes they turned on her.

And so she had finally acquiesced to Mary's gentle prodding and allowed the woman to dress her as an Englishwoman.

Mary did not have the finest garments—something she apologized for with much clucking and tutting as she shook skirts and sleeves in the sunshine, beating wrinkles and dust from the wool. But they would do.

Pocahontas was made to stand still with her arms outstretched while Mary tried this bit of fabric or that, letting out laces, tucking in folds. At last she stepped back, nodded, and said with a proud smile, "There you are, Princess! Now just try a few steps, see how it all feels."

Pocahontas lowered arms that felt as if they had been wrapped in coils of birch bark. Elbows and wrists refused to bend. When she forced them to move against the strange stiffness of the cloth, gathers of wool pinched at her sensitive skin. The skirt was as heavy as a dozen gourds of water, and it dragged about the floor, catching beneath her bare toes, for she could not manage to lift the hem and take even strides at the same time.

"Now then," Mary said, "let us lace up your bodice."

Mary pulled the strings dangling at Pocahontas's waist. The bodice constricted like a snake feasting on a mouse; it squeezed at her ribs and stomach with a vicious pressure and forced her back as upright as a spirit post. She could draw only small, shallow breaths. She grimaced and gasped. "Take it off!"

Mary loosed the strings at once, and the panels of the bodice fell away. Pocahontas staggered to her little three-legged stool, where she sat holding her sides with trembling palms, feeling tender and bruised.

When she had recovered, Pocahontas consented only to wearing a shift, an accommodation to the absurd English fear of nakedness that she felt was quite generous. But Mary covered her mouth, scandalized, and explained that showing the entirety of one's shift was nearly as shocking as going about nude.

Pocahontas would give no more ground. "If you try to dress me in a bodice and sleeves, I shall tear them to pieces!"

The shift was made of a soft, grainy cloth that Mary called linen. Strings drew the ends of the sleeves snug about her neck and wrists, but otherwise it was voluminous, white and flowing as sailcloth, even down her arms. It was warmer than the bare skin she was used to, but not as stifling in the summer heat as a full dress and sleeves would have been.

And best of all, it worked. Men still stared at her, but their hungry leers vanished. Now they looked at her with the same wide-eyed shock as women when they caught sight of her shift billowing in the wake of her confident stride. Mary said she raised a scandal, but she preferred inciting gossip to feeling a white man's unsettling gaze fall upon her breasts and bare limbs.

Something startled Pocahontas; she glanced about the chapel, her awareness of the hard, rough bench through the thin linen of her shift returning suddenly. Reverend Whitaker was gazing at her with that soft smile, but his brows were raised quizzically. He had asked her a question, and was now patiently awaiting an answer.

"I beg your pardon," she said quickly.

"I asked how you are getting on with the widow Mary."

"Well, thank you."

"If you would be happier with another companion, I can find you . . ."

Pocahontas shook her head and cast her eyes down to the chapel floor. The wood was so polished and smooth from so many feet that it looked like deep water in the dim light.

"It's only that you seem so despondent."

"I don't know that word."

"It means *sad*."

Her spirit crumpled like a dry leaf, and she thought she might weep. But then, in one quick, hot heartbeat, anger leaped up to take the place of her sorrow. She lifted her chin and stared at the reverend with an expression more imperious and haughty than any Winganuske could ever have worn. "Why should I not be? I am a captive, and my father has abandoned me." It was the first time she'd admitted aloud what she knew in her heart. Powhatan would not send for her. She would be left to her fate. She swallowed hard to drive away her tears. "Would you have me caper and sing?"

The reverend made a little huff, a self-deprecatory chuckle. "Of course not. But I had hoped you might find some happiness here, some small comforts. We do not intend to harm you, Pocahontas, nor to make you sorrowful."

Pocahontas's jaw clenched. She did not know who made her more sorrowful or whose harm cut deeper—the white men's or the Real People's. Months had passed since she had been sold for the price of a kettle, and here she still was, languishing in Jamestown while the world went on turning through its seasons, moving, breathing, living without her. Children were born in the long-houses of Tsenacomoco, but none were hers. White beads broke over clasped hands, but now that she had been gone so long from Kocoum's hearth, her own marriage was shattered—vanished.

She ached to spit a curse at Reverend Whitaker, to mock his endless stories of the god named God, who sent his priests to far-off lands to teach sinners the way of righteousness. *Whose people sin?* she longed to shout. *Mine, or yours, who hold women captive and stare at their flesh?* But Powhatan had sent no ambassador to bargain for her freedom, as she had once bargained for Naukaquawis. Nor had he summoned any *tassantassa* to his territory to discuss how Pocahontas might be freed. However she had imagined her freedom might come, she had remained in the white men's hands.

Powhatan had sent a simple admonishment that Lord De La Warr should treat Pocahontas gently—that, and nothing more. To her ears, her father's message sounded like the barking of a toothless dog.

"I will cease to be sorrowful when I am returned to my home, Reverend Whitaker."

His smile faded. "It may be some time before that comes to pass."

"So be it. I shall be miserable until then."

Her words seemed to take the reverend aback. A tender, wounded expression crossed his face, a naïve pain like a child who has only just learned that a wasp will sting. Then the smile

returned, spreading above his neat beard slowly, with a thoughtful air.

"Perhaps, Princess, you would like to learn something new."

"I would like to learn how I might return to my home."

He spoke on as if he had not heard her. And perhaps he had
not, for his dreamy eyes gazed past her, looking into the distance
for inspiration. "Some new skill, some task to take your mind from
your troubles."

Pocahontas waited.

"If you will permit it, we can teach you to read."

"Read?"

She knew what reading was, of course. The English kept their
records and stories not in the rhythm of chant or the rhyme of a
song, but as little black marks in their books. They were meticulous
keepers of their lore. It seemed nearly all of them recorded even
the most mundane events of their days on sheaves of paper and
stored them carefully in boxes. If she understood how to decipher
the strange English markings . . . if she could access their words of
power . . . perhaps she might find some way to win her freedom; a
spell or a chant or a prayer that would unlock the vaunted mercy
of the god called God. She sat forward eagerly.

"I can see that the idea appeals to you," the reverend said.
"Well, then, come to the chapel tomorrow at the same time. I
believe I know just the teacher for you."

A fierce midday heat beat upon Pocahontas's back as she leaned
against the chapel door. It opened with a soft groan. The interior of
the church was dim, almost cool. The air stirred as she closed the
door behind her, rippling the dusty hem of her shift. She thought
to hear Reverend Whitaker's familiar welcome, and looked expectantly toward the altar below the great wooden cross. But the
chapel was empty, save for a man seated in the second pew, head
bent over his clasped hands. Waves of thin, dark hair brushed his

shoulders. He wore a shirt of white linen with a spill of ruffled folds at the neck. The shirt was spotless and neat.

She moved down the aisle carefully, fingers reaching for the straight wooden backs of each row of pews. Her unshod feet were silent on the cool plank floor. When she reached the second row, she gazed down it toward the man. His lips were moving in silent prayer and his eyes were shut tightly, his brow pinched in an expression of hopeless pleading.

Pocahontas eased herself onto the bench. Six or seven people could have filled the space between her and the praying man. She waited for the man to finish beseeching his god.

When he did, his eyes rose to her face directly, as if he had known she was there.

She almost said, *wingapoh*. She stopped herself. "Good day."

A hat lay beside him on the pew, the same type of felt cap she had seen Chawnzmit—no, Mary had corrected her pronunciation of his name—the same type of cap she had seen John Smith crushing and twisting that long-ago day in the garden. John Smith had warned her then, told her she must stay away from white men, for they would ever after be a danger to her.

Self-conscious, the man pulled the hat onto his knee. "Good day. You are the princess Pocahontas?"

It was an absurd question, for who else in Jamestown had the rich copper-earth skin of a Real Person? What other woman roamed the village wearing nothing but the scandal of a linen shift? But the man seemed nervous as a shorebird. She did not wish to frighten him with her usual haughty anger. She was tired of frightening people, tired of glaring her hatred at Jamestown, its people and its palisade walls. She was only weary now—weary and alone.

"I am Pocahontas."

"Reverend Whitaker has asked that I teach you to read. My name is John Rolfe."

As Pocahontas took to her lessons, the weeks sped by, full of new work and new words. Summer passed its peak and coasted toward less stifling days, smooth and easy like a canoe drifting downriver. Autumn gathered silently, as though it had been waiting at the edges of the marsh beyond the walls of Jamestown. Pocahontas filled her hours with the cool quiet of the chapel, the shaft of golden light that fell through its narrow window onto the knife-graven desk, and the peaceful, gentle ways of her tutor, John Rolfe.

At first she hated him, just as she hated all the English, save for Mary. He was a part of Jamestown, and therefore complicit in her captivity. Her disdain for him simmered just beneath her weariness. Often it boiled over, when his lessons taxed her mind and the marks on the pages seemed to blur together in a meaningless black streak, and she raged at him. At times, when she felt too keenly her own ignorance of English words and ways, she mocked him.

But John bore her outbursts and her mockery with patient understanding, and before the summer had come to a close, her forbidding airs melted away like a snowflake on warm skin. At first she had welcomed the daily lessons for the break they provided in the monotony of her captivity. But soon she'd begun to look forward to John's slender finger sliding along the page, his quiet voice guiding her, and she greeted him with an eager smile.

Now and then Reverend Whitaker would join them in the chapel, poring over his sheaf of record papers and scratching at them with a long plume. The reverend would look up from his papers occasionally and appraise Pocahontas's progress. When she caught his eye upon her, she would blush and watch John's finger tracing the page, but not before she saw a beam of pride and affection light the reverend's face.

Usually Pocahontas and John read alone. Her voice filled the chapel with hesitant sounds as she stumbled over a syllable that was sharp and hard as stone, and John, patient and soft, corrected her. In those moments she would pause to hear the faint echo of their voices fading together from the empty church. Then she would try the word once more. When she was correct, John would nod, his eyes shining.

One afternoon, in the warm, angling light of the month John called September, Pocahontas felt a hollow growl of impatience in her middle. It was nearly suppertime, and she craved a bowl of Mary's rabbit stew. But this restlessness was more than just hunger. In all her reading, her careful poring over the Holy Book of the white God, she had found no spell or song to release her from Jamestown.

John turned a page, laid his finger at the start of a new verse. But Pocahontas shook her head.

"I don't want to read that one."

"This verse, then," John suggested, touching another.

"No."

"Then which will you read?"

"None!"

John sat back calmly, bracing for another of her storms.

But she did not rage. She only stared at him, wide-eyed, hoping he could read the want of her spirit. She dared not speak her desire aloud, for fear he would tell her that there was no verse to set her free, no magic in this book that could end her captivity.

"Well, then," John suggested placidly, "open to any page you please, and read to me the first verse you see."

Pocahontas jerked her chin into the air, as if he had thrown out a challenge he did not believe she could meet. She lifted a large, thick bundle of pages and flipped them over.

"'And he answered and said unto them, Have ye not read, that He which made them at the beginning made them male and female, and said, For this cause shall a man leave father and mother, and shall cleave to his wife: and they twain shall be one flesh? Wherefore they are no more twain, but one flesh. What therefore God hath joined together, let not man put asunder.'"

A cold knife stabbed deep into her spirit. She had not thought about Kocoum all summer long—had forced the memory of him from her mind. If it had remained, she would have spent all her days weeping, and Pocahontas had vowed not to weep before the eyes of her captors again. But now, as she heard the words spilling from her own mouth, the image of her husband returned with brutal force. She recalled him bending to set the bag of food into his canoe the last time she had seen him. She wondered if he had found the sweet dumplings she'd hidden for him inside.

Pocahontas pressed both hands to her hollow stomach. She folded, bending around the ache like a cornstalk breaking, until her forehead fell upon the open page.

John's voice was wavering and distant, a cry underwater. "Pocahontas?"

"Oh!" The sorrow, long stoppered and buried, burst from her spirit in that single, painful word.

John's hand took her shoulder and gently pulled her upright. She rocked on the rough, hard bench, mouth twisted with silent weeping.

"You have lost someone you loved," John said.

She did not answer. She hid the tears behind her hands.

"I know how you feel," he told her.

"You cannot know! You are just as cruel as the rest of them, feigning friendship while you tear my life apart. You are only another wolf in the pack, John Rolfe."

"My friendship is not feigned, Pocahontas. I know what it is like to feel your life torn apart. May I tell you a story? It is a sad story, but I should like for you to hear it."

She turned her face away from him.

He took her scorn for permission. "Four years ago, I set sail from England with my wife, Sarah, and many other people. There were more than one hundred of us packed onto a small ship called the *Sea Venture*, all with hope in our hearts that we might settle the New World, by the grace of God. None on that voyage was more hopeful than Sarah. She brimmed over with optimism and light. She cheered everyone on board—led the women in singing, played games with the little children. Sarah raised all our spirits, though the ship was cramped and the going difficult. She even loved the sea. She laughed and whooped when the waves were rough, as if she were riding a tame pony.

"Sarah discovered early in the voyage that"—John glanced at Pocahontas, and his face colored—"that she was soon to become a mother. We were both full of joy, as you can imagine. Each night as we huddled together on our narrow bed, we whispered of our precious hope. She looked like an angel in those moments. I swear she glowed in the darkness belowdecks, with that dear life sleeping inside her.

"As we approached the islands to take on fresh water, the ship encountered foul weather. The storm was terrible—even Sarah found no amusement in it. We all of us hid in the stifling darkness, listening to the waves pound our little ship. The sea thrashed us about. We could hardly lay flat, and were thrown about the hold. All was screaming and terror, and terrible smells, and Sarah clinging to me with her little hands in the darkness.

"In time, the captain sent a man down to tell us to brace, that he had no choice but to run the *Sea Venture* aground on the rocks. If all went as planned, we would take the landing boats and row for a nearby shore. Everyone was terrified—even I. There is no shame in admitting it. But Sarah put the place in order, moving about the hold with a soft word and a gentle touch. She rallied our courage, got every person braced tight in no time, packed together and wedged between barrels and crates like straw in a tick.

"And then the impact. Oh, how can I tell you of the noise? The tearing, the rending of the wood . . . the scream of nails and planks and people, and the cold sea roaring on the rocks. But we made it from our hold to the deck, and with Sarah and the captain keeping order, boatload by boatload we made our way ashore."

Her resolve to remain aloof crumbled. Pocahontas was watching John Rolfe intently now, caught up by the fear and wonder of the story. "Were any killed?"

"No," he said gruffly. "By the grace of God, all hundred and fifty souls aboard made it safely to land." He gave a short, sharp laugh. "Even the ship's dog was saved."

John stared into the depths of the chapel. His eyes, stricken and bleak, rested on the cross. After a moment he went on. "We knew it would be some months before we could expect another English ship to approach the islands and rescue us. With Sarah setting the example, we went about the business of constructing our own small colony there in the tropics. We salvaged wood from the wreck of the *Sea Venture*, and supplies, too. Life was not simple, of course. The clime was harsh and the naturals of that land were exceedingly dangerous if not approached with great care. But we managed, and even found some happiness in the closeness of our community.

"In time, Sarah . . . well, her day to bear the child was at hand. You cannot imagine how I fretted and paced and begged God to be merciful, for we had no physician, and only three women of our number had ever birthed babes before." John's face colored again, as hot and bright as *puccoon*. "I . . . I apologize for speaking of such indelicate . . ."

Pocahontas tossed her head impatiently. The English fear of a woman's magic was even more extreme than any Real Man's. "It makes no matter. Please, go on."

"Sarah came through the ordeal well enough—or so I thought that first night. They laid the baby at her breast—a girl, perfect and whole, and beautiful as a star. I loved the child the moment I saw her. I knew God had blessed me, had blessed us both, for Sarah seemed happy and strong.

"But the women gathered around her, waiting for something. I could tell they were anxious. I don't . . . I don't know precisely what the matter was. Something was . . . some part of the process was not complete. The women would not tell me what they were waiting for, but as they continued to wait they grew ever more worried. They would not let the babe sleep, but insisted Sarah put her to the breast, thinking to encourage some . . . some function or other. Sarah was as weary as the babe. Soon she could no longer keep her eyes open, and the women grew more frantic.

"I thought at first that they were being ignorant or superstitious, for Sarah's color and breathing were good, and she smiled as she slept. But when she woke hours later, she was in the grips of a terrible fever."

The afterbirth. Pocahontas had seen few babes come into the world, but even she knew the danger to a woman if part of the afterbirth was retained. The right herbs and spells—and a newborn's suckling—could make a woman's womb contract and rid itself of any scraps. But if that potent magic was left behind, it could fill the body with warring spirits. Many women did not survive such an ordeal. No wonder the white women did not tell John the truth of it. Afterbirth was blood magic in its purest, most intense form—nothing for a man to meddle with, especially not a fearful new father.

"They did not have the right herbs," Pocahontas ventured.

"No. We knew so little of the islands. If any medicine grew there that might have helped my wife, none of us knew what it looked like or where to find it.

"She lingered for two days before God finally took her. The babe lasted only a few hours more." John lapsed into silence again. His face was gaunt with pain, both fresh and remembered. "Before Sarah died, we decided together that we would call our daughter

Bermuda, after the island where we found ourselves. It seems an especially fitting name now, for I buried them both on that island, and left my heart in the ground beside them. Bermuda is my whole world, and I shall never see it—or my wife and child—again."

When the story ended, Pocahontas could not meet John Rolfe's eye. Shame pulsed through her—shame for having assumed a man such as he could feel nothing, and shame at having unearthed his painful memories. Another emotion twisted about that bare framework of shame, shrouding it like a passion-fruit vine. It was *kinship*. John Rolfe did indeed know what it was like to lose a beloved partner, to have one's world torn way. He even knew the pain of losing a child—a loss Pocahontas felt keenly, mourning as she did for the children she would never bear at Kocoum's hearth.

John sighed. He slumped on his bench, staring at the open Bible between them. Behind him, the shaft of golden light fell through the chapel's small window. Motes moved in a swaying, swirling dance like women dusted in mica, unaware of the private sorrow John and Pocahontas shared. His hand moved of its own accord and turned the Bible's page, hiding the painful verse from sight. But he did not read on, and neither did she.

Pocahontas's hands twitched in her lap. She twisted her fingers together, recalling John Smith's admonition that white men were dangerous and would only cause her pain. But what pain could be worse than this terrible loss, the pain only John Rolfe understood?

She unclasped her fingers and reached across the Bible. Gently, Pocahontas took John's hand in her own.

From the pinnacle of the watchtower, Pocahontas stared out from Jamestown's wall across the marshland, pale and brittle beneath the climbing moon, to the dense black palisade of the forest. The moon was deep ochre, hanging heavy in the sky. It tipped the canopy of the forest with a pale-golden glow.

It was the final moon of *taquitock*. Somewhere, far upriver at Orapax, a ring of torches was gathering in the wood, drawing tight like the strings of a leather bag. In the center of the ring of light, already knowing they were lost, already feeling the arrows that would pierce them, the deer lifted cloven feet of obsidian and swiveled ears as broad as cupped hands—a last delicate dance in this world before they fell where the ground was dark and cold, and their spirits lifted like white smoke to leap through the forest of the night sky.

Somewhere, in Orapax or in Pamunkey, in Paspahegh or Werowocomoco—somewhere, everywhere, in all the territories of the Real People, Kocoum drifted like a ghost, searching for her. She imagined the spirits of Sarah and Bermuda, John Rolfe's dead family, trailing Kocoum and weeping, their hands clutching for the mantle of flesh he still wore. He was warm. His feet stirred the earth's blanket of dead leaves as he searched. Theirs did not. The baby girl had copper skin and black hair. Sarah's face was a dry, featureless smear of ash.

The steep, narrow stairway creaked. Pocahontas glanced around without interest. Another man climbed up to join the two others who waited at a respectful distance on the lookout's platform. She was accompanied everywhere she went in Jamestown, but on the watchtowers especially. She supposed the English thought she would throw herself off the wall, and both Captain Argall and Lord De La Warr wanted her unharmed. But there was no longer any chance of that. She was beyond despair. She had settled into a mood of perpetual contemplation.

It was not just any man who ascended the steps. The Reverend Whitaker rose onto the platform and nodded a silent greeting. He looked at her quizzically, inquiring without words whether he was intruding.

Pocahontas turned back to her view. After a moment, the reverend dismissed the men who watched over her with a quiet word and then joined her, his uncallused hands folded on the wall beside her own.

"A picturesque evening, though it must be cold for a woman dressed only in her shift."

Pocahontas said nothing.

"It will be winter soon enough, child."

She nodded.

"You take yourself up to this watchtower often. I wonder at your thoughts when you are here."

She turned to him with some amusement. "Do you mean you wonder whether I will fling myself from the wall? I will not. You may set your mind at ease, Reverend."

He smiled. "That is good to hear, but that was not what I wondered. No, Pocahontas—I sincerely wonder what worries plague you. Perhaps I might help."

"Not worries—not often, at any rate. I come here for memories."

"Ah."

The reverend was silent, allowing her the comfort of memory. She would have preferred that silence, yet some unknown force goaded her to speak.

"It is the last moon of *taquitock*—the season of the turning leaf."

"Autumn," said the reverend.

Pocahontas insisted. "*Taquitock*. Tonight is the last night of the hunt. My people are gathered at the hunting camps. The deer carcasses have been carved—all but the last, which will fall tonight. The meat is smoking. The hides are rolled and tied for carrying home, for scraping and tanning. There is so much work to be done."

"And you are here."

"Yes."

Silence again. She dipped into it as she had so often dipped into the river, bathing at each sunrise no matter what the season, in spite of the cold. The moon slid golden over the violet trees.

"Tell me more about the hunt," the reverend said.

She smiled. "There is dancing every night. Not the regular kind—wild dancing, happy dancing. I miss it. I don't seem to know who I am without dancing and songs, without the chants and rituals."

That seemed to trouble him. A slight frown creased his face, but he did not elaborate on his displeasure. "You may not know who you are, but God knows you, child."

She shrugged. "So you say. But I have never seen your god. How can I be sure of him?"

The reverend glanced at her in surprise. "You *have* seen your old god?"

"He is not my *old* god, and he is called the Okeus. And yes, Reverend, I have seen him." She recalled with a shudder the Okeus's fearful grimace, the white eyes staring out from the flames as Uttamussak burned. And she did not know whether it was the god that frightened her, or the fire. "You must be a great priest indeed, Reverend Whitaker, if you are able to see this god of yours."

The reverend gave a dry chuckle. "In truth, I do not see him—not with my eyes. But I am not a great man, Pocahontas. I try to be humble, and God knows it is not always easy. But I know that I am far from great."

She gazed down at her hands, nodded her understanding. "I am also far from great, though once, greatness was all I aspired to."

"Oh?"

"When I was a child, I was wild and selfish, and full of ambition. I did all I could to serve my own ends, but in the end, it brought me only grief. Worse, it brought grief to everyone I love. I think I shall never be able to forgive myself for that . . . that *sin*."

She had heard him talk of sin often enough. The familiar word seemed to brighten him. "Sin is a terrible burden, and ambition always has a sting. But there is forgiveness. Through Christ, we are granted redemption for even the worst of our sins."

Christ. Reverend Whitaker spoke often of the half god. John Rolfe was fond of Christ, too. Pocahontas did not understand what made the English deity so noteworthy, and if Christ was so quick to forgive the English for the terrors they had wrought throughout Tsenacomoco, she wanted no part of him, even if he could remove the burden of guilt from her spirit. But John and the reverend both seemed sincere in their Christ belief, and both men were kind to her. She was willing to grant a small, tentative peace to Christ, for their sakes.

"I understand your difficulty," the reverend said. "At least, I sympathize with it. You feel you have no place here; you are caught between two worlds. You cannot even bear to don the full garments of an Englishwoman."

She turned to him sharply. "I am *not* an Englishwoman, and besides, the full garments are terrible. Have you ever worn a bodice and sleeves, Reverend Whitaker?"

He chuckled. "Of course not. In truth, they do seem quite terrible. But one can grow used to them."

"One can grow used to anything, I suppose. Even captivity."

"Never you, though. You tolerate this . . . this circumstance, but you are not used to it."

"No. I have no choice but to tolerate—until I am finally returned home."

Reverend Whitaker drew in a breath and moved his head as if to speak, but held back his words. An owl called into the pause, distant and small.

"Perhaps there is a place for you here, Pocahontas. A true place, not this uncomfortable captivity. A way for you to have a home again . . . at least until you are returned," he added hastily.

"What do you mean?"

"John Rolfe has grown very fond of you over these months you have spent together."

She waited, digging her fingernails into the wood of the wall.

"He has approached me about the possibility of marrying you."

Pocahontas burst out laughing. It tasted bitter and scornful. "Marry me! I am not a fool, Reverend. It is only a ploy to tie me down, to bind me tighter to Jamestown. To keep me longer, and never let me go."

Reverend Whitaker sighed. "Sometimes," he said, "Christ provides his redemption wrapped in packages that at first glance make little sense to us."

"I don't know what you mean. You must speak plainly to me."

He answered her tart challenge with gentle words. "There is no stopping what has already begun, Pocahontas. The English will not go away. We will not leave your land. If your people and mine are to live side by side, we must find some way of forging a peace. Do you understand?"

Pocahontas swallowed hard, and did not answer.

Reverend Whitaker laid a hand gently on her own. "Think on what I have said, child. Only think on it—that is all I ask."

He turned away, leaving her alone on the watchtower.

Somewhere deep in the forest, a ring of torches drew tight. She felt the deer's foot lift, felt its ear turn. She felt the arrow fly from the bow.

"My girl," Mary chided, "won't you wear shoes? It snowed overnight and the ground is as cold as ice! Mercy, it *is* ice. Be sensible, please."

Since the summer had drawn to a close, Mary had made it her most vital task to force Pocahontas's feet into the stiff leather of a proper Englishwoman's shoes. Pocahontas had accepted the wool stockings readily enough. They itched, but when layered they were nearly as warm as good fur-lined leggings. The shoes, however, she could not tolerate. They held her feet in a rigid grip just as fearful as the bodice. The few times she had tried to walk in them, she had hobbled and pitched like an ancient grandmother leaning on a stick.

"Stockings are warm enough for me."

"You'll catch your death," Mary said, not for the first time, and threw up her hands in surrender.

The earth was indeed cold, but so hard-frozen that Pocahontas's feet remained dry in her woolen stockings. Together with Mary and a handful of other women, all of them bundled in fur capes and thick scarves, she made her way toward the palisade gates.

For the first time since her arrival, she would go through the gates. Someone, Reverend Whitaker, or perhaps John Rolfe, had convinced Lord De La Warr that Pocahontas could be trusted not to flee. Indeed, how could she flee without a canoe to carry her upriver? Besides, now that most of the Real People had retreated to distant villages, the nearest occupied territory was Pattawomeck, home to the very people who had sold her into captivity. Nonoma would rejoice to see her again. She could claim another copper kettle if she returned Pocahontas to the fort.

As they crossed the plank pathway at the fort's center, Pocahontas kept her hand in the crook of Mary's elbow, enjoying the warmth of her friend's furs. She had often watched as the women of the fort "took the air," gliding along the river in their skirts like upturned baskets, smiling and laughing. Sometimes they gathered herbs along the edges of the marsh, or in the summer picked flowers for their tables. Now and then the women would fall silent and stand gazing downriver—dreaming, Pocahontas thought, of their far-off home. Men were always close at hand with muskets slung over their shoulders and their watchful eyes on the forest. Taking the air seemed to be an important ritual of womanhood. As strange as these English wives were, with their restrictive clothing and shyness, their aversion to hard work and their hours of idleness, Pocahontas was pleased to be included at last among their rituals. She caught sight of the gate ahead, looming between two rows of cabins, and her heart quickened.

Pocahontas squeezed Mary's arm. "Come—let us go faster!"

"Patience, child. Plenty of time to . . ."

A shout rose up beyond the gate. The men on the watchtowers readied their muskets.

"God have mercy," Mary muttered. "What is it?"

The voice called again: a male voice, angry and indignant. "I seek Lord-del-a-wair." He spoke English with a heavy, stilted accent. It could only be a Real Person.

One of the men on the watchtower waved his arm in a gesture of the trade language. *Go away.*

Pocahontas dropped Mary's arm and ran toward the gate. The men on guard shook their heads and warded her back with their hands. "I'm sorry, Princess," one said. "It's not safe to go out just now."

"That man—I can speak to him."

"Lord's orders, my lady. The gates stay closed."

She moved along the flat face of the gate until she found its hinge. The gap was wide enough here that she could peer through. The thick wood of gate and palisade restricted her vision, but she could see brief flashes of a body crossing her narrow view: a man was pacing outside. She caught a glimpse of Pattawomeck tattoos. A messenger from Japazaws? Or had Powhatan bought the loyalty of a Pattawomeck and hired him to carry a message to Pocahontas? Her hands pressed helplessly against the gate.

"Message," the man called out.

"No message now," came the answer from the watchtower. "Come back at night."

The messenger did not understand. He must have rehearsed the sound of his few English words, but knew nothing of what the white men shouted back to him. In frustration he cried out in the Real Tongue. "Let me in!"

The man waved his arms, shook a fist, all to no avail. At last he started toward the gate.

"Back!" one of the white men shouted. "Halt! Come no closer."

The Pattawomeck messenger came on. His face was determined. It filled Pocahontas's vision.

A shot cracked in the cold morning air. She felt the vibration of it leap through the earth and the wool of her stockings burned against her skin with the shot's reverberation. The man's face froze and he dropped out of sight.

Pocahontas sprang away from the gate, gasping. Mary was at her side, clutching her, pulling her face against the fur swathing her breast.

"Come away, Princess. Come away!"

She fought her way free of Mary's embrace. "Open the gate!"

Men were gathering, milling about; they would go out to the man now that they had felled him—now that it was too late to hear the message he carried.

Somebody said roughly, "Get the women away from here."

Mary tugged at her hand, but Pocahontas rounded on the men. "You shot him! He wasn't even armed!"

"You don't know that," Mary whispered.

"I saw the man! You killed him for no reason!"

"Widow Mary, keep the princess well back. There may be more savages out there."

Hands closed on her wrists, took her by the shoulders. Not only Mary's but many soft hands—the women of the fort, closing around her in a sympathetic ring.

"Poor dear," one of them muttered. "Come away. You'll only make yourself miserable if you stay to see."

The circle of women shuffled her back, tucked her against a cabin wall, and held her there. Pocahontas stared about wildly as the palisade gates opened. Men edged through, arms at the ready, but when they were certain there were no more Real People to be found, they relaxed. Pocahontas peered between the women's cloaks while the men moved around the Pattawomeck's body.

One of them bent and lifted the knot of the man's braid. The messenger's head rose at a sickening angle and then fell back again. When the bells in his braid chimed, the Englishmen laughed. One lifted his head again and let it fall, like a child idly playing with a poppet.

The women of the circle hid their eyes in distaste, but Pocahontas pushed at them, shoving past their grasping hands until she was free. She ran across the frozen ground, her white shift flying. She opened her mouth to shout, but another voice stole her words. She halted in wonder.

"Stop it! In Christ's name, show some respect for the dead." John Rolfe came rushing from another direction, still pulling his cloak about his shoulders. Pocahontas pressed herself against the wall of a cabin and watched as John berated the men, driving them back from the messenger's body with a hard stare. The men slunk away like dogs. John stooped, touching the Pattawomeck gently here and there, and then closed the man's staring eyes and stood over him a moment with head bent in silent prayer.

A familiar hand slipped into Pocahontas's own.

"Mary."

"Come, darling. There is nothing you can do for the poor man. John Rolfe will see to him—he'll see that the fellow is treated proper."

That night, after she had helped with the washing up from a supper she hardly tasted, Pocahontas slipped from the cabin to pace the lanes of Jamestown. She would have liked to climb to the pinnacle of a watchtower, as she often did when this sad, pensive mood came upon her. But the Pattawomeck man had been shot from one of those towers, and tonight she could not bear the view. She would see nothing from that vantage but the messenger, small and vulnerable against the ground.

She dallied at the well, listening to the soft echo of water shifting underground. She watched clouds creep like spreading stains across a pale, distant moon. The moon was ringed with a halo of white. There would be snow again soon.

Pocahontas moved aimlessly, letting her feet carry her where they would. She wrapped her arms about her body to ward off the chill. She would have to ask Mary for a cloak. English cloaks were very long and, like all their clothing, restrictive. But at least the cloaks were flowing, like her linen shift. She would be warmer, without yielding to the captivity of bodice, sleeves, and shoes.

She passed shuttered windows through which the barest flickers of firelight danced, seeping from the cracks, moving like ripples of water against the black of old wood. Women and men slept behind those shutters. Soon Jamestown would fill with children—and more women and men would come, riding the waves on their great ships, an unending flood spilling over Tsenacomoco. She thought of the Pattawomeck man, dead because he did not understand, and hot tears stung her eyes, burning as they slid down her cold cheeks.

Her feet found the smooth-worn threshold of the chapel. She looked up at the door uncertainly. It was late—perhaps Reverend Whitaker was not within.

A wind gusted down the lane, tearing at her shift and stinging the bare skin beneath. She wrapped her arms more tightly, and when the wind died away, she pushed the chapel door open. Even if the church was empty, at least it would be warmer there than the alleys of Jamestown.

Inside, a circle of yellow light spread upon the far wall. Reverend Whitaker sat at the little table where she took her reading lessons, writing in his record book with a white plume. The stub of a lone candle burned on a shallow dish at his elbow.

He greeted her with his soft, distracted smile. "Pocahontas."

She moved carefully through the pews, feeling her way in the half darkness with hands numb from the cold, and sat across from the reverend.

"What brings you here tonight?" he said.

"I am troubled in my spirit."

He laid down the plume. "What troubles you, child?"

"A man was killed today. A Pattawomeck."

"I have heard. A sad tale. You are grieving for him—is that it?"

"Yes." She studied the tabletop. She could read the carvings now: *T.S. 1611. R.W. shot a savage Apr. 1612.* Her eyes slid away. "John Rolfe is a good man, Reverend Whitaker."

"He is indeed." The reverend laughed softly. "What brought on that thought, I wonder?"

"Today, when the man from Pattawomeck was shot, John Rolfe stopped the other men from . . . from disrespecting the body. He did this not for me—not because he knew how my heart broke to see it. He did it because it was right."

The reverend waited. More words balanced on her tongue, tipping this way and that, deciding whether they would topple out of her mouth or fall back down her throat into silence. She swallowed. She was not yet prepared to speak further of John Rolfe.

But she did speak on. "I want redemption, Reverend. I want to make whole what I can—what can still be saved from breaking—if anything can be saved. If it is not too late."

"I believe much can be saved. I believe it is not too late—not for all. Not for you."

"I do not do this for me. I have no ambitions anymore, no dreams of greatness for myself. When I became a woman, I took a new name, and I asked the Okeus to grant me a loving and generous heart. What I do, I do for others—for my own people. Let no more be killed. Let my sacrifice keep them safe."

"Someone has surely answered your prayer, whether my God or your own, for yours is a loving, generous heart indeed."

His smile said it could be only his God who had granted her wish. But it was a kindly smile, so she did not correct him.

She lowered her lashes. "I will accept your Christ as my god. I will be content to live among your people, here at Jamestown. Baptize me, and I pray that your God will make me a bridge between our two worlds, so that all men may go in peace."

"A noble prayer, Pocahontas."

At the sound of her name—the old name, long lost—she looked up. "I ask one thing of you. Among my people, we take new names at times such as these. When boys become men, and girls become women. When warriors become chiefs, or when a person has a great and true vision."

"I see."

"Grant me a new name, Reverend Whitaker, for this is a time when I stand at a fork in the trail. I have chosen my path. I turn my back on the other. Give me a new name to carry with me as I walk."

"Naming a person is a fearful responsibility. How are names chosen among your people?"

"Dreams. Visions." She eyed him. The guttering candlelight touched his face and then receded, the shadows moving about him. "Or priests. I would pray for my name, but I do not know if Christ will hear me."

"He will. But if you like, I would be honored to choose your new name, child."

She stood. "Then I will see you in the morning, Reverend Whitaker."

When dawn broke, Pocahontas rose from the warm blankets where Mary stirred, muttering in her sleep. She washed in the cook pot, as she always did, and when Mary rose to stoke the fire, Pocahontas opened the trunk where the dresses lay folded with sprigs of fragrant herbs crumbling among the wool. She pulled the items out one by one and laid them on the neatly made bed. Mary watched her in open puzzlement, but when Pocahontas held the panes of a green bodice up to her own chest, Mary quickly loosened the strings so she could slide it down over her head.

The bodice was tight. Pocahontas's breath came in shallow gasps, and her head swam. But perhaps she would have been light-headed and fluttering even without the hard panels gripping her, the laces as strong as braided sinew. The sleeves made her arms stiff, and left her feeling as thoroughly wrapped as a bundle of venison in a cellar pit. The folds of her heavy skirt dragged, hiding the unyielding shoes and the hem of the linen shift. The weight of it all slowed her. She moved through the world like a dreamer still asleep.

Mary accompanied her to the chapel, beaming and offering an arm whenever Pocahontas lost her balance beneath the strange sway of fabric or in the forced, stilted shortness of her strides. But they made the threshold of the building before the sun had climbed above the palisade wall.

Reverend Whitaker beckoned. Mary helped Pocahontas kneel at the altar, and the green wool of her skirts pooled and billowed around her like an eddy on the river. She felt as if she were sinking into water, up to her pounding heart, over her head.

"There is a woman named in the Bible," the reverend intoned, holding a small bowl in his hands, "who left her family to travel to a land she did not know. There, in a strange place, trusting the judgment of her own heart, God blessed her, and she became the mother of two nations.

"That woman's name I shall give to you today."

He dipped two fingers in the bowl and raised them, dripping, to her forehead. The water was cool as he drew the sign of the cross on her skin.

"Rebecca Powhatan, I baptize thee in the name of the Father, and of the Son, and of the Holy Spirit. Amen."

POCAHONTAS

Season of Cattapeuk

When the wind took the sail, the lone mast of the shallop creaked like an ancient oak in a storm. The sailors leaned against their lines, calling to one another, trimming the great white wing until its curve became as shallow as the blunt end of an eggshell, taut as a new bowstring. The breeze shifted Pocahontas's skirts, pressing them against the backs of her legs. They flowed before her, snapping like the flag bearing St. George's Cross rippling at the peak of the mast.

She stood near the prow. There was no room to sit, but still it was the most comfortable place she could find, far from Captain Argall, whom she still did not trust, and far from the captive Real Men, who did not trust Pocahontas. She felt their eyes pressing at her back like the wind, bearing down upon her cold and hard. She felt the weight of their judgment—their appraisal of her *tassantassa* clothing, the hair she had grown long and twisted up in a knot at the nape of her neck, just like a white woman's.

She lifted her chin. They could not see the serene determination on her face, but their judgment made no matter. They did not understand why she did what she did—she could not expect them to understand. On the night she became Matoaka, the Okeus had made her a lone creature, a woman apart. And God had confirmed her path on the morning she became Rebecca.

Her sacrifice seemed to have some effect. While violence against the Real People had not completely abated, English attacks had become less brutal and destructive, and almost no one had been killed. The Real Men who crouched together on the deck of the shallop, glaring at Pocahontas's hair and dress, were proof of her success. Had she not agreed to become an Englishwoman, to take on English ways and the English god, those men would be dead, not captives.

The Real People, too, had cooled their hostility. They still intercepted white men whenever they had the chance, but the men were allowed to live—and to send proof of their condition to the fort in the form of notes scribbled on scraps of bark, begging Lord De La Warr to trade whatever goods the Real People demanded for their freedom.

It was not a perfect peace. Not yet. But it was better than open war.

John Rolfe lingered on the deck, a comforting, quiet presence, standing apart but always close enough that she could catch his eye and receive his shy smile. He made her feel braced, prepared for what the day might bring—though in truth, she had no idea what to expect as the shallop made its way upriver toward Pamunkey territory. Perhaps the Real People would be hostile, even knowing that their own kind rode the shallop with the *tassantassas*. Perhaps the sight of her, so clearly given over to white ways, would goad them to worse anger. She could only wait. She watched the forest for signs of the Real People as she prayed.

Just before midday the first scouts accosted them. She saw them first as streaks of brown and red speeding between the trees, keeping pace with the shallop's progress. Then a voice called across the river in the clear tones of the Real Tongue. "What do you want, *tassantassas*?"

John stepped to her side. "Come away from the rail, Rebecca. They may be dangerous to you."

They might indeed. She hesitated a moment longer, watching the warriors shifting among the undergrowth with a pang of regret. Ahead, a narrow point of land jutted into the river. A Real Man stood there, holding his war club high, his chest bright with *puccoon*. She could not make out his cries, but she felt the rising tension in the air.

Pocahontas nodded and allowed John to lead her to the shallop's rear. There, she sank to her knees among a few crates and barrels. John stood over her, arms crossed, watching the commotion on the shore with tense, wary eyes.

Captain Argall knew a few words of Real Tongue—gleaned, no doubt, from his interactions with Japazaws. The captain called out to them. "We come to trade."

"No trade!"

"We have your men. Unharmed."

A pause while the shallop drifted nearer the spit and the painted warrior who waited for them. Argall cried again to the man, "We have your men. They are whole. We seek Powhatan. Where is he?"

The man on the spit gave a whoop of laughter. "Powhatan!"

"We have his daughter."

Pocahontas peered between two kegs. They were nearly broadside with the warrior now. He strutted and tossed his club lightly. The flat paddle-like end flickered in the sunlight as it spun. "Who doesn't have a daughter of Powhatan?" the man mocked.

Argall shook his head. "Can't understand the devil," he muttered in English.

The hard wood of the deck dug into Pocahontas's knees, even through the thick padding of her skirts. A barb dug into her heart that was no less painful. *They mock my father openly now. Has his power fled so fast? How it would shame him, to know what this war-rior says!*

She stood carefully. John put out a hand to stop her, but she stayed him with a gentle touch. "Please, Captain Argall," she said, "tell them you seek a man called Opechancanough, not Powhatan."

Argall glanced at her skeptically, but turned back to the warrior as the shallop slid past. "Opechancanough. We come to speak with Opechancanough."

"Better for you if you didn't."

"I have Pocahontas aboard."

The laughter and shouts in the forest ceased abruptly. The man on the spit tossed his club one more time, and then waved them on. "Go, then. Opechancanough waits at his capital. Pamunkey gives you safe passage."

When the shallop anchored at the shore of Pamunkey-town, John Rolfe would not agree to remain aboard. He stood over Pocahontas like a bear over her cubs, all but roaring at the other men, and went down the ladder into the landing boat first so that he might help her in. He guided her feet with his hands, which made him blush and scowl. But it was well for Pocahontas, for she could not see the rungs of the rope ladder past her voluminous, deep-blue skirts.

"Thank you," she said with a tight smile as they settled onto the plank seat.

John nodded. He looked as anxious as she felt. A tinge of sickly green showed around his pale mouth.

"Don't be afraid," she told him quietly, so the sailors at the oars could not hear and shame him later for his weakness. "It's quite safe." She hoped it was the truth.

As she suspected it would, word had sprinted through the woods faster than the shallop could sail. A group of men waited for them on the shore. As the landing boat drew nearer, she could see the crossed bows of Pamunkey tattooed on their chests and arms. She felt her own tattoos, hidden by her long sleeves, itch at the sight of them.

The men eyed her in wary disbelief as John helped her from the boat. He alone would go ashore with Pocahontas to face the *werowance* of Pamunkey. The mud of the riverbank was slick and treacherous beneath her rigid shoes. She lifted her skirts high and stepped slowly.

"Take me to Opechancanough," she said.

Words in the Real Tongue seemed to jar them out of their reverie. One of them jerked his head; the shells and bird claws adorning his knot clattered as he turned to lead her into the heart of Pamunkey.

Pocahontas swept through the lanes of the village on the heels of her warrior guide. The man's strides were too long and fast—too angry—for her to easily keep pace in her heavy skirts and shoes. She was obliged to take quick, short steps, nearly running. She would not ask the man to slow to accommodate her white woman's clothing. Her breath strained against the tight laces of her bodice, and sweat trickled from her armpits down the insides of her sleeves.

Women crowded out of their longhouses to stare in unconcealed confusion as she made her way past. Children exclaimed and dropped their chores. They ran to throng the lanes, naked and giggling.

John Rolfe remained close at her side, his hand never straying far from the hilt of his short sword. She had begged him to leave his gun on the shallop, and was relieved when he relented. She knew the sight of her in English garb was already more than Pamunkey could bear. When her uncle looked upon her, his anger was sure to ignite, and Pocahontas wanted no shots fired from musket or bow.

The warrior who led them came to an abrupt stop outside a massive longhouse. It could only be the great house of a chief—of a *mamanatowick*, though she suspected no one yet called

Opechancanough by that title, nor would they while Powhatan still lived. But the luxury in which Opechancanough lived spoke louder than any title could. Pocahontas hesitated, eyeing the door flap, struggling to catch her breath before entering. Her feet burned from the pain of her rapid march.

"Thank you," she said to the warrior, the Real Tongue still coming easily to her lips. She lowered her face like a proper low-blood Real Woman.

He grunted and pulled the flap aside.

Pocahontas bundled her skirts about her knees as she ducked through the narrow door. The odors of the longhouse struck her such a fierce, sharp blow that she gasped, still half-crouched in the deep shadows. She was not prepared for her heart's response to the scent. She tugged at the neck of her bodice, struggling to draw in deeper and deeper breaths of this rich, earthy smell—the smell of home.

John straightened as he came through the door, and bumped against her. "Pardon," he murmured.

Pocahontas dashed the tears from her eyes before John could see them.

A resonant voice called from the end of the great house, where the heart fire glowed red and hot. "Is that my niece? Come, Matoaka."

Pocahontas shared an uneasy glance with John. His face was dim in the umber hues of the longhouse, but there was no mistaking his fear. She forced a smile and led the way down the row of bedsteads and hanging furs, past stacks of baskets and gourds to where Opechancanough waited.

The heart fire's ring of light seemed to grow as she walked, reaching its red arms wide. Light from the roof's hole stabbed downward, a white spear of sun and smoke thrust into the earth.

Pocahontas took one shallow, shivering breath, and revealed herself in the firelight. A thick silence fell. It seemed to muffle even the sound of the logs popping and sparking. Opechancanough's shock at her appearance was no greater than her own surprise. The tableau spread before her was a scene she had viewed many times before around the heart fire of her father's *yehakin*. The handful of men ranged in a circle, the fire flickering between them, the peace pipe, already smoked, lying on its square of rabbit skin. She glanced at the women crouched against the walls, ready with food and water, their eyes fastened to her in stark disbelief. And Opechancanough himself, perched upon the largest bedstead, leaning forward, the fire lighting his features from below. *He is the very image of my father. He has already taken over, in all but name.*

Opechancanough shook his head slowly, and she half-expected to see long silver hair spill over his shoulder like a strip of wolf's pelt.

No one spoke.

Pocahontas drew the deepest breath her bodice would allow. "I have come on behalf of the *tassantassas*, seeking a trade. Their captives for yours."

"I can see you do come on behalf of the *tassantassas*."

She did not miss the barb in her uncle's voice. Pocahontas lowered her eyes, and realized with a start that one of the chiefs who stared up at her from his place by the fire was her half brother Naukaquawis. She slid her eyes quickly from his face, too.

"What do you mean by coming to my *yehakin*, to my territory, dressed like a *tassantassa* woman?"

"I mean no ill, *werowance*. I have only come to negotiate . . ."

"I do not negotiate with *tassantassas*." His words were not spiteful, not even heated. They were a simple dismissal. He had brushed her from his life, from the very reality of his world, with no more thought than a child brushes gnats from his skin.

Pocahontas clutched her skirts in hard fists. *To think of what I have lost, what I have sacrificed for the Real People, and he dismisses all I have given with the wave of a fly whisk?* Her sharp, dimpled chin lifted. In that moment, Rebecca the baptized Englishwoman had never existed, and even Matoaka, anointing herself beside the lone fire of her womanhood, fell away. Amonute, the fearless, insufferably bold girl-child, strode from the shadows of the past and stood unashamed before the Great Chief.

"Perhaps I will become a *tassantassa*," she said, "since neither you nor my father ever saw fit to exchange me. No, far better to allow a daughter and niece to languish in captivity than to part with a few precious bits of stolen steel. How brave our chiefs are! How willing to sacrifice young women to the mercies of our worst enemies!"

The air seized around her. Shocked tension seemed to spill from the chiefs, catching her in a web tighter than the laces of any bodice. *Now he will spring up and strike me*, she thought in a panic, *and John will leap to defend me, and he will be killed.*

But Opechancanough rumbled with sudden laughter. "Is that little Amonute I see before me?"

The *werowances* around the fire relaxed slightly; there was a fractional easing of tension, like a bow lowered but still nocked and drawn.

Pocahontas lowered her lashes, but not her chin. She caught Naukaquawis's eye, and pleaded with him silently, praying to the Okeus, if the Okeus still cared for her at all, that Naukaquawis would understand.

The spirits were merciful. Naukaquawis raised a palm, and then stood slowly. "Uncle, you know my sister has always been hotheaded. Allow me to speak to her for a moment. It has been long since I have seen her. We have much to say to one another."

Opechancanough jerked his head, a silent dismissal.

Naukaquawis brushed past Pocahontas, avoiding the reach of her skirts, and led the way down the dark hall to the fresh air outside.

"What's going on?" John whispered.

Pocahontas felt a shriek of hysterical laughter building in her chest. She pushed it down. "I don't know."

Naukaquawis led them to the garden near Opechancanough's longhouse. It was prepared for planting, with new mounds of black earth heaped at neat intervals across the clearing, the proliferation of springtime weeds pulled and waiting in pale, dried heaps to be gathered up and burned. A group of children crowded on the platform of the crow tower, jostling and whispering as they stared down at Pocahontas and John Rolfe. Naukaquawis hissed and threatened them until they scampered down the scaffolding and ran for their homes.

When they were alone, their voices covered by the wind in the forest canopy, Naukaquawis turned to her with a look of concern in his keen dark eyes.

"What is all this, Pocahontas? Tell me truthfully."

"It is exactly what I told Opechancanough. I will be staying with the *tassantassas*."

"But why?" He glanced past her shoulder at John Rolfe, who hovered around her like a mother fox fretting over her kits. "And who is the white dog who follows you?"

"My guard."

Naukaquawis squinted at John, his face twisting with skepticism. "Listen, Sister. I know there has been tension between us in the past, but I don't wish to see you harmed."

"The white men will not harm me."

"But look at you, dressed in *tassantassa* clothes, barely able to walk . . . It's an insult to your dignity as a Real Woman."

Pocahontas sighed. "Please, Naukaquawis, understand what I do. I am making a sacrifice—I *am* a sacrifice, for the good of our people."

She took a deep breath, and then continued, "You have seen how their numbers grow season by season. Even when the white men were at their weakest, when they starved and had no food but the flesh of their own dead . . . even then, we could not defeat them. They are a force we cannot stop. I have lived with them for a year now. Believe me—I know better than anybody does."

"Opechancanough won't like to hear that. It is better if you don't say those words to him. He still dreams of running them out, finding their weakness, some means of destroying them, or driving them back across the sea."

"He might as well dream of commanding the tides to ebb and flow at his whim."

Naukaquawis hung his head. "I know. At least, I have suspected as much for many months now, and you have confirmed my worries." He looked up at her. A sad smile curled his lip. "I have wondered, all this time, whether you still lived, and whether they were treating you well. Father was distraught, you know, when we heard you'd been taken."

"But he never tried to free me."

"He has no power anymore," Naukaquawis said, shaking his head. "Okeus preserve me from such a fate. Fading into uselessness—wasting away. Take me in battle, Okeus, or in the hunt. Not like that."

"Where is Father now?"

"In Orapax. Still in Orapax."

"And yet so many of the Real People are here."

"Opechancanough is here," Naukaquawis said, arching one brow.

"And Winganuske?"

Naukaquawis frowned. "What an odd question. But she is here, too, in Pamunkey. How did you know?"

"I suspected she might leave him . . . might follow Opechancanough as his strength increased. Poor Father."

"It went hard on him. You taken, and then Winganuske leaving . . . He is not a shadow of the man he was at the height of his power, but only the shadow of a shadow."

A painful lump rose in Pocahontas's throat. She wanted to ask, *And where is Kocoum? How does he fare?* But he might be dead, and if he were not, he would surely be married again . . . and she did not know which would hurt her worse.

She closed her eyes tightly. "It has gone hard on us all. None of us are the people we once were."

Naukaquawis took her hand and squeezed it. She smiled. He had never shown her such brotherly affection before.

"You are wise, now that you are a woman," he admitted. Then he squinted at her slyly. "Even if you are a white woman now."

She laughed and held up her hands. "I am not. You can see for yourself. No matter the clothes I wear, or where I make my hearth, I am still Real."

Naukaquawis's face grew serious again. "If we cannot stop them, Pocahontas, what can we do? For there must be something. I won't believe that the Okeus has abandoned us. There must be a way to . . . *survive.*"

A cloak of shame darkened his eyes. She saw what it cost him, the admission that the Real People could not defeat this foe—that he, young and strong, a warrior and a chief, was powerless.

"If anyone can find out how they might be stopped, Naukaquawis, it is I. If they have a weakness—any kind of weakness at all—who is better placed to know it than one who lives among them? Do you see now why I stay at the fort, why I wear their clothes and take on their customs?"

"Yes, I see," Naukaquawis said, rubbing his chin thoughtfully. "Perhaps it is best, after all."

She did not tell him the rest: when a bridge is laid across a deep ravine, it is easier for men to come and go. She knew that once she had offered herself up to be that very bridge, their two worlds would bleed together and merge faster than anyone could try to stop it, like streaks of paint thinned by too much oil. As years passed, much would be lost of the Real way of life. Already so much had changed. The *tassantassas'* glass beads, which had once been precious, were now nearly as common as shell. No one looked twice anymore at a copper cook pot or an iron digging hoe. She thought of Nonoma, sitting in a chair and sipping her stew from her *tassantassa* spoon, and she wanted to laugh—or cry. This was not the survival Naukaquawis longed for, but it was a *kind* of survival. And it was, she believed, their only hope.

Oh, my brother, she thought bitterly as she watched his brows furrow in a frown, *I will not be the last Real Person you see wearing* tassantassa *clothing. Perhaps one day even you will don trousers and a shirt, because you must. Because it is survival.*

"Since I have lived among them," she said, trying to make her voice light, "there have been fewer deaths. On both sides of the palisade."

"I have noticed."

"It seems to help them, to see me there, to know me. They are less cruel to our people because they believe I am good."

She stared out across the garden, at the smoke hanging over the tops of Pamunkey's longhouses. She remembered the dream on the night she became a woman—remembered the people drawing close to her small but glowing fire. How strange to think that only now, when she had been named Rebecca, would she truly become Matoaka as the Okeus intended.

She drew another deep breath, straining against her laces. "I believe that if I marry a *tassantassa* man, I can plant a peace more firmly in the soil, and it will take root. The war will end for good."

Naukaquawis's eyes flashed. "Marry one?"

She was careful not to look at John Rolfe. "Why not? Did Powhatan not unite the tribes by marrying the daughters and sisters of powerful men? If the *tassantassas* cannot be driven away or killed, we must seek unity. Endless fighting will only see us all in our graves, sooner or later. Is love not better than war?"

Naukaquawis grunted. "Only a woman would think such a thing." His face softened. "But you might be right. Just don't tell the other men I said so. I'd have my braid cut off and hung up for shame on Opechancanough's longhouse."

"So I have your approval?" Not that she needed it. Pocahontas was determined to weave unity between her two worlds whether her family saw the sense of it or not. But she would like to know they approved.

Naukaquawis shrugged. "I suppose, since Kocoum . . ." He hesitated at the stricken look on her face. "Pocahontas, he did not survive."

Her body went cold, then numb, but she did not weep. Perhaps, in some small way, she had already known it. It could not be otherwise. All would be as the Okeus willed—she was to be Matoaka, the fire burning for all people—and nothing, not even her love for Kocoum, would be allowed to prevent it. She said a silent prayer for his spirit, and for hers, for its empty, burning ache.

"One thing only," Naukaquawis said. "Will you remain loyal to us above the white men? A woman takes on the identity of her husband. If he is Paspahegh, she becomes Paspahegh. If he is Appamattuck, she becomes Appamattuck. But you must remain Real, no matter what clothing you wear, or how long and ridiculous your hair looks."

In spite of her pain, she smiled. It surprised her that she could. "I swear it by the ashes of Uttamussak. I will always be loyal to the Real People. I am forever a Real Woman, no matter who my husband is."

"Then I approve," he said, "and will pledge to Opechancanough that you will be true and faithful to our people, and will work for the greater good. But you know he won't like this."

She gave a small puff, a faint exhalation of breath. "I know." She pulled again at the neck of her bodice. "Naukaquawis, you cannot imagine how uncomfortable these clothes are. They told me I'd get used to them, but I know I never will. I hope you appreciate what I'm doing."

He laid a hand on her shoulder. "Come. Let us face our uncle together, little Mischief."

When they returned to the longhouse and Pocahontas stood once more in the ring of light before the chief, she was grateful for the thick skirts that hid the trembling of her knees. Naukaquawis was as good as his word. He immediately voiced his support for the marriage.

But Opechancanough rose silently from his bedstead, face stony and cold. He stalked about the fire like a cougar waiting for the right moment to spring.

"Marry a white man?" Opechancanough said. The hoarse quiet of his voice was more frightening than any shout could have been.

Pocahontas swallowed hard. She summoned the child Amonute to her spirit, before the last of her courage could fly away, clattering and shrieking like a flock of birds startled from a marsh. "I am going to do it, Uncle, whether you will it or no. I do not ask permission—only your blessing."

Even Naukaquawis glanced at her in surprise. Surely this time Amonute's boldness would be her undoing.

Opechancanough glared at her, wordless with fury.

"It's this man I will marry," Pocahontas said, indicating John Rolfe, who stood watching Opechancanough with unconcealed fear. When she translated her own words into English for his benefit, happiness warred with terror in his bloodless face and wide eyes. "Give us your blessing, and trade your captives for ours, and I shall leave happy."

Opechancanough turned his back on her and Pocahontas felt Naukaquawis flinch. "Trade the captives—yes," Opechancanough said. "But approve of such an abomination? Never. Do not ask me again, woman. It will never be."

.   .   .

Opechancanough's flat refusal hovered over Pocahontas's spirit like a thunderhead, black and oppressive. As she and John were rowed back to the shallop, she felt the chief's rejection weigh heavy on her heart. It stayed with her as she watched the exchange of captives from the rail of the shallop, and even John, quietly beaming as his fear dissipated, could not draw her from her dark reverie. As the anchor was raised and the shallop turned toward Jamestown, Pocahontas turned her face resolutely away from Pamunkey, thinking to shut Opechancanough from her heart, to move as swiftly and easily toward her new life and new work as the ship glided on the current.

But her uncle's grave displeasure clung to her like a burr in doeskin fringe. As Pocahontas stood with arms out, allowing Mary to measure her for alterations to her dress, Opechancanough's scowling face was never far from her thoughts. Reverend Whitaker called Pocahontas to the chapel and spoke with her in earnest tones of the things expected of a Christian wife. But she heard him with only one ear. The other ear still rang with the anger of her uncle's words, his tones of disgust and rejection.

It makes no matter, she told herself again and again, whenever she caught herself growing sorrowful at the thought of the chief's disapproval. *I do what I must for the Real People, not for Opechancanough.*

Ten days later, on a morning bright with promise and sweet with the scent of plum blossoms, Mary escorted Pocahontas to the chapel of Jamestown. Her best dress, the green wool, had been carefully embroidered at the hem and sleeves with a line of white flowers and yellow, starlike spangles of flying birds. Mary had even added, to Pocahontas's tearful, grateful surprise, the fire ring and heron from her old buckskin apron, picked out in stitches as red as the best *puccoon*.

The chapel was crowded with smiling faces, all the people of Jamestown she had come to know and trust: the women in their best and brightest dresses, the men bowing their heads as she passed. From the altar where he stood beside the reverend, John Rolfe gave his shy, quiet smile.

Reverend Whitaker directed her to stand opposite John, and then raised his voice in prayer. He prayed for a long time, speaking of their union, declaring it evidence of Christ's mercy and God's great and unknowable plan. He called the marriage a genesis of peace. At that, Pocahontas sighed with satisfaction.

A murmur sounded from the rear of the chapel, near the open door. It grew into a burst of exclamations. Pocahontas opened her eyes. There was fear in those voices. She turned to stare back down the chapel's aisle.

For one fearful heartbeat, she thought she was still sleeping. A tall man strode down the aisle, his head raised at a haughty angle. His apron was a confusion of black-and-red shapes and symbols, the fringe of a *werowance* swaying about his knees. He clenched something in one hand, but there was no knife in the tie of his apron, no bow slung on his shoulder.

Pocahontas blinked, and then her mind reeled out of its fog. It was her uncle.

Opechancanough stood before the altar and looked at Pocahontas calmly.

"*Wingapoh*," Opechancanough said. He opened his tight-clenched hand.

A string of white beads lay curled on his palm. No, not beads: pearls.

She raised her eyes to his face.

"I was told you would be married today," he said quietly in the Real Tongue. He nodded once to John, then turned back to Pocahontas. "I bring the blessing you asked for. This plan you have—I have thought about it often since we last spoke. It is a good plan. Just be certain this man treats you well."

"I will."

"If he is unkind to you—too impatient, too cold, too caught up with fighting or hunting to see to your heart—leave him."

She nearly laughed. "I will. Thank you, Uncle."

Trembling, Pocahontas turned to Reverend Whitaker with a nod. The reverend instructed her in the vows, which she repeated carefully in English. She smiled when John stammered over the words of his own pledge. At last the reverend joined their hands together, and laid his own hands upon their heads to seal their vows with prayer.

At the close of the prayer, Pocahontas glanced shyly into the reverend's eyes. "May my uncle give his blessing, too?"

"Of course, my dear," the reverend said.

She spoke a few quiet words to Opechancanough and he held the pearls up, stretched between his two hands. He glanced at the reverend, a questioning look, but the reverend only stared back uncomprehendingly.

Pocahontas gripped John's hands tightly. "Do it," she said in Real Tongue, smiling.

Opechancanough broke the pearls over their hands. When the string snapped and the tiny white globes scattered, a laugh of joy escaped from her throat. The sound of it filled the chapel and rebounded from the walls, rolling like pearls across the dark wood floor.

THE FOURTH NAME

Rebecca Rolfe

SMITH

October 1615

He was far away, reclining on a bed of cool silk, tidewater drying on his skin. The window was unshuttered. No, not shuttered—it was a woven mat, rolled and raised like a curtain tucked high against a window frame. A breeze carried a scent into the dark dome of the longhouse; rosemary and the rich perfume of Constantinople; pine smoke, buckskin, ancient incense from a temple on fire; fish offal, salty and sharp; the earthy tang of red paint licked from sweat-beaded skin. When Antonia moved from behind her screen and the water fell like stars over her curved hip, he saw that she had shaved her scalp from hairline to crown, and her long dark hair was a braided rope wound with copper and pearls, hanging down her honey-brown back.

She spoke, but Smith could not make out the words. Another sound muffled her voice; it pulsed and rose, faded and rose again—a persistent, gravelly sigh. When he moved he felt cold, so he held still and watched Antonia slash at him with a pair of antlers that spread from her forehead like oak limbs in winter. He stepped away from the sharp points, and this time when he moved he was not only cold, but wet, too.

Christ preserve you, Chawnzmit, Antonia said, *if you don't get dry you'll die. It's a wonder you aren't dead already.*

Smith sat up. He was in a small boat that rested at a steep slant among jagged rocks and clinging brown weed. Bilge pooled against the low side. Smith had lain in it for God alone knew how long. His trousers and tunic were soaked through. The paddle end of one oar tossed in the surf nearby, its broken handle showing like sharp teeth in a white smile.

Smith clutched frantically at his wet tunic. The packet was still there, wedged between this clothes and his sodden, burn-scarred body. He pulled it free and unwrapped the oilcloth, choking back his trepidation. When he saw that the pages within were dry—or at least, not too badly damaged by the damp that had managed to seep through—his relief was so great that he nearly wept.

He wrapped the pages once more in the oilcloth, tucked them under his arm, and pulled himself carefully from the wrecked boat. He was stiff with cold, and his back ached fearfully, but he seemed unhurt.

Step by careful step, he made his way over the rocks toward a low dune. Its back was crested with wet gray grass, which hackled in the seaside wind like a wary dog. The driving salt mist had compacted the sand, and he climbed it easily, if slowly. From its top he surveyed his surroundings.

The sun was just rising. It spread a smear of wan light, fighting through a curtain of low cloud, the kind of cold, thick-smelling bank that hangs over the shores and never moves inland, no matter how the wind pushes at it. He could not quite determine where the sun was, and so he could not orient himself. Christ knew how long he had rowed in that storm, and once he'd dropped into the hull of the skiff, senseless with exhaustion, not even Christ could say how long or how far he had drifted. His throat burned with thirst.

From somewhere in the near distance, in a stand of trees half-concealed by fog, Smith heard men's voices calling.

"Ohé! Êtes-vous blessé?"

French. He would have dropped to his knees to thank Christ they were not Spanish, but now that he was aware of his thirst, it was rapidly taking hold. He feared that if he knelt he would never make it back to his feet again. He forced himself toward the copse, one foot and then the other, holding his packet of papers like a drowning man clings to a plank.

The Frenchmen met him at the edge of the trees, and all he could see were the waterskins hanging from their shoulders. They made him sit and held a wooden spout to his lips. He seized the skin with weak, insistent hands, as a greedy infant grabs at the teat. But then they pulled it away after one mouthful, making him drink slowly, one sip at a time. The men tried to speak to him, but all he could think of were all the words for "water" he had ever known.

Eau. Νερό. Su. Água.
Suckquahan.
Suckquahan.
Suckquahan.

As he recovered, he grew more aware of his surroundings. His senses broadened like a net expanding underwater to scoop at the drift and detritus of the world. There were two Frenchmen. They carried muskets and wore the pointed caps of hunters and a certain polished nobility. Out to bag a boar, and instead they'd felled a shipwrecked Englishman.

One of them stooped and braced Smith's arm with a firm hand. It took Smith some time to parse the French words he spoke. "We have food back at our lodge. You look like you could use a bite. Come along, friend."

Thank God, the lodge was not far away. They helped him stagger through the forest until they came to a stone building with a roof of new thatch. Smith collapsed onto a bench inside and laid his head back against the plastered wall, shivering. He accepted their dry blankets with gratitude, and watched as they stoked a fire and hung his clothes beside it. The room filled with the odor of wet wool and steam. An ocean dripped from his clothing to puddle on the clean-swept flagstones of the hearth.

Wine came first, blessedly hot, thawing his gut and bones. Then bread, which he dunked in the wine, and a knob of hard cheese.

"Now then, fellow," said one of the hunters, "tell us how you came to be here."

"My French is poor."

The hunter waved a hand. "It's serviceable enough."

"And you will not believe me, even when I tell the tale."

"You already strain credulity, washed up on our beach like a half-dead eel. You may as well tell whatever tale you please."

"Very well," Smith said. He settled into the warmth of his blanket and began.

Late in the summer of his final year in Jamestown, a mishap with a horn of black powder left him badly injured. His chest and abdomen were a mass of blisters and broken, weeping skin. His beard was singed away, leaving the reek of burnt hair in his nostrils whenever he had the misfortune to drift out of merciful unconsciousness.

During his weeks of suffering, Smith heard the men who tended his wounds opine over his immobile body that the president of the colony had finally met his match in a horn of powder; John Smith was not long for the world of the living. When they carried him aboard the *Susan Constant* for her return voyage to England, it was clear they all expected him to find a watery grave somewhere between the New World and the Old.

Instead, to the consternation of the ship's captain, Smith recovered.

He clawed his way back to life, and then, with a scarred hide to prove his bravery, Smith clawed his way into a captaincy of his own.

Back in England, he found himself, to his wonder and satis-faction, the foremost authority on the New World. It was a turn of events that would have curled Edward-Maria Wingfield's pointy little beard. That knowledge alone pleased Smith to no end.

Even more pleasing were the offers with which he was liber-ally peppered by all manner of investors, each of whom sought his expertise. Over the following years, he led a handful of expeditions: mapping the coast of the New World, tracking the movement of the whales that yielded precious oil and ambergris, seeking silver and gold, chasing the elusive ghost of a passage to the Indies. Most of these, Smith readily admitted, were not great successes, but his investors didn't seem to care. The moment he returned from one expedition, an offer was already at his door for another.

The most recent trek was the dearest to his heart. Under the direction of investors who meant to compete with the Virginia Company, Smith was to lead a mission of colonization. The colony would establish itself somewhere north of Jamestown.

It seemed a promising venture when they cast off lines in London, but from the start, the expedition was plagued—perhaps even cursed. Lines broke or were blown away in freak squalls. The compass malfunctioned. A pernicious illness of the bowels swept through crew and colonists alike, and two people died before they had even left the European coasts to strike out across the open sea.

Worries truly began, though, when they reached the Azores, where the ship was dogged for two days by French pirates. The crew wanted to surrender, but Smith would have none of it. He had never feared the French. He declared that they would fight. If they lost, Smith swore to ignite his kegs of powder and destroy his own ship rather than allow it to fall into the hands of pirates.

With the promise of a fiery end for motivation, Smith's crew fought admirably. They shook off the French, but barely a day later ran afoul of two more vessels flying the colors of French privateers.

Smith perceived that it would be better to bargain with them, if a bargain could be struck. He commanded his men to raise a flag of truce. They tied their ship to one of the pirate vessels, and Smith went aboard to parley. There he discovered with great relief that the privateers were after Spanish and Portuguese ships, not English. They hadn't wished to capture his ship—only to question him. Once they were satisfied he'd seen nothing of any Spanish ships, they agreed to let him go in peace.

However, while he was engaged with the captain in his cabin, his crew had done him an ill turn. Still reeling from the previous day's threat, they had already cut the lines and sailed on without him, rather than risk being blasted apart by their own supplies of powder.

Smith was left a prisoner of the French privateers.

They treated him well enough, providing better accommodations than Wingfield had offered in the cramped brig of the *Susan Constant*. He wanted for nothing; the pirate captain even provided him with paper and ink, and in his month of confinement he wrote his memoirs of Jamestown.

Smith had assured the captain of the *Don de Dieu* quite convincingly that England would pay a good price for his return. The captain was intrigued, and promised that once he had collected a few bounties on Portuguese scoundrels, he would return Smith to London and trade him for gold.

As the summer dragged on, though, the *Don de Dieu* worked its way ever farther from English shores. With each hint of a Portuguese ship, every gleam of white and red on a hazy horizon, Smith's ransom grew fainter in the captain's mind. Soon Smith was all but forgotten, a forlorn specter haunting the deck of the *Don de Dieu* in helpless silence.

Until the storm.

It blew up from the southwest, a wall of cloud towering over the sea like the shoulder of God himself. As the storm approached, the water grew dark and angry, and soon Smith knew, as the captain knew, that the *Don de Dieu* could not outrun it.

Smith bundled his memoir into a packet of oilcloth, slipped it beneath his clothing, and waited. When the captain was distracted, shouting orders to his fearful crew, Smith slipped into the man's quarters and found a dagger hidden in a mahogany trunk.

As the men hunched against the rain and wind, working frantically at the lines, Smith sprinted across the deck. He slashed the ropes securing one of the small landing boats, and flipped it over the rail. He leaped after it, barely pausing long enough to be sure his aim was sound.

Thank God, the oars were lashed against the hull. He cut those lines, too, and rowed as if the devil himself swam in his wake. A small part of his mind knew that a rowboat could not outpace the *Don de Dieu*, yet Smith could not countenance staying aboard the French ship, doing nothing to save his own skin. The crew battled on, unaware that several pounds' worth of English gold had just disembarked the ship.

Smith rowed, orienting himself first by the sight of the *Don de Dieu* floundering among the violent waves, and when he lost track of the ship, he kept going in the same direction, or so he hoped, pulling evenly on the oars, praying he was headed toward land. He knew it lay to the east, but determining which direction might be east was an exercise in futility. Now and then he pulled his compass from his leather pouch and peered at its dim face in the storm, but the needle lurched and wobbled as his boat tossed in the waves, and he could never be sure of his orientation. He was obliged to bail often with a little copper scoop that was tied to the boat. Each time he dropped the oars to bail, he begged Christ not to turn his boat around in the pitching, frothing, roaring mountains of waves. He rowed until his arms turned limp and useless, and then he rowed on still. When his body finally collapsed into the hull of his boat, he was already dwelling in the unsettling mist of his dreams.

"And that is the last I recall, until you found me washed up on your beach."

The hunters glanced at one another across their table.

Smith sipped his wine. It had gone cold, but he felt somewhat recovered from his ordeal, and the coolness of it was pleasant on the tongue. "You don't believe me?"

One of the hunters gave a shrug, elegantly uncaring in that special manner only the French can affect, sinuous and half-asleep. The other gave a tentative chuckle.

Let them laugh. Laughter changes nothing.

The only thing that mattered to Smith was the manuscript, still wrapped in the oilcloth, safe on the table beside him.

But later that afternoon, as Smith lay dozing on one of the hunter's cots, the manuscript safe beneath his pillow, a thin, high shout of amazement broke through his slumber.

Outside the lodge, the hunters stood on a distant dune, calling to him, their arms waving, slow and small like the filaments on an insect's head.

Smith felt stronger as he crossed the stretch of land between the lodge and the beach. Sandy earth rose up to meet each step, cradling him, propelling him forward with a fast and confident stride.

The hunters rushed him along a narrow trail, barely more than a deer track that clambered along a high bluff. The foliage brushed his face. It smelled of salt spray and wild things.

They emerged on a promontory of bare gray stone, high above the pounding sea. Smith walked to the edge. Wind pulled at his hair, carrying the smell of low tide and a chalky, sour gust of guano.

Below, where the surf beat itself to white foam against a fist of jagged rock, a dark shape lay smashed like a child's dropped toy.

Smith squinted until he could read the letters on the prow, burned into the wet wood, leafed in scratched and peeling gold: "Don de Dieu."

He turned to the hunters. "There's gold in it for you," he said in his dismal French, "if you can get me back to England."

POCAHONTAS

March 1616

When the wind moved through the tobacco leaves, they whispered, a broad-leafed murmur of music that was almost like corn in summer. Pocahontas liked the plants. Even now, just sprouts pushing from the dark earth, their leaves were glossy and cheerful. The pale sun of early spring glanced off the leaves and all around her the field glowed as she moved through the rows on hands and knees, crushing the first grubs of the season between her fingers.

The grubs covered her hands in their sticky brown juice, and she plucked a tobacco leaf and scrubbed her palms and fingers. It smelled fresh and bright, faintly spicy. It scoured away the residue of the grubs and left a tingling sensation on her skin.

This was not the tobacco she had known in childhood. The sacred leaf of the Real People grew in shady dells, with jagged-edged leaves and tiny, forked flowers of violet blue. This—the plant that dominated the cleared fields around her home with John Rolfe— loved sun and grew shoulder high, spreading its leaves in dense clusters like the canopy of the forest. The flowers clustered long and white, with flared petals that looked like the trumpets the boys at the fort sometimes blew.

John had brought the plant all the way from the southern islands. Sometime after he had buried his wife and daughter, he had obtained a bag of rare seeds from one of the naturals of Bermuda. He had carefully preserved the seeds ever since that day, keeping the bag tightly sealed and periodically spreading them on a bit of cloth to ensure damp did not take hold and ruin them with mildew. He had shown them to Pocahontas, and she had convinced him to plant the seeds. By that autumn a drying rack, thick with wide, brown tobacco leaves, stood proudly before the Rolfe home.

Even better than the harvest were the seeds Pocahontas had collected after the last of the white flowers had withered and dropped. The original bag from Bermuda could not contain them all, so she wove a tight basket to store them in, and dug a small cellar behind the house where the tobacco seeds slept through the winter, dreaming of the warm soil of spring.

The tobacco was not the only thing that sprouted and grew. Her son, Thomas, had now seen nearly eighteen months. He ran shrieking through the garden, chasing flies and cabbage moths, his black hair and the hem of his little gown streaming behind. He had only just begun to speak, lisping half-formed words, and he demanded to know the name of everything his bright-black eyes touched. When her work was done, Pocahontas would sweep Thomas up on her hip and carry him about the fields, and everything he pointed at she would name, first in English, then in the Real Tongue.

Sometimes when she looked at her son, she thought she could see an echo of Kocoum in his features, and she often wondered whether the spirit of the child she should have borne to her first husband had found its way to the world after all, in the body of little Thomas Rolfe.

She picked herself up from the earth as Thomas came running toward her with his arms outstretched. The hems of her long skirts were tucked in the edge of her bodice, which she had loosened for work. Pocahontas brushed the soil from her knees and hands, and then pulled the skirts free so they swung about her feet. Thomas squealed and buried his face in the wool.

She lifted him, pressing her face against his sun-warmed hair, breathing in his fresh, sweet smell.

"What?" he said, pointing.

"Leaf," Pocahontas answered. *"Attasskuss."*

Thomas pointed across the field, where John dug into the earth with his long-handled hoe. She watched his strong back bend, his arms straighten and pull, his dark hair brushing his broad shoulder.

"Father," she said. *"Kowse."*

It had taken Pocahontas many months to grow used to the sight of John working in the tobacco fields. She could not fault his industriousness; the man never ceased working. But among the Real People, the garden was the woman's domain. The field was her sacred space where no authority was greater than her own—not even her husband's. Seed and root were female mysteries, like the magic of life-giving blood. Yet John had always insisted on working his own land. "My wife will not toil like a slave while I take my ease," he had said when she protested. And he kissed her protestations away.

And even if he did prefer to spend his days gardening rather than hunting or fishing, he yielded to her superior knowledge of plants and the rhythm of the soil. Husband and wife worked together, always under Pocahontas's direction. Before Thomas's first birthday their small estate near the village of Henrico, not far from Jamestown, was green and flourishing.

The fact that they could stake a plot of land outside the bounds of Jamestown, or any of the other stockades that ringed the new English settlements, was a testament to the success of Pocahontas's marriage. Her union with John Rolfe had enforced a peace across the land. There had been no ambushes by Real People, and no firing of English cannons or burning of longhouses. Now, two years after he had broken the white beads in the Jamestown chapel,

Opechancanough had even resumed trading with the white men. Pocahontas was pleased, and rejoiced that her sacrifice had even brought her happiness. John was a gentle, thoughtful husband, and Thomas filled her heart like nothing had before.

But Pocahontas could not help feeling sad now and then when she looked out from the door of her house across the stretch of her fields. The Rolfe estate stood in Appamattuck territory, on land that belonged by rights to Oppossu-no-quonuske. The old *wero-wansqua* had traded it to the Rolfes for an ample share of English goods, but Pocahontas never felt as if she owned it. And she wondered how many more estates would spread across the land. What would the Real People do when the boundaries of their territories constricted? Where would her people go, as her husband's people continued to spread across Tsenacomoco?

Such musings made her sick at heart. She tickled Thomas to chase her sorrows away. He laughed and squirmed in her arms, as soft and happy as a pup. Then the boy suddenly pointed toward the beaten track that led down to the Rolfe estate from the village of Henrico.

"What?" Thomas demanded.

Pocahontas watched the man as he wandered out of the wood. She could just make out his neat, ash-colored beard against the dark of his tunic.

"Friend," she said. "*Netap.*"

She eased Thomas to the ground. The boy followed her out onto the lane, where she greeted Reverend Whitaker with a smile. "It has been a long time," she said.

"I'm pleased to see you looking so well, Rebecca. And young Thomas—my word, how you have grown!"

Pocahontas called John in from the field, and set about preparing the midday meal while the reverend entertained Thomas with a story about Christ walking on the surface of the sea. When they gathered at the table and the meal was blessed, the reverend looked somberly at John.

"The latest shipments have come in at Jamestown."

"So soon?" John said, crumbling corn bread into his stew. "Did they bring anything of note?"

"I should say so. I've received a letter from the Virginia Company, directing me to implore you, John Rolfe, to bring your lady wife to London so that she may be seen among society."

John sat back. His hands were pale and flat on the surface of the table.

Pocahontas watched him uneasily, but did not speak.

"Society?" John said at last. "What is the meaning of this?"

"It seems your wife has become quite popular in London. Now that Jamestown Colony has been declared a success, everybody desires to meet Lady Rebecca Rolfe, the princess of the New World."

"But," Pocahontas ventured, "I'm not a princess. Not in the way the English mean it."

"I know," Reverend Whitaker said, chuckling deep in his chest. "But all England is convinced that you are royalty. Your name flies about the tables at parties and balls, or so I hear."

She shook her head, bewildered. "How can they even know my name?"

"I confess I do not know how they've learned of you. Some letter from the colony, perhaps. But the Virginia Company was most adamant. London will not be satisfied until it sees you for itself. All your expenses will be paid, of course. Courtesy of the V.C."

"No," John said. "No. Whitaker, you know this is only a ploy. The Virginia Company thinks to parade my wife at parties and at court, like some prize milk cow with ribbons about her neck, so they might secure more funding for their ventures. That's all this is—surely you can see that."

"Likely," the reverend admitted. "But alas, the king and queen have gotten wind of the idea. Queen Anne especially has expressed her great desire to host and entertain the Lady Rebecca. I don't know that you can refuse them, John."

"We simply won't respond. Letters are lost all the time. They'll believe we never saw their letter."

But Pocahontas leaned forward with sudden interest. Opechancanough would want to know about the white *mamanatowick*—how he lived, how he might be reasoned with. How the tide of white men might be stemmed. "Meet the king and queen? Oh, John, we must!"

John sighed. "Rebecca, I do not think it wise."

She clasped John's hand, but turned to the reverend. "Do we have some time to ponder it, before we send our response?"

"Of course."

"Then let me at least take the news to my family. I believe it will be of interest to them."

Pocahontas watched from the rail as Jamestown receded, a gray smudge against a deep blue-green palisade of trees. Thomas rode on her hip, clinging to the laces of her bodice, staring wide-eyed about the deck of the *Lady Grey*. The commotion of the ship's crew was enough to silence even his chatter. All about them, sailors chanted as they hauled on lines. From the vantage of the great wheel, the captain shouted his orders.

John lingered uncertainly in the shade of the mast. Pocahontas knew he still had his hesitations about the voyage to England, but he had accompanied her to Orapax the week before, and had seen for himself how keen the old *mamanatowick* was to send his daughter to England.

Powhatan had seized eagerly at Pocahontas's proposal. His dream of possessing guns was now only a distant and foolish memory. A far more urgent need now haunted Chief Powhatan's spirit:

he wished to know how many English there were. There must be an end to them—an end to this flood of *tassantassas* that seemed to run deeper and faster with each passing season, scouring more and more of Tsenacomoco away.

"Go," Powhatan had told her. "I cannot believe what the white men tell my chiefs when they sit down to trade. But I know I can rely on your account, Pocahontas. Learn what you can of the English, of their *mamanatowick* and his designs. Think on what you learn, and tell me what we can do if their ships keep coming. Tell me what of our world we might save."

When John understood Powhatan's desperate need for knowledge, he took pity on the old man and relented. "It's naught but a ploy by the Virginia Company," he grumbled as he helped her pack a pair of trunks, "but if you are certain it will do your people some good for you to see London with your own eyes, well . . ."

Pocahontas was not the only Real Person who would look upon the capital of the English king. She glanced over her shoulder to where Utta-ma-tomakkin crouched on the deck beside John. The priest's dark eyes flickered along the riverbank as the ship made its way swiftly toward the sea. Pocahontas had convinced him to don white men's clothes for the sake of blending in, and the priest looked awkward and uncertain in his trousers and linen shirt.

She had already begun schooling him in the English tongue. The charge Powhatan gave the priest was nearly as important as her own task: Utta-ma-tomakkin was to find the English god, to look upon the deity, and learn all he could about its power. Understanding the white men's god might provide the Real People with some small advantage as the tide of *tassantassas* continued to rise. Or so Powhatan and Opechancanough hoped.

As Pocahontas watched him, Utta-ma-tomakkin clutched at a large stick thrust like a sword through his *tassantassa* belt. He had been instructed to count the English by notching the stick with his knife each time he saw a white face. Pocahontas frowned as she watched Utta-ma-tomakkin worry at the stick. She suspected a whole forest of sticks would be needed to tally the English in all their numbers.

Matachanna made her way across the deck to Pocahontas. She, too, had agreed to wear *tassantassa* clothing, though, like Pocahontas in her days as a captive, Matachanna found she could not tolerate the restrictive bodice and sleeves. Pocahontas had given her a linen shift and it flowed about Matachanna's bare feet as she stepped with exaggerated care. The pale linen made her face sickly and green.

Matachanna held out her arms for Thomas. She had offered to care for the child while Pocahontas observed the English in their own lands. Pocahontas planned to learn all she could of London and the king—she knew she would be busy in England, and was grateful she would not be obliged to hand the boy over to an Englishwoman to tend. Thomas was learning his words faster than ever now, and she wanted him to speak the Real Tongue as readily as he spoke English. But she was more grateful still that she had a friend—her sister—with her. Matachanna understood all that was at stake for the Real People.

Pocahontas handed Thomas over to her sister with a smile. "You look ill already. One would think you'd never been in a canoe."

"This is no canoe," Matachanna said direly. "It's the size of two longhouses. The Okeus never meant for man to travel in such a way."

"John tells me the real adventure begins when the ship leaves the river and rides upon the open sea."

Matachanna stared downstream. The river was vast here, opening lazily to the salt water. The comforting, forested banks were far distant to either side. Far ahead, the land fell away entirely, and an endless blue curve of ocean waited beneath a sunlit haze.

"Spirits help me," Matachanna muttered, and held Thomas tightly against her.

When the *Lady Grey* did gain the sea, Pocahontas did not smile quite so easily. The first several days went hard with her. The pitching, heaving roll of the ship confused her senses. She hardly seemed to know which direction was up. She was plagued by nausea, and resisted the sailors who implored her to come out of the hold and take air on the deck. They swore her sickness would abate if she could see the horizon, but she refused to believe it. After her second day of retching into a pot and listening to poor little Thomas wail, she finally climbed the ladder to the open air.

The sailors were right. Almost at once she felt better, and chided Matachanna up onto the deck, too. Thomas recovered himself and giggled at the flock of white birds that trailed the *Lady Grey* like a plume of bright smoke, but Matachanna huddled into her shift, wedging herself between two crates. She could not be brought out of her misery.

The tang of the sea air sent a thrill racing through Pocahontas's blood. Even when the skies were gray and the waves rough, she spent her days on the deck with Thomas and John, only retreating to their small quarters in the hold when rain drove her below. She watched great silver fish with pointed snouts, which John called *dolphins*, leap and play in the spray of the ship's bow. In the mornings, when the sun was still rosy over the sea ahead, misty pillars of whales' breath would rise in the distance and hang dissipating over the sleek black arches of their backs. She grew so fond of sailing that one warm, mild day the laughing crew hoisted her up the foremost mast in a rope sling. She hung there, calling out and waving to John far below, while the mast swayed gently side to side like the crown of a massive tree in a summer wind. All around the flanks of the *Lady Grey*, the vast sea stretched and stirred, rippling endlessly like a huge blanket shaken between uncountable, unseen hands.

At last the *Lady Grey* found European waters. They tracked north along sere brown coasts, and then found the land growing lusher, painted in shades of green. Finally, early in the month of

June, they were surrounded by a great whirl of birds that made Thomas laugh until he was breathless with delight, and they coasted into the harbor of Plymouth.

"Thank the Okeus," Matachanna muttered, hitching up the hem of her shift. "If I didn't want to return to Orapax so badly, I would never set foot on an English ship again."

POCAHONTAS

June 1616

The coach bounced and squealed on its springs as it left the dirt road for the hard-packed gravel of London's outer lanes. Pocahontas lifted the coach's shade to peer out at London and felt a jolt of horrified awe. The city was a solid mass of stone stretching as far as she could see, clinging to the banks of a dismal, treeless river. Smoke hung like a fogbank over the pointed roofs of uncountable houses. And everything—from walls to steeples to roads, from the puddles the horses splashed through to the people they passed—was gray.

Plymouth had been a large enough village, but at least she could see green fields stretching away from the homes, and forests beyond the fields. Pocahontas gaped at the stifling grayness of London. How did these people eat? Where did they find food, if not in gardens and forests? There were neither fields nor forests anywhere near.

She sat back, gazing around the interior of the coach, at a loss for words. Matachanna was huddled close to Utta-ma-tomakkin, whose stoic silence could not mask his turmoil. Even in Plymouth he had realized his counting stick would be useless. He had abandoned the task after cutting the hundredth notch with his knife. But London seemed as large as a thousand Plymouths.

Pocahontas turned to John with wide eyes. He reached across her to tug the shade closed again.

Only the sounds and smells of London intruded as the coach maneuvered through its crowded streets, but that was intrusion enough. The coach rocked as they turned, and voices called out from all sides. "Cockles! Cockles by the pound! Fresh cabbages!" There was a burst of breaking pottery; a man cursed, and a woman screeched insults. She heard the rising snarls of two dogs fighting, and men laughing and shouting their wagers. There was a thick odor of horse dung and human urine, of musty wool and rot. It clung to Pocahontas like a shroud.

Thomas slept on Pocahontas's lap. She envied the boy's ability to slip into the peace of his dreams amid the shouting and chaos. *I shall never have a restful dream again*, she thought sadly, stroking her son's black hair. She tried to imagine what she could possibly tell her father when she returned to Tsenacomoco. Her thoughts were bleak and wearying. He had spoken of a flood of *tassantassas* and wondered how to quell it. But she now knew the sea could not be quelled.

She closed her eyes to ward away the threat of tears.

When they arrived at their inn, the horses came to a stamping, blowing halt. A footman in a patched blue coat opened the carriage door. Pocahontas took the man's hand and stepped down into the inn's courtyard, glad to be on her feet again after the long ride from Plymouth.

She looked about the square yard. The wings of the inn surrounded the court entirely, blocking the view of the London streets. Patches of thin grass reached like an old, worn buckskin fringe between the cracks of paving stones. A row of weedy roses straggled along the rough-made bricks of the building, dropping yellow and pink petals among the thorns. She recognized the flower from the books John had shown her, but when she bent to sniff a pale bloom, it had none of the sweet scent the books promised. It smelled wan and thin as an overused cloth. The eaves above the upper story were overhung with tendrils of some twining plant, not unlike the passion-fruit vines of Tsenacomoco. Swallows darted in and out among the vines, the sun glinting on their blue-black wings despite the smog that tried to stifle its warm rays. A thick line of white droppings showed clearly in the grass below the swallows' nests.

John stepped down beside her, the still-sleeping Thomas now propped against his shoulder. He glanced up at the inn's door and frowned. A veil of anger, tightly controlled, darkened his features.

Pocahontas followed her husband's gaze. A red sign swung from an iron bracket above the door, and she squinted at the letters painted in curling white script. She seldom read script, and it took her a long moment to puzzle out the inn's name.

The Bell Savage.

"A fine jape," John muttered, "courtesy of the V.C."

A small troop of men in faded blue coats carried their trunks and bags inside. The inn's hostess, an old woman with white hair drawn up in a voluminous bun, showed them to their rooms, tutting and fussing as she went. When their trunks were deposited in their rooms and the old woman withdrew with a final hen cluck of warning—"Meals are served at the times indicated, and sharp, too!"—Pocahontas shut the door with a sigh of relief.

Matachanna took Thomas from John's arms. She lay with the boy on the bed, a great canopied thing with yellow velvet drapes. The bed creaked beneath Matachanna's slight weight, and when she tried to tug the drapes closed—to hide the sight of her tears, Pocahontas suspected—a great puff of dust rose up beneath her hand.

"Let's have some fresh air," Pocahontas said in the Real Tongue. She pulled back the curtains that covered the room's window. Their quarters were on the third floor, the highest. She could look down from her window to the narrow street, flanked as far as she could see by three stories of dingy brick. Across from the window, a crooked alley wound between two dark-sided buildings, affording a glimpse of a flat gray expanse of the river, and, spanning it, the arches of a huge stone bridge. The road that ran along the bridge was crowded on either side with houses as tall and thin as saplings and wooden stalls where merchants hawked their wares. A rapid movement in the alley caught Pocahontas's eye. A small dog with a coat like moth-eaten wool trotted down the lane, dodging the puddles of muddy water that gathered in the alley's pits and divots. As she watched, a man staggered out of a door, singing in a broken, howling voice. He opened his trousers and urinated against the wall.

Pocahontas turned away.

John was bent over a trunk—not one of theirs, but one far finer, with brass bands and a polished and carved mahogany face. He lifted the lid tentatively. She could see a bright fold of cloth inside.

"What is it, John?"

He held a folded piece of parchment up to the window's light. "*For Lady Rebecca Rolfe: It is our pleasure to provide you and your retinue with these tokens of our esteem, for the duration of your stay in London. Signed, The Virginia Company.*"

John propped the trunk's lid open. Together they lifted out and examined several gowns and other articles of fine clothing. Matachanna, distracted from her misery by the bright fabrics, joined them in laying out the garments. They laid finespun wool atop soft linen, and sturdy, bright velvet side by side with the cool smoothness of silk. There were skirts and sleeves in every shade of blue, and greens as rich as a forest in summer. Pocahontas compared a deep-gold silk with a russet wool while Matachanna toyed with a black braid edging a cream-colored bodice.

But the more they examined the garments, the more apparent it became that they were not especially fine—or at least, their finest days were behind them. The nap of a velvet sleeve was crushed and worn thin at the elbow. One side of a wool skirt was subtly sun-faded, and a silk hem was pale with frayed threads. Pocahontas surmised they were the cast-off gowns of some gentleman's wife.

The women let the drape of a skirt fall between their examining hands. John shut the mahogany trunk and sank down on its lid, his frown deepening.

Three days later, just when Pocahontas began to feel that if she did not escape from the stifling rooms of the Bell Savage she would climb the dusty curtains in frustration, the first of the expected invitations arrived. John read it out loud to them: supper and a ball at the London estate of Lord De La Warr, to be hosted by his lady wife in the absence of the lord.

Pocahontas held her breath. Her eyes locked with Matachanna's own.

At last Matachanna said, "Are you going to go?"

"I don't believe I have a choice. Not truly."

"But De La Warr . . . he's the one who . . ."

"Wowinchopunck's wife and sons—I know."

Matachanna helped her into the newest-looking dress they could find. The bodice and skirts were of a soft sky-blue silk. Stiff, wire-framed cuffs jutted from the shoulders to hide the ties of the sleeves. The gown's low, rounded neckline, edged in an intricate lace, did not entirely conceal the tattoos across Pocahontas's chest. She surveyed herself in the room's tall mirror and turned to John, touching the edge of one tattoo, a question on her lips.

"Leave it be," John said before she could speak. "They'll like to see your markings. Makes you more of an oddity." He turned away with a sigh.

Pocahontas could not manage the fashionable hairstyle on her own—the high, voluminous coif swept back from the brow. The innkeeper sent up her niece, a blushing, quiet girl named Abigail with hair as fine and pale as corn silk. Abigail set to work with a pair of combs, teasing and coaxing Pocahontas's hair into a thick, dark cloud around her face. Matachanna snorted with laughter at the sight, but when Abigail pulled the cloud into a heaped crown and pinned it, even Matachanna exclaimed at the transformation.

"You do look a proper London lady," John admitted. His eyes warmed, and his smile had none of the cynicism that had twisted it since the day they set sail from Jamestown.

As Lady De La Warr's supper was to be "a garden delight," Abigail insisted on adding a tall white hat to Pocahontas's tower of hair. "'Tis only proper for a married lady to wear a cap out of doors," the girl said as she secured the hat with a long pin.

Matachanna shook her head. "You look as if you've got your head stuck inside a water gourd."

"Curious," Pocahontas said in the Real Tongue, "that is exactly how I feel." She turned her head very slowly to examine her reflection, fearful the hat might topple off. But Abigail had done her job well; it kept its place on her lofty cloud of black hair. "I look completely ridiculous." She said to Abigail in English, "I thank you kindly for your assistance."

The estate of Lord De La Warr lay beyond the gray clutter of London proper, amid a patchwork of rolling parks and gardens. Pocahontas was pleased to see that not all the land here had been turned to stone and ash, but even London's most scenic dells could not compare with the rugged, fierce beauty of Tsenacomoco.

John, refined and foreign in a deep-green coat with a stiff, high collar, helped her down from the carriage into a great courtyard of pale stone that curved out from a manor house. Pocahontas had to roll her eyes upward to see the entire ivy-shrouded height of it. She dared not tip back her head; she still felt as if hair and cap alike might slide from her scalp and collapse in a heap on the ground.

From behind the house, the soft strains of harp and flute lifted and moved on the breeze like birds in lazy flight. She had heard the English instruments a time or two, when she and John had gathered at Jamestown or Henrico for happy occasions. The sound made her melancholy for home. The air was languid with a sweet scent. *Roses*, she thought. *That must be the smell of a proper rose.*

They moved toward the steps of the estate. Beneath the tight stays of her bodice, Pocahontas's gut twisted with anxiety. She lifted her silk skirts to ascend the steps, but before she could, the dark wooden doors of the home swung open. Lady De La Warr appeared between them in a sudden eruption of sound and color.

"My dear Rebecca Rolfe," she cried. Her voice was loud but melodious, and seemed to come from deep in her middle, from the narrowest point of her squeezed-slender waist. Her dress was made of bloodred silk, and shimmered with hundreds of flowers embroidered in golden thread. She flung her arms wide in welcome. "What a delight to meet you at last. And your honorable husband—do come in, do come in!"

Pocahontas hurried up the steps and sank into the smooth curtsey she had practiced before the mirror at the inn.

"Now, now," the lady said, "let us have no formalities between us. We must be the best of friends, you and I." She beamed. Her chestnut hair was formed into a column even taller than Pocahontas's own. A stiff collar of lace fanned out below her chin, so that her head with its soaring pile of hair seemed to float above her graceful shoulders. "You must call me Cecily."

Pocahontas dipped her head as far as she dared. "And I am Rebecca. I am pleased to make your acquaintance."

A cluster of ladies in bright gowns milled in the hall behind Cecily, barely visible past the impressive jut of the lady's lace collar. They whispered behind their hands, peering out at Pocahontas.

"My goodness," Cecily said, "your elocution is simply superb. I confess I did not think to find a natural of Virginia so articulate."

Pocahontas felt John stiffen beside her. She laced her arm through his to calm his temper.

"But look at me," the lady went on, stepping back from the threshold, "keeping you out on the step. Please, be welcome."

The home of Lord De La Warr and his voluble wife was the most elaborate setting Pocahontas had yet seen in England. Every surface, every object, gleamed. Afternoon sun lanced through the windows, its warm glimmer dancing on polished wood floors and gold-leaf frames surrounding portraits painted in bright colors. A cut-glass vase on a table scattered rainbows across a wall. A brown-and-white spaniel wove its way past men's legs and women's skirts, and even the little creature's neck glinted with a golden collar that sparkled as the dog danced on its hind legs for tidbits from the ladies' fingers.

Soon enough John was engaged with a circle of gentleman, telling them all he knew about the cultivation of tobacco. Cecily pulled Pocahontas away from her husband and led her toward the staring, whispering women.

"You must tell us," Cecily said, "all about Virginia. Oh, how I desire to see it!"

The ladies murmured their agreement. A few of them fluttered fans before their faces, and behind the wispy barriers of their bright plumes, Pocahontas saw the ladies' eyes travel to her neckline, staring at the black lines of her tattoos.

"Surely you know my husband, Lord De La Warr, president of Jamestown."

Pocahontas clenched her jaw. "Yes," she said carefully, "all of Tsen . . . that is, all of Virginia knows his name."

"Have you met him, dear Rebecca? Do tell me, what is your impression of him?"

She thought of Wowinchopunck's wife and children. A swell of illness rose in her stomach. "He is . . . very bold," she managed.

Cecily's chin lifted with pride, which only heightened the unearthly floating effect of the lace collar around her face. "He is a great man, and no mistake. His mother's father was treasurer to

Queen Elizabeth, you know, and . . . but Rebecca, you look pale. Is aught the matter?"

"The journey from Virginia was long," Pocahontas said. "I suppose I am still weary—that is all."

"Fresh air will do you good. And supper. The musicians are already playing, and the garden is splendid in the afternoon light. Come, one and all! Let the feast begin!"

It was past midnight by the time they returned to the inn. A sickly crescent of moon rode dim and low in the sky, barely shining through the thick smog that blotted out all but the brightest stars. Pocahontas leaned on John's arm as they climbed the steps of the Bell Savage. Her feet ached in her fine slippers, and her scalp was tender with the weight of her piled hair and its ridiculous white crest of a hat.

She sighed at the sight of her bed, but she could not climb into it still dressed in the blue silk gown. She woke Matachanna, and together they undid Pocahontas's finery by the flickering light of a candle.

"And how was the garden delight?" Matachanna said through a yawn.

"Somewhat less than delightful."

"Oh?"

"Lady Cecily—that is, Lord De La Warr's wife—seems to have taken the same liking to me that she takes to her little pet dogs. She kept me by her side the entire evening, and all she wanted to hear was how much I admire her lord husband."

Matachanna met Pocahontas's eyes in the mirror. Her look was flat with disgust.

"You can't imagine how I longed to tell her what I truly think of him. And whenever she was not speaking of that *manitou* she calls her husband, she was asking insulting questions, or making ignorant remarks about the 'savagery' of the Real People."

Matachanna tugged the pins from Pocahontas's hair. Pocahontas hissed in pain as the black tower collapsed. Her sister's gentle fingers massaged her scalp until the throbbing ache abated.

"It made me feel sick," Pocahontas went on, "to be so false. But what could I do, except tell whatever kindly lies I could think up about Lord De La Warr, and answer Cecily's silly questions with dignity? If I turn the English away with rudeness, we may not learn what we need to know."

Matachanna nodded. *How to stop them*, her sober eyes said.

"And what do you suppose you'll tell our father when we return home?" Matachanna said quietly.

Pocahontas sighed. "I wish I knew. I ask myself the same question a hundred times each hour. He won't like to hear anything I can tell him. He wishes me to find some weakness to exploit, but as far as I can tell . . ." She fell silent, staring at the candle flame but seeing only the image of Powhatan. He looked in the vision as he had looked the last time she saw him: old and weak, reclining on his bed of furs, his lined face alight with one final hope that Pocahontas would return from England with the secret of the *tassantassas* clutched in her hand like a shining fish in an osprey's talons.

"They have no weakness." Matachanna finished the dark thought for her.

"No," Pocahontas said. "They must. All people do."

"After all, we have only been here a few days, and you've barely begun to go out in society. There is still time to learn, to find the secret we need."

"Oh, yes." Pocahontas stood, allowed Matachanna to slide the sleeves from her arms and loosen the ties of her bodice. Together they wrestled the skirt off Pocahontas's hips. "There will be many more opportunities.

"*Ever so many more*," Pocahontas imitated the Englishwoman. "Cecily intends to pack me all over London like a babe in a cradleboard, showing me off at every supper and dance and grand event she hears of.

"I'm terribly popular now, you see."

Matachanna frowned. "Just as you always wished."

"Don't tease. It's unsettling. It seems someone has written a book."

"A book? Who wrote it?"

"I don't know. A man from Jamestown, who returned to London. Some claimed it was John Smith, but how can that be? He is dead."

"Another man, then," Matachanna said sensibly. "Nearly all these *tassantassas* are called John. Cecily and her friends might have confused one John for another. The Okeus knows I can hardly tell them apart."

"That must be it," Pocahontas said. "Whoever this John is, he wrote about me, and now all of London thinks I'm a princess. Oh, Matachanna, all the suppers and parties to come—Lady Cecily and her friends will all expect me to act just like one of their royal princesses. How will I do it?"

Matachanna watched Pocahontas pull on her nightshift. "You must bear up. These suppers and dances will allow you to earn the *tassantassas*' confidence. You'll find good news for Powhatan, Sister. I know it."

When Matachanna had returned to her own room, John slipped back inside. He blew out the candle and turned down the dusty bedcover, holding up its corner so that Pocahontas could slide beneath the linen sheet. In the dark of their close, melancholy room, she curled against her husband's body and let her silent tears fall on his skin. Outside, the sounds of drunken song and slurred shouts of anger broke the stillness of the night. John stroked her hair until her breathing was smooth and regular, and then he settled himself against his pillow to sleep.

Pocahontas lay awake. Her tears were spent, but the heaviness of her spirit remained. Tomorrow night she was expected at another ball, and there was nothing she felt less like doing than dancing.

Two days after Pocahontas's first encounter with Lady Cecily De La Warr, she looked down from her window to see a large coach swinging into the courtyard of the Bell Savage. It was as dark and glossy as a blackbird's wing, pulled by three pairs of matched white horses, their bridles and harnesses decorated with swaying red plumes.

The coachman called to the inn's staff. "I have come for Lady Rebecca Rolfe."

John peered over her shoulder. "Has Cecily De La Warr sent for you again?"

She shook her head. "I was not expected—not that I know of."

They soon learned that the coach was sent to convey the Lady Rebecca and her retinue to lodgings of much better quality and vastly higher repute than the Bell Savage. Their trunks were loaded aboard—all but the chest of threadbare gowns provided by the Virginia Company. The coachman insisted that he had strict orders to leave behind any "shabby alms offered by the fine and thoughtful gentlemen of the V.C."

Pocahontas paused at the coachman's words. They seemed rehearsed, as if he had been instructed to repeat them exactly if he were challenged. Something about their cadence and air felt strangely familiar. Thomas was fussing inside the coach and would not settle until he was cradled in her lap, and so she relented, and left the chest of Virginia Company clothing to a very pleased Abigail in thanks for her good service.

The six-horse team moved swiftly through the streets of London. Along every lane, people stopped to watch the fine carriage pass, and soon they were crossing the impossible span of the bridge. The crowded houses flashed by and even merchants in their stalls stared in the carriage's wake.

On the far side of the river, the spacious estates and brick theaters of Southwark spread like a hide of plush fur, warm, inviting, and luxurious. The perfume of carefully tended gardens overtook the looming, sour stink of London and the dismal Thames. At the corners of every lane and beside the doorways of the fine houses grew shrubberies and flowering vines in green profusion.

The coach carried them to their new lodgings, a small but lovely estate at the crest of a low hill. It was as serene and secluded as any house in a city might be, dreaming quietly behind an ivy-covered wall, buffered by an expanse of manicured hedges and glossy green lawns.

"Who owns this place?" John asked of the butler who greeted them.

"Lord Markley of York, sir. But he never visits anymore. He is very old, you see. He was most pleased to make his London home available to you, at the request of your benefactor."

"Our benefactor," Pocahontas mused. "The Virginia Company?"

But the elegant man was already calling orders to the house staff, directing their trunks to this room and that.

Pocahontas shared a cautious glance with her husband. John lifted one dark brow.

In her rooms, Pocahontas found a great standing chest of polished red wood, its doors flung open. Cascades of fine embroidered silk and rich velvets spilled from its hooks and shelves.

Matachanna cried out in wonder and, setting Thomas down to toddle about on the room's patterned carpet, she buried her hands in the velvet. "By the Okeus! Look at these colors. I know nothing about *tassantassa* clothing, but even I would swear these are all new-made."

Pocahontas held up a brilliant-yellow sleeve, examined the neat stitches of the embroidery and the thick cuff of lace turned up at its end. "This certainly looks new. And very fine."

"Where did it all come from?"

"I wish I knew. John doesn't think it's a gift from the Virginia Company."

"I suppose it doesn't matter. You'll look as fine as *tassantassa* royalty in any of these dresses. You'll shine among even the best-dressed ladies, just like one of Winganuske's copper bells!"

The English summer yielded to a bright, fragrant autumn, and Pocahontas and John attended a supper party nearly every evening. Now and then they accompanied this lord or that investor to one of the many Southwark theaters, Pocahontas charming them between acts with her poise and her stories of life in the wilds of Virginia. Each morning Pocahontas would walk with Matachanna through the gardens of Lord Markley's estate, watching Thomas chase cats and sparrows while they discussed the English in hushed, careful tones.

Months had passed, yet Pocahontas had learned little that might be of use to Powhatan. She despaired to Matachanna. Despite the peace of the estate, she could not help feeling the weight of London pressing all around her like a bodice laced far too tight. Sometimes, as she and John waited for a coach to carry them off to another ball or masque, Pocahontas would lean from the house's upper window and watch the dark stain of London spreading beyond the Thames. She thought she could see it growing larger, growing denser, with its choking press of *tassantassas* day after endless day. *For all I know, every last one of them wishes to leave this place and take up residence in Tsenacomoco. The English must outnumber the Real People a hundred to one.*

Often when she strolled with Thomas in the gardens, following the erratic path of his lively, dimpled legs, her laughter would fade from her lips, and Pocahontas would find herself staring after her son in the grip of a sudden, hopeless sadness. For many days she could not identify the peculiar sorrow that cut so deep into her spirit. But at last the pain formed itself into words. She whispered them after Thomas as he ran.

"Where is your home, my son? Where do you belong? And if you belong in Tsenacomoco, will your home still be standing by the time you are a man?"

Abruptly, the image of Werowocomoco came back to her, the way it had looked on the night she had become Matoaka: the vines clinging to its exposed bones, and the bones as black as char, as black as still, cold water.

She caught Thomas up in her arms, holding him close to her heart so she could press her face to his hair and breathe in the comforting scent of him. But he did not smell like the tobacco fields or the turned, damp earth and the pine smoke of their home fire. He smelled like London. It was a bitter, hard smell. But it smelled like certainty—like a future. *A form of survival*, she thought, recalling with a bleak tremor Naukaquawis chasing the children from the crow tower while she stood at his side, cloaked in the disguise of an Englishwoman. *But not the survival you had hoped for.*

She let Thomas slide from her arms again, and stood still while he bolted down a gravel path, away from her, into the English landscape. After a time, when he had disappeared from sight, Pocahontas lifted the weight of her skirts and walked resolutely after her son.

The bright autumn faded rapidly to weeks of cold drizzle, and finally to a scattered, wet snow that bent the branches of the garden's hedges beneath its gray weight. Robed in thick velvet and soft furs, Pocahontas, Matachanna, and Utta-ma-tomakkin walked along the garden's central path. Tiny birds flickered and hopped within the icy palisades of the hedges, chanting *chip-chip* as Pocahontas passed. But their lively voices did not cheer her. She had spent six months in England, and she was no closer to learning what might quell the flood of *tassantassas* to Tsenacomoco's shores. In the dark, cold days of winter, she felt surer than ever before that it could not be done.

She took Matachanna by the hand. Her sister's palm was warm against her own. "It has been a long six months. Long and tiring."

Utta-ma-tomakkin huffed through his nose. "It has indeed."

Pocahontas glanced at him from the corner of her eye. "Whatever became of your counting stick? The one Powhatan instructed you to notch for every *tassantassa* you saw?"

"That," Matachanna said darkly. "He broke it into pieces and tossed it in the fire back at that dirty house where we first lodged. Didn't you, Tomakkin?"

The priest shrugged. "It's no use counting them. There isn't a name for a number so large."

"And what of your other task," Pocahontas said, "to see their god, to learn whether God has a weakness?"

"I have conversed with many of their priests, discussed their rituals, talked my way into temples to observe their worship. Their god has no form—he is invisible. How can the people of an invisible god be so . . ."

Great. She was afraid to say the word aloud.

They walked on in silence, but a furious current swelled in her heart, a rising rush of words and fears that beat at her spirit until she feared she would scream, or laugh. Or run.

She breathed unsteadily, and then said, "Many of the people I have met here—Cecily De La Warr and others—have asked me if I don't intend to stay in London."

Matachanna grunted in disgust. "For how much longer?"

Pocahontas stopped walking. "For all time."

"Of course you said no."

Pocahontas chewed her lip.

"Oh—Pocahontas! You can't even consider it. Tell me you're not considering it."

"Hear me, please."

But Matachanna dropped Pocahontas's hand. She balled her fists and gripped the folds of her winter cloak. "It's the love they show you, isn't it? You haven't changed a bit since you were a child, chasing power—hungry for attention."

Utta-ma-tomakkin laid a hand on his wife's shoulder. "Let her speak."

"Matachanna, you've seen London with your own eyes," Pocahontas said. "You've seen their ships in the river, gathered and waiting to sail for our land." She swept her arm out across the stillness of the garden, but they all knew that she indicated what lay beyond its walls—the dark stain of stone and coal dust creeping across the land. "There is no stopping this, Matachanna. There is no going back. And I have my son to think of. What life shall I give Thomas? Shall I send him back to Tsenacomoco, to watch his people driven out of their territories? To watch children thrown from the decks of ships and shot like deer in a fire ring? At least here, Thomas can be . . ."

"A *tassantassa*," Matachanna said.

Pocahontas shook her head. "Safe. Happy."

"How can you expect anyone to be happy in London? Stone walls, no trees, no fields . . . and an invisible god, a god your son can never see . . ."

"I just want him," Pocahontas said, eyes filling with tears, "to have a home. I want him to have a land he can always return to, no matter where he might travel . . . A home he knows will always be there, waiting for him, as it ever was." She covered her face with her hands. The cold of winter scraped her knuckles. It bit at her skin. "*We* no longer have that, you and I. You know how much Tsenacomoco has changed since the white men first came. It's not the same place it once was. We aren't the same people we were.

Look how our father was forced to slink to Orapax to avoid the English."

"Opechancanough isn't in Orapax—not anymore. He's returned to Pamunkey for good, and he holds his tribe strong in the face of the invaders."

"That was true when we left. But we've been away six months. Does Opechancanough still live? Does our father live? We can't even know whether there's a longhouse left standing in the forest! That uncertainty—I cannot wish it on my son."

"But what of you? What of your spirit? Can you truly stay here, and idle with Lady De La Warr, talking of how admirable her husband is? Can you allow yourself to be so false? Pocahontas, please. Think of what you're saying."

"I can do anything for Thomas. I *will* do anything, to give him a future. I will endure whatever must be endured, to shelter him from the loss of all that's dear to me."

Utta-ma-tomakkin took her gently by the arm. "But it is dear to you. The villages, the temples, the Okeus. The songs and chants— our ways, our land. Shouldn't your son know these things, too?"

Pocahontas scrubbed at her eyes with the edge of her cloak. "I'd rather he never knew our way of life at all, if he must lose it—if he must feel the loss I have felt. I would rather he be all English, and not Real at all. I would rather raise him knowing nothing but English ways, for losing the world as it was is a pain too great for any heart to bear."

"There may yet be a way . . ." But Utta-ma-tomakkin trailed off into silence. They all had seen the realities of London, the uncountable mass of the English. They all felt how fragile, how tenuous, their hope was now. It was a wisp of vapor. It was the thread of a spider's web, beautiful and bright, and strained to the point of breaking.

Matachanna's breath was ragged and faint. "I can't quarrel with you, Pocahontas. I love you too much to argue." She wrapped her arms around Pocahontas's shoulders, and Pocahontas pressed her face against Matachanna's neck. She wept openly.

"You are right," Matachanna said. "Tsenacomoco may not be standing now. And if it is, it may not remain whole for long. But it is *our* land, *our* way of life. And Thomas is not only English. He is a Real Person, too. Think on that, before you decide."

Pocahontas glanced up, past the short fringe of Matachanna's hair. Utta-ma-tomakkin stared into the depth of the garden, his eyes distant and pained. In his *tassantassa* clothing, the priest looked stunned and half-complete. It was as if the majesty he carried in the temples of Tsenacomoco had been wrenched from him like an arrowhead ripped from wounded flesh. The pale light of winter reflecting from the snow surrounded him in unaccustomed light. It beat back the shadows of the temple, the cloak of mystery that was his source of power. In the stark light of London, the powerful young priest looked as broken as an old pot discarded by the river.

POCAHONTAS

January 1617

The maid drew a long steel pin from a wooden box. The pin flashed in the light of the candles, a momentary glint of silver like a fish rising to the surface of the river. Pocahontas closed her eyes as the maid bent to her work, securing the requisite hat within the high, mounded nest of black hair. She breathed deeply, seeking the smell of the river, the salty ripple and flicker of fish among the weeds. But the air of her room smelled of candles—warm, dripping tallow; oily smoke—and nothing more.

John rapped at the door and entered when she bade him. He looked nothing like the tobacco farmer he was. His brocaded doublet was alive with embroidery, bright twists of vine and flower against dark crushed velvet. Rows of gold buttons decorated the sleeves from cuff to elbow. At his upper arm, the slashes in the fabric allowed the linen of his undershirt to peek through, a match to the wide ruff of lace that draped in triple thickness across his shoulders. It was difficult to imagine such a man hoeing and planting and, in the season of harvest, tying the fans of tobacco leaf high on the racks to dry.

The change suits him, she told herself. *He looks dashing—winning.* Yet she preferred him with earth on his hands and sweat soaking through the dingy cloth of his shirt.

We must grow used to this new life. It is best for Thomas—it is secure. There could be no growing of tobacco in London, of course. What land would they farm? And at any rate, John had learned at their parties and suppers that King James was in opposition to the stuff. The king might soon seek to outlaw it. *We shall find a new livelihood.*

Or perhaps they would have no need. The benefactor who had first rescued them from the Bell Savage had continued in his kindness, sending the best of food, fine horses and a private coach, toys for Thomas, and more ornaments and fine fabrics than Pocahontas could ever hope to wear. Perhaps the mysterious stranger's support would continue, and Thomas would grow up in ease and luxury, with no need to fear for his survival.

The maid finished her work. Pocahontas stood, then smoothed and tucked the pleats of her skirt where they fell from the rounded point of her bodice's stomacher. Her dress was made of brocade, as rich and red as *puccoon*. A stiff wire choker supported her fine lace collar, which spread below her face like wings, delicate and transparent as a spider's web.

"You look lovely," John said. His voice was low, nearly sad. "I never would have guessed that half a year ago you were crushing grubs in a tobacco field."

"I was thinking the same of you only a moment ago."

"I never crushed grubs. You reserved that sport for yourself."

She smiled, but looked away. "John, I think . . . I think we ought to remain in London."

Silence filled the room. She dared to glance at him—his face was still with shock.

At last he said, "Have you grown to love the city so well?"

"I am only thinking of our son. He will have more opportunity here, more security. And he won't be made to watch as his mother's people are driven away. Or worse."

"But there has been peace in Virginia since you and I married."

"Is there still? We have been away so long. And if there is, how long can peace last? When I was a child, I thought my people were great. We were so numerous, no force in the world could stop what my father had created. We were one powerful force, made of many parts." She gave one sad laugh that was nearer a sob. "*Many*. But now I know what that word truly means. There is no stopping the English migration, John. I know that now.

"We came to London so that I might find some way to salvage our world. But now I see clearly. There is no saving it. We might only hope to delay what cannot be stopped. Perhaps it is better— not only for Thomas, but for all of us—to accept the world as it will be, rather than fight to save what is doomed to die."

He came to her and touched her face gently. Pocahontas closed her eyes tightly so that he could not see her tears.

"Are you sure?" John said.

"I can never be sure of it. My spirit cries out to me. It tells me to go home. It . . . *commands*. But Tsenacomoco was *my* home, and one day it will vanish like mist in the morning. What place can my son call home? What place calls to his spirit?"

He kissed her hand. "Rebecca, my sweet lady—my good, brave wife. Don't think on it now. We've time yet to decide."

But as they boarded the coach, as they made their way down the hill and through the brightly lit theater district of Southwark, Pocahontas stared beyond the Thames to London. Dim lights flickered amid the dense blackness, an unbearably wide swath of them. The lights were too many to count, as numerous as seeds spilled from a basket, as numerous as stars.

There is no time, she thought, and turned away from the sight of London to take John's hand.

The king's Twelfth Night Masque was to be the grandest affair of the season. It was held at the royal banqueting house of Whitehall, a lush structure of white stone two stories high. It glowed in the winter moonlight. Pocahontas and John were shown at once to their seats—the finest in the house, save for the royal seats, the steward assured her. She sank into her chair, cushioned with deep-blue velvet, and stared.

Even through her troubled fog, the banqueting house impressed her. It was a long hall with a smooth, dark floor, so well polished that the rows of marble pillars along its edges reflected like birch trunks mirrored in a still forest pool. A railed balcony stretched high along the walls. Ladies in bright gowns clustered there, swaying and nodding like a field of wildflowers, whispering behind the rays of their fans. High above her, the soaring ceiling was a glory of gold leaf and carving and paintings of Christian heroes and saints. Pocahontas gazed in wonder at the ceiling's pinnacle, where a great oval of gold ringed a gathering of angels, painted as if they stood upon a pane of glass and gazed past their bare toes at the people crowded in the hall below.

At one end of the hall was a stage, layered with lush drapings and set-piece panels. Their seats were very near the stage, and Pocahontas watched it eagerly for signs that the masque would soon begin. In her time in Southwark, Pocahontas had come to appreciate plays and other theater performances. At first, they had confused and frustrated her. She couldn't understand why the people on the stage did not simply *tell* their stories in the proper way, rather than being deceitful and acting as if they lived in the world of legend. But with time she understood that this was simply the English manner of storytelling, and she was soon caught up in the tales of treacherous kings and conquering heroes, of weeping maids and scheming wives.

"And so," a rather high and casual voice called, "I see our Virginia savage has joined us."

John was already rising to his feet before the man stopped speaking. He helped Pocahontas out of her seat and led her by the hand, a few short steps away to where a slight figure sat poised on an ornately carved chair. The man had a long, thin nose that was as flushed and ruddy as his bony cheeks. His sharp, daring eyes were deep sunk. As he raised a hand to stroke a pointed chestnut beard, a few pale crumbs fell onto his doublet.

John bowed deeply and Pocahontas, following his lead, sank into a curtsey.

"Your Grace," John said.

Pocahontas stole a second glance at the slender man: *King James, the* mamanatowick *of England.*

Beside the king's chair sat a low table on which rested a silver tray with an array of delicacies and an enameled decanter of dark-red wine. On the other side of the table, Pocahontas caught the glimmer of thread-of-gold embroidery against lush ivory silk. She lifted her gaze a fraction more and saw the skirt and bodice of an exceptionally well-dressed woman. Above the woman's winged lace collar was a serene face. Queen Anne's once-golden hair was dulled by gray, but her skin was still smooth and fine. She caught Pocahontas's eye and smiled graciously before Pocahontas gasped and dropped her stare to the floor, face burning as red as her bodice.

"John Rolfe," said King James, "fresh from the colony."

"Not so fresh, I think, my king," the queen said quietly. Her voice was musical and gentle. "They have been in London half a year."

King James selected a small cake from his tray, which he ate before continuing. It left a smear of honey on his beard. "And Lady Rebecca, the wild princess of the forest."

Queen Anne looked pointedly away from her royal husband. "It is a pleasure to make your acquaintance, Lady Rebecca." The queen extended her hand. Pocahontas took it and curtseyed over it as she had been taught.

"Thank you, Your Grace," she said as John bent to offer his courtesies to the queen.

"You must come to court, Lady Rebecca, and share with me all your stories. I so long to see Virginia with my own eyes. Is it very beautiful?"

"We haven't anything in Virginia as fine as this hall," Pocahontas said, "but the land itself is unrivaled in beauty. It is as rich as any tapestry, Your Grace."

"Rich," the king grunted sourly. "That it is *not*. Though the good Lord knows how the Virginia Company have tried to convince me otherwise."

Pocahontas stood with hands clasped at her waist while John answered the king's queries about Virginia—its soil, its crops, its distressing lack of gold, and its unsettling ability to nurture the tobacco that King James so abhorred, and which he feared would make its way across the Atlantic in ever greater quantities to swamp his Godly kingdom with vice.

She surreptitiously watched the king: his curt gestures, his pinched red face, the crumbs speckling his doublet and beard. His manner was short and ungracious toward John, dismissive and nearly mocking toward Pocahontas herself, though his wife did what she could to soften the king's verbal blows. A queasy sensation built beneath her heart as the king spoke on. *This is your* mamanatowick *now, the man to whom you must always be loyal and true.* She thought of her father in his younger days. Even in old age he possessed a regal strength. She thought of Opechancanough, fierce-tempered but wise, made to lead men and lead them well.

Pocahontas turned her face away from the king.

The crowd swelled—a mass of whirling skirts and glinting doublets, of ruffs bouncing on shoulders and goblets rising in the sun-gold light of hundreds of candles. Musicians took their places beside the stage, and the tentative chords of tuning harps and violins wafted about the hall, chased by the assertive, reedy voice of the curtal. Here and there, Pocahontas gleaned bits of conversation, as she had done at so many parties before, sifting through the stray words for any secret she might carry home to Powhatan.

"How is your husband, Lady Grace?"

"He has been most unwell, I am sorry to say."

"It isn't the flux, is it? I've heard it has made its way back into the city."

"Christ protect us, let us hope not."

A flicker caught Pocahontas's eye—a flash between the shoulders of two laughing men. Her spirit filled with the prickling sensation of recognition. She peered more sharply into the crowd, but whatever specter had taunted her memory was gone.

The tuning orchestra fell silent. King James dismissed them to their seats and turned eagerly toward the stage. As she dropped once more into a curtsey, a figure moved at the periphery of Pocahontas's vision—stocky, strong, with a dark-golden beard and a characteristic swagger. She looked about anxiously as she and John found their seats once more.

"What is it?" John said.

"I thought I saw . . ." But she hushed, for candles throughout the hall extinguished. The branches of light surrounding the stage seemed to leap and flare.

With a burst of music, the stage came to life. Curtains and sets dragged apart, revealing not the actors Pocahontas was used to seeing but strange creatures in gaudy costume, with heads of bright, bobbing plumes and trailing fabric tails. They chanted and sang of the delights of the garden. But the sets that grew up around them were grotesque parodies of fields—tall and spindly stalks, flowers that shouted in rhyme, leaves that unrolled across the stage like long green parchment scrolls. Masked figures stepped from hidden doors and uncovered their faces to reveal yet more masks beneath. And on and on the chants went, praising beauty while all about her an excess of color and sound clamored in a show of vulgarity that made Pocahontas shrink into the velvet cushions of her seat.

This was not the English storytelling she had come to know and love. There was no clear story here, no moral message, not even a single character whose tale she could follow. It was nothing more than a parade of riches, crude in its ostentation.

When the time came for the traditional comic reprieve, the antimasque performers came tumbling from behind their doors, crowing and waggling their overstuffed codpieces. They made coarse jokes, cavorting through the rows of onlookers, trailing glittering silk as they ran. While her wary eyes watched them, the stage was reset, and she turned back to find that nothing looked as it did before. Pocahontas usually enjoyed the respite of the anti-masque, the relief from the masque's heavy themes—but now she gripped her husband's hand as a new onslaught of garish visions overwhelmed her.

At last, three hours later, the final scene came to a close. The actors froze in a tableau as a great length of painted black silk unrolled from the ceiling, covering the stage in a blanket of stars, the Chariot of Night flying like a brilliant moon across the banner. Pocahontas tried to steady her breathing as the audience applauded.

John eyed her with concern. "Are you well?"

"Tired," she said faintly. "Only tired."

"I'll call for the coach, then."

As they stood to take their leave, Pocahontas's eye lighted on a mask that had been discarded by one of the actors. It had the shape of a bird's face, beaked and feathered. It leered up at her with piercing, mocking eyes. No natural bird looked that way—no bird of Tsenacomoco. She watched it warily for a moment, as if it might spring from the stage, crying with the voice of a thousand crows. The mask did not move, of course, but her skin prickled with apprehension.

She lifted her skirts and hurried after her husband.

.   .   .

Pocahontas's head nodded as the coach made its way back to Lord Markley's estate. She could not lean against John's shoulder and sleep—not with the wide lace collar about her neck nor with her hair heaped beneath the tall white hat. But all the way through the quiet blackness of the Southwark night, Pocahontas's spirit hovered in an uneasy half dream.

The brazen figures from the masque crowded around her, gripping her with hard hands so that she could not pull away. She looked into their faces. She stared beyond masks of feather and fur, of glittering gems and golden braid. The eyes that stared back at her were sunken and sharp like the eyes of King James. In the black pupil of each, she saw a flicker of red fire, and she remembered the Okeus burning.

At the estate, the doorman rushed to the steps to intercept them.

"Please, Master Rolfe, begging your pardon. You have—that is, the Lady Rebecca has—a visitor."

John and Pocahontas stared at one another.

"A visitor?" John said. "What do you mean?"

"He waits in the drawing room, sir. He only just arrived, moments before you."

Pocahontas seized her skirts, willing her weary feet to rush up the stairs.

"Here, Rebecca," John called after her. "Wait!"

But she swept into the drawing room before her husband could stop her.

There he stood in the spilling light of the fireplace, already half turned toward the drawing room door, as if he'd expected her to be there. Gone were the old woolens, the mail shirt that smelled of rust and oil. He wore a fine coat now, with slashed sleeves and bright embroidery, and well-tailored breeches tucked into boots that reflected the fire's flicker and dance from their burnished surface. The hair and beard were the same, thick and golden. He had tamed them somewhat, neatened them with scissor and comb.

John Smith clasped his hands behind his back and smiled at her. It was a timid smile—an expression she had never before seen on that bold, haughty face.

"*Wingapoh*, Pocahontas."

The sound of the name raised a hard lump in her throat. She turned away from him abruptly, all the words chased from her mind, both English and Real.

"I . . . I am happy to see you looking so well," Smith ventured.

She shook her head and would not meet his gaze. She felt as though the beings in their masks crowded around her, reaching out from the firelight, striving to pull her into the flames. She planted her feet to the drawing room carpet and went on shaking her head, silent and resisting.

John Rolfe eased himself into the room. He glanced from Pocahontas to Smith, and then extended his hand to the visitor. "Come, friend. Let us give her some time. She will speak when she has found the words."

When her husband had shut the door softly and Pocahontas was alone with the firelight, she clawed at the collar around her neck. The wires bent and she tore it free, hurling it onto a nearby table. She found the steel hatpin with trembling fingers and tugged it away. A dozen ebony hairpins followed. They clicked against the table when she dropped them. She worried at the knots of her lacings until her bodice loosened, and she sank onto an ivory-colored settee, gasping and raking her hair with her fingers until it hung straight once more, draping over the red brocade of her gown.

For a long while, Pocahontas held herself apart from all thought and all emotion. She was as stunned as a rabbit in torchlight, glassy-eyed and staring, conscious of nothing but her beating heart. Then, slowly, tentatively, she examined the vision again of Smith standing beside the fire, waiting for her to arrive, knowing she would soon be there. Was it truly his face, or just another false mask? Were those his eyes that looked at her, or was it the piercing stare of King James, with the smoke of Uttamussak darkening his gaze?

Your new mamanatowick, *your king.* She raked her hands through her hair again, pulling it, and felt a silent cry tear at her throat.

When she had finally composed herself, her mind flooded with words. Her tongue burned to speak them.

She found the two men in the parlor. A fire blazed in its hearth, and they conversed over cups of wine. Both looked strained and weary. Their conversation ceased when her red skirts filled the parlor doorway. The wine cups returned to the table with unison clinks.

"The two of you have much to discuss," her husband said, rising from his chair. "I'll leave you." He paused a moment to squeeze her hand as he left.

The fire crackled in the silence.

"What am I to make of you, standing here in my parlor?" she said at last. Her voice shook, but she did not care.

"Pocahontas . . ."

"They told me you were dead. The men at the fort . . . at Jamestown."

"They believed it was so. I nearly believed it myself. I was badly injured, and they sent me back to England to die."

Her face began to crumple as she fought back the tears. "Are you here? Or are you some vision from the masque? I cannot tell the difference anymore—what is real and what is not."

"I'm here. Little Sister, I'm here." He stepped toward her with his hands out, as if she might grasp them to verify his reality.

But Pocahontas stepped back. "It seems I cannot be sure. Nothing is certain anymore. My father sent me to England to learn the truth of your people—whatever truth I could find on my own, for none of us can trust what an Englishman says."

"And what did you learn?" Smith asked gently.

Pocahontas drew a long, careful breath. It felt good, to breathe so deeply with the laces of her bodice hanging loose like a buckskin fringe. "That there are too many of you."

Smith lowered his eyes. A ripple of shame obscured his features, as if she were looking at him through a drifting veil of smoke.

She tossed her head. "So it was you. You at the masque—I thought I saw you. And you all along: the gifts, the fine carriage, this estate . . ."

"Yes."

"You once called Powhatan *father*, when you were the stranger in my land. And now you care for me as if I am your child. Shall I also call you *father*, then?"

"Please," he said, "don't be angry. I meant no insult by it. It only seemed the right thing to do."

"Right in what way?"

"After I returned to England, I wrote of my experiences with the Real People . . . with you. The book was published. I'm afraid it made me something of a celebrity. When I learned you were in England, it seemed only just to share my wealth with you, in whatever way I could."

"So it was you after all, who wrote the book. Your book is the talk of all London, but I refused to believe it could truly have been you who wrote it."

"I have heard," Smith said, grinning sheepishly, "that you have been the most sought-after guest at every affair in London."

"Oh, yes." She laughed bitterly. "It seems I fit right in. I may as well delight my gracious hosts and become their countryman— swear my allegiance to King James." She stared into the fire.

"Are you truly considering it?" Smith said after a pause.

When she looked up at him, hot tears broke and streaked down her face.

Smith's eyes went dull with sudden, stunned pain. His mouth opened as if he might speak, but he held his peace.

Then he took up a small velvet pouch that hung from his belt. He reached inside. A necklace of white beads rose from the bag like the first smoke of a newly kindled fire, delicate and pale. Smith placed the beads in her hand.

Pocahontas lifted them to the firelight and let the smooth, cool beads slide one by one through her fingers. She noted the red yarn they were strung on, and her breath caught in her throat. She looked up at Smith with a sudden, hot rush of gratitude.

When they said their awkward farewells, Pocahontas knew— in the same way she'd known it about Kocoum—that she would never see John Smith again. She wandered the sleeping halls of the estate, pressing the old, worn bead necklace between her fingers, until she found her husband. John had left the double doors to the garden open wide. A wisp of snow curled into the house, stirred by a nighttime breeze. John stood among the blue-gray pathways, his doublet cast away, the simple white linen of his shirt stark and bright against the black lines of the hedges.

Pocahontas went to him, twining the beads around her fingers as she walked. They were cool as the river in the morning when it rose to the level of her heart. They were as white and hard as the bones of a *werowance*, laid in the silence of the temple.

John looked at her expectantly.

"I have decided," she said, and wrapped her arms around his warmth.

POCAHONTAS

March 1617

The weather was not fair enough for sailing until many weeks later, and, when it cleared, the illness that had crept through London's streets and gutters, through its theaters and fine houses, had laid a strong hold on the city. Even isolated as they were in Southwark, on their borrowed estate, the Rolfe household did not escape the flux.

First Matachanna fell ill, then little Thomas. Pocahontas cared for them both devotedly, and joined with Utta-ma-tomakkin to sing the chants that would drive the demons of illness from their bodies.

She feared for them, especially for the boy, who was so tiny and pale in his sickbed. She had heard rumors that the flux sometimes brought on a fever, and that children who managed to survive the terrible purging of the flux were nonetheless struck blind by the heat of their own suffering bodies. But the sound of Utta-ma-tomakkin's rattle kept up her courage, and the scent of holy tobacco smoke comforted her with its biting sting.

The spirits were merciful. Thomas rebounded from the illness as bright-eyed and full of questions as he had always been, and, several days later, Matachanna felt well enough to walk in the weak sunshine of the garden.

"Compared to crossing the sea," she said, laying a hand to one still-pale cheek with trepidation, "the flux was like dancing at a harvest festival. Are you *sure* you don't want to stay in London, Pocahontas?"

Pocahontas squeezed her sister's hand. "If you feel well enough to tease me, then we are certainly going home."

"I'm glad of it. Even if it means crossing the sea once more. Even if . . ."

Matachanna did not finish her thought, but she had no need to speak on. Pocahontas knew what her sister would say. *Even if there is nothing left.*

On a fine, blue spring day, they boarded a small ship called the *George*. Pocahontas watched London drift away as the ship rode the Thames's current out to sea. Her heart was light, and as she watched Thomas chase the gulls along the ship's rail, her spirit sang a soft, hopeful song of homecoming.

But before they had left English waters, a shivering weakness crept into her bones, and her bowels cramped with every step she took and every lurch of the *George* against the waves. When she refused to climb the ladder and rest on the deck where the air was fresh and the seabirds screamed, John asked the captain to turn the *George* back toward land.

They found harbor at the village of Gravesend. John located a house that was happy to board the Virginia princess and her retinue, then Utta-ma-tomakkin carried her to her bed. As she looked up from his strong arms, the priest's face was hard with concern. She spoke to him, telling him not to fear, that she would see Tsenacomoco soon—they would all see it soon, and the forest would be full of longhouses, as round as ripe fruit, and the smoke would hang above the treetops, and the canoes would move like lovers in the night, their torches shining double on the water— *you'll see, Utta-ma-tomakkin, you'll see.* But her words sounded like a sigh, and the priest's eyes were distant, staring among the spirits as they always did.

Pocahontas could feel the spirits. They moved about her, flashing as they passed, like silver fish turning on the surface of the river.

The bed where they laid her was broad and soft. It was made of lashed saplings, piled high with mats as warm and plush as rabbit fur. She turned to Matachanna, to ask her how she had made such a fine bed in an English house, but Matachanna's face was wet with tears, and she only shook her head and clutched Pocahontas's hand. She would not answer.

John was there, holding her hand whenever Matachanna dropped it, pressing the backs of her cold fingers to his forehead. She brushed back his dark hair and felt soil against his skin. His smell was tobacco and earth and the sweat of a day's labor. His smell was the bed they shared at Henrico, the mingled scent of their two bodies, the flesh that had made their son.

Matachanna bent over her and kissed her forehead. *Oh,* Pocahontas said, startled at the weakness of her voice, *you've made a mess of my yellow paint.*

She did not know how much time passed. Days, perhaps, or hours, while she sank into the depth of the sleeping mats and the longhouse settled on its frame. The umber shadows soothed her, surrounding her with the odors of pine smoke and drying herbs and the musty, feral scent of furs.

Utta-ma-tomakkin's rattle shook like rain above her head. It spoke like thunder in a dream, hollow and rolling. The rattle and the chants never ceased—until they finally did, and the priest fell onto a high-backed chair with his head in his hands.

Get up, Matachanna said, her voice high and distant, the voice of a girl who has not yet entered the sweat lodge. *You're sleeping, and there is work to be done.*

Pocahontas rose up. Someone had painted her arms and chest with *puccoon*. The paint seemed to lift her, driving the weakness from her limbs—the paint, and the incense of tobacco, which filled the air, pungent and rich.

There is work to be done.

Yes. There was work to be done—there were words welling in her spirit, clamoring on her tongue.

She looked around the room. John was bent and weeping over the frail brown hand still clutched against his forehead. Matachanna rocked, head back, her mouth open in a cry of pain Pocahontas could not hear. The priest was slumped and spent. At his feet lay a long stick carved all about with notches, an uncountable number incised into the pale flesh of the wood.

Pocahontas moved past them. She felt the cool dry whiteness of clay dust on her face. In the bright light of the garden, the hedges were alive with the shiver and flash of spirits. They danced in a thousand colors; they whispered together like a forest in the wind.

Thomas played in the grass, chasing thrushes that waited for him to come, and then sprang into the air and glided farther down the lawn. Thomas—his black hair, his wondering eyes. His skin was the color of earth, of tanned hide, of cornstalks when the season is spent.

She went to him and lifted the boy in her arms.

The words that had filled her spirit loosed. They moved like a flock of blackbirds, clamoring, winging, rising to the pinnacle of a bright and vibrant sky.

My son, she whispered, *the Okeus calls to you. Go back to your home.*

For however long it remains, yours is the land of the forest, of the river that rises and falls with the pulsing heart of the sea. Yours is the longhouse, the temple, the face carved on the spirit post.

For you are one torch in a circle of fire; you are the deer that lifts its feet in the ring.

For you are earth and spirit, ochre and fire. And tidewater is your blood.

HISTORICAL NOTE

and Author's Remarks

I wrote *Tidewater* in record time, considering it's twice the size of my previous books and I was still working at a full-time day job for the first half of the novel's creation. I started it on March 15, 2014, and finished the final edits (for the self-published edition, at least) and the formatting on July 14 of the same year. From March through May I brought the book to eighty thousand words, and on June 1, I quit my job to write full time. I completed the first draft of *Tidewater* before the end of June, accumulating another eighty thousand words in twenty-five days of nonstop work, and I sent it off to my editor on June 26.

How can it be that I could write a novel of this scope with relative ease, but I can't find a sensible place to start the historical note? When I think about *Tidewater*—the novel and the history behind it—I feel overwhelmed. Perhaps that is a natural emotion for a person who has just written and revised 160,000 words in 119 days.

But I think it has less to do with the workload and more to do with my emotional response to this crucial and tragic bit of American history. And so I am not going to try to make this a straightforward historical note full of fact and rationality, as my notes usually are. I feel I can't talk about this piece of history without some emotional involvement, so I'm giving you a historical note injected with a bit of my personal feelings and something of the story of how *Tidewater* came to be.

The idea of writing a novel about Pocahontas first sparked in my brain in 2011. My now husband, then boyfriend, Paul, was deployed to the Middle East, and I was working at a used-book store. I often seized the opportunity to restock the history and biography shelves, as I'd frequently find obscure books on fascinating subjects that filled my head with all kinds of potential novels-to-be and kept my mind off the danger Paul was in—for a while, at least. I unearthed a book about Pocahontas and her family during one such restocking adventure. It was *Pocahontas, Powhatan, Opechancanough: Three Indian Lives Changed by Jamestown*, by Helen C. Rountree.

I perused it on my lunch break, flipping here and there through its pages, and it was all pretty fascinating stuff. But for some reason, the description of Powhatan people's fashion really grabbed me. Perhaps it was because the reality of what these people wore and how they did their hair was so unlike the way Disney represented them in the 1995 film. But for some reason, I couldn't get the image of these people out of my mind: wearing virtually nothing but leather aprons, tattooed and painted, with their heads half-shaven and their hair done up in knots displaying the most extravagant ornaments.

I came up with many other ideas for historical novels during my bookstore days, but I've forgotten or abandoned most of them. The lavish hairstyles of the Powhatans, though, stuck with me. I began reading about Pocahontas obsessively—all the books I could find (listed at the end of this note, for curious readers who would like to explore the truth of this historical tale). And as I came to learn more about her and her people, I was shocked by how different the truth was from the popular myth of star-crossed lovers that has made Pocahontas immortal.

I was shocked, but I really shouldn't have been. The Western world has a long history of treating indigenous peoples with varying degrees of disrespect. On one end of the spectrum, they were and are treated with open hostility and racism. On the other, they are seen as morally flawless, enlightened beings, "noble savages" who had it all right until those white guys came along and screwed up utopia. I find the latter just as inappropriate as the former, because it lumps a huge variety of cultures into one generic category. It strips from these people their real identities, their true heritage. It makes Native Americans of the past, like Pocahontas, into morality lessons instead of celebrating them as individuals whose lives changed the course of history, and whose influence still echoes today. It places a featureless mask onto all of them—the Natives of history and those living now.

As I read several books on the Powhatan Algonquians—Rountree's and others'—I knew I wanted desperately to tell Pocahontas's story—the story of an unavoidable clash between two vastly different cultures; a clash which could never end in fairness for both sides of the conflict. It was a story fraught with intense conflict and tragic figures who were determined in the face of a fate they surely knew they could not hope to escape. It was big, dense, complicated history—the kind of stuff historical novelists can't resist. But I wanted to do it *right*. I wanted to represent the people of the Powhatan Confederacy as they probably were, not as the stock characters Western culture so often demands of Native American figures.

Chief Powhatan, for example, was not the most ethical man. He definitely does not fit with the pop-culture caricature of a Native, living in harmony with all around him. When an alleged prophecy predicted that Powhatan would be defeated by people who emerged from the Chesapeake region, he decided to nip that in the bud and massacred the entirety of the Chesapeake tribe. He was an aggressive expansionist who maintained order in his ever-growing empire by marrying women from every family he could find, getting them pregnant, then keeping the offspring with him in his capital city of Werowocomoco, raising them to believe in his own politics. Powhatan demanded "tribute" from all his conquered tribes—a tithe of sorts, whereby he collected a portion of all other tribes' goods: crops, hunted meat, skins, and other valuables such as beads and *puccoon*. In spite of the Western desire to see all Native Americans as enlightened and harmonious people who understood how to be human better than anybody else did, Chief Powhatan most assuredly did *not* paint with all the colors of the wind.

And he wasn't the only one.

My desire to "do it right" posed a real problem, for the Pocahontas myth of popular culture is a story hugely beloved by many, many people. The myth is so widely known that I don't even need to recap it here. I can virtually guarantee that you've read it or heard it before, even if you aren't a North American, even if you haven't seen the Disney film five hundred times. It's a well-known myth.

It's also, except for a few very tiny and insignificant details, completely false.

"Pocahontas" was a nickname, meaning (in the English of the early 1600s) "little wanton," or as we would say today, "mischief maker" or "scamp." The girl's real name was, depending on whom you consult, either Amonute or Matoaka, or perhaps both. The Algonquians of the Tidewater region changed their names at momentous points in their lives, and so it is not unlikely that she was known by all three names at various points in her life. Later, when she married John Rolfe and took up Christianity, her name changed again to Rebecca—a change which Rountree posits was probably natural for her to make, since adopting a new religion and English ways was almost certainly one of those momentous points in life that call for a new name. I tried to show the Powhatan tradition of changing names in this novel without confounding the reader. It was quite a trick for an author to pull off, and I can only hope that I did it well and that you were not too terribly confused.

Contrary to the popular myth, Pocahontas was not a young woman when she met John Smith. She was a prepubescent child who likely had zero interest in romance. John Smith and the rest of the English would have been a curiosity to her, or perhaps, as I showed in my novel, she might have visited them in order to learn what she could about their culture and plans, and transmit that information to her father. She was apparently quick with languages and often served as an interpreter and negotiator on her father's behalf, in spite of her extreme youth.

So, then, if she was likely not interested in romance, why did she rescue John Smith from death? Everybody knows she threw herself across his body to save him from the war clubs before her father and his savage warriors could beat out Smith's brains.

Well—*no*.

The infamous "rescue scene" was my one concession to the myth, and the only place where I went against historical fact for the sake of fiction. I felt I truly could not exclude the scene, as it is stamped so firmly in the zeitgeist. When one thinks of Pocahontas, one pictures an Indian maiden throwing herself across the body of a doomed white man—even though Pocahontas's real accomplishments, her intellect and skill with language, her willingness to work with the English to try to forge some sort of peace—amount to so much more than the mythic "rescue."

But the real achievements of women in history are so often ignored, and we are remembered only for our relationships to influential men. In truth, it's not even a problem confined to history—it's a sad fact of our culture that persists to this day. Double that obnoxious truth for any historic woman of color, who will only be remembered for her relationships with *white* men, even if those relationships are fictitious.

While many historians have proposed conceivable reasons why the mythic rescue *could* have happened, because they want the exciting and touching myth to be true, I am thoroughly convinced by Rountree's evidence that it almost certainly did *not* happen. John Smith claimed it did, but it was not the only time he'd claimed that a besotted female in a foreign land had risked her own life to spare him from death. It was actually a pretty common theme in Smith's autobiographies, and, although Pocahontas was known in English accounts as "the favorite" of her powerful father, she was actually a girl of very low social standing, and not any kind of "princess" who might be able to stop her father from killing anybody he wanted to kill.

If her father was Chief Powhatan, the most influential and powerful man in the Tidewater region, then why was she not considered royal?

Well, inheritance in the Powhatan Confederacy was matrilineal. This means that a person's right to rule came from his or her mother, not from the father—and Pocahontas's mother was apparently a woman of no standing. Although she was the daughter of the Chief of Chiefs, she was not "royal" by Powhatan reckoning. Before she could ever inherit the right to rule, control of the Tidewater would first pass to Powhatan's brothers, then to his sisters (all of whom shared a mother with Powhatan), and then to the children of his sisters, male first, then female, in order of birth.

Pocahontas was about as common as dirt, and likely kept herself from a life of total obscurity by clowning and joking, thereby charming the moccasins off her mighty father—as hinted in her nickname.

"Pocahontas as princess" was also just too common a trope to interest me, in addition to being historically inaccurate. Instead, I found in Pocahontas's low social standing a mirror of John Smith, whose own lack of social clout obviously gnawed at his mind for many years.

Smith wrote prolifically about his various adventures. They are often so swashbuckling that one can never be sure whether anything he wrote was true, but according to many historians, this was not uncommon in "true accounts" of the 1600s. A "true account" was expected to have a lot of pizzazz, and so the requisite sparkle was often injected into otherwise ho-hum diaries.

I can't fault Smith or any other author of the time too harshly for spicing up the facts. I make my living writing fiction, too.

But Smith's writings are hugely entertaining, if they are not likely to be *entirely* true. His utter disdain for the highbred members of English society reaches across the centuries and rings loud in a modern reader's ear. Wingfield and Ratcliffe both obviously rubbed him the wrong way, as did most men he encountered. He accused the men of the colony of "envying his repute" even though his *repute* was largely manufactured by his own writings. He had all sorts of choice names for his fellow colonists, and his journals are colorful and full of character; his sarcastic, self-aggrandizing voice can be heard loud and clear centuries after his death.

Smith valued hard work and intelligence above any other trait, and anybody who was industrious and clever got his respect, while a roustabout who tried to coast on reputation earned dense layers of Smith's colorful and copious scorn.

I confess I found myself liking John Smith more as I continued to read his writings. Like my fictional Pocahontas, I found some kinship with him, for I know what it means to see my natural abilities and strengths completely disregarded because I lack a pedigree—the 2014 American equivalent of seventeenth-century high English breeding being, of course, a college education. I don't have that crucial marker of societal worth, and, in fact, I don't even technically have a high school diploma or a GED, although I did complete all four years of high school. (It's a long story, and goodness knows this note is already long enough.) Suffice it to say, I am also *no gentleman*, and yet I'd like to see your average PhD write four historical novels in less than two years.

John Smith, I understand you.

Smith's two accounts of his time at Jamestown are our main sources of information about the Native people of the Tidewater region. Many of the details he recorded of Native life were corroborated by later visitors and settlers in the region, and so we know that he was mostly truthful about the Powhatans, if about little else. (Smith and other observers recorded virtually nothing about Powhatan women, and so I was obliged to invent many of the details of their lives. Pocahontas's coming-of-age ceremony, for example, is entirely fictitious.)

The stories John Smith recounted about his interactions with the "Naturals" and "Salvages" (*sic*) were so rich and amusing that I had a very hard time selecting which scenes to include in *Tidewater*. This book could easily have been twice as long as it was, if I'd included them all.

Particularly enticing was the story of a certain "dreadful bridge," a thin sapling spanning a ravine-like creek bed that the Indians could cross with ease in their moccasins, but which the English found awkward and dangerous in their stiffer clothing. The "dreadful bridge" became a persistent nemesis of the English, and I left it out of this book with real regret. I can't tell you how I adore the image of a bunch of young Powhatan men standing around laughing as the *tassantassas* try to cross a narrow, wobbly log.

Also left out with great remorse were the unbelievable number of times Smith's various canoes and ships got stuck in the mud when the tide went out. It happened so many times that you'd think he would have eventually learned better, but apparently he never did. "Stranded by the tide yet again" was a common reason for Smith's various perils. I surmised that if I used it more than once, readers would think I was a very uncreative author whose well of ideas had run dry. They never would have suspected that it's real history (according to John Smith, anyway).

In fact, there were so many points of this abundant history I had to exclude for the sake of pacing a good fictional tale. In other cases, I had to merge multiple characters into one, for the cast was growing far too large by the time I hit *Tidewater*'s midway point, and I still had yet to cover Pocahontas's abduction and her integration into English life. The establishment of the Jamestown Colony affected so very many lives and had such far-reaching consequences that I simply could not contain it all in one novel—not even a novel the size of *Tidewater*. You begin to see why I feel overwhelmed by this (far too long) historical note.

And of course, these characters' stories didn't end where *Tidewater* ends. Not even Pocahontas's story ended with her death. She became a legend, adored by the English for her conversion to Christianity and her ability to be "civilized." She was proof that colonization would be successful, that the Natives of the New World would (eventually) welcome the English with open arms. Later, she was distorted out of all recognition by the myth of her love for the dashing John Smith. (I do not think he was particularly dashing, although I will concede that his mustache and beard were quite spectacular.)

But we all know about *that*. What happened to the rest of the characters?

John Smith went on to enjoy a career as a writer. He still made a few expeditions now and then, mapping and exploring—but his tale of Pocahontas rescuing him from certain death made him into a celebrity. The Pocahontas myth became a popular story in Smith's own time and remained in the English imagination for some time afterward. Many plays and novels were written about her (and Smith's supposed rescue) in the seventeenth and eighteenth centuries. There has been much speculation that Smith's account of Pocahontas might have inspired Shakespeare to write *The Tempest*.

In any case, Smith achieved the high status he always seemed to covet by riding the very coattails he sewed for Pocahontas.

Powhatan died a year after Pocahontas did. He was an old man, likely in his eighties or possibly even his nineties. When news reached Virginia that Pocahontas had died on the voyage home from England, the delicate peace she had wrought began to crack. Powhatan probably died knowing that the violent and unwinnable conflict with the English would soon return and that he could do nothing to preserve his remarkable empire or protect the people who depended on him.

He was succeeded by a brother, Opitchapam, who did not appear in this novel for simplicity's sake. Opitchapam ruled only a short time, and, upon his death, Opechancanough took control of the Tidewater—a transition that was already subtly beginning while Powhatan still lived.

I won't go into too much detail about Opechancanough's achievements. His rule of the Tidewater region was spectacular in bloodiness and desperation, a last-ditch effort to preserve the Real People's way of life before it was altered forever by the flood of English immigrants.

Opechancanough is one of the most fascinating and underappreciated historical figures I've ever encountered, and if *Tidewater* is enough of a success, I intend to write a sequel about him and his daughter Cockacoeske, a *werowansqua* who actually witnessed the true disintegration of the Real People's way of life after Opechancanough's death. If I get around to writing that book, it won't be until 2016, and I will try to keep it well under the 160,000-word mark.

John Rolfe seems to have been truly in love with Pocahontas. He wrote letters to Reverend Alexander Whitaker expressing his desire to marry her, seeking permission from the priest. He tried to disguise his desire and affection for her by insisting that he only wanted to marry her to bring her closer to the Gospel—for, in that time, it was inconceivable that a white man could truly love a Native woman, and in order for such a union to be acceptable, it must be done for missionary purposes. However, his infatuation with Pocahontas couldn't be so easily hidden.

He was apparently devastated by her death, and insisted that little Thomas remain in England under the care of an uncle until he was older, for Rolfe was afraid that the child, who was still recovering from dysentery, would not survive the voyage home. Rolfe had already seen the death of two beloved wives and one child—he would not risk Thomas's safety, too.

Rolfe maintained good relations with his Powhatan in-laws even after Pocahontas's death. His tobacco farm prospered, and he soon became a very wealthy and influential man. He attracted a new wife, an Englishwoman, whom he married in 1619. But in 1622, Rolfe was killed, and his tobacco plantation was destroyed in a concerted and widespread attack by the Native Americans.

But Rolfe's legacy of tobacco farming lived on, and the crop brought incredible wealth to the colonies spreading across Virginia and, later, great political power to those who controlled the tobacco. Had Pocahontas, with the natural farming skills of a Real Woman, not shown John Rolfe how to nurture the plants in Virginia's climate, the entire history of North America might have been very different, for tobacco was, in its day, just as potent a political force as King Cotton during the Civil War.

And that leaves Thomas Rolfe. John Rolfe died when Thomas was about seven years old, and by this time Virginia was so war torn that it was no place for an orphaned child. Thomas remained with his English uncle until he reached the age of twenty. When he finally returned to Virginia, it was a very different world from the one he had left as a child carried in his loving mother's arms. He had to petition the president for permission to visit his Powhatan relatives, and he struggled against societal expectations that he, an

Englishman by nurture if not by nature, avoid the dangerous and untrustworthy Natives.

Throughout Thomas's life, English conflict with the Powhatans escalated. Thomas was torn between two worlds, a fact that touched me deeply as I wrote the scenes with this energetic little boy, so well loved by both his parents.

Thomas Rolfe inherited a large amount of land from his father and may have been gifted a tract of land by Opechancanough, too—a testament to the duty the Powhatans felt toward Pocahontas and her only child. But with his land ownership came greater responsibilities toward Virginia. In 1644, he entered military service, defending the various forts in the area against Native attacks. No one knows how Thomas felt about training his gun on his own people—individuals who were perhaps even his blood relatives. Maybe by that time, after so long entrenched in the conflict between his two cultures, he was inured to the idea and resolved to preserve his own interests in a world that grew more hostile with each passing year.

Thomas Rolfe died sometime around 1680, in possession of vast portions of Virginia. Due in part to the value of Rolfe land, the names of Rolfe and Pocahontas are still used to conjure in the Tidewater region. Thomas Rolfe's descendants—the descendants of Pocahontas—are greatly influential in regional politics and commerce to this day.

I am deeply indebted to the following authors, whose works I relied on heavily in researching and creating this novel: Helen C. Rountree (*Pocahontas, Powhatan, Opechancanough: Three Indian Lives Changed by Jamestown*; *John Smith's Chesapeake Voyages, 1607–1609*; *The Powhatan Indians of Virginia: Their Traditional Culture*; *Before and After Jamestown: Virginia's Powhatans and Their Predecessors*; *Pocahontas's People: The Powhatan Indians of Virginia Through Four Centuries*), David A. Price (*Love and Hate in Jamestown: John Smith, Pocahontas, and the Start of a New Nation*),

Camilla Townsend (*Pocahontas and the Powhatan Dilemma*), and Frances Mossiker (*Pocahontas: The Life and Legend*). This last book is an older work and reflects an earlier sensibility about Native Americans, with far more myth than fact. However, it was entertaining and provided some useful insights into English perspectives. I only encourage readers who try it out to take it with a grain of salt.

A massive load of thanks to Dorothy Zemach, editor of the self-published edition of *Tidewater*, who kept the semicolons to a minimum. This book is undoubtedly better because of you. Thanks as well to Jodi Warshaw, acquisitions editor at Lake Union Publishing, who looked past *Tidewater*'s unimpressive indie launch to see its true potential. Kristin Mehus-Roe was my developmental editor for the Lake Union edition, and Michelle Hope Anderson was my copy editor. Both of them did a fantastic, thoughtful, and detailed job with a very long manuscript, and I am grateful for their hard work. Lane Brown created the gorgeous original painting for the self-published edition's cover—I am convinced that *Tidewater* never would have found its way to Lake Union without the aid of Mr. Brown's spectacular art, and for that I will be forever indebted to him.

Always my biggest and most sincere thanks to my readers. I literally could not do this without you. I am aware of that fact every single day, and I'm absurdly grateful to you.

Thanks to the many people who are spreading the word about the quality and variety of indie writing: bloggers, Twitter-ers, fellow authors, and readers around the world. You are pioneers, and I hope you feel exactly as awesome as I know you are.

And thank you, Paul, for everything. I love you.

—L.H.
Seattle, Washington
July 2014

Glossary

of Powhatan Words and Pronunciation Guide

ama: AH-ma. Mother—a word invented by the author, as no recorded incident of the Powhatan word for *mother* exists (that the author could find).

Amonute: am-oh-NOO-tee.

Anawanuske: ah-na-wa-NOO-skee.

Apocant: APP-oh-cant.

Appamattuck: app-a-MAT-tuck.

attasskuss: a-TASS-kuss. Leaf.

cattapeuk: cat-a-PEE-yuk. Season of fish runs; spring.

Chawnzmit: CHAHN-zmit. A bastardization of "John Smith." "Chawnzmit" was first proposed as a possible Powhatan "interpretation" for John Smith's name by Helen C. Rountree in her book *Pocahontas, Powhatan, Opechancanough: Three Indian Lives Changed by Jamestown*. I thought it was clever, so I used it, too.

Chessiopiak: chess-ee-oh-PEYE-ack. The tribe known today as the Chesapeake.

Chickahominy: chick-a-HOHM-i-nee.

Chiskinute: chiss-kih-NOO-tee.

Chopoke: choh-POH-kee.

Coanuske: coh-a-NOO-skee.

cohattayough: co-HAT-a-yoh. Late spring/early summer.

Frawh-say: An invented Powhatan bastardization of *Francais*; French.

huskanaw: HUSS-ka-naw. The physical trial of violence and privation that ushers boys into manhood.

Iroquoian: eer-oh-KWOY-an.

Japazaws: JAP-a-zawss.

Kocoum: KOH-koh-um.

Koleopatchika: koh-lee-oh-PATCH-i-ka. The English noted that Pocahontas had an aunt called "Cleopatra." This was undoubtedly a bastardization of a Powhatan name, and "Cleopatra" was the closest the English could manage. "Koleopatchika" is an invented name, one that I imagine the English might have misheard as "Cleopatra."

kowse: KOW-see. Father.

Mackinoe: MACK-i-no.

Mahocks: MAH-hocks.

mamanatowick: mam-a-na-TOW-wick. "TOW" rhymes with "now." The title means "Chief of Chiefs."

manitou: MAN-i-toh. An ill-tempered spirit; a demon.

Massawomeck: mass-a-WOH-meck.

Matachanna: mah-ta-CHAH-na.

Matoaka: mah'-toh-AH-ka.

Mattaponi: mat-a-POH-nee.

Monacan: MON-a-can.

Musqua-chehip: musk'-wa-CHEH-hip.

Naukaquawis: nock-a-KWAH-wiss.

nepinough: NEP-i-noh. "The earing of the corn"—late summer/ early fall.

netap: NEH-tap. Friend.

Nonoma: NO-no-mah.

Okeus: OH-kee-uss.

Opechancanough: oh-pee-CHAHN-ka-no.

Opossu-no-quonuske: oh-poss'-uh-no-kwoh-NOO-skee.

Orapax: OR-a-pax.

Pamunkey: pa-MUHN-kee.

Paspahegh: PASS-pa-heeg.

Passapatanzy: pass-a-pa-TAN-zee. The capital city of Pattawomeck territory.

Pattawomeck: pat'-a-WOH-meck.

Pepiscunimah: pep'-i-SKUN-ih-mah.

Pocahontas: pohk-a-HOHN-tuss. A nickname that means, roughly, "Mischief."

popanow: POP-a-now. Winter.

Powhatan: POW-a-tan. More a title than a true name. The federation of tribes is also called Powhatan, in honor of Wahunse-na-cawh, the Powhatan known to history and featured in this novel.

puccoon: puck-OON. A bright crimson pigment made from a plant. Very difficult to procure, and only available via trade with the southern tribes, it was a visible sign of wealth and status.

Quiyo-co-hannock: kwee'-yo-co-HAN-nock.

rahacoon: rah-hah-COON. Raccoon; we get the English name for the critter from the Powhatan word.

roanoke: ROH-a-noak. Tubular shell beads.

suckquahan: SUCK-wa-han. Water.

Taka-way-wemps: tah'-ka-WAY-wemps.

tanx-werowance: tanx'-WAIR-oh-wanss. A subchief; a chief of lesser status.

taquitock: TACK-wih-tock: "The fall of the leaf"—the hunting season; fall.

tassantassa: tass-n-TASS-a. "Stranger."

Tsenacomoco: senn'-a-KOH-moh-koh. The whole of the region; the Tidewater.

Tsena-no-ha: senn-a-NO-ha.

tuckahoe: TUCK-a-ho. A bland, starchy tuber that grows in marshy areas.

Utta-ma-tomakkin: u'-ta-mah-toh-MOCK-in. The first syllable is pronounced with the same soft "oo" sound as in "foot."

Uttamussak: u'-ta-MUSS-sack. The most sacred temple in the region. The first and second syllables are pronounced with the same soft "oo" sound as in "foot."

Wahunse-na-cawh: wah-HUHN-sen-a-caw. The "real" name of Powhatan.

werowance: WAIR-oh-wanss. Chief.

werowansqua: wair'-oh-WANSS-skwaw. A female chief.

Werowocomoco: wair'-oh-wo-KO-mo-ko. The capital city of Powhatan's empire.

Winganuske: wing'-ga-NOO-skee.

wingapoh: wing-GAH-poh. A greeting.

Wowinchopunck: woh-WIN-choh-punk.

yehakin: YEH-ha-kin. Longhouse.

ABOUT THE AUTHOR

Photo © 2014 Paul Harnden

Libbie Hawker was born in Rexburg, Idaho, and divided her childhood between eastern Idaho's rural environs and the greater Seattle area. While working toward a career as a novelist, Libbie held an array of jobs, including zookeeper, yarn dyer, and show-dog handler. She loves to write about character and place and is inspired by the striking natural beauty of the Rocky Mountain region and the fascinating history of the Puget Sound. She would choose high mountains, sage deserts, and heavy rain clouds over a sunny, sandy beach any day of the week. When not writing, Libbie enjoys hiking, painting landscapes and portraits with pastel and watercolor, and exploring the western United States. She now lives in Seattle with her husband.